THE YEAR OF THE RUNAWAYS

SUNJEEV SAHOTA was born in 1981 in Derbyshire and continues to live in the area. He is the author of the critically acclaimed debut novel *Ours are the Streets*.

Also by Sunjeev Sahota

OURS ARE THE STREETS

THE YEAR OF THE RUNAWAYS

SUNJEEV SAHOTA

PICADOR

First published in India 2015 by Picador India
an imprint of Pan Macmillan India,
a division of Macmillan Publishers India Private Limited
Pan Macmillan India
707, Kailash Building
26, K G Marg, New Delhi – 110 001
www.panmacmillan.co.in

Pan Macmillan, 20 New Wharf Road, London N1 9RR
Basingstoke and Oxford
Associated companies throughout the world
www.panmacmillan.com

ISBN 978-93-82616-68-9

3 5 7 9 8 6 4 2

A CIP catalogue record for this book is available from
the British Library.

Printed and bound in India by Gopsons Papers Ltd.

CONTENTS

WINTER

1. ARRIVALS

Randeep Sanghera stood in front of the green-and-blue map tacked to the wall. The map had come with the flat, and though it was big and wrinkled, and cigarette butts had once stubbed black islands into the mid Atlantic, he'd kept it, a reminder of the world outside. He was less sure about the flowers, guilty-looking things he'd spent too long choosing at the petrol station. Get rid of them, he decided, but then heard someone was parking up outside and the thought flew out of his head.

He went down the narrow staircase, step by nervous step, straightening his cuffs, swallowing hard. He could see a shape through the mottled glass. When he opened the door Narinder Kaur stood before him, brightly etched against the night, coat unbuttoned despite the cold. So, even in England she wore a kesri. A domed deep-green one that matched her salwaar kameez. A flank of hair had come loose from under it and curled about her ear. He'd forgotten how large, how clever, her eyes were. Behind her, the taxi made a U-turn and retreated down the hill. Narinder brought her hands together underneath her chin – 'Sat sri akal' – and Randeep nodded and took her suitcase and asked if she might follow him up the stairs.

He set her luggage in the middle of the room and, straightening right back up, knocked his head against the bald light bulb, the wire flexing like a snake disturbed from its tree. She was standing at the window clutching her handbag with both hands.

'It's very quiet,' Randeep said.

'It's very nice. Thank you.'

'You have been to Sheffield before?'

'My first time. What's the area called again?'

'Brightside,' he said.

She smiled, a little, and gazed around the room. She gestured towards the cooker.

'We used to have one like that. Years ago.'

Randeep looked too: a white stand-alone thing with an overhanging grill pan. The stains on the hob hadn't shifted no matter how hard he'd scrubbed. 'There is a microwave, too,' he said, pointing to the microwave. 'And washing machine. And toaster also, and kettle and sofa-set . . . carpet . . .' He trailed off, ridiculous to himself. 'The heater works fine. It's included in the rent. I'm sorry there's no TV.'

'I'm used to it.' She looked to the wall. 'Nice map.'

'Oh. Thank you. I thought . . .' What did he think? 'I want to visit every continent of the world.' She smiled politely, as if he'd said he wanted to visit the moons of Jupiter. 'It's one of my dreams.'

There were only two other rooms. The bathroom was tiny, and the pipes buffalo-groaned when he forced the taps. In the centre of the greenish tub the hand-held shower lay in a perfect coil of chrome, like an alien turd.

'And this is your private room,' he said, opening the second door.

She didn't step inside. There wasn't much to see: a double bed, a rail for her clothes, a few wire coat hangers. Some globs of Blu-Tack on damp, loose wallpaper. There was a long, hinged mirror straight ahead which they found themselves staring into, him standing behind her. She didn't even reach his shoulders. It was cold and he noticed her nipples showing through her tunic. Frowning, she pulled her coat shut and he averted his eyes.

'I'm sorry,' he said. 'It's too small. And dirty. I'll look for something else tomorrow.'

'It's fine. Honestly. Thank you for finding it for me.'

'Truly?' He exhaled relief. 'There is a bus from the bottom of the hill that can take you into town.'

'And that hill will keep me in shape.'

'And this isn't an area with lots of apneh.' Her lips parted, but she didn't speak. 'Like you asked,' he reminded her. 'And the gurdwara's only a few stops away. In Burngreave. I can show you? If you like?'

'We'll see,' she said. 'It's late. Can I call you tomorrow?'

'Of course. But you should know that the flat downstairs is empty. So no disturbances.' He smiled, pleased with himself. 'Yes, this flat was a special find. Especially at this time of year, it is not easy. We were lucky.' That 'we' was problematic and knocked him off balance. 'But I should go,' he said hastily. He took up his red tracksuit top and zipped it to his chin, pushing the short sleeves up to his elbows.

She walked him to the stairs, saying, 'You should probably bring a few of your things and leave them here.'

He nearly blurted out that his suitcase was just outside, in the gennel. 'I will bring some. But I will telephone you first.' He wouldn't be one of those boys who turned up at a girl's house unannounced and unexpected. Then he remembered about the meter tokens. 'The light.' He pointed down the stairs. 'There is a meter underneath. It takes the pink electric tokens. Not the white ones. The pink ones. There is a shop around the corner. The aunty there sells them.'

She looked confused. 'Do I have to collect these tokens? Like vouchers?'

'Collect them from the shop, yes. Only be careful you put the cards in straight. Would you like me to show you? The meter?'

She'd never heard of electricity being pink, or white for that matter, but she was tired from the journey and said she really did just want to sleep. 'But thanks for everything, Randeep.'

She used his name, without 'ji' and to his face, which hurt him a little. But this was England. 'No problem. And do not worry. You won't need any for a while yet. I put lots in before you came.'

She thanked him again, then – perhaps out of nerves, needing her fingers occupied – retightened her chunni over her turban and under her chin. It made her eyes look bigger, somehow.

Randeep opened his wallet and held out some notes to her. 'Next month's.' He was looking away. He hated doing it like this. At least when she lived in London it had gone by post. She too seemed embarrassed to take it.

He said goodbye. Halfway down the stairs he stopped, looked

round. 'I hope you don't mind, but is everything all right? You are not in any trouble?'

'Oh, I just need to rest. I'll be fine tomorrow. Can I call you?'

'Of course you may. Of course.' He smiled, then went down the remaining steps and opened the door. He nodded a final goodbye. She leaned forward out of the doorway, arms folded. She looked uncertain.

Randeep held his suitcase across his lap on the bus ride home. Of course she wasn't going to ask him to stay. It was stupid of him to have thought she might. If anything, he wondered now if she'd seemed eager for him to leave her alone. He spat coarsely into his hankie and worked out a bit of dirt on the brown leather of his case, which still gleamed, in spite of the coach to Delhi, the flight to London, and now three months spent wedged on the roof of that disgusting wardrobe.

He got off right outside the house and saw the grey-blue light of the TV flickering behind the closed curtains. He'd hoped they'd be asleep by now. He went the long way round the block, stopping off at the Londis for some of those fizzy cola-bottle sweets.

'You are leaving?' the singh asked. The suitcase.

'I was helping a friend move only.'

The TV was still on when he got back. Randeep turned the key gradually, wincing at the loud final snap of the metal tongue, and went straight up to his room on the second floor. He sat there polishing his workboots with toilet roll and after that he changed the blanket on his mattress, taking care with the corner-folds. Then he lay down, the darkness roomy around him, and with no real enthusiasm reached for the toilet roll once more.

It was near midnight when the clanging of the gate woke him up. He hadn't meant to fall asleep afterwards and the scrunch of sticky toilet paper was still in his hand.

Downstairs, he went through the beaded curtain and found Avtar gulping straight from the tap. The back of his uniform read Crunchy Fried Chicken. Randeep stood in the doorway, weaving one of the long strings in and out of his fingers. There was a calendar of tropically naked blonde women on the wall by the fridge. Someone would have to get a new one soon.

Avtar turned off the tap, though it continued to drip. 'Where is everyone?'

'Asleep.'

'Did someone do the milk run?'

'Don't think so.'

Avtar groaned. 'I can't do everything, yaar. Who's on the roti shift?'

Randeep shrugged. 'Not me.'

'I bet it's that new guy. Watch, they'll be bhanchod burnt again.'

Randeep nodded, sighed. Outside the window, the moon was full. There were no stars though, just an even pit of black, and if he altered the focus of his eyes, he saw his vague reflection. He wondered what his father would be doing.

'Do you think Gurpreet's right? About what he said this morning?'

'What did he say this morning?'

'You were there.'

'I was asleep.'

'He said it's not work that makes us leave home and come here. It's love. Love for our families.' Randeep turned to Avtar. 'Do you think that's true?'

'I think he's a sentimental creep. We come here for the same reason our people do anything. Duty. We're doing our duty. And it's shit.'

Randeep turned back to the window. 'Maybe.'

'And I asked bhaji, by the way, but there's nothing right now.'

The job, Randeep remembered. He was relieved. He'd only mentioned it during a low moment, needing solidarity. One job was enough. He didn't know how Avtar managed two.

'How'd the thing with the girl go?'

'Nothing special,' Randeep said.

'Told you,' and Avtar picked up his satchel from where it rested against the flour barrel. He took out his manila college folder and wriggled up onto the worktop.

Randeep had learned by now that when Avtar didn't want to be disturbed he just ignored you until you went away. He let the beads fall through his hands and was turning to go when Avtar asked if it was true that Gurpreet hit him this morning in the bathroom queue.

'It was nothing,' Randeep said.

'He's just jealous, you know.'

Randeep waited – for sympathy? for support? – but Avtar curled back down to his book, trying out the words under his breath, eyes glinting at the end of each line. Avtar's posture reminded Randeep of the trips he used to make between college and home, his own textbook open on his lap.

In his room, he changed into his tracksuit bottoms, annoyed he'd forgotten to warm them against the oven, then slid inside the blanket. He knew he should try to sleep. Five hours and he'd have to be up again. But he felt restless, suddenly and inexplicably optimistic for the first time in months. Years? He got up and moved to the window and laid his forehead against the cool pane. She was somewhere on the other side of the city. Somewhere in that dark corner beyond the lights, beyond that pinkish blur he knew to be a nightclub called the Leadmill. He wondered if she'd noticed how he'd spent each evening after work scrubbing the doors and descaling the tiles and washing the carpet. Maybe she was thinking about all he'd done right now as she unpacked her clothes and hung them on the rail. Or maybe she'd decided to have a bath instead and was now watching TV, thick blue towels wrapped around her head and body the way British girls do. His forehead pressed harder against the glass. He was being ridiculous again. There was no TV, for one thing. But he couldn't lose the sense that this was a turning point in his life, that she'd been delivered to him for a reason. She'd called him in her hour of need, hadn't she? He wondered whether she'd found his note yet, the rose-scented card leaning inside the cupboard above the sink. He cringed and hoped she hadn't. At the time, in the petrol station, he'd convinced himself it was the sophisticated thing to do. Now, he exhaled a low groan and closed his eyes and forced himself to remember each carefully written word.

Dear Narinderji, I sincerely hope you are well and are enjoying your new home. A beautiful flat for a beautiful person. And a new start for us both maybe. If I may be of any assistance please do not hesitate to make contact. I am at your service day and night. In the interim, may I be the first to wish you, in your new home, a very Happy New Year (2003).

Respectfully yours, Randeep Sanghera.

It was gone 2 a.m. and Avtar was still sitting up on the counter. He'd long set aside his college notes. His ankles were crossed and the heels of his trainers lightly tapped the cupboards. He could feel his eyes start to close, a shallow dark descending. He jolted himself upright. 'Come on, come on,' he said, half to himself, half to Bal, the guy he was waiting for. He checked his phone. He recounted the money. He had enough, had earned enough. Then his phone rang, too loud for that time of night. It was them.

'So we come to yours?'

'No, no. Keep to the gardens.' He didn't want them knowing where he lived.

He zipped up his jacket and sneaked out of the house and down onto Ecclesall Road, heading away from the city. The shabby restaurants were all closed, the pound shops shuttered. He liked this road in the day, a place of business and exchange, a road that seemed to carry on into the hills. Tonight, though, there was only a scrappy silence, and the city at his back, the countryside glowering ahead. He gripped the top of the zip between his lips, flicking it with the end of his tongue, and breathed out puffs of air that hung briefly in the cold. He turned up towards the Botanical Gardens and saw them sitting in their rich black BMW, faces flooded by the car's interior light. The engine was still gunning. Bal got out, the eldest of the three brothers, all long leather and shaped facial hair. The gold ring on his right hand was the size and shape of a fifty-pence piece. Avtar nodded, jogged to meet him.

'Why so late? I have work soon.'

'True what they say, man. Fuckin' cold up north.'

'You were held up?'

'By another one of you chumps. In Birmingham. He won't be doing that again.'

Avtar handed the money over. 'It's all there. So tell your uncle not to bother my family. Do you understand?'

Bal counted it, note by note. 'Good. It's just my share, then.'

'Arré, go fuck a cow. I can't pay extra every—'

He slapped Avtar. 'It's two o'clock in the bastard morning, I'm in the arse-end of nowhere and you want to argue the fucking toss?'

Hand on his cheek, Avtar looked over to the two in the car, the baseball bat he knew they kept in their boot, then back at Bal's heavy face. The height, which stretched the fat out of Bal's body, couldn't do the same for his slabbed cheeks and jaw. He took three more notes from his pocket and threw them across. 'If we were in India, bhaji, I swear I'd break all your bhanchod bones.'

Bal feigned confusion. 'What would I be doing in India?' Then he laughed and pinched Avtar's cheek, as if he were a child.

Three hours of sleep later, Avtar forced his stiff second pair of socks up over the first and pulled on his oversized workboots. He stuffed the sides with kitchen towel until they fitted. Then he picked up his rucksack, his hard hat and reflector jacket, and locked the door quickly. He was late.

He and Randeep were the last of the twelve to come down the stairs. They mumbled a quick prayer over the smoking joss stick and rushed out. Avtar didn't mind: it meant they got the nearest waiting point. The street lamps were still on, spreading their winter yellow. The chill was sharp as needles.

'So cold, yaar,' Randeep said, and tucked his gloved hands into his armpits.

They turned onto Snuff Mill Lane and waited beside a twiggy hedge near the Spar. The National Lottery sign reverberated in the wind. Any van pulling up would look like it was only delivering the day's newspapers.

'There used to be a flour mill here,' Randeep said. 'Hundreds of years ago. I read about it.'

'Yeah,' Avtar said, too tired to really talk.

They took out their Tupperware boxes and peeled off the lids. Avtar held up one of his chapattis: a brittle misshapen thing full of burn holes. 'No joke, I genuinely think my cock could do better.'

Randeep smeared the chilli gobi around his roti, then rolled it all up like a sausage.

The white Transit arrived and they climbed into the back and squeezed onto the wheel arches. The others were already in there, eating, or asleep on the blankets that covered the corrugated floor. Randeep squashed his bag under his knees, behind his legs. Opposite, Gurpreet was drawing on his roll-up and looking right at him.

'Did you wear that jacket all the way down the street?' Gurpreet asked, rocking side to side. 'Do you bhanchod want to get seen?'

'I was in a hurry.'

'In a hurry to get us all caught, eh, little prince?'

He'd have to take some of his clothes over to her soon. He concentrated on that.

'So what was she like, then?' Gurpreet asked. 'Our Mrs Randeep Singh?'

Randeep pretended not to hear.

'Oy! I asked you something.'

'Nothing. Like any girl.'

'Oh, come on. Tall, slim, short? What about . . . ?' He mimed breasts.

Frowning, Randeep said he didn't notice, didn't care to notice.

'And she didn't let you stay?'

'I didn't want to.'

Gurpreet laughed. 'Maybe one day you will.'

'Leave him alone,' Avtar said, strongly, eyes still closed.

'Where are we going today?' Randeep asked quickly.

Vinny – boss, driver – spoke up: 'A new job, boys. We're off to Leeds.'

They all groaned, complaining about how late they'd be back.

'Hey, ease up, yeah? Or maybe I need to get me some freshies who actually want the work?'

Someone in the back closed his fist and made the wanker sign, a new thing that had been going round the house recently.

The proposed hotel site was directly behind the train station. A board so white it sparkled read, *Coming soon! The Green: a Luxury Environmentally Friendly Living Space and Hotel in the City of Leeds*. But right now it was just a massive crater, topsoil scraped off and piled in a pyramid to one side. At least all the bushes and trees had been cleared.

They assembled in the corner of the station car park, looking down onto the site. Another vanload joined them. Mussulmans, Randeep guessed. Bangladeshis even, by the look of them. A man approached, his hard hat askew on his big pink head. He went straight to Vinny and the two spoke and then shook hands.

'All right, boys,' Vinny said. 'This is John. Your gaffer. Do what he says and you'll be fine. I'll pick you up at seven.'

The van reversed and Vinny left. Randeep moved closer to Avtar: if this John was going to pair them off then he wanted to be with him. But John began by handing out large pieces of yellow paper, faintly grid-lined. Avtar took one, studied it. Randeep peered down over his shoulder.

'These are the project plans,' John said, walking back and forth. 'As you can see there's lots to do, lots to do, so let's just take it one step at a time, yes? You understand?'

'We could do this with our eyes closed,' Avtar muttered. 'Saala bhanchod.'

'Oy! No, bhaji!' John said, bursting into Panjabi, pointing at Avtar with the rolled-up paper. 'I no longer fuck my sister, acha?'

Avtar stared, open-mouthed, and then everyone was laughing.

They put on their hats, smoothing their hair out of the way, chose tool-belts and made for the footings stacked in neat angles on the wooden pallets. John called them back. He wanted stakes in first.

'But it will take twice as long,' Avtar said.

John didn't care. 'We're doing this properly. It's not one of your shanty towns.'

So Avtar and Randeep piled a wheelbarrow with the stakes and bumped on down to their squared-off section of the site. 'You put in the stakes and I'll follow with the footings,' Avtar said.

Randeep dropped onto one knee and held a stake to the ground. With a second glance towards the plan, he brought down his hammer. 'Like last time?' He wasn't going to fall for that again.

'It'll take all week just to do this,' Avtar said. 'It's as big as one of their bhanchod football grounds.'

At lunchtime, they found their backpacks and joined the others sitting astride a large tunnel of aluminium tubing, newly exposed from the dig. Beside them, a tarpaulin acted as a windbreak. They slid off their helmets. Their hair was sopping.

Afterwards one or two pulled on their coats and turned up their collars and sank into a sleep. The rest decided on a cricket match to stay warm. They found a plank of wood for a bat and several had tennis balls handy. They divided into Sikhs and Muslims, three overs each. Gurpreet elected himself captain and won the toss. He put the Muslims in to bat.

'No slips, but an edge is automatic out,' he said, topknot swinging as he ran back to bowl.

He was knocked for fourteen off the first over, the last ball screaming for a six. Gurpreet watched it arc above his head and land somewhere in the car park.

'Arré, yaar, there's something wrong with that ball.'

'Right,' Avtar said. 'The fact that it is being bowled by you.'

Randeep laughed but when Gurpreet glowered he fell silent.

They needed thirty-one to win and came nowhere near, with Avtar going for glory and getting caught, and puffing Gurpreet easily run out.

'These Mussulmans,' he said, throwing aside the bat. 'Cheating is in their nature.'

John approached and for the first time Randeep noticed his gentle limp.

'Bohut good work, men, bohut good work. But come on, jaldi jaldi, it looks like you'll have it all khetum in no time.'

Avtar and Randeep stowed their lunchboxes and trudged down the site. Another six hours to go.

Vinny was late that evening.

'Some of us have other jobs to get to, yaar,' Avtar said.

'Sorry, sorry,' Vinny said. 'I had to go to Southall.' He was forced to turn left. 'Crazy one-way system in this city.'

'Is there work in Southall?' Avtar asked, up and alert.

'Hm? No, no. The opposite. I've found another one of you slackers. You'll have to make some more room back there.'

No one spoke. It was nothing new. They came and went all the time.

Soon they hit the motorway. Someone asked if Vinny Sahib had heard anything about any raids? Because one of those Mussulmans, you see, he was telling that the raids have started again.

Vinny whistled a single clean note while shaking his head. 'I've not heard a thing. Why would I? Far as I'm concerned you're all legit, ain't you? You all showed me your papers. Nowt to do with owt, me.'

The van continued in the slow lane, the tyres rumbling away under Randeep, a vibration that felt vacantly erotic. Then something made him sit up. At first he thought it was rain but it was too slow and gentle to be that. Then he understood, and touched his fingertips to the back window. 'Mashallah,' someone said, as Randeep felt them all brimming up behind him, pressing and jostling to stare at the sky, at the globe of tumbling snow around each street light.

At the house, Avtar persuaded Vinny to drop him off at the chip shop, leaving Randeep to eat alone in his room. Soon he was in bed, too exhausted to call Narinderji, too exhausted even to sleep, and he was still awake when he thought he heard a door sliding shut, like a van's side door, and the downstairs bell being rung. He swiped clear a patch in the window – Vinnyji again? – and went down the first flight of stairs. Gurpreet and the others had edged into the hallway, shushing one another.

'It's Vinnyji,' Randeep called down but no one seemed to hear him.

Gurpreet bent to the letter box, just as Vinny's voice came through, shouting that he was freezing his fucking kecks off out here. Quickly, the door was opened and he hurried in. He was hunched over, looking shorter than usual, and each needle of his spiked hair was topped with a bobble of snow. Behind him was someone new.

Randeep joined them in the front room, glancing around for Avtar. The others were all there: some perched on the mattress laid over the metal trunk, two squatting on an upturned milk crate, several flopped into the Union Jack deckchairs nicked from a garden a couple of weeks ago. The TV was balanced on a three-legged stool in the middle of the room, playing their favourite desi call-in show.

'This is Tochi,' Vinny said, his thumb chucked towards the new guy. 'Starts tomorrow, acha?'

He was very dark, much darker than Randeep, and shorter, but he looked strong. The tendons in his neck stood out. Twenty-one, twenty-two. One or two years older than him, anyway. So another he'd have to call bhaji.

'I've got a spare mattress in the van. He'll be staying in yours, OK, Ronny?'

It wasn't really a question but Randeep said he was absolutely fine with that.

He and Tochi carried the mattress up the two flights and leaned it against the wall. They'd have to take out the wardrobe first.

'Wait,' Randeep said and placed his suitcase to one side, out of harm's way.

'Cares more about that fucking suitcase . . .' Vinny said.

They bullied the wardrobe out and shoved in the mattress and then Vinny said he had to go.

'Have a beer,' Gurpreet said, joining them on the landing.

Vinny said he couldn't. 'Was meant to be back an hour ago. She'll have the face on enough as it is.' He turned to the new guy and made a star of his hand. 'Five sharp, you understand? These lot'll show you the ropes.'

When the three of them were left, Gurpreet folded his arms on the shelf of his gut, slowly. 'So. Where you from?'

Tochi walked into the room and closed the door. Gurpreet stared after him, then pushed off the banister and huffed downstairs.

Randeep waited. He wanted to make a good first impression. He wanted a friend. He knocked and opened the door, stepping inside. The guy looked to be asleep already, still in his clothes and boots, and knees drawn up and hands pressed between them. He'd moved his mattress as far from Randeep's as was possible in that small room: under the window, where the chill would be blowing down on him, through the tape.

'Would you like a blanket? I have one spare,' Randeep whispered. He asked again and when he again got no reply he tiptoed forward and folded out his best blanket and spread it over his new room-mate. Downstairs, there were still two rotis foil-wrapped in the fridge. He heated them straight on the hob. He liked the froggy way they puffed up. Then he coated them with some mango pickle. He didn't want to join the others in the front room, where he could hear the TV blaring, but he didn't want to disturb his new room-mate either. So he stayed there, marooned in the middle of the kitchen because there wasn't a single clean surface to lean on, tearing shapes out of his roti and feeding himself.

By 3.15 the next morning Randeep was awake and washed and dressed and in the kitchen binning the previous day's joss stick and lighting a fresh one. He said a quick prayer, warming his hands by the cooker flame, and set about getting what he needed: frying pans, rolling pin, butter and dough from the fridge, a cupful of flour from the blue barrel. He dusted the worktop with the flour and tore a small chunk from the cold brown dough, softening it between his palms. He had just over an hour to get sixty rotis done.

He paced himself and rolled out the dough-balls methodically. Four rolls up, turn it round, four rolls more, a pinch more flour, three more rolls on each side and then into the pan. He found himself whistling even as his upper arms filled with a rich, dull ache. There was movement around the house: radio alarms, the thrust of a tap. He quickened up and once the rotis were done and wrapped he dumped the frying pans in the sink for whoever would be on washing duty that night and replaced them on the hob with four large steel pans of water, full gas. He added tea bags, cloves, fennel and sugar and while all that boiled he gathered up the five flasks and dozen Tupperware boxes stacked on the windowsill. Each box bore a name written in felt-tip Panjabi. He found an extra box for his new room-mate, Tochi, and spooned in some potato sabzi from the fridge. As he carried a six-litre carton of milk to the hob, Gurpreet wandered in, the bib of his dungarees dangling half undone. He was pinning his turban into place.

'All finished? Thought you might have needed some help again.'

Randeep flushed but concentrated on pouring the milk into the pans.

'Clean the bucket after you wash, acha?' Gurpreet went on, moving to the Tupperware boxes. 'None of your servants here.'

He had cleaned it, he was sure he had, and his family had never had servants. He didn't say anything. He just watched Gurpreet moving some of the sabzi from the other boxes, including Randeep's, and adding it to his own. He wondered if he did this with everyone or only when it was Randeep on the roti shift.

'Where's your new friend from?'

Randeep said he didn't know, that he went to sleep straight away.

'His name?'

'Tochi.'

'Surname, fool.'

Randeep thought for a moment, shrugged. 'Never said.'

'Hmm. Strange.'

Randeep didn't say a word, didn't know what he was driving at, and stood silently waiting for the pans to come to the boil again. He had the twitchy sensation he was being stared at. Sure enough, Gurpreet was still there by the fridge, eyes fixed.

'Bhaji?' Randeep asked. Gurpreet grunted, seemed to snap out of it and left, then the hiss of the tea had Randeep leaping to turn off the gas.

Soon the house was a whirl of voices and feet and toilet flushes and calls to get out of bed. They filed down, rucksacks slung over sleepy shoulders, taking their lunchbox from the kitchen counter; next a rushed prayer at the joss stick and out into the cold morning dark in twos and threes, at ten-minute intervals. Randeep looked for Tochi but he must have gone ahead, so he paired up with Avtar as usual. Before he left the house he remembered to take up the pencil strung and taped to the wall and he scored a firm thick tick next to his name on the rota.

Overnight, the ground had toughened, compacted, and at the end of the morning they were still staking it out while Langra John – Limpy John – and three other white men went about in yellow JCBs.

'Wish I had that job,' Randeep said, closing his lunchbox. 'Just driving about all day.'

Avtar clucked his tongue. 'One day, my friend. Keep working hard and one day we'll be the bosses.'

Randeep leaned back against the aluminium tunnel. He shut his eyes and must have nodded off for a while because the next thing he heard was the insistent sound of Gurpreet's voice.

'But you must have a pind. Was that in Calcutta too?'

Tochi was sitting against a low wall, the soles of his boots pressed together and knees thrown wide open.

'I'm talking to you,' Gurpreet said.

'My pind's not in Calcutta.'

'Where, then?'

Tochi swigged from his water bottle and took his time screwing the top back on. He had a quiet voice. 'Bihar.'

Gurpreet looked round at everyone as if to say, Didn't I tell you? 'So what are you?'

Avtar spoke up. 'Arré, this is England, yaar. Leave him.'

'Ask him his bhanchod name.'

Shaking his head, Avtar turned to Tochi. 'What are you? Ramgarhia? Saini? Just shut him up.'

'Ask him his bhanchod name, I said.'

Tochi made to get up, frost crackling underfoot. 'Tarlochan Kumar.'

Randeep frowned a little but hoped no one saw it.

'A bhanchod chamaar,' Gurpreet said, laughing. 'Even the bhanchod chamaars are coming to England.'

'Who cares?' Avtar said.

'Only backward people care,' Randeep said, but Gurpreet was still laughing away to himself and then John limped up and said they better get a move on.

'Do you think he's got a visa?' Randeep asked, when they started up again.

Avtar looked at him. 'When did you last meet a rich chamaar?'

'His parents might have helped him.'

'Janaab, don't go asking him about his parents. He's probably an orphan.'

That evening Gurpreet knocked on their bedroom door and said he and a few of the others were going out, so Randeep and Tochi would have to help with the milk run. 'You've got Tesco.'

'Where are you going?' Randeep asked and Gurpreet made a fist and pumped it down by his crotch.

'And stop buying those bhanchod cloves and whatnot. We don't have money to waste, little prince.'

Randeep waited until he heard him on the stairs, out of earshot. 'He's that ugly he has to pay for it.'

Tochi was threading his belt around himself. The swish of it sliced the air. 'You'll have to do it yourself.'

'I can't carry all that milk. Do you know how far it is? Can't you help me?'

'Join one of the others.'

'But we can't all go to the same place. The gora gets suspicious.'

Tochi said nothing.

'I respect you, bhaji,' Randeep said. 'Can't you help me?'

On Ecclesall Road the roadworks still hadn't finished and the street was all headlights and banked-up snow. Randeep pulled his woolly hat lower over his ears and marched through. Tarlochan only had on his jeans and a shirt which kept belling in the wind. His jeans had no pockets, as if they'd been torn, and his hands looked raw-white with cold, like the claws of some sea creature.

'Next time I will insist you borrow my gloves,' Randeep said. 'You can have them. I have two pairs.'

As they passed the turn-off for the Botanical Gardens, Randeep pointed. 'That's where Avtar bhaji's second job is. Through the gardens and carry on straight.'

'Whose garden is it?'

'No one's. Everyone's. Maybe the government's. But they're pretty. I always think it's like we have the city, then the gardens, then the countryside.' He nodded towards the hills, made smoothly charcoal by the night. 'Shall we go there one day? To the countryside?'

'How many apneh work with your friend?'

Privately, Randeep felt 'apneh' was perhaps a little too far, given their background. 'A few, but no one else from the house. You looking for a second job too?'

He didn't say anything. Instead he turned sharp left down a road, his head bent low. Randeep yelled his name, then ran to catch up.

'Police,' Tochi said, still walking.

Randeep turned round and saw the blue lights revolving by. 'No visa, then.'

'I guess not.'

'How did you get here? Ship or truck?'

'On your mother's cunt.'

Randeep stared glumly into a dark coffee-shop window. It didn't seem to matter how hard he tried.

'Sorry,' Tochi said. He looked annoyed with himself.

'I'm on a marriage visa.' Randeep expected a reaction but got none. 'I got married,' he went on, aware he was starting to blather.

'To a girl. She came over to Panjab. From London. But she's here now. In Sheffield, I mean.'

'So why not live with her?'

'She's Sikhni. But I'm not that bothered, if I'm honest with you, bhaji. I'm going to take some clothes over soon but that's it. It's just one year, get my stamp, pay her the money, get the divorce, then bring my parents and sisters over. It's all agreed with Narinderji.' And he wished he'd not said her name. He felt like he'd revealed something of himself.

They bought milk, flour, bread, potatoes and toilet roll and went back to the house. Others were returning with their milk and shopping too, and it all got piled into the fridge, done for another week.

*

Randeep took a step back from the door and looked up to the window. The light was on. He rang the doorbell again and this time heard feet on the stairs and Narinderji appeared on the other side of the thick glass – 'I'm coming, I'm coming' – and let him in.

'Sorry. I was in the middle of my paat.'

'I didn't realize,' Randeep said, following her up to the flat.

With each step his suitcase hit the side of his leg, and, as he entered, the gurbani was still playing. She hadn't changed anything much. It was all very plain. The single plain brown leather settee. A plain tablecloth. The bulb was still without its shade. Only the blackout curtains looked new. A pressure cooker was whistling on the stove, and the whole worktop was a rich green pasture of herbs. In the corner, between the window and her bedroom door, she'd created a shrine: some kind of wooden plinth swathed in a gold-tasselled ramallah, and on top of this both a brass kandha and a picture each of Guru Nanak and Guru Gobind. In front of the plinth, on a cushion, her gutka lay open, bound in orange cloth, and beside that a stereo player. The gurbani began to fade out and the CD clicked mournfully off. Randeep set his case by the settee.

'How have you been?'

'I'm getting used to it.' Her hands were clasped loosely over her long black cardigan.

'You are getting to know your way around?'

'Yes. Thank you.'

'At least the weather is getting a smidgen better now. I thought the snow would never stop.'

She gave a tiny smile but said nothing. Randeep wondered if she just wanted him to hurry up and leave again. He knelt before his case and thumbed the silver dials until the thing snapped open.

'Well, as I said on the phone, I've brought some clothes and things for you to keep here.'

He draped a pair of matching shirts across the creased rump of the settee, along with some black trousers and starched blue jeans, all still on their bent wire hangers. He took a white carrier bag tied in a knot at the top and left this on the table. 'Shaving cream, aftershave, that kind of thing. And also some underwear,' he added in the casual manner he'd practised on the way down. Then he reached back into his suitcase and handed her a slim red felt album. 'And these are the photographs I think we – you – should hang up.'

He watched her palming through the pages. The first few were taken on their wedding day, in a gurdwara outside his city of Chandigarh. The later ones showed them enjoying themselves, laughing in a Florentine garden, choosing gifts at a market. 'They look believable to me,' she said.

'Vakeelji sorted it all out. He said sometimes they ask to see where we went on holiday.' He sidestepped saying 'honeymoon'. 'There are dates on the back.'

'Are there stamps on our passports?'

'It's all taken care of.'

Suddenly, her nose wrinkled and she held the album face-out towards him: the two of them posing in a busy restaurant, his arm around her waist.

'Vakeelji said there have to be signs of – intimacy.' He'd looked past her as he'd uttered the word.

'I don't care what Vakeelji said.' She shut the album and dropped it onto the settee. 'This isn't what I agreed to.'

He felt himself getting riled, as if discarding the photos in some way reflected her feelings towards him. 'Look, can't we just do what Vakeelji said? I'm the one with everything to lose here.'

'I've put a lot at stake too.'

'Yes. I'm certain you have. And I'm very thankful for all you're doing. I'm sorry if that isn't clear. We won't use the photos.'

The silence seemed calculated, forcing her to relent.

'Most are fine to use,' she said, and he nodded and retrieved the album.

'I only hope we've got enough. I'm hearing rumours of raids.'

There was a sort of frozen alarm in her face which thawed to incomprehension. 'You think this place will be raided? By who?'

'It's just people at work talking. And there are always rumours. But it's better to be prepared. Maybe I should come and live here?' he said, testing the water a little.

The shock of the suggestion seemed to force her mouth to open.

'I was not being serious.'

'It's too small. And the weather,' she said, randomly.

'I understand completely,' he said, layering smiles over his disappointment. He couldn't remember the last time he'd been so warm in a house, with food smelling as good as that on the cooker.

She made to walk him to the door.

'Shall I help you with this first? It's not fair to leave you to pack it all away.' Delay tactics. She said she'd do it later. That it wasn't a problem. Reluctantly, Randeep followed her down the stairs. As she opened the door he took the notes out of his pocket and handed them to her.

'Another month,' she said. 'The year will be over before we know it.'

'Yes!' he replied, shaking his head, as if amazed how quickly the time was passing, when really it seemed to him that each new week took on the span of an entire age.

After he'd gone, she collapsed onto the armrest of the settee, face hidden. This was too hard. This was too much to give. What had she got herself into? She lifted her head out of her arm and was met with the images of her gurus. They spoke to her, reminding her that she always knew it was going to be hard, that doing the right thing is never the easy choice, but to remember that Waheguru is her ship and He would bear her safely across. She felt Him beside her, and felt her resolve return, as if the blood was pumping more thickly through her body.

She fetched from the drawer the map she'd picked up from the station and zoned in on her street. The surrounding areas didn't sound like places she wanted to visit: Rawmarsh, Pitsmoor, Crosspool. Burngreave. Killamarsh. They sounded so angry, these northern places, like they wanted to do you harm.

Across the city, Randeep lay on his mattress. Everyone had eaten early and gone to sleep, tired out from a whole muddy week of shovelling up and levelling out cement. No one had even mentioned his second visit to the wife. He replayed their conversation and was more or less pleased with how it had gone. They seemed to understand each other and if the year carried on like that everything would be fine. He was hopeful of that. He heard the downstairs door go and the kitchen beads jangling. Probably Avtar would stay in the kitchen for an hour, eating, studying, counting how much money he had, or didn't have. Randeep wouldn't join him. The last few times he had gone downstairs he'd got the impression he was only getting in the way.

Rain pattered against the glass. He turned his head towards Tochi. Yesterday, Tochi had moved his mattress out from under the window and turned it at a right angle, so he and Randeep now lay parallel to each other, the door at their feet. Randeep guessed it was so he could sleep facing the wall. His boots were crossed at the ankles and were the only part of him that poked out from under the blanket. Randeep's blanket. Which he'd not even been thanked for.

'Bhaji, are you awake?'

Nothing.

'Bhaji?'

'What?'

Randeep didn't know what. He hadn't had a conversation planned. 'I can't sleep.' Then, a minute or so later, 'This is strange, isn't it?'

'Go to sleep.'

'I mean, when you were a kid, did you ever think you'd be working in Sheffield, in England, and living in a house like this? I'd never even heard of Sheffield.' There was silence and Randeep asked, 'Do you still have people back home?'

Tochi didn't reply. The rain seemed to be plashing harder and Randeep drew his blanket up around his neck.

'Bhaji?'

'What?'

'I like hearing the rain outside.'

A pause, and then Tochi: 'Me too.'

2. *TOCHI: AUTORIDER*

Tarlochan Kumar was bent double under the last huge sack of fodder. He shook it into the buffalo trough and moved away as the animals nosed hungrily forward. He was seventeen; it was his fourth year in Panjab, his third with this family. He'd miss the place.

He crouched by the pump at the side of his hut and washed his arms, soaping off the grass and sweat. Then he changed into a clean white kurta pyjama he'd that morning left to dry on a branch. As he made his way to the big house, the sunset streaked the horizon.

The solid iron double gate was closed and its blue rivets still hot to touch. Inside, in the courtyard, his sahib sat cross-legged on his menjha, speaking to a local usurer. The sahib's wife was napping beside him, her head flopped back over the love seat, and on the floor their daughter crushed herbs in a small ceramic mortar. Once the usurer was dismissed, Tochi knocked on the metal gate and was invited in.

'How many times?' the sahib said. 'Treat this place like your home.' He was in a good mood, which was something.

'Sorry, sahib,' Tochi said.

He noticed the wife half open her eyes and tap her foot twice against her daughter's back. The girl lifted her chunni up over her head, screening her face from Tochi.

'I have to go home, sahib. My papa is not well. I got a call yesterday.'

His sahib uncrossed his legs so just his toes touched the floor. The taut hairy ropes of the menjha had striped deep red marks over his feet. He watched them fade. 'It's the height of the season. You could not have picked a worse time.'

'I know.'

'Why are you chamaars so unreliable?'

Tochi said nothing.

'How ill is he? Will he not get better?'

'Both his arms are gone.'

The wife clucked her tongue in sympathy and muttered a waheguru.

'What colours God shows us,' his sahib said. 'You understand I'll have to get someone else. I can't keep your job for you.'

'I know.'

Tochi nodded, turned to leave.

'Don't forget your food,' the memsahib said.

He thanked her and picked up the thali of leftovers on his way out.

The next day, his sahib was waiting outside the big gate, wages in hand. Tochi accepted the wad and bent to touch the man's feet.

He walked the two hours to Jalandhar, his belongings in a brown rice-sack slung across his shoulder. At the depot the buses were parked up in their rows, the iron grilles blurring into each other in the mellowing dark. He found his bus, but the conductor sitting on the roof ground out his beedi and said they wouldn't be leaving until it was full, nine o'clock, at least, so he should pass his luggage up to guarantee his place. Tochi kept his bag with him and went and sat in the station's chai-samosa dhaba. He ordered some tea and made a cradle of his arms on the table, nestling his head down and closing his eyes.

It was past noon before the conductor blew his whistle. As they laboured out of the compound, the passengers were rocked from side to side and the man sitting next to Tochi clanged the tiny cymbals tied to his wrists and whispered a prayer under his breath. He was a young man, in a cheap white cotton shirt and faded black trousers. A burgundy folder lay across his lap. He was going for an interview, he said. To be a ground clerk. Tochi nodded as if he knew what that was and told the man he was going home because his father had lost both his arms. Grimacing, the man clanged his cymbals and didn't speak again, as though he didn't want Tochi's bad luck to rub off on him.

The conductor steadied himself against the pole while he

punched Tochi's fare into his machine, tearing him off a stub from the tape-roll of pink chits. Then, rice-sack clasped against his stomach, Tochi allowed himself to swing in and out of sleep until it was gone midnight and they were pulling into Meerut station and the young man next to him was saying he wanted to get past.

Outside the depot, tall double-headed lampposts ran up the spine of the road, and traffic swarmed, though no one seemed to be getting anywhere fast. The connecting bus wasn't leaving until the morning, so Tochi dodged across the road and carried on down the street, hoping to find a hostel amongst the cement stores and Airtel operators. In a two-storey shack with red and green fairy lights all over: '*AARTI HOTEL*', he paid the boy watching a Bollywood film at the counter. Then he went up to a thin metal bed and fell asleep to the snicker of cockroaches.

He couldn't get on the coach direct to Patna – other passengers priced him off – so he waited the morning out under a narrow tree, making a cola and two rotis last until he climbed onto the afternoon bus to Shahjahanpur. He played cards with a young boy sporting a sandalwood mark on his forehead. The boy was sitting across the aisle from Tochi and they used their knees for a table, but when the boy asked Tochi his name – 'No, your full name' – and Tochi told him, the boy's mother made some excuse and switched places with her son.

He spent three nights in Shahjahanpur, sleeping on the ground behind a mandir, head on his sack of clothes. On the fourth morning he asked the pandit for a bucket of water. He washed himself, then dipped his clothes into the bucket, wrung out the water and put them straight back on. He could almost feel them crisp and shrink against his skin. He went again to the station, and this time the conductor said there were enough passengers for the journey, but only as far as Allahabad. The bus was full of Sikh women, pilgrims with round turbans and small knives. No one said a thing the entire journey, and Tochi sat at the back, staring out at the young green corn. He wondered how they'd coped in the year since his father's accident. All his brother had said was that money was running out, work drying up. To come home, please.

Dawn arrived grainy in Allahabad and Tochi joined the long queue for the Patna bus, his fourth. He'd got to perhaps six or seven from the front when the conductor announced they were full and everyone would have to wait for the evening ride. Tochi went down the windows each side saying that his father had lost both his arms and would someone please exchange tickets with him. Most passengers turned their heads, but a young man with a professorial look jumped off and cheerfully told Tochi to take his place. He even offered to pay for his ticket but this Tochi politely declined.

Slowly the heat dwindled. When the bus crawled into Patna, finally there were landmarks Tochi recognized: Vaishali Talkies, Bhavya Emporium, Market Chowk. He stepped off and bent to touch his hand to the soil and then to his forehead. For the final hour-long journey he flagged a packed bumblebee-painted auto-rickshaw and hung onto the side of it, feeling his body curve as the thing juddered out of the city. Tochi jumped off at his village gate, opposite Bicky's Friendship Store, and as he passed under the arch he again bent to bless himself with dirt from the ground.

He walked the long white strip of road, past some kids playing with a stick who stopped to watch him. The vast field of wheat either side was still in the hot air. Butterflies flew reed to reed, wide-winged, cabbage-green and peacock-spotted. He turned off into an alley where the sewage moved in sluggish plates in front of the wooden doorways. It was darker here. He came to a red panel, the paint flaking to reveal the green underneath, and he lifted it aside and ducked and turned sideways to squeeze himself through the thin gap and into the room. The sun streamed through holes bored into the back wall and fell like scattered treasure across one half of the stone floor. On the other side, in thick shade, he could see his father asleep on a mattress woven from coconut leaves. His head was turned to the wall and the sleeve of his grey tunic lay empty at his side. The pink shelf his sister had put up was still there but the things on it were new to him: a gold pen, a ration card, an address book still in its plastic wrapping, a picture of a white girl with straw-coloured hair hugging a dog in front of a thatched cottage.

There was an English inscription on the picture of which he only knew the word 'home'. He dumped his clothes in the corner and went back outside. Further up, the lane forked and at the junction was a large broken fountain now filled with sand. Beyond it were a few shops made from sleeves of tin that seemed to be held together by nothing more than God's benevolence. The tailor – Kishen – was still there, cross-legged at the sewing machine, under a ceiling fan which made the sheets of fabric displayed behind him ripple. They'd gone to school together, briefly, back when the state had attempted a literacy drive. They shook hands.

'Your brother said you were coming back.'

'How's business?'

'Running. Papa died last year.'

Tochi swatted a fly hovering by his ear. 'Is there work?'

Kishen said there was nothing. 'Even Chetan and his sons went to Danapur. They heard there was land there.' He measured out some tiger-print cloth, looped it back and sliced it in two with scissors tucked beneath his thigh. 'They came back. Nothing.'

Tochi looked at the pyramids of hot yellow bricks, at the two rat-thin dogs weaving primly between the wheels of an oxen cart. Some bare-chested kids played cricket in the arid field, and beyond them was a mountain of sewage, looming like a black cliff face. Nothing seemed to have changed.

He shook hands with the people he passed, confirming that he was back and that he had found work in Panjab. And, yes, hadn't he grown? He walked slowly, wanting them all to get a good look at him, to understand that there was once again a man in the house, that it wasn't just the cripple. The villagers understood this. They would have done the same.

When he had completed his circuit and arrived back at the sand-filled fountain he saw his brother coming down the road. Dalbir. His brown shorts were tattered and his white school shirt not much better. He carried a sack of grain about twice his size. So they had taken him out of school. Tochi approached but Dalbir shrugged him off: 'I can carry it.'

'Never said you couldn't.'

Dalbir was looking to the ground. His eyes were wet.

'I didn't bring you anything back. I'm sorry. I said I would, but I didn't.'

'That was four years ago,' Dalbir said. 'I'm fourteen now.'

Tochi stepped aside and watched his brother turn into the field, where brown buffalo were feeding. In the house, his mother was unpacking his clothes, shaking them out and hanging them on a thin wire she'd tied across the back wall.

'Geckos will climb in if you leave them on the floor like that.' The gold wedding hoop in her nose glinted in the daydark.

Tochi crouched beside the door. He took off his boots and placed them against the wall. He heard his father shuffling and turned to see him wriggle upright, using his shoulder-stumps as a kind of motor. There was a glass of whisky on an upturned bucket level with his face and he laboured to catch the straw in his mouth. When he finished he breathed out gratefully. 'Why'd you tell him? What good is he here?'

'Was he drunk when it happened?' Tochi asked.

His mother moved to the mud oven, squatting. 'He thought he'd switched the machine off.'

'When can you go back?' his father said, slurred. 'You need to go back and work.'

'We need a man in the house,' his mother answered. 'I can't even get a proper rate for the milk any more.'

Dalbir stepped under the doorway – he still didn't need to duck – and slid down the wall opposite his brother, copying his pose: crouched on his backside, knees pitched up and arms draped loosely over the top. Palms cupped. And then Palvinder, their sister, arrived, her salwaar covered in cuttings from the crops she was helping pull up. She touched Tochi's forearm as she passed and joined her mother in the corner of the room, and both women started blowing into the cave of the mud oven in an effort to get the cooking-fire going.

The dhal was thin and barely covered the shallow plate, the potatoes few. Tochi tore his second roti in two and threw half across to his brother. His sister passed round glasses of hot tea, the side of each glass stamped with a cartoon mouse. Tochi blew across the rim of his glass, while his mother and sister used the ends of their chunnis as gloves. Afterwards they rolled out the wicker mats and Dalbir went and lay beside his father. Palvinder shook her mat out by the back wall, furthest from the door, and Tochi was to sleep across the entranceway, in case of intruders. His mother pulled her chunni over her head, hiding her face, and said she was going to check on Devi Bai down the lane, because her son was off looking for work and the daughter-in-law wasn't behaving as a daughter-in-law should. Tochi listened to the starry rustle of her clothes as she stepped away.

'What d'you have?' his father asked. His eyes seemed redder through the dark.

'Is there none left?'

'Did you not save any?'

'I sent it all to you.'

His father sighed and turned his face to the wall. Tochi stood and went outside, jumping the fat river of sewage that ran in front of their home. The night sky shone so bright it made silver splashes in the drains. He could hear drills somewhere. He heard his mother returning, too, coming through the night like a nearhand ghost. She stopped beside him. She looked older than he remembered. The hair thinner. Still that overbite which had passed on to her daughter but not her sons.

'I'll look for work tomorrow.'

'We need you in the field. We're running out of time.'

Tochi kicked his heel into the muddy lane, making a divot. 'I'll still look.'

'They've refused Palvinder's hand,' his mother said.

He nodded and, arm outstretched, reached for his mother, and she held his hand and rested her small head lightly inside it.

He'd slept with his head on his wrist, and now his wrist ached, but he didn't move. He just lay there with eyes open. He could see his father naked to the waist and Palvinder squatting beside him, washing him with the tin bucket and strawberry soap. He was all torso, the stumps of his arms skinned over. Skinned over and shrunk and wrinkled like meat. Tochi closed his eyes, then opened them again. His mother held out a glass of tea and a salted paratha. He sat up and ate.

'Where's chotu?'

'Working,' his mother said.

'He's early.'

'It's because you're here,' Palvinder said, looking at him over her shoulder, still soaping their father. 'I usually have to drag him up by his ankles.'

It was just past seven and children were heading off to the village school, hands looped around the straps of their dusty backpacks. Tochi made for Babuji's house. No doubt the old man was aware of his return – someone would have informed him soon enough – but Tochi wanted to pay his respects in person. To thank him for organizing his father's treatment and to assure him that this quarter's rent would be on time. But Babuji had gone to Calcutta on some business for one, maybe two months, and Tochi was told by the servant to return then.

He walked to the field, bending to enter the concrete hut. His scythe was still hanging from the rusty hook by the motor switch, as if it had not moved in the last four years. He took it up, along with three rough brown sacks, and stepped back out into the green-and-blue morning. Dalbir was many yards down a row of cut wheat, the crops lined neatly behind him. He'd already done two rows, nearly three. He'd set off too fast. He'd learn. Tochi reached up for a tree branch and brought his scythe down upon it. The branch fell cleanly across his feet. He tied his white dhoti up between his thighs and headed off, away from his brother.

He went at his own pace, a regular hacking once on each side of the root before twisting the whole thing out with a sharp turn of his wrist. It was only around mid morning, when he squatted to start on his eighth row, that his thighs began with that familiar ache. His brother was slowing. Each time Tochi looked back from under his armpit, Dalbir seemed to be moving with heavier feet, flicking the sweat from his brow, breathing harder. By noon Tochi had finished his half, and even filled the brown sacks and carried them to the hut. Dalbir still had at least one-quarter of his to go. Tochi took up his scythe and started at the other end, and a little over an hour later they finished together.

'I could've done it on my own,' Dalbir said.

'Never said you couldn't,' Tochi said, and he picked up three steel buckets, two in one hand and one in the other, and made for the path, to where the buffalo were tied to their trees.

'Already?' Dalbir called after him, panting.

'Already.'

They measured the milk into metal canisters and carried them home for their mother and sister to sell around the village. Done for the day, Tochi found a clean white shirt and brown trousers and went down to the village pump to fill a bucket with water. He bathed in front of the entrance to their shack, using his old dhoti first as a screen and then a towel. He used the same water to wash the mud from his sandals.

The next village, Jannat, was about two miles away and he was there under the half hour. A hunched old woman with a blue hydrangea in her hair squatted beside the entrance arch, a wicker basket of almonds and cherries displayed before her. It was a village even tinier than his own, boasting just one road and ten, maybe twelve, huts. But the fields looked rich, Tochi thought; they still needed tilling. He passed under the arch and carried on towards the house with the big red metal gates, knocking once. A male servant materialized on the balcony. He asked Tochi his name, then told him to wait a few steps from the gate. Madam didn't like them getting too close to the house.

Nearly an hour later, the gate yawned open and the landowner stepped nervously outside. Tochi got up from where he'd been crouched in the roadside shade and waited for the man to beckon him forward. He was tall, elderly, his olive-green robes rippling over a full round belly. He asked Tochi what his business was. Was he causing trouble with someone from this village?

'No, sahib.'

'Because I hear there is a lot of trouble about.'

'My family live in peace, sahib.'

'I won't stand for any trouble, you understand? Keep your goonda-giri away from my village.'

'Yes, sahib.'

The man slapped at the back of his neck. A midge, maybe. 'It is the elections. Every time. They send people mad.'

Tochi said nothing. He wasn't expected to have a view on such things. A donkey came clip-clopping up the road behind him. The landowner walked down the slight incline to his gate and raised his hand to stop the tangawallah. He spoke to the man on the cart – something about a land dispute between two local brothers – and then climbed aboard. He told Tochi he'd be back in a little while. Tochi nodded and went back to wait in the shade of the roadside tree.

Another hour later, three young men took shape on the road, beedis glowing palely in the heat and dhotis tucked up around their groins. As they neared they kissed the air, prompting Tochi out of the shade and into the white sun. The men took his place, chatted a while, crushed their beedis under their feet and went on their way again.

It was nightfall by the time the landowner returned, whistling to himself. He seemed a little drunk. Tochi stood and moved into the moonlight. The old man looked surprised, frightened even, and his hand went round to his back.

'I have a gun,' he said.

'I'm from Manighat, sahib.'

'Are you here to cause trouble? I have a gun.'

'I'm looking for work, sahib.'

'You can't buy my vote. You Sena logh think you can buy anything. I have a gun.'

'I will work very hard, sahib. I have a brother also who can work if you need him.'

There was the *squeak-squeak* of a metal bolt being simultaneously twisted and yanked, and then the gates opened. It was the servant. 'Shall I put your food on the table, sahib?'

'Has everyone else eaten?'

'They are waiting for you.'

The landowner started up the incline to his gate.

'Sahib, about any work . . . ?' Tochi said.

The landowner stopped, turned round. 'There's not even enough for the men from this village. Maybe try further on.'

The old man made to leave again, but Tochi dared another question. 'Could I trouble your kindness for a suggestion, sahib?'

'Villages nearer the city, maybe. Most of their sons have gone to work in the town.'

The servant closed the gate behind his master, and Tochi heard the bolt being forced back across.

The next day he put on the same clothes and headed out again, past Jannat and on to the next village, another dirt-driven plot of huts and flat fields of wheat and corn. He could see fields of high cotton, too, bending demurely in the sunlight. The landowner was in his house, completing his ablutions. Tochi was asked to wait in the courtyard. He stood beside a large tulsi plant and reached over to stroke its velvety leaves. It felt nice. When he heard a door open, he returned his hands behind his back.

The landowner sat on his charpoy in just a white vest and lunghi while one of his granddaughters knelt behind massaging mustard oil into his hair. He listened to Tochi, then said he was sorry, but there would be uproar if he gave work to someone from outside the village, especially in these times.

'I have quick hands, sahib,' Tochi said. 'I'll get all the cotton before it dries.'

'Sorry, kaka,' the man said, and slid his eyeballs up, his brow constricting in the effort to meet his granddaughter's looming face. 'Tell your dadi to give this young man five rupees. He's come so far to hear bad news.'

Tochi said there was no need, and, if sahib would give him the gift of his permission, he would prefer to get on his way.

The next village was six miles further on and it was past noon when he arrived at the gate. But the landowner had gone on a month-long pilgrimage, and his sons were spending the day in the city.

He carried on, walking the sandy edge of the asphalt to avoid the thickening traffic. The roadside shacks turned from mud to tin, and he passed a petrol garage where two attendants in grubby IOCL overalls lazed against a pump. He was on the fringes of the city. He entered Randoga, the biggest village in the district, with a skyline of wooden balconies and red Airtel satellite dishes.

A wide dirt track separated the fields and their farmhouses from the mazy central bazaar. He passed a man leading a herd of wet black cows and asked him who were the main landowners around here. The man pointed to a few farmsteads, but said he doubted they'd be in at this hour. Tochi made for one of the houses anyway, cutting a diagonal through a field of wheat. He stopped at the open gate. A woman, bent at the waist, was cleaning the courtyard with a charoo. She was too glitteringly dressed to be the lagi. Tochi tidied his shirt into his trousers and wiped the sweat from his face with the inside of his collar. He tapped his knuckle twice against the metal gate, then took a step back and put his hands out of sight. She twisted round, still bent over, and asked him what he wanted.

'Please forgive me, memsahib. I wondered if sahib had a minute, please?'

'What do you want that only takes a minute?'

So he wasn't in, or at least not within earshot, and she sounded like trouble. 'I'll be on my way, memsahib.'

'I said what do you want?' She stood, queenly, and dropped the charoo to one side. She looked young. There were red ribbons strewn through her hair-bun.

'I'm looking for work, memsahib.'

'Oh, well, that's what you all say, but when you get it . . . Look! We have to clear up after your mess.'

'I'll leave you in peace, memsahib.'

'Come here.'

'I need to find work.'

'Here,' she said again.

He started towards her, her face ageing with every stride: the lines showing through her powder, the smear of henna beneath her hairline, the thick bristle around pencilled eyebrows.

'What kind of work?'

'Farm work, memsahib.'

'Where are you from?'

'From the city,' he lied. He didn't want any trouble following him home.

She stared for a while. Then: 'We do have work. Lots of it. But sahib has gone to the bazaar.'

'Acha, memsahib.' He turned to go.

'You can wait inside.'

He didn't say anything.

'Did you not hear?'

'Memsahib, I need to find work.'

'I told you there is work. Just wait inside.'

He didn't move.

Her hard face hardened further. A shadow over a stone. 'Things easily go missing from these houses. It's an open entrance, isn't it? I wouldn't want anyone in this village to think you weren't trustworthy.'

Tochi went through a large green door inlaid with gauze against the mosquitoes. He waited beside the charpoy, covered in its white sheet. He heard a door swinging open, clattering shut, and a tap running. A minute or so later she entered, her make-up now all gone. 'That sheet stains so easily,' she said, and started unbothering herself from her sari.

Afterwards, he walked back round the dirt track and on to the pale stone lanes of the bazaar. A parade was on: Sita in her Rajasthani red, dupatta pulled forward like a deep hood and led by a single boy in white turban and tunic, miserably banging his drum. Tochi picked his way through the singing crowd, slipping into the spaces vacated by others, always moving ahead. No one seemed to notice him. He emerged into a side alley crammed with wedding-card manufacturers and moved away as some girls rode past, quacking their scooter horns. The alley spread into a paved square where four young men were playing cards on an unstitched brown sack, the kind used to transport crops. Their lunghis were rolled up around their knees and their calves covered in mud and field cuttings. Tochi crouched beside them and at the end of the hand asked if there was work around here. They said there was lots of work, but also lots of people looking for it.

'What should I do?'

'Go and register at the dhak-khana,' one of them said. He seemed the youngest of them, with a fluffy moustache above thin lips. 'They'll add you to the list.'

'It'll be a long list.'

He made a so-so motion with his head. 'A year. Maybe six months if you give him enough. And have a phone for your home.' By which he meant steal a phone for your home.

Tochi nodded. So they could call him if a job came up. 'Do you know anything? Any work going?'

'Yaar, if I did do you think my brother would be sitting at home counting his fingers?' They laughed and dealt the next hand.

'Thank you,' Tochi said, standing.

'It's these elections,' the young man said. 'People are scared to hire us. The Sena logh have scared them.'

In the western corner of the bazaar, he found the post office, between a liquor store and an open-air stall selling electric fans. There was no door, only a rusting metal shutter rolled up and held in place with a wooden pole wedged at each end. Inside, he couldn't see anything of the walls: they were hidden behind the immense rows of shelving that gave slightly under the weight of all those paper files. The postmaster sat at his table, writing into a blue ledger. With one hand he held his hair off his face. His cuffs were checked neatly back, revealing a silver bracelet on one wrist and a gold wedding thread around the other. Tochi waited to be noticed. The postmaster looked up, raised his eyebrows and kept them there.

'I'm here to register, sahib. For work.'

'Six months,' the postmaster said and bent back down to his book.

'I don't mind what the work is, sahib. Farm work would be best, but I don't mind as long as it's work.'

'Six months.' He didn't even look up.

Tochi took out from his back pocket a twenty-rupee note. 'It's all I have, sahib.'

When the man didn't reply, Tochi returned the note to his pocket and made to go.

'You don't have a family?' said the man.

'I have a father, a mother, a sister and a brother.'

'Your father doesn't work?'

'He has no arms.'

The man clucked his tongue. 'There's not much work for you people in this district. The elections, you know.'

'Thank you for your time.'

He closed his ledger with a dusty thud and reopened it at the first page. 'Three months. There's work – farm work – in Danapur in three months. Shall I put your name down?'

'Do you think they might give me an advance on my wages, sahib?'

'Definitely not.'

'Then you should not put my name down. I need money now.'

'Get an auto. Lots of business. Especially with the rains coming.'

'I can't afford one.'

'Since when has that stopped anyone?' And with that he stretched behind for a file, then sat up straight again, the front chair legs banging the stone floor. Clearly, Tochi was to leave now: he'd taken up enough of his time. He wound back through the bazaar and to the main road. Soon he could see buses up ahead, their fuzzy red lights pitching through the slow dark. He walked three or four miles, maybe, past a newly built hotel and several others not yet finished. Then he was weaving through the city herds of cars and lorries, crossing the chowk to get to the mandi. He stopped outside the market. All the shutters were pulled greyly down: he'd find no auto drivers here. He made for Patna Junction, hands pushed deep inside his pockets and arms rod-straight, shoulders hitched up to his neck. There were no lights here, just the muted silver of the moon trailing the alleys.

He kept his head low, not looking at the men stalking the night for drink and women. Rounding a corner too quickly, he felt his stomach dip and his left side sink warmly down. A drain. He could feel his sandal dredging off. He fetched his toes together and yanked his leg out of the sewage. It emerged in foul sludge and without its sandal. He rolled his sleeves to his shoulders and moved onto his knees, feeling his hand carve its way through the black waste. He closed his eyes and constricted his nostrils, lowering his shoulder to deepen his reach. He couldn't find it. His arm was dripping great cones of black filth like some diseased and shedding creature. He wiped off as much of it as he could and carried on up the lane, limping with his heavy leg and one sandal. He knew he stank – even the women on the balconies made *chi-chi* noises.

In time he took off his other sandal and left it at the side of the road. The ground was warm underfoot. Not far from the train station he stopped outside a theka, a liquor store. The owner had a yellow towel slung around his neck, each end held in his fist as if he was a boxer's mate. He stood there staring out at the night and at Tochi as if all his life he'd been waiting for Tochi to pass. Tochi asked if he might clean himself up. He was searching for a job, he said, and didn't think he stood much chance looking like this. The man jerked his head to the side and said there was a tap round the back. Soap too.

'Thank you,' and Tochi followed the wall down, twisting side on to slip between two giant pipes that climbed into the darkness. He had to grope to find the tap and after maybe a minute or two water started coughing out. He washed his arm as best he could and removed his trousers and scrubbed them roughly. When he put them back on, the stiff blackness remained, and his arm still gave off a thin smell of rotting sewage. He closed the tap and went round to thank the owner.

'Where are you going?' the man asked.

'I'm looking for work.'

'What kind of work?'

'Rickshaw work.'

The man looked doubtful. 'You can afford one?'

Tochi thanked him again and turned to go.

'If you want to make money quick, lots of boys are taking an operation. We could do a deal.'

The man seemed to smile with only one half of his face, which frightened Tochi a little, and he apologized and said he really had to go.

He heard a coal train shrieking to its stop on the other side of a building up ahead. He rounded the building – a cinema – then crossed the rail lines and climbed. The auto drivers were all outside the station, most of them asleep in their taxis while they waited on the morning crowd. One driver stood with his back to Tochi, singing.

'Bhaiya, can I ask for your help?'

The man turned round, in no hurry. He was shorter than Tochi, and his small moon of a face and thin legs seemed a wrong fit for the rest of his body, as if all the fat in him had deposited itself in a wide belt around his waist. His hair was slicked back. 'Kya?'

'I'd like to speak to someone who will sell me an auto.'

The man looked Tochi up and down, at his ruined clothes. 'Autos don't come cheap. Who did you rob?'

'Who do I speak to?'

The man made a dismissive gesture with his hand. 'No more licences in the city. Find some other work.'

'Just tell me who I need to speak to.'

'You need to speak to me, and I've told you already.'

Tochi remained where he was, looking at the man. 'Maybe I should ask someone else.'

The man chuckled and turned his head to the side. 'All this government support must be going to their heads. Now they want to work with us, too.'

From the autos came a couple of sleepy, smoky laughs.

He spat at the ground, right between Tochi's feet, and stood there smirking, arms crossed over his chest as if waiting for Tochi's next move. Relenting, Tochi returned to the station platform and was about to cross the tracks when a voice called him back. A body pieced itself together through the dark, chest uncovered, an orange lunghi twisted expertly around waist and thighs. The man asked if Tochi was the one looking for an auto, because he had one for sale, or at least his brother did.

'Where is it?' Tochi asked.

'You know the clock tower? By the maidaan? Meet me there in the morning,' and before Tochi could ask anything else the man turned and hastened up the platform.

Away from the station, he breathed in a clear, great draught of air, looked up and asked God to please let this chance be real.

He checked under each stairwell he passed for a place to lie down, but they were all full, and soon he realized he was near the river. He crossed the flyover, spookily quiet at this hour, and scrambled on down. The water looked seductive, its dips aglow with moonlight. Off to his left was the simple outline of the long red bridge. At the river's edge, he took off his trousers and shirt and washed them in the water, then returned to the wall in his wet clothes. There were already people bedded down for the night, bodies lying low against the bricks, sheltered from the wind above. He found a space further along and lay on his side, facing the river. It didn't take long for his eyes to feel heavy, and the last thing he registered was the fat honk of a tugboat gliding darkly by.

He was at the maidaan not long after sunrise and already the place was filling: shoeshine boys setting up for the day, office men strolling to work, nuns on their morning constitutional. He couldn't see the man anywhere. His eyes moved to a tidy saffron crowd gathered in the shade of an apple tree. They were sitting around a man who kept pointing to a piece of paper in his hand. Some sort of protest, maybe. Tochi looked up at the clock tower. He wished they'd agreed on a specific time.

He was woken by someone shaking his shoulder, and rushed to his feet.

'Where's the auto?'

'Come with me.'

As they walked, they could hear the man under the tree: 'We need a strategy to install Hindutva! They can't keep holding us down!' A bright white banner twisted itself across the brambles: *Bharat is for the pure of blood and blood we will shed to keep it pure.*

The auto man fluttered his hand by his side, indicating that Tochi keep his distance from the crowd. 'These Maheshwar Sena people,' he said.

Tochi waited, hoping for something further, but the man left it at that and they carried on over the maidaan and through the iron gates.

The auto was a broken, paint-peeled thing, the yellow roof bevelled with dents. Tochi pointed to the ruptured front tyre. 'Is there a spare?'

'Under the seat.'

Walking round the vehicle, he noticed *Om* stickers plastered to the rear grille-window and pictures of Sai Baba. 'How much?'

The man turned his head, calling, 'Bhaiya?'

Tochi hadn't spotted the man sitting inside the auto, hidden by the deep grime of the window. His brother, Tochi remembered, as the man shuffled to the side and with some effort levered himself out. For balance, he kept one hand on the doorframe. He looked ill, and his voice, when it came, was the voice of a man decades older.

'Whatever you can afford, bhaiya.'

'I can't afford anything. I'll pay you from what I earn each day.'

The first man shook his head. 'Do you think we're stupid?'

'Now, now, nikku,' the brother said.

'You'll never see him again, I promise you that.'

The ill man looked at Tochi. Tochi said nothing. He just stood there in his stiff river-washed trousers and mouldy white shirt.

'We'll see,' the man said.

'You're crazy!'

The ill man smiled. 'Please excuse my brother-in-law. But the auto's yours if you would like it.'

They agreed on the time and place Tochi would come each

evening to make good on his payment, and then the man held out the keys and licence, and a list of regular pick-ups.

'I hope it brings you better luck than it did me,' he said.

Tochi lay in the auto, at the end of the slim gully that led to his house. He kept the keys in his fist and his fist hidden inside his armpit. He'd felt almost criminal driving home, as if he'd expected someone to halt him and point out how ridiculous it was for his family to own such a thing. Children throwing marbles into the fountain had stopped and stared. Even Kishen had looked up from his tailoring, tape measure clamped between his teeth, and asked if Tochi had taken to robbing banks.

Lovingly, Tochi ran his hand over the handlebars, the leather old and bristly against his palm. He heard something, and saw that it was Dalbir stepping out of the dark lane. He was carrying a steel bowl with a spoonful of dhal, and a single roti. He handed this to Tochi.

'I'll bring your tea later,' Dalbir said, climbing in beside him. His wide eyes made a slow tour of the vehicle, neck arching as though he was inside some huge temple.

'I can't remember the last time Ma was so happy.'

'Who's asking you to?'

'I'm asking myself.'

'Don't.' Tochi passed him half of his roti.

'I've eaten.'

'Eat some more.'

At dawn, he filled a bucket with water from the pump and bought on credit a bar of crumbling strawberry soap from Bicky's Friendship Store. He started at the back, scrubbing off the stickers, slowly working his way round. At some point, Dalbir came and asked for the spare rag.

It was far into the morning when the last of the polish had been applied. Tochi went back to the house and wrapped a shawl around his father's torso. Then he helped him outside and sat him on a chair in front of the auto. Tochi's mother and sister followed, heads covered and holding a bowl of yoghurt and a saucer of holy water Palvinder had fetched that morning from the gurdwara. She dipped her fingertips in the water and went round the auto splashing drops. Then his mother fed Tochi a spoonful of the buttery yoghurt. Tochi touched her feet and she asked God to bless her son with success.

He drove into Pankaj Flats Colony, joining the squiggle of autos already parked by the gated compound, and climbed out into the hot afternoon. He'd never been to this quiet corner of the city before. A chowkidar sat dozing in his chair, thumbs hooked into his belt-loops, and on the other side of the gate, where the sun burst across the apartment blocks, Tochi could hear children playing. The other drivers were hunkered down in the shade of the wall, reading a paper or listening to the cricket. Tochi crouched down too, on the flats of his feet, rounding his back closely over his knees and threading fingers together tight across his shins, curling himself up into as small a target as possible for the sun. He wasn't sure when the woman was going to come out. Any time between two and three, the list had said. Someone offered him a beedi, which he declined.

'So you've taken Ashok Bhai's auto?'

'Bought.'

The man smiled. 'That's what I meant.'

His name was Susheel, he said. From Jannat. That was his auto over there, the one with the lucky red ribbons tied to the grille. He seemed younger than Tochi – the softness of his beard, a certain confidence.

'If you need anything, just ask for me. Everyone knows who I am.'

Tochi nodded, thanked him, but perhaps he hadn't seemed sufficiently impressed.

'Ask anyone. Susheel. That's me.'

There was a loud banging on the metal gate and a call for it to be opened. The chowkidar rolled up onto his feet, leisurely, stretching. He said he was coming, madam, coming. The drivers all stood up too, but when the gate flushed open to reveal the woman, most of them sat back down. She stepped forward, her hand a shield against the sun. Tochi didn't know if this was her, and he didn't want to approach and ask – it might look like he was in the business of stealing someone else's pick-up. But then Susheel confirmed that this was his ride, or one of Ashok Bhai's old ones, at least. Tochi walked to the woman, salaamed, and explained that he'd bought Ashok Bhai's auto and if she would permit him to lead her to his vehicle he'd take her wherever she needed to go. There was a sudden silence, and Tochi could feel the drivers staring at him. The woman nodded and said, 'Of course. Please, after you.'

He waited for her to be seated before rousing the engine and reversing out of the compound. 'You should have brought the auto to me,' the woman said.

Tochi nodded. He'd worked out as much already. 'Sorry, madam.'

She laughed. 'No matter.'

Twenty minutes later he parked outside a modern-looking building with 'Sheetal's' embossed across the window in a spiky green diagonal.

'Wow, that was fast,' the woman said, throwing aside her magazine.

She gathered up the pleats of her crimson sari and stepped gracefully onto the lumpy tarmac. A sliver of her nut-brown midriff was briefly exposed.

'Two hours, acha?'

Tochi nodded, and watched as the peon beamed and opened the door, and she swished up the marble steps and hurried inside, away from the heat.

Tochi drove to Kumhrar Road, where he caught a couple of fares: two white-saried widows carrying trays of unlit dia lamps to the Radha Krishna Mandir, and then a father and son who wanted to fly their kites on the ghats. When he got back to Sheetal's, he still had to wait a full fat hour before the peon opened the door and the woman came down the steps, talking over her shoulder to a friend who followed. They stopped beside the auto, still talking. Something about someone's kitty party. Tochi couldn't be sure: their tongue was half English. He wanted to try for a few more fares before the evening grew too thick and he had to go home. He looked at the glassy timer in the centre of his handlebars, and maybe the woman's friend saw him looking and made some sort of gesture with her eyes, for he heard Madam say, 'Oh, he's just a scheduled.'

There was an excruciating silence, and the woman's friend smiled in a squeamish way and said she'd see Radhika next time, later in the week maybe. Madam waved and reluctantly turned round. She was biting the corner of her lip, like a schoolgirl. She got into the back without once looking at Tochi and asked quietly if he wouldn't mind going next to St Joseph's Sacred Heart School. They needed to pick up her son.

The next day, Tochi drove right up to the gate where Madam was waiting for him. Her chin was up, eyes peering down her nose, and she climbed into the back of the auto in a single swift movement. Determined not to speak, it seemed, as if to illustrate the proper relationship between driver and Madam. It didn't last long. Tochi had only turned onto Ganapathy Drive when she flopped forward, elbows on knees.

'Acha, I'm sorry. But it's so hard to know what to say these days. I mean, are you even still called chamaars? Legally? Am I allowed to say that?'

'You can call me what you like. I only want to drive you and get paid for it.'

'So what should I call you?'

Tochi said nothing.

She fell back, sighing. 'I'm not a horrible person, you know. I do feel sorry for you people.'

Through the rear-view mirror he could see her looking out the side, agitated, frowning, as if again her words had come out wrong.

When he returned to pick her up, she appeared at the window, waving far too excitedly, and suddenly the door was thrown open and she was coming down the steps, sari hitched up and six, seven, eight women pushing up behind. They arranged themselves around the auto, beaming at Tochi. Collectively, they gave off a pinkish, fruity scent.

Madam spoke calmly, though there was something strained

about her face, as if she were trying to check her delight: 'Can you fit us all in?'

Tochi asked where they were going.

'Bakerganj,' said one.

'The maidaan,' said another.

An obese and middle-aged third shunted her friends aside. 'The Women's Shelter. I'm patron of their birth-control programme. Actually, I should tell you that we have a real problem with birth control in your caste group. Are you married?'

Tochi twisted the key and the engine puttered up. 'I'm only allowed to take four.'

All nine forced themselves into the auto, sitting on each other's laps, standing, singing, as if this was a great adventure.

He skirted potholes and speed humps, avoiding police checkpoints, and as each passenger alighted they gave their address and a time to collect them the following day.

'Most of us have sold our private cars,' Madam said. 'We want to help the poor in society instead.'

It was just her and her son left. The boy bounced about in his white shirt and fire-engine-red tie. Twice his mother pressed upon him his sunglasses, and twice he threw them off. At the compound gate, he jumped out and ran towards a waiting kulfi cart. His mother gathered his satchel into her lap.

'Same time tomorrow? Or are you too busy now?'

She was smiling, pleased with herself. Tochi just said he'd come tomorrow as normal.

*

He got to know the city well. All the branching bazaar alleys that hid the frilly-roofed salons and Danish-style tea rooms. After dropping Sarasvati Madam off at Charlie's Chai Corner, he'd take the newly built flyover and collect Bimlaji from Nalanda University and go from there to Sheetal's, via Radhika Madam's compound. That used to make him late delivering Jagir Bibi to the gurdwara, but once Susheel shared with him the tanners' lane shortcut Tochi could avoid the bulk of the afternoon mandir rush and the old lady would be at the gurdwara well before the ardaas. The late afternoons were busier still, full of school pick-ups and last-minute runs to the market. Over time, passengers began to recommend him to others: an opportunistic friend and his daily visits to a dying 'oil-in-law', a father whose driver had taken to drink. It felt as if no sooner had he washed the auto and set off from his village, than the next time he paused and looked up from the road the sun was sinking away, and he'd again forgotten to eat the rotis his sister had packed, and the night was starting its smoky occupation of the sky.

'I hear you're doing well,' Susheel said.

They were at the Drivers' Dhaba, sipping sweet tea.

'Maybe you'll earn as much as me one day.'

Tochi nodded. 'How old are you?'

Susheel's face turned serious. He understood. 'Seventeen, bhaji.'

'Family?'

'Just my ma and papa. My ma's ill.'

Tochi nodded.

His last stop in the city before heading home was always to pay the brothers their share of the day's takings. They lived in a one-roomed shack under a stairwell, behind a new hotel, with both their families. At least eleven different faces he'd counted over the weeks. He'd duck to enter and the children would huddle off into a corner to give this uncle room to sit. A sister handed him tea and as he drank the brothers liked to hear of his day. Where he'd been, who he'd taken. Afterwards, they'd say that the auto truly was proving much luckier for him.

*

He slept in the back of the auto, as a precaution. One night, Dalbir lay collapsed over the handlebars. He'd been working in the field and, Tochi noticed, had forgotten to wash the mud from behind his ears.

'We should buy another auto so I can be a driver too,' Dalbir said.

'Who'll work the land?'

Dalbir thought on this. 'I'll hire a manager.'

He heard a woman rustling down their lane. It was Palvinder. She brought Tochi a glass of milk – they could afford to drink it themselves now – and collected his dirty bowl and plate.

'Ma is asking for you,' she said to Dalbir.

'Why?'

'Since when did you start asking "why"?'

'I have my rights.'

'Go,' Tochi said, and, grumbling, Dalbir rose and went slouching up the lane. Tochi gulped at his milk, handed back the glass. 'Did Ma tell you?'

Palvinder nodded.

'And you're happy with the match?'

'Would it make any difference if I wasn't?'

Tochi nodded. 'I'll see what they say tomorrow.'

She stood the emptied glass upside down in the bowl and followed her younger brother.

The servant showed Tochi through to the breakfast room, where Babuji was sitting at the scoop of a long kidney-shaped table, spooning sugar into his tea. When he glanced up, sunshine seemed to fill his face and he reached for his walking stick.

'Don't get up,' Tochi said, touching the old man's feet.

Babuji tapped his stick against the nearest chair and Tochi sat down, balancing on the lip of the seat. 'I came as soon as I returned. But you were away.'

'Calcutta business,' the old man said dismissively, because what he really wanted to hear was what Tochi had been up to. Where he'd been and what he'd done and how long he'd been back. Was it true he'd bought an auto? Tochi said it was.

'Wonderful! Well done! You're moving in the right direction.'

He'd aged in a grand way. His hair had turned as white as milk and the skin was terrifically lined, making a noble feature of the large loose face that many still said reflected too soft a character. His hands clasped the ivory handle of his stick and the hem of his silver kurta made a valley in his lap. He'd known Tochi's grandfather. They'd been great friends, Tochi's mother had said. Babuji had even attended Papaji's funeral pyre, and as far as anyone in the village could remember that was the first time a landowner had attended the rites of a chamaar. But that was all back when they'd worked for the family, in the years before Tochi's father had asked Babuji if they might quit their servant jobs and instead rent some land.

'I wanted to let you know we've found a good match for Palvinder.'

Babuji nodded. 'So I hear.'

'I'm sorry I didn't come and ask for your permission first.'

'Oh, those days are gone, Tarlochan. Is the girl happy with the match?'

'If the match has your blessing, then the rest of us don't need to question it. They're from Jannat.'

'On the Margiri side? I know the seth who owns the land. They're a good family.'

'I've no doubt. But he's the only son and if we can't pay the full dowry they say they'll refuse. And she's already been refused once. She won't get another chance.'

Babuji sighed. 'It's a monstrous business. "I want five motorbikes and ten cows before your daughter can marry my son." But it's the way these things work.'

'I just wanted to check that you think their demands are reasonable.' He paused, then decided to add, 'If they insist I'll of course pay.'

'I think it's monstrous, like I said, and I hope one day it changes and we all start practising the religions we preach. Until then . . .' He opened his hand in a gesture of resignation. 'If you find you can't pay, we'll give them my Contessa. It still drives like a dream.'

'I didn't come here to ask—'

'I know you didn't.'

Tochi nodded. Somewhere in the house a clock chimed out the hour. He'd be late for his first job. He put on the table the following quarter's rent. 'It's the same as before I left. Aren't you ever going to increase it?'

'Can you afford it if I do?'

'I'll just have to give them one less motorbike.'

Babuji feigned horror. 'Not the motorbike. People will think we're animals if we only give four.'

That afternoon, Radhika Madam asked why he wasn't going the usual way, via the maidaan, and Tochi explained it was because of the election. There were rallies. This way would be quicker.

'I'll be glad when election season is over,' Madam said, fanning herself with the end of her pallu. 'And the rains are taking so long, na?'

He took the hairpin turn onto Lohanipur Road and sped towards the bazaar. But it looked like here, too, there was a rally, and he gently braked into the crowd. He tried intimidating his way through, delivering long bursts on the horn.

'Might be quicker to walk, Madam.'

'In this heat? And give his mother more reason to complain I'm not fair enough? I'll wait, thank you very much.'

So he forced his way to the side, parking beside a few other drivers, and switched the engine off.

It was the Maheshwar Sena. And the same white banner Tochi had seen at the maidaan all those weeks ago now hung in a taut smile across the entrance to the bazaar: *Bharat is for the pure of blood and blood we will shed to keep it pure*. Three, four, five people were on the stage, dressed in saffron and passing between them a microphone boxed in an orange collar. Their words boomed – loud and fuzzed with static – through speakers tied to tree trunks all around. They spoke of the need to regain control. That their religion was becoming polluted, the gods were being angered. The land was increasingly infested by achhuts, churehs, chamaars, dalits, adivasis, backwards, scheduleds – whatever new name they decided to try and hide behind. They needed to be put back in their place. Not given land and handouts and government positions.

'Maybe I will walk and you can go,' Madam said.

'If you want.'

Clearly she didn't, and stayed put. 'Such backward logh. And how useless is our government that they can't do anything? Do you know, our maid, Paro, told me that one of these goondeh made her husband get off the bus and walk home?'

Tochi said nothing.

'They've no shame.'

'Who?'

'Don't be clever.'

Though there were shouts of support and one or two tatty saffron flags above the roving mass of heads, mostly the crowd was impatient and kept calling for the swamijis to move their holy backsides out of the way. 'I've got work, bhanchod!'

'Let there be no doubt,' the speaker went on, as if someone had turned up the volume. 'We will fight to keep our country pure. We will shed blood. We will not back down. Let's put it even more plainly: we will kill.' The crowd quietened a little. The speaker seemed pleased by this. 'There will be revenge for the murder of our brothers by the Maoists. There will be a purge. No one can stop it. And it will start at the beginning of Navratri. In respect for our murdered brothers and sisters, on the first day of Navratri we will allow none of the impure to work in the city or be seen about the city. It will be a day for the pure only. So the pure can enjoy the parks and the streets as Ishvar intended. Anyone going against us will be exterminated.'

Anger flamed inside Tochi, and Radhika Madam was tapping his shoulder, urgently. 'Please, let's go. This is too awful.'

On his way home he stopped at the village of Jannat. He knew it was one of the houses behind the Hanuman mandir, but it took a schoolboy scoffing toffees on the temple steps to point it out. Tochi knocked and a voice – an old man's voice – asked who he was. Inside, he took a seat on the low stringy charpoy, pulled down from where it stood against the wall. The house was dark save for the candles and their intimate light. There were just the two rooms, with an empty doorway between them. Tochi could see the mirror in the second room and reflected in the mirror was a woman lying under a blanket. At her side was Susheel, hands on his knees. The old man was busy apologizing for asking Tochi who he was, but there was so much trouble about these days, what with these Sena logh. Only two days ago he'd heard they'd killed a man because he'd refused to take part in their protection racket.

'It'll pass,' Tochi said.

'This is your first time to Jannat?'

'I came three months ago. Looking for work.'

'Did you speak to the thakur?'

Tochi said he did.

'He's getting old. Forgetful. But a good master. He gives us no difficulty.'

'The land is good here. Rich.'

'We work hard on it. Though not hard enough, it seems. I like your auto.' His lips thinned into a sly smile, his pinched little face made even more so by the ratty white turban.

Susheel came forward to shake Tochi's hand and pass him a cup of tea. His hair was parted to the side, the usual quiff flattened down. Despite the cockiness at work, he seemed like a caring boy. A good match.

'You know my son,' the old man said.

Tochi nodded. 'Did you have a date in mind, uncleji?'

'When would suit you?'

Tochi understood the inference. When would he be in a position to fulfill the dowry? 'I'll speak to my parents. I just wanted to ask if you had a date in mind. Or if you had any other demands.'

The father shook his head. 'I'm sorry if we're asking for a lot. We're not greedy people. But he's my only son. You understand?'

Tochi said he did.

'And his mother is not well. But I promise you that, if you perform your duty, we will perform ours and your sister will be treated well here. You'll have nothing to worry about.'

Tochi shook hands with them both and folded back out of the doorway. He was about to drive off when Susheel appeared at his side.

'Bhaji, I wanted to say I'm sorry if my father offended you. He doesn't mean to, I promise.'

Tochi nodded.

'And would you please . . . ?' Tentatively, smiling embarrassedly, Susheel held up an envelope.

He'd only been home a few minutes when his sister arrived with his food.

'Quick today,' he said. He made a plinth of his knees and began mixing the white butter into his sabzi. Palvinder stood there holding his glass of water.

'You can put it down.'

She did. Still she stood there.

'You going to stay there all night?'

'Uff, just give it to me.'

He gave her the letter, asking how they managed to contact each other, but she was skipping up the lane and out of his sight.

*

The Maheshwar Sena were more and more on the city streets. It seemed as if around every corner there was a jeep loaded with men in saffron bandanas. They spoke through megaphones, reminding people of the upcoming day of the pure. Any low castes, or anyone protecting a low caste, would be committing a crime against Hindutva, would be spitting on the burning bodies of their murdered brothers and sisters, would be dealt with. Some shops had already been targeted. A jeweller's was destroyed, the glass bangles smashed on the road, the cash register launched through the window. And one day Tochi saw a suit-boot man with a briefcase stopped and badgered for his ID. He tried to look imperious as he handed it over, only to receive a wide stinging slap and an instruction to make sure he didn't leave his house on Navratri.

Radhika Madam asked if he shouldn't just stay at home until all this madness passed over. He said he couldn't afford to do that.

'Well, at least you won't be working on Navratri.'

Tochi remained silent.

'Tell me you're not?'

They'd arrived at Sheetal's. Madam stepped out, hitching up her sari with one hand.

'You know, money won't buy back the dea—' She caught herself, perhaps thinking how easy it was for her to say that.

For days they all urged him to not work on Navratri. Bimlaji, Jagir Bibi, Saraswati Madam. None of them would be leaving the house – no one would – so what was the point in coming into the city? Didn't he understand that? Especially now things were getting worse. Rumour was that a poor young man had his hand chopped off for hitting one of these crazy orange-brained dacoits. And now it seemed the Maoists were getting involved.

'As if one set of murderers wasn't enough,' Radhika Madam said.

His mother, too, begged him not to go into the city now. 'Wait a while, na? Work in the field for a few days. With us. You can make up the money afterwards. I'll help you.'

But Tochi said it wasn't the money.

'What use your pride when we find you dead in the street?'

But it wasn't pride, either. Or not just pride. It was a desire to be allowed a say in his life. He wondered if this was selfish; whether, in fact, they were right and he should simply recognize his place in this world.

The night before Navratri, on his way home, he stopped outside Kishen's. His friend was pulling the shutter down.

'You going into the city tomorrow?' Kishen asked.

'Do you think I should?'

'I think you should at least leave your licence at home. And anything else with your name on it.'

'Mera naam he tho hai.'

'Vho he tho hai mera naam,' Kishen finished. A schoolyard phrase, about their names being all they owned. The tailor took up his folded newspaper and flicked it twice with the back of his hand. 'Our brothers-in-arms. The Maoists. They say they'll fight fire with fire.'

Tochi shoved into gear, driving off. 'The pyres! The pyres!'

—

He didn't go. He stayed at home and went into the field with his brother. They worked all day, hacking, twining, carrying. Every hour he stood and slicked away the sweat from his forehead with the hem of his dhoti. Over the city, the sky was clear. He could see no column of smoke and he could hear no cries. All was silent save for his brother's scythe a few rows back.

His mother beheaded and cooked a whole chicken for the evening meal and afterwards Tochi returned to the auto, lying on top of the yellow roof with his hands behind his head. The sky was delirious with stars. The air was damp. The rains couldn't be long. He heard his mother coming down the lane and turned to look. She was holding something; a box, which she placed on the rear wheel arch. She unfurled a long iron key from the end of her chunni and rattled the tin open, lifting it up to Tochi because she didn't know how to count. He sat up on the roof, legs out in a wide V, and made equal piles of the notes.

'Two more months,' he said. 'Maybe three.'

'Shall we set a date, then?'

He nodded. 'I'll speak to them.'

Three days after Navratri, the rains came, blasting the red earth. Scooters began to lilt in the softened ground and dogs yelped under jeeps. Tochi rushed back from tying down the auto's rain-covers and stood shivering wet in the doorway, watching the manic fall of water and the sewage running fast beneath his feet. He said tomorrow he was going to the city. He couldn't wait.

'So soon?' his mother asked.

'This is when we earn.'

He was right. The first day back and he couldn't go ten metres without some man waving his briefcase at him, a woman calling for him to please stop before her umbrella collapsed on her. People fought over him, proffering double, triple the fare. It was the same the next day, and the one after that, and he motored through the splashy streets while the single black wiper did its squeaky work. Each day he kept a lookout for the Maheshwar Sena, but all he'd seen were two men in orange standing under the dripping awning of a tractor repair shop, waiting for the rain to lessen. Radhika Madam said the weather had forced them off the streets, and, anyway, they'd not achieved anything with their so-called day of the pure. Thank God.

'I could see them from our window. The whole time they spent getting drunk in their jeeps. Some revolution!'

Tochi knew otherwise. He'd driven through the alleys leading off Gandhi Chowk and seen the burnt-out tanning yard. And he'd heard his passengers talking: it seemed that at least three men had been killed, and maybe even a child.

Palvinder and Susheel were wedded that winter in an open-air ceremony and travelled to Shimla for their honeymoon. Then, not a year married, Susheel called to say he was bringing Palvinder back for the birth of their first child. Tochi's mother ordered that a new charpoy be bought – one in the double-weaved style – and placed this in the room they'd added to the rear of the house last summer.

'Tochi must be doing well,' Palvinder said when she arrived, testing out the bed. 'And what's this about using hair gel? You becoming a goondah now?'

'Doesn't she look different!' Dalbir said.

His mother said that of course she looked different. She was carrying a child inside her.

Tochi thought Dalbir meant something else, though, something to do with not looking like a girl any more. Perhaps that was why for the first time ever he'd heard her using his name, to his face.

Outside, a couple of kids were arguing with a passing dhol-player, pestering him for a go on his drum, and somewhere a man was selling hot peanuts and chai.

'It's nice to be home,' Palvinder said, a hand on her belly. She gestured for Dalbir to come sit beside her, saying how tall he'd grown and that she'd heard he was back at school now. No time even to call his old sister?

'I'm a busy man,' he said.

She laughed and held his face. 'Have you started shaving?'

Their mother came back and shooed the boys out. She wanted to speak to her daughter in private.

All month Tochi stopped off by the buffalo on his way home because his mother insisted Palvinder have fresh milk every night. She refused to reheat what was left from the dawnlight milking Dalbir completed before school. One evening, during Navratri, as

Tochi drove back with the milk, his mother met him halfway. The baby was coming, she said calmly, so he needed to go find Prakash Kaur from the next village and bring her here. Tochi passed her the bucket of milk and turned his auto around.

At the gate to the neighbouring village, two women stood chatting, baskets of winter spinach on their heads. Tochi asked if Prakash Bibi was at home. They said she wasn't, that she'd been doing seva at the city gurdwara all week. Tochi frowned. He'd been careful all day, after the havoc of last year, and didn't want to return to the city now, with the night looming.

'Is there any other midwife?'

They looked at each other and shook their heads.

As he raced off he heard them shouting their blessings for the newborn, perhaps mistaking him for the father.

The city roads were still quiet, too quiet for Navratri. Thankfully, Tochi found Prakash Bibi in the gurdwara canteen, scraping huge steel vats with wire wool. The sleeves of her widow-white kameez were rolled back into the fat of her elbows. When she saw Tochi she seemed to understand immediately and from a knot in the end of her chunni handed him a list of items to fetch from the Vishwanath Medicine Store.

'It's near the bus station. Come back here with it all and we'll bless it before we go.' She asked him if he needed money. He'd already turned for the door.

He followed the river, past the ghats, where vendors were clearing away their unsold shoes and handbags. Two beggar kids came dancing through the night, excitedly shouting, 'Khoon kharaba! Khoon kharaba!' Tochi turned up Tanners' Alley, engulfed in its sudden dark. The ground was uneven, forcing him to slow-swerve around the dust heaps. A couple of men were slumped against the exit. He thought they were drunks, then noticed one of them clutching his head, blood running down his wrists. There were voices, too, chanting, coming from the centre of the city, near the maidaan. He'd thought this might happen and reversed and went the long way round to the medicine store. But its shutters were down and it didn't matter how hard Tochi banged, no one opened up. Suddenly, four, six, eight motorbikes roared past, two men on each bike, a third standing at the back. They were whooping, holding aloft makeshift orange flags that cracked in the air. Across the city, fingers of smoke began to rise and spread. He knew of one other large medicine store, near Gandhi Chowk, but when he got to that roundabout some twenty or thirty motorbikes were circling it, revving their engines and pulling wheelies. A crowd watched on. He got nowhere trying to barge through a side gully – it was too narrow, too packed with exhilarated children and anxious adults. He headed back to the chowk, looking for another exit. Then a man ducked into his auto and asked to be taken to the train station.

'Unless they've been scared off by these hooligans, too. They make things so difficult, yaar.'

Tochi asked what had happened and he said it was the damn Maoists. They'd dumped a truckload of Brahmin bodies in the maidaan a few hours ago, all wrapped in an orange sheet painted *Happy Day of the Pure Anniversary*. But this was only what he'd heard. None of it might be true. The cheers and calls for revenge amplified, and more rioters appeared from the direction of the maidaan, displaying what looked like green petrol canisters.

'The poor chamaars are going to get it tonight,' the man said, tutting, and then perhaps he noticed Tochi's name on the licence card because he held Tochi's shoulder and told him to go home and look after his family. 'I'll walk. You go. Go now and I pray may God be with you.'

Villages burned as he sped out along the city road. Orange flames were thrown up everywhere and great flakes of ash drifted against the windscreen. Parents were dragging their children into the fields. He braked at an abandoned PCO and called Babuji, who said the world was going crazy and that he was on his way in the Contessa. If Tochi got there before him then he was to get his family and come to the big house at once. He'd left the rear gate open for them. Tochi hurried back into the auto and soon saw that his own village was on fire. He drove harder – 'No, no,' he kept muttering – and forced his way through the rush at the gate. He found Dalbir shaking at the end of the lane, beside their father in his wheelchair.

Tochi told them to get in, then ran up and ducked inside the house. His mother was in the new room padding a wet poultice against Palvinder's brow.

'What's happening? What's this shor-tamasha?' his mother asked.

He said they had to go. They rolled Palvinder onto her side and put their shoulders beneath each armpit and hefted her up. They walked like that up the lane, Palvinder counting her breaths and both arms circled low around her huge belly. She sat in the back with her parents while Dalbir jumped in the front, their father's wheelchair folded on his lap.

Tochi kept the headlights off. All around him huts were ablaze, and from within the burning shacks came screams. He stopped at the fountain, inside which a woman lay dead – she must have tried to douse the flames by rolling in the sand. Beyond her more orange-clad rioters were charging through the arch, banging their canisters together. And amongst it all was Babuji's silver Contessa, honking, stuck in the crush. Tochi turned round and drove past Kishen's and past their lane and made for the fields, urging the auto up onto the long dirt road. The track was full of half-submerged rocks and each sharp bump had Palvinder calling out for her mother.

'Where are you going?' Tochi's father asked.

He didn't reply. He knew the track would eventually lead them to the river but from there he didn't know what they would do or where they would go. Branches whipped across the roof. He heard his sister say she was scared and his mother said not to be, that it was all going to be fine. He ripped his licence card from the dashboard and threw it outside. Then he looked at his brother: Dalbir was staring straight ahead, his hands gripping the wheelchair.

'Bhaji?' Dalbir pointed. There were buffalo, tethered to the trees. And people standing around. Motorbikes, too, and a jeep. Tochi slowed right down. If he turned round he wouldn't be able to outrace them.

'Just say God's name and all will be well,' Tochi's mother said.

The men were calling to him, brazen and gesturing with their bottles. He shunted the auto on until they were ten or so metres away. 'Kapoor,' he whispered, and left the engine wheezing as he stepped outside. They were six or seven in number, smoking and drinking. Orange sashes were belted through their jeans and they'd dressed the buffalo in big floppy orange bow ties which gave the whole scene a grotesquely comic edge. One of them slid down the bonnet of his jeep and walked with expansive steps out from under the trees. Looped around his wrist, a small stereo crackled jazzily. A Bollywood song: *tu cheez badi hai mast mast* . . . He asked Tochi where he thought he was going.

'Doing my job. Getting our people away from the dirt.'

The man – the leader – nodded and said that was good, very good. Then he jutted his chin at one of his men who now walked past Tochi and towards the auto.

'What's your name?'

'Tarlochan.'

The leader waited.

'Kapoor.'

The man at the auto called out, 'Arré, she's having a baby.'

'What's his licence card say?' the leader said, still looking only at Tochi.

But he said he couldn't find it. 'It's not here.'

'Stay here,' he said to Tochi and went to the auto. Tochi followed behind anyway.

The leader peered in, his forearms on the roof, the stereo dangling its song. *Yeh pyar bada hai sakht sakht* . . . 'Is this your husband, sister?'

Palvinder was crying into her mother's neck.

'Are you going to the hospital?'

She nodded.

'Let us go,' Tochi's father said.

The leader walked round to Dalbir. 'What's your name, chotu?'

'Dalbir Kapoor,' he said, no hesitation.

The leader sighed. 'I better let you go, then.' He gave Dalbir the stereo, a gift for being brave, then with that long careful walk of his rejoined the others.

Tochi waited, then edged back into the auto. He spoke quietly, clearly. 'When we get around that bend, I want you all to get out and run into the trees.' Dalbir nodded. In the mirror he could see his sister and mother, foreheads pressed together, praying.

'Arré, aaja,' the leader called. 'She's having a baby!' Someone laughed from further back in the trees. Someone else looked down and nodded.

Tochi clicked the auto into gear and inched forward. As they passed the motorbikes and orange-bow-tied buffalo, the leader salaamed and wished them well. Tochi tracked them in the mirror, shrinking, until he rounded the wooded curve and they slid out of view. He slowed, but didn't stop. 'Go.'

Dalbir vaulted out, then ran round and prised his sister away from their mother. He tried to pull his mother out too, but she said she couldn't leave their father behind.

Tochi looked left, at his brother tunnelling into the night, leading his sister by the hand. He applied his foot to the pedal and pressed, and the harder he pressed the more the auto juddered over the rocks. Already he could see their headlights in his mirror. Star-shaped bulbs easily closing in. He thought it was the jeep, but then the headlights split off into motorbikes and came up on either side of him. They were dousing the auto, inside and out. His mother screamed and shouted for them to in God's name show some mercy. Tochi swerved towards one of the bikes, but the rider laughed and dodged out of the way. A rag was lit and thrown and there was a sudden whooshing upthrust of flame and noise. Tochi stopped and as he tried to pull his parents out, arms snaked around his waist, his neck and legs, and hauled him back. The smell of the fumes stunned him. They held him down, his cheek pressed hard into the road. He felt their knees all over him and could hear something being unscrewed and then the thick glug and plash of petrol pouring onto his back. He fought to breathe, arching his neck as if sucking up the pale moonlight. In front of him the crops flickered in fiery shadows and all around he could hear the blister and the pop and two voices becoming one, and a third, perhaps his own, joining them.

To lift the basket of bricks onto his head he had to squat so deeply that his knees flared out and his arse touched the ground. He tottered the length of the factory and stacked the bricks in the vault of the lorry in piles two bricks wide, alternating longways and crossways. On his first day he'd been told that would stop them toppling over. His first day – when the scars had still stung. He returned indoors, the shallow basket lolling by his side, and rejoined the queue at the brick mound.

At midnight the green bulb flashed and the conveyor belt groaned to a stop. The production team began to take off their gloves and dust masks, heading home. He figured there were still a good forty baskets left: he'd become expert at judging how many trips to the lorry remained after the belt had closed. He organized the bricks into his basket and raised it towards his head. But his arms were trembling and then his right hand collapsed and it took two men to rush up and steady the thing.

'Arré, go home, yaar,' one of them said. 'Don't kill yourself in your last week.'

He walked out, the brick dust ticklish in his hair, all over his face and clothes. He used to wonder what he might look like, a grey ghost stepping through the night. He passed the marble palace, built for some dead English queen, and stopped outside a hole in the wall for his one-rupee cup of mishty doi. It had been a fellow worker's tip: a cup of this sweet yoghurt after work and he wouldn't be coughing up dust through the night. He handed the empty clay cup back to the kid-vendor and crossed the tramlines and into the alley. He stuck to the middle of the dark lane, between cheap guest houses on one side and sleeping rickshaw drivers on the other. Past the Nepalese cafe was a large door of solid metal, a square hatch cut into it. He slid aside the bolt and bent through the hatch, entering a small, weedy courtyard. In one corner was a black arrangement of rubber tyres. He hooked one of these over his shoulder and made his way up the open stairwell at the rear of the yard. He could hear people talking behind the doors. Children, grandparents. A television. On the roof everyone was asleep already. The fire was out. He took the knife from his back pocket and drove it into the tyre, tearing along the central seam, wheeling the tyre round with his free hand. He cut the rubber into strips and made a pyramid of them to his left, and then he found some matches in the pocket of one of the men asleep, and on his third attempt the rubber caught and he got a little corner fire going. His stomach was contracting emptily, but he was tired enough that it didn't matter.

He waited on the factory floor outside the shift manager's office. The spinners were on full tilt that evening, filling the air with their grinding. The door opened and Mr Rao came out and said he was sorry to have kept Tochi waiting but Chief Manager Sahib had rung out of the blue, desperate to get his opinion on a most delicate work matter. 'Great changes afoot. But I have probably said too much already!' Tochi handed in his folded-up overall, and Mr Rao gave Tochi his weekly wad of notes, saying he couldn't believe the time had flown by so quickly. Was he going back to his village? In Orissa, was it?

'Bihar, sahib.'

'Exactly.' The phone rang inside. 'Excuse me. That's probably him again.'

Tochi picked up his sack of clothes, said a few goodbyes, and walked out. The gurdwara was only a short distance through the city gardens and there he bathed and ate. Then he waited outside the prayer hall. Inside, a turbaned old man was sitting behind the palki, reading from the book. He ended the verse with a long waheguru and gestured for Tochi to follow him through a side room and to a tall cupboard with a Chinese dragon print on its black lacquer. The old granthi turned the key and reached for Tochi's leather satchel. It contained everything he'd earned.

'Count it,' the granthi said.

'Thank you, Baba.'

'Is your bus tomorrow?'

'Tonight.'

The old man nodded. 'I've never seen you once pray. Not once have you entered the darbar sahib.'

Tochi touched the man's feet and begged his leave.

'I don't know what you've suffered, but you mustn't blame Him. It's too easy.'

Tochi looked to his left, to the rectangle of light in the doorway. He thanked the old man again and walked straight towards it. It had been two years. He was going home.

The local bus routes must have changed in his time away because he had to get off at the neighbouring village and walk the last two miles home. It was dawn, though stars still showed low in the sky. A white government van, a green cross on its side, stood under his village gate. He remembered it from the days after the massacre, just as he remembered the four bespectacled men and women who, two years on, were still sitting around with their clipboards and pencils. The woman smiled and made an approach, but he walked straight past, down to where Kishen's store used to be and over the sand-filled fountain. Some kids were playing cricket in his lane and he gave one ten rupees and told him to go ask Babuji if Tochi might come and see him any night this week.

Inside the house, there was nothing left save for his sister's red-and-gold chunni, coiled up in a corner. She'd left it behind in the rush to get out and he'd not felt able to touch it. Everything else he'd burned. He put down his sack of clothes and his satchel of money and went to the water pump behind the house. He worked the lever with one hand and splashed his face with the other. Then he heard a bolt slide open and a neighbour from the lane opposite brought him an iron bucket and a bar of streaky green soap. The man's wife stared from her doorway, curious. He filled the bucket, watching the soap sink cloudily to the bottom, then carried it inside. He undressed and squatted and used his cupped hands to pour the water down his back. These days he washed his back again and again – the absence of feeling meant he could never be sure how thorough he'd been.

He was asleep when the door opened and sunlight invaded. Blinking, he sat up and saw Babuji, walking stick in hand. Tochi said he'd have come to see him, that Babuji needn't have made the trip.

The old man gave a little dismissive shake of his stick. 'How was Calcutta? Everything OK in the factory? They treated you well?'

Tochi said they had.

'And the hotel was happy to have you? No trouble?'

'None,' Tochi lied.

'Excellent. So now you've got that out of your system, there's plenty of work here to do. When can you start?'

Tochi said nothing.

'Because I've been thinking and it'd be good to try and get three lots out this year.'

'Babuji, about what we talked about before I left?'

The old man grimaced, revealing perfect dentures. 'I was hoping you would have changed your mind.'

'Did you find out?'

'I found out that it's very expensive.'

'I think I've earned enough.'

'So what? Do you plan to live over there in hiding forever?'

'I will come back. I'll come back a rich man who can choose his own life.'

Babuji told him that, yes, he had found a man in Patna who did this kind of thing regularly. His fee was heavy – too heavy, as far as Babuji was concerned – but he said he could get you anywhere. Europe, England, Canada, America. Guaranteed.

'But you have no idea how hard it will be. Here you have a job, food, somewhere to sleep. You'll be sleeping on the streets over there. It won't be all playing cricket in their parks.'

'Where can I find this man?'

Babuji banged his stick. 'You are not thinking properly!'

Tochi stayed silent for a while, then repeated his question.

Shivroop Skytravel: a small glass-fronted building with a life-size cut-out of an air stewardess in the doorway. Tochi pushed inside, into the freeze of the air conditioning. A dark woman, a perfect strip of vermilion in her parting, looked up from behind her desk. She asked if she could help. She didn't smile.

'I'm here to see Mr Thipureddy.'

'What is it in connection with?'

'I'm here to see him about flights abroad.'

She sighed, seeming to understand, and leaned heavily to one side, perhaps pressing a button. Several minutes passed before a man stepped through the curtain at the back of the office. He was short, even darker than the woman and with a jumped-up little moustache whose tips pointed to God. The woman said something in Tamil and then the man clicked his fingers and told Tochi to come upstairs.

An hour later and Tochi was back on the street, his money-satchel lighter. Two weeks, the man had said. He'd called someone in Delhi and said that Tochi could be on a flight to Turkey in exactly two weeks. After that he'd be trucked as far as Paris, which was in France, and from there Tochi would be on his own. Did he understand?

'Yes,' Tochi said.

'Of course, I'll come with you as far as Delhi. Part of the service.' And then Mr Thipureddy took out some forms from his little Tamil drawer and snatched up the pen leaking in his shirt pocket. There was a map on the wall behind him.

'Where is France on there?' Tochi asked.

'Hm?' Mr Thipureddy twisted round. 'Oh, no. France is in Europe. That is South India. I am from – ' he reached back and jabbed his pen into the map – 'there. Kanyakumari. The southern-most tip of India. The end of the country.'

Tochi nodded.

'It is the only point in the world where three oceans meet. So you see it was in my blood to help people straddle the seas.' He gave a little laugh. It sounded like something he said often. 'Anyway. I expect you will be wanting to make payment.'

Mr Thipureddy met him twice more in the next ten days to go over what he called Tochi's itinerary, and the night before departure he confirmed by phone what time they were to meet at Patna Junction. Tochi switched off his mobile – Babuji's leaving gift – and sat on the plastic suitcase he'd bought that afternoon. There was nothing to do now but wait. He took out a tennis ball and bounced it against the ground and wall opposite, watching its yellow sheen glimmer and die as it ricocheted through the dark. He thought again of that place called Kanyakumari. The place of ends and oceans. It seemed amazing to him that there could be an end to India, one you could point to and identify and work towards. That things needn't go on as they are forever.

Later that night, Susheel came to say goodbye. He gripped the keys to his motorbike in his fist and said he'd heard bhaji was back. That he was leaving again, this too he'd heard. Tochi told him it was true.

'When do you go?'

'Tomorrow.'

Susheel nodded, looked down, looked up. He gave a nervous smile. 'Papa has arranged for my wedding next month. I thought you should know.'

'I'd heard,' Tochi said.

'Oh.'

The breeze picked up, disturbing the silence.

'I have to wake up early tomo—' Tochi began.

'Why did they find her in the trees?'

He moved a hand down his face. 'Because I told them to run away. Both of them.'

'All three of them,' Susheel corrected.

'All three of them,' Tochi repeated, barely moving his lips.

'Where are you going?'

'I don't know. Europe.'

Susheel looked to the lane beyond the open doorway. 'Away from here. Good.'

Tochi didn't know what that 'good' really meant.

'How did you earn enough?'

'I worked.' He didn't mention the money Babuji had given on his parents' death – a pseudo life-insurance payout – or what he'd made from selling the rental contract on the land. Even with all that, he'd only just enough to cover all of Mr Thipureddy's costs.

'My papa's been trying for fifteen years and still can't afford to go.'

'I guess I was born lucky,' Tochi said.

Susheel smiled, wry, and extended his hand. 'Papa asked me to invite you to our house. But it seems we were too late.'

Tochi shook his hand. 'Good luck.'

'Good luck.'

Tochi heard the motorbike being kick-started at the end of the lane, and then the sound of the engine withdrawing. He'd been dispatched to ask if he could join Tochi, or if Tochi would send for him, or make some provision for him once he was safely fixed up abroad. Susheel would've known that Tochi understood this. But the boy hadn't asked, for whatever reason. And no doubt he'd go back home and tell his father that Palvinder's brother hadn't been in and the door had been locked and that he'd waited as long as he could. And the father would sit there swirling the dirty ice cubes in his whisky, wondering how much to believe his son.

The coach station at Delhi's Indira Gandhi International Airport was so blazingly floodlit that Mr Thipureddy changed his mind and told the tuk-tukwallah to drop them off in the cargo park instead. That had been over an hour ago.

'She's always late,' he said and flipped open his phone.

'No need to call, uncle. I'm here.'

She approached through the smoky lilac air, the skirt of her sari held away from the dirt.

'Madhu,' Mr Thipureddy said.

Her shiny plastic waistcoat looked crimped in the moonlight

and from the lanyard around her neck hung a whistle and perhaps a security pass. The niece, Tochi thought. She asked how her aunty was, if Aanjay's marks had recovered sufficiently to get into college this year. Only then did she say hello to Tochi. 'You've heard of Russia? Because we're going to have to go via Ashgabat, which is pretty much the same thing.'

Mr Thipureddy kissed the air. Tochi wondered if he'd have to hand over more money.

'No choice,' she said. 'They moved Annie. Too much flip-flopping in Customs these days.'

She showed her uncle the new tickets and asked if he'd got all the papers officialized. He gave them over.

'Which route?' Mr Thipureddy asked.

'B. Ashgabat to Turkey. Then Europe.'

'You don't get seasick, do you?' Mr Thipureddy said to Tochi. 'But Arhan will look after you.'

The niece looked up from palming through Tochi's documents. 'It's Deniz now. How long since your last carry-over?'

'Not since that business with the food on the plane.'

She said to Tochi, 'The food on the plane is free. Do you understand? Don't try to pay for it. Don't cause a scene – just eat it.'

Tochi thanked Mr Thipureddy, who wished him the best of luck, and followed the niece into the airport. She talked him through what to expect, what he'd have to do. It sounded like a routine she was ploughing through, even where she said she was going to repeat the key points because she could tell he was nervous. She gave him a small red rucksack to hold over his shoulder – 'A book, toothbrush, socks. Motor magazines. I don't know why you boys never bring hand luggage. It looks so suspicious' – and a bright green-and-gold ribbon to tie onto the bag before he got to Turkey. It was how the driver would recognize him.

'Won't that look suspicious?' he asked.

'On a plane with Indians? It'll look restrained.'

She asked if her uncle had shown him how to use an escalator – moving stairs. He said he hadn't and she made a frustrated noise.

She looked at the watchface on the underside of her slender wrist. 'We don't have time now. You'll have to just work it out.'

They checked in his suitcase, where a woman name-badged Annie stamped his ticket and fake passport and wished him a safe flight. He put the red rucksack through security and rejoined the niece on the other side of the beeping electronic arch. She checked the boarding time and pointed out the gate. Then she extended her hand and wished him very good luck.

'If anyone stops you or asks you anything, just remember what I told you. But Annie will be on the flight.'

'Thank you,' Tochi said.

She seemed about to go, half turning. 'I was sorry to hear about your family.'

Tochi said nothing.

She sighed. 'Well, let us know how you get on.' And she walked back, ignoring the security guard who laughed and asked her how much she'd pocketed this time.

The boarding call was announced and her instructions started to churn in his mind. He looked to the floor, fighting his nerves, then got on the plane and found his window seat and belted himself in. Somehow – the graceful stewardesses, the exasperated passengers, the hard, straight seats – it all looked as he'd expected it to. An elderly Sikh man in a three-piece suit sat next to him.

The plane began to move. He looked out of the window at the dirty white span of wing veering away and beyond that to the floodlit luggage men playing cards on the bottom step of a mobile staircase. Then the plane started to speed up and there was a savage oncoming roar as Tochi felt himself forced back into his seat. He could see the luggage men clasping their cards to their chest and their trousers yapping wildly about their ankles and then the ground tilted away and the dark sky opened, beckoned, and a sense of being freed, of freedom, poured beautifully through him.

He didn't see Annie again until they arrived in Ashgabat, when he took up his rucksack and followed everyone out of the plane and into the airport. She was sitting behind a glass counter, as though she'd always been there. People were reaching for their documents and joining one of two queues. He waited in Annie's line. She had a serious face, which complemented the way she stamped tickets and dispatched passengers on their way. When he gave over his documents, she glanced up briefly, then applied the circular green stamp and moved on to the next.

He filed into the waiting room: a small, sorry place with rows of rudimentary grey seats and an old-style black-and-white ticker board that looked broken. There was a bar at the back playing American-sounding music, and a barman who was punching open boxes of snacks and stacking them high. There was no one at the bar, though. Everyone was sitting on the seats and quietly waiting. He'd seen lights and cars on the descent, but now it felt as if they were all stranded here in this Russian desert. He rested his head on the rucksack.

It was still dark outside when people started to queue at the airport's only boarding gate. He half rose out of his seat, then saw Annie at the bar, tidying her skirt over her knee as she talked to another girl. *She'll let you know when it's time,* Mr Thipureddy's niece – Manju? Mandip? – had said. So he sat back down.

Two hours passed and more flights had departed before Annie came down in her high heels and announced that the flight to Gaziantep was now boarding. She spoke first in English and then, with almost smiling slowness, in Hindi.

He stayed awake all through the flight. The flickering map on the beige-boxed screen at the front of the plane made little sense to him and he spent most of the time watching the slow dissolving of the night, the way the heavy black-blues hung on and hung on until finally relenting to the turning world and the first faint pinks of daybreak.

Though the landing wasn't as smooth as last time, and passengers gasped and lurched, the pilot's voice came over and he said something which made everyone laugh. Out of the plane, he noticed Annie up ahead, in front of all the other stewardesses. He kept his head low, trying to keep up. Suddenly, the moving stairs appeared in front of him, like a cliff drop. He didn't have time to wonder how the thing worked – he could feel people at his back – and put one foot onto the grille and gripped the rail, his left leg somehow following. He felt a little dizzy, as if he wasn't sure if the stairs were carrying him down or if the ground was floating up. He focused on the man in front and tried to copy him off the thing.

The hall was large and carpeted red and his fellow travellers were taking out their passports. Once more, Tochi joined Annie's line. She didn't look at him as he passed and when he turned round, she'd gone. A gum-chewing man with a glistening bald head called him forward. Tochi handed over his passport, and as the man flicked through, a tricky smile came to his lips.

'So you're paying my rent this month, ha?' he asked in bad Hindi.

Tochi said nothing.

'Which of Annie's are you? Germany? UK?'

'France,' Tochi said.

The man nodded, tapping in some numbers. 'Good. I hate the French.'

He collected his luggage, dragging it off the belt, and headed straight out of the automatic glass doors and into the new world.

The niece had been right: his ribbon was one of the least colourful, and it took some time before a short, heavyset man with surprisingly quick strides approached. His yellow shirtsleeves were squared around his elbows, sunglasses on his head.

'Tar-lo-chan, Indien?'

He followed the man outside. A dry, sandy heat filled the day and two great whorls of sweat swelled out from the man's armpits, almost meeting in the centre of his back. As if reading Tochi's mind, the man twisted round and said, 'No air con outside.' He spoke reasonable Hindi and said his name was Deniz and welcome to Antep.

They sat in silence on the dinky airport bus that dropped them in the middle of an industrial estate. They walked along the perimeter fence, beyond which women in headscarves and red-stained overalls were eating pastries in the shade. Deniz shouted something across to them and some of them laughed and raised their hands. They seemed to be wishing Tochi good luck. Rounding the corner, some sort of depot came into sudden view, pallets strewn, and Deniz pointed out his truck – the only truck there – a reassuringly huge twelve-wheeled monster. Its black tarpaulin bore a giant image of wet tomatoes on a vine. Deniz gestured for Tochi to wait while he went inside. He returned ten, fifteen minutes later, stapled papers in his hand and a yellowing pillow squashed under his arm. He said it was time to go. Tochi moved to the rear of the truck, but Deniz threw him the pillow and told him to climb in the front.

A beeping sounded as they reversed, then Deniz changed gears and took the road out of the estate. Tochi stared. He'd never felt so high up in a vehicle before. He could see all the way back to the airport, where a plane was taking off, climbing its ramp of air.

He waited outside the cemetery gates, ready to leave, his two months in Paris just as Deniz had predicted. They'd been on the deck of the ferry to Brindisi when the Turk warned that France was the wrong choice for him. London would be much better.

'London? You understand me?'

The waters looked free and magical, the sun breathily warm on Tochi's face. He wondered if this was what it would feel like to stand on that southernmost tip of India. The calling sea beyond.

'Very racist, the French are. Horrible people. The English are much nicer. You should have paid a little more and gone to England.'

'As long as there's work.'

'Not much work in Paris for you men these days.'

Later, as they'd crossed into Austria, or maybe France, Tochi asked him if he meant what he said, about there being no work in France?

'Did I say that?' He shrugged. 'It's true, anyway. You'll find out soon.'

'How much for you to take me to England?'

They agreed on a price and a date. And when Deniz dropped him off at Bobigny gurdwara – 'All the Indians spend their first night here' – he reminded Tochi to be waiting outside the cemetery gates and to not tell anyone. He didn't want half of Bangladesh climbing into his truck and ruining his tomatoes.

He completed a second circuit of the cemetery in case Deniz had meant some other gate, but there was only the one. He sat on his suitcase, rucksack between his legs, and ran a thumbnail in the leather creases of his boots, where foot met shin. Sleeping in the park. Less than one week of work. He was glad to be going. The traffic was sparse, the road lonely. There were apartments for sale in the window of the shop opposite, and there, in its dull reflection, he saw Deniz coming up behind him. His sunglasses shone and on the chest pocket of his red T-shirt a black horse pranced.

'So! Ready to leave, my friend?'

For the ferry to England, he hid in the back of the lorry. Europe was no problem, Deniz had said, but these English types could be very difficult. Tochi hunkered down, knees tight to his chest and head tucked in. It was as dark as a well. Metal barrels surrounded him – right above his head, too – their clinking the only sound. He fell asleep. At some point he lifted his head off his knees and felt a deep stillness inside him. The barrels weren't wobbling. The engine wasn't running. All was peace and darkness. He closed his eyes, though the insides of his lids were painted with images of dying and the dead. He was woken by the rear shutter rattling up. He held his breath, didn't move. Daylight made a faint blond entrance. There were voices, Deniz's among them, and knuckles being rapped on the containers. More voices, white-sounding, until the shutter clattered back down. A little later the engine roused and he felt the truck's clunking descent.

'This is England,' Deniz said, when at last Tochi was able to wriggle out. They were in some sort of car park. Shops, white people. Nearby, the grey noise of fast traffic. The sky looked the same as in Paris. Deniz fetched them a plain baguette each and they got back in the front and rejoined the motorway.

'I thought you said it would only take an hour?' Tochi said.

'From Calais. They do less checking in Dieppe. Why, was it uncomfortable?'

'It was fine.'

Deniz said he'd drop Tochi off in Southall, in London, unless he had anywhere else in mind. 'My wife's brother is always saying how he needs waiters. He has a restaurant.'

Tochi stared out of the window. The roads seemed impossibly straight and flat, the fields perfectly hedged in.

'What do they grow here?'

Deniz said he didn't know.

'It looks like spinach.'

'Perhaps.'

He looked closer. 'It is spinach.'

'Why, does it remind you of home?'

'It reminds me of spinach.'

Two hours later they arrived, parking the lorry half on the pavement. A car beeped, swerved past.

'There's your temple,' Deniz said. He nodded towards a gold dome, princely and Indian against the coming dark. 'And this is the main road.'

The bus stops – Tochi guessed they were bus stops – showed filmi posters, while passing women retightened cardigans over their kameez, salwaar-bottoms puffed out in the wind like legs of mutton.

'Are they all illegal here?'

'No, just Indian.'

He followed Deniz out of the driver's side, past a travel agent's called IndiGo and a shop display of sari-draped dummies. Deniz halted outside a fast-food place, cartoon chickens on the window, and told Tochi to wait there a minute. He watched Deniz enter and shake hands with a fat man who kept wiping his nose on his apron. They spoke a while and the fat man lifted his shoulders heavily and gestured around him, in a move that suggested either there was more than enough work, or not enough as it was. As Deniz came back through the door, Tochi stepped away.

'I've got to go but wait inside and Marat will take care of you.'

'Is there work?'

'Maybe. He's not sure. Just wait.'

They returned to the truck so Tochi could collect his bag, his suitcase, and pay Deniz the balance.

'I hope you make your millions,' Deniz said, restarting the engine, saying good luck, goodbye.

Inside the restaurant, the fat man – Marat – brought Tochi a can of cola and showed him to a table. He moved his hands so that Tochi understood he should wait there while Marat used the telephone. Tochi nodded, said thank you in English.

It was a busy night. White people, Indian, black, everyone seemed to eat food from here. Even Indian girls came blustering in, in tight tops and skirts. Tochi stared. Another fat man worked with Marat at the counter, while further back two younger men in sleeveless T-shirts operated the fryers. He could easily learn that, Tochi thought.

The chicken clock on the door said ten past eleven and Marat untied the apron from behind his back and lifted it over his head. He said something to the others and indicated that Tochi come with him, flicking the lights off on his way out. They turned down a side street where Marat pointed to a long window bordered with red conch shapes. The glass in the front door had the same pattern.

'Bangladeshi,' Marat said.

Tochi followed him round to a small yard where a shallow sports car was parked. A tall man with a shaved head and a gold bracelet leaned on the bonnet, chatting into his mobile. He saw them waiting, yet made no move to end his call. Eventually, he and Marat exchanged some words and the tall man looked over.

'Where you from?'

'Bihar.'

'How'd you get here?'

'Truck.'

'Can you wash dishes?'

'If there's water I can.'

The tall man nodded at Marat, who looked relieved as he left.

'How old are you?' the man asked.

'Twenty-six.'

'Course you are.'

He said his name was Sukhjit and he took Tochi back through the restaurant and to the kitchen at the rear. The floor was tacky against his feet.

'Start with the dishes and work your way round.'

'Where do I sleep?'

'On the floor. Tomorrow, I'll bring a mattress. And then you better move in with Sheera.'

He put down his bags and got to it. Work on day one. This was good. Maybe it was true what they said about England. That this was where you could make something. He was on to his third stack of dirty plates when he sensed someone watching him. He looked over his shoulder. It was a waiter, his head curled around the door-frame as if sneaking a look.

'I'm Munna. What's your name?'

'Tarlochan.'

'Tarlochan Singh Sandhu?'

'No.'

'I'm Munna Singh Sandhu. But Munna's not my real name. It's my baby name. Are you a friend of Sheera Uncle?'

Tochi said nothing.

'He's not very nice.'

Slow, backward, he looked about seventeen. A two-note car horn sounded, the second note more belligerent than the first, and then the boy disappeared and Tochi heard the front door opening, closing, locking.

When he woke he had to peel his cheek off the damp steel flank of the cooking range. It was still dark – there were no windows in the kitchen – and he didn't know what the time was. If he listened, he could hear the noise of passing traffic. He couldn't hear any movement from the restaurant, though. Perhaps they were asleep, the other workers. Gently, he opened the kitchen door and blinked in the sudden bright. A giant wing of pale, wintry sun rested across the room, over the dark wood tables and the chairs turned upside-down on them. There was a counter to Tochi's right, with a cash register at the far end, and behind the counter were glasses and bottles and fridges. Through the window, he tried to work out the shops on the other side of the road. Fruit, one of them. Mobile phones another. Then the sari place. And next to that a shop where men stared up at a TV screen, watching horses race. He heard a noise, a wailing like the ambulances in Patna. Cars slowed and set themselves aside as two police vans came flying down. Tochi flattened himself against the wall until the wailing retreated, then returned quickly to the kitchen and closed the door behind him.

Hours later, he heard the restaurant door unlocking and the muffled creak of feet on carpet. He stood up and waited to be discovered. It took a few minutes – there was first the clinking of glasses, then the complicated beeps of the cash register. When the man came through the kitchen door he paused mid-sip and stared at Tochi over the rim of his glass. His eyes were red and small. He finished necking the drink – whisky – and went round the kitchen switching things on: the tandoor, the oven, something under the sink that made nasty crunching sounds. The crown of his head was so bald it shone, but the hair around the sides was long and landed in greasy curls about his collar. He went back out into the restaurant and next Tochi heard a sustained hungry growl. He opened the door and saw the whisky man pushing around the room some sort of cleaning machine.

The backward boy – Munna – arrived at the exact moment the oven timer rang out four o'clock. 'I'm on time again, Sherry,' he said. 'That's three times this week.'

Behind the bar, the whisky man was pouring himself another peg. He'd changed into his chef's whites. 'Call me that again and I'll rip your tongue out.'

Tochi went out into the yard. It was already dark. He rested against the wall and slid down to a crouch, T-shirt riding up to his shoulder blades. He put his head in his hands and it took a few moments to recall the name of this place he was now in. He just had to work, he told himself. Keep working, keep earning, and he'd get there, wherever there was. When he came back through to the kitchen, onions were being violently chopped, mustard seeds popping. In the restaurant, tables were dressed in burgundy polyester, a steel boat of ketchup marooned in the centre. Munna waited by the door ready to greet the guests. Sukhjit was here too, and with him a kid whose narrow sideburns, amazingly, met in the cleft of his chin. Like Munna, he was buttoned up in white satin shirt and black trousers.

'This is him,' the boss said.

The kid approached, all swagger, holding out his fist. Tochi did nothing and the kid grinned and reached for Tochi's hand and closed it into a fist and touched his own with it. 'Like that, see?'

'My nephew: Chikna,' Sukhjit explained.

'Chico,' the boy said. 'It's Chico.'

'Actually, it's Charandeep Singh.'

The boy frowned. 'Thanks, chacha.' Then, to Tochi: 'So you a fauji or a scooter?'

The door opened and a couple in matching leopard scarves blew in. Munna beamed and took their coats and said that, yes, winter was definitely on the way, and Tochi went back into the kitchen, where several steel vats were already humped into the sink.

He got into routine. First he scraped off the leftover chicken or curry or mint sauce or rice into the bin he'd wheeled in from the yard. Then he rinsed the dishes in a tub placed to the left of the sink, before plunging them into the sudsy water and scouring until he heard squeaks. Lastly, he passed them through a second tub on his right, in water made faintly green by a thimbleful of disinfectant Munna had shown him how to use. His fingers shrivelled and the plate of skin between his shoulder blades ached. It was two o'clock when he heard the last of the diners waved off, and the waiters took a bowl of chicken curry from the chef and started back for the restaurant, calling for Tochi to come and join them.

They ate with their fingers, moulding the rice and chicken into little balls. The chef came through with his own thali and sat alone by the long window.

Charandeep spoke. 'Chacha says you're from Bihar, yeah? Blitzed it over truck-style?' He had to repeat himself, in Panjabi.

Tochi nodded, not looking up from his bowl.

'Proper outlaw,' Charandeep said, approvingly.

'Are you here for a holiday?' Munna asked.

Charandeep smiled. 'Kids, eh?' He went on: 'Same as Chef. Trucked it over time ago. Sixties, maybe.' He leaned in. 'Sent him a bit doolally, though. What's your tonic, alcoholic? Know what I mean?'

A car with a fierce exhaust parked up. 'Uncle's back,' Munna said.

Sukhjit swung through from the kitchen, rubbing his hands warm. 'Too cold for love out there. How's things? Sherry?'

'I have to call him Ardashir or he'll rip my tongue out,' Munna said.

'As long as it's out of hours,' Sukhjit said, singing open the cash register.

One by one they dumped their bowls in the sink. A car horned and Munna left; then Ardashir pulled on his long black coat, and Sukhjit and Charandeep said they were going too and turned off the lights and locked the door. Tochi returned to the kitchen. He changed the water in the sink and started again. It was nearly four when he wheeled the bin out and spread his blanket beside the still-warm range. Sukhjit must have forgotten about his mattress.

*

Most days he stayed in the restaurant, going no further than the window, though once a week he'd proceed onto the road, with its big red buses and busy faces. He'd journey to the end of the street and around the corner, from where he could see the green tops of the old gasworks. He always paused outside a shop that sold homes, calculating how long it might be before he could afford one.

He was paid on Sunday nights. He'd be called into the yard, where Sukhjit held out his notes through the window of his red Alfa, the engine thrumming. It was about a tenth of what he'd expected, yet he said nothing. He used his first wage to buy some proper soap. The rest he folded into his rucksack, which along with his suitcase he stowed in the gap between the fridge and the wall.

On his third payday his suitcase was stolen. He'd been taking down the chairs in the restaurant when Munna rushed in from the kitchen shouting about some goreh robbers. Tochi sprinted into the yard so fast a doornail ripped off his jeans pocket, but there was only the rear end of a white hatchback skidding round the corner. The microwave lay cracked on the kitchen floor, dropped in the getaway, and the drawers were all tipped open, Tochi's suitcase missing.

He picked up his rucksack and checked his money was still there. He had one other shirt and pair of trousers but the rest of his clothes had been in the suitcase, along with his blanket and towel. He got his fist around his remaining jeans pocket and ripped that off too.

'Fuckin' chiefs,' Sukhjit said, that evening. He passed Tochi his notes. 'These things happen, eh?'

Tochi said nothing.

'Why aren't you living with Sheera? It's raid season, man – Sherry, staying with you from now on, yeah?'

Ardashir was putting on his coat. 'Never stopped him.'

It was a few minutes' walk, a run-down part of the neighbourhood Tochi had never been to. Most of the windows were grilled over and behind one of the grilles twinkled a dwarfish tree. Ardashir went down a flight of thin stone steps, Tochi following, and once through the front door he tugged on some string dangling from the ceiling, which brought on the light. Sink, cooker, fridge, boiler. Three chairs – one straight, two orange plastic – stood against the wall with several empty bottles of whisky huddled around their legs. Beneath the long net of the window was a single bed on tiny gold wheels. Tochi dropped his bag to the floor and took a piss in the bathroom, on the other side of the kitchen. When he came back Ardashir was pulling sofa cushions from under the bed and arranging them in the middle of the room.

In the morning, lying awake on the sofa cushions, he watched Ardashir at the sink, pouring whiskies and chucking them back one after the other, growling as each peg hit the spot. He was in trousers only and the heavy slack of his stomach pressed against the worktop.

'If you get caught, you don't live here.'

Tochi nodded.

'You don't know me, you understand?'

'It's your house.'

Ardashir gave a little snort. 'Yeah.'

They didn't bother one another. Soon as Tochi woke he washed and left to look for a second, daytime job. Sometimes he asked the Turk, Marat, and often he trudged to the gurdwara in case fruit-picking had started up. He was back at the restaurant for midday, time enough to vacuum and dress the tables. Ardashir would arrive an hour later and change into his whites, and they'd work together in the kitchen, quietly, peaceably, making the midnight walk back to the basement flat in silence, and in this way the seasons shifted and the months passed.

The restaurant closed on Christmas Day – the one day in the year when it did – and Tochi spent the morning lying on the floor, on the blue sofa cushions, gazing up at the damp ceiling. There was no point in looking for any work today – he'd learned that much from last year. Ardashir sat on his straight chair at the window. After a silence of almost two weeks, the older man spoke.

'How long are you staying here?'

'I can leave now.'

'In England, I said.'

'Until I've earned enough.'

'Then you're a fool.'

The afternoon was quieter still and as they sat down with the lamb curry brought back from the restaurant the previous night, all that could be heard was the dull scrape of metal on foil and the slurp and slop of eating. Sometimes a car went by.

'You're a bigger fool than me. I didn't have anyone to tell me different.'

Tochi said nothing.

'Take my advice and go back now. Before there's nothing to go back for and you're stuck here.' It was the most he'd ever said to Tochi. Perhaps it was this Christmas spirit everyone went on about. 'Thirty-three years. Didn't do my papa's rites, my biji's. Wife and children started new lives. For what? So I can sit here in this hell. No future but death. Just a body needing to be clothed and fed. Go back, you understand?'

'I've done my papa's rites. And my biji's. And my brother's and my sister's.'

Tochi's wrist began to tremble and he lowered the spoon and stared at the ground between his knees. He heard Ardashir stride past and pour the rest of his food into a black bin liner hanging off the side of the sink.

The restaurant reopened fully on New Year's Eve. Tochi worked fast, determinedly, but by the time the countdown and midnight cheer came and went he still had hours ahead of him. Sukhjit stumbled in. He was laughing and had his arm collapsed across another man's shoulder.

'Arré, Sheera, give my cousin one of your lassis, man. We're gunna be Panjabis tonight!'

'Does that mean we get to beat our wives?' the other man said.

Sukhjit put a finger to his own lips. 'They'll hear you. Ears like an elephant.'

Soon, Sukhjit rounded everyone out the door, saying it was over to his place for whisky and poker, and in less than a minute all the noise of the night evaporated and the restaurant door locked shut. Ardashir joined Tochi at the sink, grabbing a wire-wool scourer of his own.

It was past five when they made it to the flat.

'Thank you,' Tochi said.

'You won't get anywhere working like a dog for him. Earning shit money.'

He arranged the blue sofa cushions in the middle of the room.

'Take the bed,' Ardashir said.

'I'm good here.'

'I said take the fucking bed.'

The next day, Tochi was pulling down the chairs from their tables when Ardashir answered the restaurant door. It was the same man who'd come into the kitchen with Sukhjit. He stood there shaking the cold off his small shoulders, flicking out his feet. He seemed to hate standing still. He even spoke fast.

'What you doing, man? It's New Year's fucking Day.'

'Do you want a drink?' Ardashir said.

'Not all alkies, dude. So where is he? This him?' he asked, looking at Tochi. 'You got your NI card?'

Tochi looked to Ardashir who said he'd get one in the week. 'As long as you get his CSA card.'

The man shrugged. 'Coming out his pay, in any case.'

'How much?' Ardashir asked.

'That's between me and Freshy Jo here.'

'How much?' he asked again.

'You his fucking pimp?'

They agreed on a figure, which was about four times his current wage. They shook hands.

'I'm Virender. Vinny. And you're lucky, you know that? I've just got a new contract. A top-of-the-motherfucking-range hotel. Should knock the smile off Sukh's face.'

'When can he start?' Ardashir asked.

'I'll speak to Sukh. But say I'll pick him up next Saturday. I'm down south anyway. Have your suitcase ready to go. Acha?'

On his last morning Tochi tidied away the sofa cushions and sat on the straight chair, red rucksack at his feet. Ardashir placed a pair of leather workboots on the floor. They looked old and used but stronger than his own.

'You'll need them.'

'I'll buy some.'

'I'd like you to take them, but suit yourself.'

He sat on the bed and swigged from his bottle. They said nothing until a few hours later when a white van parked outside and the horn sounded.

'I told him not to do that,' Ardashir said, standing up. Then, to Tochi: 'You should go.' With that, he disappeared into the bathroom behind the kitchen, leaving his bottle on the worktop.

Tochi hooked the rucksack over his shoulder and took up the boots and walked out of the room and door and up the stone steps. The day was cold and bright. He opened the van door and nodded at Vinny and climbed in.

3. SETTLING IN

The Sheffield snow had nearly gone. Grass showed darkly through and only a few white sleeves remained on the roofs of the houses opposite. Moving away from the window, Tochi prised off the workboots Ardashir had given him and put on his cheap trainers instead. He took the half-roti he'd saved from his lunch and, on his way downstairs, crushed it all into his mouth. The kid, Randeep, he could hear in the kitchen, complaining to someone about the cement their gaffer had ordered: 'It'll take forever if we can't use the jib. Maybe if—' Tochi closed the front door and bent his head low against the cold.

He turned left on Ecclesall Road, not right as Randeep had shown him, and strode past all the places he'd already tried twice in the last month. He walked efficiently, never meeting anyone's eye. Once he was through the city centre, the terrain rose steeply and from the top of the hill he could see the blue dome and sprawl of that shopping centre they all spoke about. He couldn't remember the name. It didn't matter. There'd be no work for him in a place like that.

There was a Nooze 'n' Booze a little further along, windows grilled over, manned by a bearded sardar type. Tarlochan waited for a couple to leave with their bottles of wine. The uncle looked older this close up. In his sixties, at least.

'Sat sri akal.'

The man smiled. 'Sat sri akal, puth.' Son.

Tochi explained that he was new to the area and looking for evening work. He'd be happy stacking shelves or working behind the counter or cleaning. Anything really. Whatever it was, he'd put his heart into it.

'Fauji, hain?'

Tochi nodded.

'Pind?'

'Manighat.'

The man tried to place it.

'It's in Bihar.'

A sigh, a nod. 'Acha. Well, good luck.' And the man gestured for the turbaned girl behind Tochi to come forward. 'Third time this evening, beiti. Is it still not working?'

Outside the shop, Tochi made a fist and banged the grille-shutters, shaking everything. The shopkeeper came out. 'Any trouble and I'll call the police.' His voice wobbled. Tochi moved on a few feet, then stopped, his forehead to a lamppost.

'Are you all right?'

It was the girl. From the shop. In her hand some pink meter tokens. He glanced up to her turban, then spat on the floor.

'He wasn't fair to you. He didn't treat you well. I told him so.'

'Right.'

'We're all equal before God.'

He wished she'd go away.

'I'm new to the area as well.'

He nodded.

'It's not easy. It's very lonely. I get very lonely. Especially at night.'

She seemed an odd mixture of strength and innocence, with little idea of how she might be misconstrued.

'Do you know where the gurdwara is? If you're lonely you can go there. I do. Or if you need food.'

'What if I need a woman's bed?' he found himself saying, needing to hurt her the way he was hurting.

She remained perfectly still, yet he could see her mind turning away from him. 'God can't provide everything,' she said, and wished him well in his search for work.

The kid's friend, Avtar, was leaving the house as Tochi arrived back. On his way to his evening job, going by the orange uniform. He nodded at Tochi and held the front door open for him, and Tochi nodded back and passed inside. From the dimly lit hall, he could see into the front room where a few of them were watching a Tamil porno, Gurpreet urging the man on. Upstairs, the kid was sitting on his mattress, writing into something. The glow from the streetlights seeped through the curtain edges and made a vase on the wall, above the boy's head. Tochi lay back on his own mattress, undoing the Velcro straps of his trainers but keeping the shoes on because the floor was so cold. He closed his eyes. A pleasant darkness enshrouded him. All he could hear was the scratch of the boy's pen.

'I'm writing a letter home,' the kid said. 'Better than phoning.'

Tochi felt he nodded, eyes still closed.

'I've mentioned about my new room-mate.' A pause. 'That's you.'

'Give my salaams.'

'And I'm including some photos of me and Avtar bhaji. We took them at a booth in the station last week. You get four in a row. And it's not too expensive. I can show you if you like.'

Silence.

'I mean, if you want to send some to your family.'

Tochi laced his hands together behind his head. 'I'll think about it.'

*

The foundation concrete had cured and they'd spent the morning making a start on the brick posts. It was donkey work, really. Around them, yellow cranes manoeuvred into place, driven by professional-looking white faces. Tochi secured the final brick into his section and jumped onto the wall, confirming everything was flush and bedded down. From here, he could see across the whole site. There were almost three times as many people now as when he'd first arrived. Project managers, floor planners, site officers, water operatives. A roving swarm of hard yellow hats, fenced in by the short brick posts that at last seemed to be giving the site some sort of shape. He saw the kid's slim figure far across the way. He had his hands on his knees, peering into a turning barrel of cement as if he'd lost something inside it.

That evening, he changed route, passing the Botanical Gardens and the small moonless wood. There were fewer shops this way –

instead, the further he went, the bigger the houses became, the wider the avenues. The air felt greener, as if this was where all that countryside started insinuating itself. The something district, they called it. Even their green spaces sounded urban. He walked for perhaps an hour and found himself in a village, in front of a little, pretty convenience store. Inside, a brown kid in several layers and a baseball cap idled at the counter. Tochi made his usual pitch.

'You want a job?' the kid surmised. His Panjabi was poor, Hindi-inflected – 'Aap job chaiyeh?' – and he'd probably understood little of what else Tochi had said.

He slid open a wooden panel behind him and called up the stairs for his mother. Tochi heard her coming down, mumbling that everything was price-marked, Manvir, why don't you look before interrupting her all the time? A small woman, who might have been handsome if it wasn't for her long jaw, she stopped as soon as she saw Tochi. 'Oh, sorry.'

The boy said something and then the woman sent her son upstairs and turned to Tochi. 'You're looking for work?'

Born back home, clearly. Probably came over to be married. 'Ji. In the evenings. Cleaning, shelf-stacking, I can do anything.'

She thought a moment. 'I'm guessing you're illegal.'

Tochi nodded.

'Pind kerah?'

'Mojoram.' It was the name of the Panjabi village he'd worked in. She asked him his name and again without hesitating he said, lied: 'Tarlochan Sandhu.'

'Jat, then?'

This time he paused. 'Ji.'

She said her husband was in India for a few weeks but they had been looking for someone. Especially now they were both getting on a bit. It was just so hard to find someone honest, you know? You couldn't trust a gori and her sons weren't interested. Tell them to stand in the shop for even an hour and you'd think they'd been asked to reverse the cosmos.

Tarlochan asked if that meant he had a job.

The landlord knocked on the first working day of every month. A compact forty-something, he had neat, short popcorn-coloured hair and his long nose made his eyes seem deeper-set than they probably were. He was called Mr Greatrix and he always wore the same tie.

Narinder handed him the rent, which he took with a resigned sigh and counted out very slowly.

'This is all very cumbersome,' he said.

'I'm sorry?'

'I have to come here to collect it and then I have to go to the bank. It's all very . . . cumbersome.'

Narinder didn't know what to say. She wished he'd turn round and go down the stairs and leave.

'Do you not have a bank account?'

'Sorry.'

'What about your husband?'

'I'll ask him.'

'Don't you know?'

She said nothing.

'I'm going to have to up your rent.'

'Pardon?'

'For the costs I incur in coming here.'

Narinder looked to the wall over the man's shoulder, at the cracks in the plaster, like branches. 'No. I'm sorry.'

'You what?'

'I don't think you're doing the right thing.'

He nearly laughed. 'I rather think that's for me to decide.'

'Imagine it's not me standing here. Imagine it's your sister or your mother. Would you want them to be treated like this?'

'But you're not, are you? Either my sister or my mother.' Adding, muttering, 'Thank the good Lord.'

'But if I was. How would you feel if someone was trying to use them in this way?'

He pressed the silver top of his pen, so the nib disappeared. 'I think we're going off point.'

'I think you have to be fair, Mr Greatrix. To treat people as kindly as you'd want those closest to you to be treated. I might be your tenant but I'm also your friend and neighbour.'

Someone once said to her that when she spoke she made people feel naked against the world.

'Maybe we can discuss this another time,' he said, blushing as he made his exit.

She was woken by a rattling sound, as though someone was trying to trip the lock. Momentarily, she thought Mr Greatrix was back. She sat up. Her heart was thumping. The clock-radio blinked 12:00. The light had cut out, or had been cut out. She told herself not to get like this, not to let fear take her over. She held the kandha at the hollow of her throat and listened for Him, and something like the stroke of a wing disturbed the air beside her face. She moved to the bedroom door – heel to toe, heel to toe – and opened it. She must have forgotten to draw the curtains because the main room was bathed in a geometry of light, shapely blocks of blue that made a cityscape on the floor and walls. There it was again, the rattling. She found the torch-pen she'd bought the previous week and with a rolling pin in her other hand opened the apartment door. In the dark the stairs looked even narrower, longer. It was only the wind in the letter box. Sighing, a little irritated with herself, she took a pink token from the tin under the sink and kept one hand to the wall as she went down to the meter. When she came back, she couldn't sleep, so drew out from under the mattress her letter, the one she'd a few nights ago started drafting to her father. She wanted to write a letter to her family every month. This was her second. She'd gone back home to Croydon after the visa marriage, not telling anyone. The lawyers had said it was important she had a fixed address, at least until her interview, until the visa was granted. The interview, mercifully, was short. As instructed, she said she'd met Randeep four years ago, on one of her yearly visits to India, and that they'd fallen in love and decided to get married. She had photos and witness testaments to support it. The interviewer – a kind-looking man, close to retirement – smiled and said it all looked in order and that he was happy to support her application.

Soon, she received a call from the Indian lawyer confirming that Delhi had granted the visa, and that Randeep and his family were extremely grateful, that they said it was as if she'd been delivered to them from God. Narinder could expect her first payment by the end of the month.

One month after that, mere weeks before her real wedding to a man called Karamjeet, Narinder left home. She wrote the most difficult letter of her life and secured it with a hairclip to the front of her gutka, and placed this on her dressing table. She'd not said anything about Randeep – they'd only notify the police and put an end to it all – she'd only said that she had her reasons for not being able to go through with the wedding right now but that she'd be back in one year and hoped with enough time they'd be able to forgive her. At four in the morning, an hour before her father woke for his morning prayers, Narinder carried her suitcase down the stairs and stepped outside, where a taxi was waiting to take her to the station.

Now, she attached a stamp and sealed up the envelope. Like last month's letter, this one simply communicated that she was fine, that she'd be back by the end of the year and that they weren't to worry. She folded out her map across the bed – she'd take a train somewhere tomorrow and post it from there.

She never attended the gurdwara on Sundays, always fearful of finding herself in the middle of a wedding, face to face with an overpowering aunty who knew her family. But most other evenings she took the bus from the bottom of her hill and would arrive in plenty of time to hear the evening's rehraas sahib. Unlike the gurdwaras she loved in Croydon and Ilford and Southall, the Sheffield one wasn't domed and the windows had no balconies cut with gentle fretwork. It was a plain brick building with five uneven stone steps leading to a black door and gold knocker. It could have been someone's house and, once, probably was. To the left of the door a large blue plaque was inscribed with the kandha and next to that a nishaan sahib waved its little orange flag. After prayers, she'd repair to the canteen kitchen, and more often than not to the giant concrete sinks where she'd spend the rest of the evening hosing down the dirty dishes passed her way.

One evening, she was doing just that when Randeep saw her and halted. Avtar was with him and they'd finished eating and been on their way to hand in their thalis. They didn't come to the gurdwara often but sometimes, like tonight, because there wasn't a milk run to do and because Vinny had dropped them off early, they'd put their kurta-tunics on over their jeans and bussed it up.

'What is it?' Avtar asked.

'Nothing. Here. Take mine. I need the toilet.'

'Take your own.'

'Please,' he pleaded. 'She'll see me.'

Avtar looked. It was mostly old women. There was only one who was young, scrubbing hard at the insides of some steel glasses. 'Is that our Narinderji? She does seva here?'

Randeep made a desperate face.

'Come on. What are you scared of?'

Avtar handed his dishes to one of the old women, forcing Randeep to give his up to Narinder. He held out his thali and she didn't look up and see him until he said, 'Sat sri akal.'

'Sat—' She stared for a long while, blankly, until at last she seemed to remember that her hands were meant to be doing something and she took his plate from him. 'Sat sri akal.'

'We come here sometimes,' Randeep said.

'I see.'

'Are you doing seva?' At the rim of his vision, he could see Avtar slapping his forehead.

'I try to help,' she said, rinsing the plate under the taps.

'Oh, yes. Me too.'

'I've never seen you here before.'

'I usually come in the week.'

'I'm here most days.'

'Right.'

Frowning, she went back to her cleaning.

'Well, maybe I should make more of an effort. If you're here most evenings.' He smiled.

She seemed perplexed. 'I don't see what difference me being here makes.'

'No, no. I guess I just thought it might be a good idea. If people see us together.'

He rejoined Avtar, who put his arm chummily around Randeep's shoulder and led him outside. 'There, there.'

'If you hadn't rushed me, I'd have been fine.'

'Of course. I'm sorry. Next time I won't.'

'Next time you won't be there.'

'Arré, but she's such a cutie, yaar.'

They walked a little further on. Randeep was smiling. 'She is cute, isn't she? You know, that's what my sister said, too. Lakhpreet said she's "cute as a button". That's another one of their English phrases. Did you know it already? Cute. As. A. Button.' But Avtar didn't say anything, and Randeep, still smiling, didn't notice.

That night, sitting on his mattress in the room he shared with two others, Avtar studied the four small piles he'd made of his money. The first pile was for the monthly repayment on what he owed Bal. The second for the loan taken out against his father's shawl shop. The third pile was meant to help his parents with their rent and bills and, lastly, a pile for his own expenses here in England. No savings pile. There'd never been a savings pile. No matter. Once the loans were paid off, then saving could begin. He started counting it all again when from across the room came a loud grunting snore and a turning-over. Instinctively Avtar crushed the notes together and hid them under his arms. He waited until he was sure the other two weren't faking their sleep and then he separated the money into piles again. It was no good. Bal was coming up in his BMW next week and still there wasn't enough. He took some notes from his parents' pile and split it between the first two. Still he was short. He recounted how much he had set aside for himself and took half of this and distributed it evenly among the rest.

The following day, on their way back from Leeds in the van,

Gurpreet threw in his weekly contribution and passed the tin to Avtar. Avtar slipped in half of his normal share.

'What's this?' Gurpreet said. 'You cheating us, chootiya?'

'I'm not eating for half the week. So I'll pay half as well.'

Gurpreet tutted in false sympathy. 'And two jobs he works. Spending it all on whores?'

'Your mother's not that expensive,' Avtar said, sighed. Gurpreet laughed and Avtar passed the tin on.

4. *AVTAR AND RANDEEP: TWO BOYS*

Avtar Nijjar, former student and now the youngest conductor employed by BUTA Travel, held on to the rubber loop above the door and leaned out of the bus.

'Sidhu Bangla! Geetpur! Kalawar! Jheela! Choper!'

He moved aside, arse against the windscreen, as elbows and legs clambered in. He kept one hand over his ticket machine and money bag. Thankfully, mercifully, it was the fifth and final round trip of the day. 'That diversion's not helping,' he told Harbhajan. 'Try Farid Chowk this time.'

Harbhajan sighed and draped himself across the thin hoop of the steering wheel, his new flamingo-pink turban cocked against the windscreen. 'Yaar, we should go somewhere. Goa, maybe. Imagine it. The beach. Some bhang, some money.'

Passengers were still forcing themselves on board. Avtar started to count over their heads.

'We'll take this,' Harbhajan said, patting the dashboard.

They were full. Avtar slammed the door and some of the people shut out rushed to flag autos; others stood swearing at him through the glass. 'Your papa let us take this bus? Jha, jha. You must be dreaming.'

And sighing again Harbhajan pressed on the horn for an unnecessarily long beat and urged the bus forward.

It was nearly dark when the last passengers disembarked at Harmandir Sahib and Harbhajan drove on to the shawl shop. Avtar passed him the ticket machine and the day's takings and jumped down.

'Just think about it,' Harbhajan said. 'Goa! The kudiyaan on the beach in their small-small clothes.'

'See you later,' Avtar said and slipped out of his old black shoes and bounded up into the shop. It was a single room lined floor to ceiling with wooden cubbyholes, and each hole held a neat stack of six shawls. At the back of the room his father sat cross-legged on a large fringed cushion. He had a customer with him, several cream and faintly damp-smelling Rajasthani shawls spread before her. Avtar began refolding and repackaging the many shawls that had been viewed and discarded during the day, separating them first by material and then by design and price. He rustled them back into clear plastic covers, stapled the covers secure, and returned the shawls to their cubbyholes. As he finished the customer stood up, puffing out her white-and-pink sari.

'Madam, I have one more you will definitely like,' his father called but she was already through the shop and summoning her rickshaw-wallah.

Silently, together, they shook the sequins from the groundsheet and one by one thumbed out the ten joss sticks lit before the images of the ten gurus.

'I'll bring the scooter round,' Avtar said.

'You go. There's still work to do.' It was the eighth time this month he'd insisted on staying behind. Avtar had stopped asking why, but keep counting.

'I'll come back in a couple of hours, then.'

'No, no. I'll make my own way back.'

'Papa – it's too far to walk.'

'I'll get Mohan to drop me off. Stop worrying.'

So Avtar took the small royal-blue tin with the day's meagre earnings and clipped it to his jeans and rode home.

The lift was still broken at Gardenia Villas. He returned outside and checked the four public toilets to the east of the building but none had toilet paper. He'd just have to come back down after dinner with some of his own.

He vaulted up the stairs and made it halfway up the twelfth flight before stopping for breath. It was further than he'd ever got before. He leaned against the warm wall and reread Lakhpreet's note, pouting, wondering what her 'news' would be. He didn't like surprises.

On the landing, Mr Lal, their neighbour, sat on a fishing

chair outside his front door, smoking a pipe. He'd tied a wet American-flag towel around the smoke alarm, Avtar noticed.

'Young Avtar! Kaise ho?'

'Good, uncle. Thank you.'

'Still working the buses, I see.'

Avtar smiled flatly.

'Well. Good for you.'

He'd got used to the man's way of boasting, and asked, as he knew he had to, 'Have you heard from Monty recently?'

'Yesterday.' He blew out pipe smoke. 'Lakhs he is earning. Lakhs. The way he's going, he'll have his own business in Toronto soon. And then we'll join him.'

The jealousy always got Avtar in the gut, though he tried not to let it show. 'I hope so. God willing.'

'Nothing to do with God. You just have to go where the money is.'

Avtar's mother was at the stove, struggling to spark up the hob. Navjoht, his brother, sat on the spongy two-seater, a comic open on his lap.

'How can we be out of gas so soon?' his mother said. She tucked the end of her pallu into her waist and blew across the hob, trying the clicker again. It didn't catch. 'Beita, can you go buy some before it closes?'

'I only put some in yesterday,' Avtar said.

He stepped over the urine bucket with its large plastic lid and twisted the gas pipe further into the stove valve. It slipped loose again so he lifted the stove a metre to the right, closer to the gas cylinder. Then the flame caught.

'It's too far from the window,' his mother said. 'The room will be full of smoke.'

'I can move it by the sofa.'

'I'm busy,' Navjoht said, pre-emptively.

Their mother said she needed the rice so Navjoht stood, pen clamped in his mouth, and lifted the brown sofa cushion and took up the small sack and passed it across.

Avtar gathered his pillow and rug from on top of the sofa and moved through the shower curtain they used to screen the main room from the balcony. He rolled out the padded rug, arranged the pillow, and lay with both knees pitched up to the sky, for the balcony was too short for him to lie at full stretch. Hands behind his head, he closed his arms around his ears so all he could see was the blue above, all else in the world blocked out. He stared hard at the sky until the familiar alchemy occurred and it felt as if the blue was lifting him away. He smiled and closed his eyes.

When his father arrived, twilight had fallen and the bulb on the wall cast the balcony in bronze. Avtar hadn't meant to fall asleep and turned on his side, drawing his knees to his chest. The shower curtain was thin enough to see through and Navjoht was clearing away his books so their father could take the sofa. The old man told the boy to carry on working but Navjoht said he'd 'continue' in their bedroom. Probably, on hearing their father, Navjoht had switched the comics for his schoolbooks.

'Another English word?' their father said, lowering into the cushions. He kept his hands on his knees and rested his back. 'Smells delicious, Shanti,' he managed, still breathing hard from the climb up.

He was as white-haired and aged as his wife was youthful. *Smells delicious. The flat looks nice. That colour suits you.* Sometimes Avtar thought that each compliment contained an implicit apology for the twenty-year difference in their ages.

Later, after the small collapsible table had been folded and stowed under the sofa and the dishes washed, and after Avtar had been downstairs and back to empty the urine bucket and use the toilet proper, his parents retired to their room and Navjoht rolled out his sleeping mat with something of a waiter's flourish. Avtar returned to his own rug on the balcony. Through the rusting white fretwork he stared out at the spread of the city. Above him, the amrood tree dangled its branch and he propped onto his elbow and broke off the fruit. Bitter. Still maybe a month too early. He threw it over the top and into the dark.

—

When he thought his brother had fallen far enough asleep, Avtar rose to a crouch, then slowly onto the balls of his feet. He watched him breathing, curled up in a moonbeam, and took one step into the room. When he let go of the curtain behind him, the dark shadow closed across Navjoht like a cupboard shutting. He stepped over him and toed the urine bucket to one side so he could get at the door. Then he retracted the lock with infinitesimal slowness and slid into the mottled light of the corridor and down the thirteen flights of concrete steps and out into the night.

He waited in the dead-end alley beside the bankrupt Bismillah cement factory. Shards of slate littered the ground. He heard voices, low tearful singing, and a band of semi-naked pilgrims filed past with wispy-haired chests, ribcages pressing out. They played their tiny cymbals and chimtas and did not once look towards Avtar in the alley, as if they'd been dismissed from the temple in howling disgrace. Above, smog dimmed the starscape, the pale-grey heights punctured only by the red dot of a plane blinking itself away.

She arrived, nervous and beautiful. Her frock, red-blue with elasticated ribbing beneath her breasts, showed her collarbones, flaring out. Around her throat she'd tied a silk scarf. She wore these kinds of dresses more often these days. He wasn't sure how he felt about them but he didn't comment. She hung by his side until he circled an arm around her waist. She stalled and looked over her shoulder and then yielded.

A year ago he could never have thought of himself as the person he was now, someone consumed with this girl and her body. He'd been aware of girls, for sure, but he'd never associated with them. His friend circle both at school and in the one year of college he'd completed had only ever consisted of boys: like-minded, serious boys, into cricket and their studies. Not the type who spoke much about girls, let alone sex; sex, as far as Avtar was concerned, was not something boys from respectable families got themselves involved in. Respectable. That was the word Avtar had used – or its formal urdu variant 'shareef' – when she'd stopped him in the college grounds one day.

‘I’ve not seen you in class,’ she’d said, as if they were already good chums.

He’d recognized her. Lakhpreet Sanghera, from his combined studies class, the only class open to everyone. Her family had lived for a short while in the same block of flats as his, but in the larger ground-floor apartments that had their own bathrooms. She was maybe three years younger than him.

‘I’ve left. I came to pick up my leaver’s certificate.’ He indicated the cardboard folder in his hand. ‘You need it to get the coupons.’ He doubted she knew which coupons he meant. She didn’t look like the type of girl whose family needed state help. Wasn’t her father something in government?

‘Oh. That’s a shame. I liked looking at you in class.’

He felt his face stiffen, his embarrassment fuelling a sudden anger towards her. ‘Miss, I’m from a shareef family. Please don’t trouble me again.’

Later that evening, lying on his balcony, he wished he’d not been so rude. He thought of her large black eyes and her glossy lips and cinched turquoise tunic. He thought he’d lost her, but the very next day the PCO man said he had a phone call.

‘I never said you weren’t shareef.’

‘I’m sorry . . . Miss,’ he added, regretting it even as the word left his mouth. She laughed.

One month later they had sex in the bell tower of the cement factory. He held her tight against him, rubbing her bottom, her thighs, her long brown back. He loved how hot and flushed her skin felt against his, how perfectly her nipples pressed into his mouth. His own desire surprised him, but her need came as a shock, and when he lay on his back, spent, she moved on top, craving it once more.

That was months ago, and now they jumped the gate round the back of the factory and snuck up the stairs. He cleared some space among the discarded timber and spread his jacket on the ground. Behind them the tower’s big iron bell hung godly and silent. In front, a few miles away, the Golden Temple shone, a tiny intimate lantern. It was a cool September night.

He said nothing when she told him her father had won the promotion and they were leaving next month. She leaned forward and locked arms around her knees, each hand holding the other hand's wrist. Her hair screened her face from him.

'Your hair looks different.'

'I used a hair press.'

He said, 'Chandigarh's not far.'

'Four hours ten minutes by bus.'

He smiled, she did too, and they went inside the tower and started to take off their clothes.

*

The morning after he received his month's wages, Avtar buttoned up his uniform and left the flat by 6.30 so he'd have time to call at the collector's house and settle the rent. Then he waited at the bus stand for Harbhajan to come by, sipping the malati water his mother mixed for his winter cough. They completed two circuits before taking lunch at the Roti Dhal Stop, and where previously Avtar had always ordered two keema naans he'd now taken to ordering one, and a plain one at that. It was one of the ways he was saving money in advance for the bus trips to Chandigarh.

'What's her name?' Harbhajan asked. 'Otherwise why so glum, yaar?'

Avtar gave him a disapproving look and told him to finish up or they'd be late.

'I always knew you had a secret chokri hidden away.' A little later Harbhajan said, 'Let's do something. Let's hit the clubs in Delhi.'

'A few weeks ago you were lost on Goa.'

Harbhajan mopped up the last of the dhal and stuffed it into his mouth. He downed the glass of water in one and sat back and prepared to burp, but when the burp didn't come he sank a little further in his seat and looked around, disappointed. At the next table a businessman was on his mobile, facing the slightly absurd poster of a gun-slinging pelican. A second phone lingered by his elbow at the edge of the table; Harbhajan palmed it and slipped it into his own shirt pocket. Avtar glared, eyes wide, watching his friend put on his large brown sunglasses and calmly pay the cafe owner on his way out. Avtar waited until they were back on the bus and away before asking what the bhanchod hell did he think he was doing?

'He already had one, na?'

He plucked the phone from Harbhajan's pocket. 'You could buy ten of these if you wanted.'

'Where's the fun in that?'

Avtar looked at him. 'So who did you steal those sunglasses from?' he asked, and Harbhajan smiled through his thick, neat beard.

At home, his mother was flitting through some sort of pamphlet. Her hair bun hung loose down her nape, the strands around her forehead white with flour. Avtar closed the front door.

'Prove the cosine rule,' she said tiredly.

Navjoht fell back against the settee, as if exhausted. He was still in his school uniform. 'Too easy again. Ask me something hard, na?'

She handed him the booklet, saying she hadn't realized what the time was. Rising, she lifted the sofa cushion and carried the bag of rice to the stove.

'Papa?' she asked.

'Working late again,' Avtar said.

'Will you test me, bhaji? Please?'

'Later, na.'

Navjoht shut his book and, sulking, went off to his parents' room.

'Why are you late? Get the table.'

Avtar dropped to his knees – 'We have to go all the way to Chogawan now' – and pulled the table out from under the sofa. 'That kentiwallah's gone to Dubai.'

Pointedly, his mother said nothing.

'Mr Lal says Monty's earning thousands every month.'

'Mr Lal has a slick tongue. And why are they still living next door, then? Using a bucket for their soo-soo?'

'He said there's money in Toronto.'

'Avtar, we've spoken about this. Roti's roti no matter where you eat it.'

He moved to the balcony shower curtain, where his shadow loomed gigantically. His mother was still talking.

'I saw Mrs Sanghera last week and even they are moving. Tomorrow. To Chandigarh.'

It was Avtar's turn to remain silent. She added jeera to the pan and increased the flame.

'You remember them? They used to live ten, twelve floors down. They moved to that new compound by Verka last year.'

'Maybe.'

'A son and three daughters. The eldest girl is pretty.' A pause. 'Lakhpreet. A little immature, maybe, but no matter. Girls grow up after marriage.'

Avtar looked across to his mother, chopping onions. So she knew.

'I think your papa and I will go to bed early tonight.'

The Ganesh clock balanced between TV and wall said a little after eight when Avtar stole out of the flat and walked the three miles to the temple. She was waiting in the shadow of the main gate. Her salwaar kameez was blue, without embroidery or effect. Her hair she'd tied up and covered simply with a white chunni. For once, she wore neither make-up nor colour.

'You nervous?' he asked.

'I'm impatient. Let's do it.'

They slipped off their shoes and sandals and stepped through the shallow water trough. Before them, the gold temple sat in its medieval lake, the black liquid surface glimmering with grand reflections distorted by the complications of light on water. The marble was warm under their feet, and damp.

'We should wash first,' he said.

'Fine.'

It was said with an edge of irritation. He knew she was only doing this because it was important to him, because he wanted them to make a promise before God.

'So melodramatic!' she'd said. 'You don't trust me.'

'I just know what these Chandigarh goons are like. And I don't want them anywhere near you.' He took her in his arms. 'I really do love you.'

'And you? While I'm over there will you let anyone else near you?'

'I'm only human,' he'd said, and she'd blocked him in the ribs.

He watched her cross towards the female bathing room on the steps of the lake, ducking to enter. He took off his shirt and rolled his trousers above his knees. He went down the steps and into the lake and when he was waist-deep he reached under for the chain and walked further out until the water reached his neck and he could taste the salt on his lips. He held his breath and bent forward until the water covered him completely and then he rose back up and said the first verse of the japji sahib. He went under again, and again, until he had completed all five verses and then he returned, hand over hand on the red chain, shivering as he reached for his shirt. It was late, and the japji was a morning prayer, but what they were doing felt like a new beginning.

She emerged from the bathing room dressed, her face glistening sharp in the moonlight.

'You ready?' she called.

A widow in a white kameez handed them a bowl of prasad. The bowl was made of overlapping palm leaves and they held it between them and carried it up the marble pier and to the temple in the centre of the lake. Two men knelt praying on either side of the doorway. Avtar and Lakhpreet bowed their heads and said a small prayer before stepping over the threshold. The Guru Granth Sahib lay open on its bed of gold and glass. Avtar's trousers still dripped water. He placed the offering at the granth's feet and they folded onto their knees and touched their foreheads to the ground. Then they went slowly round the chamber and bowed their heads three more times, on each side of the granth. They left by the same door through which they'd entered, walked back down the marble pier, around the lake, and out of the large open gates.

'Did you make the promise?' Avtar asked.

'I said I would and I did.'

'But you're sure? I'll understand if you want to change your mind.'

She looked at him, her smooth forehead suddenly constricting. 'Will you? Will you really? And what was the point of this if we're just going to change our minds?'

'I don't want to force you.'

'Uff, janum, you forget I want to marry you. Even with your romantic delusions. I just don't think we needed to go through all this drama first.'

He nodded and, absurdly, thanked her.

She gave a little laugh. 'So next year, after I finish my plus two, we'll come back here and get married?'

'I don't think my family could afford it here.'

'It doesn't have to be here.'

They walked to Jalianwala Bagh Road and kissed for several minutes behind the gates to the museum, tongues thick, hips fighting. Then Avtar called over an idling auto-rickshaw. 'PCO me when you arrive, acha?'

'Try and come every month,' she said and climbed into the ripped seats of the auto. She was looking away. He put his hand on her cheek and turned her face towards him. Her white chunni had fallen off her head and her eyes were brimming. He went round and gave the driver her address.

*

It was four in the morning and the peppermint-roofed government car was waiting outside. The truck with their furniture had gone on ahead. Randeep tried the bathroom door again.

'Daddy, are you OK? Please just tell us if you're all right. We're getting worried.'

Behind Randeep, his mother said, 'Remind him of all the people I had to beg for this chance at a new life.'

The handle turned, the door swung in and Randeep's father stood there looking over their heads, his whole face quivering. He spread one hand along the frame and took a slow step forward. He stopped, looked down.

'I can't do this, Paramveer. I'm so sorry, dear.'

Mrs Sanghera unpinned her black shawl and arranged it around her husband's shoulders. 'You're not going to be very warm in just that vest, are you?'

She took his hand in her own, an unfamiliar intimacy that forced Randeep to look away.

'We're all here with you. The car's waiting right outside the compound. Shall we go together? One step at a time?'

He moved into the hall, head fixed straight at his feet.

'That's it. And I'm sorry for raising my voice.'

'I deserve it. What kind of a man am I?'

She looked over her shoulder and told Randeep to make sure the last two Italian suitcases were packed and that his sisters were ready. 'I'll lock up.'

Randeep took the lift down, grabbing his college satchel from where it lay propped against the door. The night was clear and the compound gardens chippered with insects. Beyond the gate, the driver rested his hip against the door of the jeep, smoking a beedi. The suitcases were strapped to the roof and folded into the back were the twins, Ekam and Raji. He threw in his satchel and asked where Baby was.

He found her sitting on a child's swing in a rubber-decked corner of the gardens. He peered over the iron railings and clinked his kara twice against the bars.

'You ready?'

'How's Daddy?'

'He's coming. Mamma's with him.'

She took a deep, galvanizing breath, as if about to meet her maker, and glided through the gardens, the gates and down to the jeep. He couldn't remember the last time he'd seen her wear a salwaar kameez. Girls, he thought. Making a drama out of a simple move.

The doors to the apartment block opened and Mrs Sanghera led her husband out, holding both his hands and walking backwards, as if he were blindfolded. At the jeep, Randeep opened the door and could only watch sadly as his father scrambled inside. Mrs Sanghera told Baby to pass her father his beads.

'Baby?' And then, louder, 'Lakhpreet?'

'Sorry, Mamma?'

'The beads.'

The driver flicked his beedi high and away, and Randeep watched the wire of orange light trace itself on the air. He got in the front and moved to roll down the window, then stopped, not sure how his father would react. The driver started the engine and asked sahib if they were ready. When his father didn't reply, Randeep quickly said they were. An owl hooted.

'Isn't that meant to be good luck?' Randeep asked brightly, into a general and moody silence.

Avtar gave up cleaning his bus's windows – he seemed to be applying more dirt than he was removing – and whistled his way round the cells of parked buses towards the glass office at the back. The light was dingier here, brownish, and though it struggled to penetrate the smeary windows of the office, it did look as if that was Nirmalji sitting at his desk today. Avtar rolled down his sleeves and applied a hand to his chest – yes, his shirt was done up; yes, there was a pen in his pocket. He knocked on the open door.

'Salaam, sahib.'

Nirmalji's head rose from his rota book and he didn't quite smile. In this pose of stillness he looked like his son: bearded, turbaned and small-eyed, full of neck and face, though with more gold rings on his hands than Harbhajan wore. Sreenath, another conductor, had packaged his neat Brahmin body onto the side bench. He was an eighty-plus bald gummy gossip who'd worked here longer than anyone else. A white tikka stippled with grains of rice seemed a more or less permanent feature of his forehead. Nirmalji spoke.

'Son, I need you to be here next Sunday. The Chabba route.'

'OK, sahib.'

'I said that farm boy would not last long,' Sreenath said. 'These pindu-logh never do.'

Avtar sat beside Sreenath and while the old man shared his gutter tales – 'They say he was seen leaving her room . . .' – Avtar mentally cancelled his trip to see Lakhpreet next Sunday. It had been the same last month. He wasn't sure when they'd ever see each other again.

A roar sounded, startling Avtar onto his feet, and Harbhajan powered towards them on a red-and-chrome motorbike, popping the air with glints of light on metal. He snatched off his sunglasses, beaming as he walked to the office, calling for Avtar to come see, come see. He made it to the door before spying his father.

'How come you're here?' Harbhajan said. There was a note of fear in his voice.

'You're late.'

'I was buying my new bike.'

'What nonsense is this?'

Harbhajan indicated to Avtar that they should get going.

'You will take it back,' Nirmalji said.

'I'm not taking it back.'

This seemed to be how they always spoke to each other: a stiff, reproachful back-and-forth. Nirmalji walked out.

'Family members must get paid more than the rest of us,' Sreenath observed.

'Oh, fuck off, you old fool,' Harbhajan flashed and walked off too. Avtar heard the door of their bus being yanked open, then slamming shut.

Sreenath chuckled and started attacking his teeth with a toothpick. 'Robbing his own father.' He tutted. 'I feel very sorry for Nirmalji. Don't you?'

Avtar told the old man about the diversions he'd seen that morning around Circular Road and to take the Gobindgarh junction instead. If he was still doing that route.

Harbhajan didn't say much on the road that week. He didn't acknowledge the other bus drivers as they passed and responded only with a tight nod to the uncles and bibis who asked after his mother and father. During breaks between routes, he bought his meal from the Roti Dhal Stop and took it outside, alone. Avtar ate his food inside the restaurant, under the half-hearted whirr of a wire-mesh fan. He knew his friend's sunken moods well enough and was waiting for the flare of madness that always followed them, like blood spreading through water.

They were finishing up one evening, Avtar counting and rubber-banding the takings, when Harbhajan held down the horn and an excessively violent sound erupted into the twilight. Avtar jumped, coins fell, and a man cycling home wobbled off his bike. Harbhajan flopped back, laughing. Avtar bent to retrieve the coins from under the seats.

'Yaar, we're going to a party next week. Friday night. Be ready.'

'I'm busy,' Avtar said.

'You're really not,' and he clicked his fingers for the money. Avtar had no choice other than to hand it over, but as the lumpy mustard-coloured bag passed between them he felt uneasy.

'Make sure you give it all to your father, acha? It's my neck on the line if you don't.'

'Of course. What else am I going to do with it?'

No more was mentioned about the party, but after work on the appointed day Harbhajan arrived at the flat, bending to touch Avtar's mother's feet.

'Ah, what a good boy. Aaja – come in.'

'Next time, aunty. We're late.' Avtar drew the shower curtain aside and was coming through from the balcony as Harbhajan said, lied, 'It's my birthday. We thought we'd go for a burger-cola. Is that OK?'

They drove straight out of the city on Harbhajan's new motorbike. The engine was fierce and Avtar gripped the metal handle behind him, feeling the warm air sear past, taking determined hold of his hair. For a minute he feared they were heading into Pakistan, but Harbhajan swerved east at the roundabout.

'Where are we going?' Avtar called.

'You'll see!'

He'd expected him to turn off the GT Road at Kapurthala – Harbhajan had been seeing a girl there – but he carried straight on and some ninety minutes after leaving Avtar's flat they slowed into the flashy nightlife of Jalandhar. Toes on the ground, Harbhajan nosed the bike through the crowds and parked it among others at a leaning rack. Above them, *Rainak Bazaar* spun in neon revolutions, the *k* dimmed out.

Avtar stalled Harbhajan with a hand to the shoulder. 'What's the place called?'

'1771.'

'Blue?'

Harbhajan grinned and carried on.

The lane seemed to strip on for miles. Then, without warning, Harbhajan stopped and said he thought he'd missed it. He turned on his heel and saw the jeweller's he'd apparently been looking for.

'It wasn't shuttered up last time.'

They snuck along the trickle of an alley down the side of the shop and at the end of this, several wider lanes branched into view. No light seemed to enter them.

'Do you think it's this way?' Harbhajan said.

'Yaar, I don't think—'

His friend walked off and, exasperated, Avtar followed.

The window of the bar was black, with 1771 gold-stamped across in a cheap diagonal. The long downstrokes of the 7s morphed into a woman's fishnetted legs. At the door, a man in a white kurta was talking sweetly into his phone of how glad he was they were getting married soon. Harbhajan clicked his fingers and showed the man some sort of card or ticket which allowed them up the stairs and through double doors with large porthole windows.

At first it seemed that there weren't many people present – Avtar counted only three women and a man at the bar. The place felt strange and he realized there was no music, only sibilant conversations and smoky laughter, and these he traced to the unlit corners of the room, where women sat with the men who'd picked them up.

The man at the bar slid off his stool and with each step his smile widened and his arms opened out, as if feet and hands and mouth were all connected by some complicated puppetry. His wide-collared orange shirt looked crisp in the dim light, and his eyes were jittery green.

'Driver sahib! I had a bet you would still come.' He looked to one of the dark corners of the room, where a pair of slender female calves were closing around a leg wrapped in its tube of denim.

'Rustom, you owe me. Our turbaned master has, after all, come.' No response came from that quarter. 'He's busy,' the man laughed.

'This is my friend Avtar. Avtar, this is Venkatesh.'

Avtar said hi, but Venkatesh just kept smiling at Harbhajan. 'What would you like to drink, friend? Anything you want. Anything.'

There was a slight rounding out of Harbhajan's shoulders as he said, 'You know what I want. Get it me.'

Venkatesh beamed, as if he'd expected to have to work harder than this. 'As you wish, huzoor. They are all upstairs.'

'I'll be ten minutes, yaar,' Harbhajan said, eyes fixed on a door at the back of the room. 'Will you wait for me?'

'What's upst—?'

Venkatesh said that of course Avtar would wait and, in fact, Sonya would look after him, won't you, baby? With that, Harbhajan strode for the door, Venkatesh rushing on behind like a little meerkat, and somehow Avtar was left standing in the centre of the floor, alone.

He moved to the end of the bar, away from the girls, and sat with arms folded on the gleaming black of the counter, his legs right-angled around a corner. He looked at his watch and decided to give it twenty minutes. Then he'd go and drag him out. It was drugs, obviously. The stupid idiot had got himself sick on drugs.

Twenty minutes came and went and then a further ten, and now again Avtar checked his watch. Another five, he decided. He sat there tapping his thumbnails together, pinching back the cuticles. One of the girls eased smoothly onto the stool beside him. She placed her glamorous purse carefully on the bar and just as carefully crossed her legs and put both hands on her knees, below where her red skirt stopped. She had big curls and pink lipstick that made her already sullen face look even more so.

'I'll have a Mumbai Sling.'

'I've no money.'

'Why did you come here with no money?'

'Why did you?'

She unclipped and unzipped her purse and held up a plastic card. 'What will you have?'

He shook his head.

'Does my money offend you?'

'Not your money. How you earn it.'

'Good. So what will you have? I have orders to look after you.'

He said nothing, then asked, 'Is Sonya your real name?'

'Harinderjeet.'

'A good name. A strong name.'

He could see her face in the bar's surface, frowning as she returned the card to her purse. 'Is Sonya not a nice name?'

He felt her leaning in.

'A sexy name?'

He flinched away. She laughed.

'Are you a pindu farm boy? Because they're usually the disgusted ones. Either they rush on their clothes and run out or they stand there telling me how ashamed I make them feel, how if I was their sister they'd definitely beat me . . . Strange boys.'

'If you were my sister I'd feel ashamed, too. But only a coward would hit a woman.'

'Ah, so you are a pindu.'

'I'm just an honest and hard-working Indian.'

She sighed, as if bored. 'You say that as if you're the only one.'

He looked at his watch, then around the room again. Nothing had changed. 'Who's up there?'

She shrugged. 'Could be anyone. Maybe even your sister.'

He slid off the stool and went round the bar and through the door. A short flight of lavishly carpeted stairs brought him to a second entrance beyond which he could hear the undefined mangle of music and chatter. The guard dozed in his chair so Avtar shouldered through the surprisingly heavy door and into what looked like a slapdash gambling den. There were flimsy card tables covered in threadbare green, and matka stands and shoot-'em-up video games and a tribe of college-looking boys intent on the money machines. He could hear other accents – UK, American – brought here by their desi cousins in a bid to impress. He saw Venkatesh first, slumped against the jukebox, head lolling low. He looked asleep. Avtar shook his shoulder hard, and slowly, as if it were a giant weight, Venkatesh rolled up his head. His eyes had lost their shimmer and as he slewed his head from side to side, gibbering, he looked amused to have found Avtar standing there.

He looked in the toilets, then did another circuit of the room, locating Harbhajan behind one of the leatherette settees, curled up like a baby. He tried waking him, but there was no point, so he hefted him up by the armpits and secured an arm around his waist. The idiot's topknot swung loosely around his head, coming undone.

'*Where-is-your-pugri?*'

Harbhajan closed his eyes, dreamily, and slopped his face onto Avtar's shoulder. He found the keys to the motorbike in Harbhajan's pocket and shoved them into his own jeans. Then he carried him out, down the stairs and through the lanes until, two hours later, they arrived at the bike. He arranged Harbhajan on the seat, then niftily, without letting go of his friend, sat down himself.

'Just keep hold of me acha, yaar? Don't let go.'

He got the engine going at the third kick and turned a few dials until an amber cone struck up before him. He said a quick prayer and haltingly, wobblingly, moved forward.

The journey back took three times as long as the journey there. Twice Avtar turned off the GT Road and made a detour through the villages because a passing autowallah warned there were police checks up ahead. So it was close to 3 a.m. when he entered Harbhajan's neighbourhood and braked outside a fish-and-liquor dhaba. He asked the owner to bring out a coffee and forced Harbhajan to drink it. It made no difference. Outside the black gates of Nirmalji's house, Avtar killed the engine. He wiped both their faces with the hem of his shirt – he hadn't realized how much he was sweating – and coaxed his friend from the saddle. Avtar had to hold him upright.

'Arré, giani, come on.' He slapped him. 'We're home. Look.'

Harbhajan opened one yellow eye, shunted Avtar away and veered back down the road, careering across the asphalt. Avtar caught up, his hands on Harbhajan's shoulders to try and still him. 'Home.'

His yellow eyes weren't blinking and with his beard and long girlish ringlets he looked like a madman haranguing the night. 'I hate it. I hate him. I hate him.' He sprinted to the gates, crashing into them, then looked up into the sky, his mouth pulled into an ugly stretch, and screamed, 'I hate you! I hate you!' He kicked the gates – 'I hate you! I hate you!' – and the iron shook and clanged. The more Avtar tried to restrain him, the louder Harbhajan screamed. 'I hate you! I hate you!' Lights came on in the neighbouring houses and the large balcony window in Harbhajan's own house lit up too. Nirmalji appeared, tightening his dressing gown resentfully as he came down the path. Harbhajan's arm extended through the bars, pointing, identifying. 'You! I hate you! I hate you!'

'Where is your turban?' Nirmalji said.

'I hate you!'

Nirmalji found his key and forced the lock open. 'That bhanchod chowkidar,' he muttered. 'Avtar, would you take him to his room, please?'

'Is everything OK, Nirmal Sahib?' a voice asked from behind. A neighbour. 'Is that young Hari?'

'It's fine, thank you. High spirits only.'

Harbhajan quietened as soon as they were away from his father. Now he complained of feeling sleepy.

Harbhajan's mother was standing inside the front door. She was a short, dutiful-looking woman, her eyes puffy, as if she'd been crying. Avtar had never met her before. He touched her feet, then with his fist at Harbhajan's back drove him into the house. 'Aunty, can you tell me where . . . ?'

'It's the third door on the second floor, beita.'

Avtar steered Harbhajan towards the marble staircase. He kept his eyes down. He felt embarrassed by how much they had. The huge dining table, the leather sitting suites. Two just-glimpsed servants exchanging looks. Harbhajan kept on wanting to turn back, saying he'd left something at the tiger's house. 'We'll pick it up tomorrow,' Avtar said and that seemed to placate him.

The bed was square and plain and stranded in the centre of the room. The left-side wall was taken up with a fish tank, the fish dingily aglow in the low blue murk. Avtar sat Harbhajan on the end of the bed and removed his shoes and socks for him, and then Harbhajan flipped over and scrambled under the covers. Soon he was snoring gently. Avtar stood up, hands on hips, relieved. The window behind the bed had a deep ledge and balanced on it was an unframed black-and-white headshot of a younger, preoccupied-looking Harbhajan, cheek scrunched up against his fist. Next to it, a fizzled-out joss stick, some rupees, dried-up marigolds to one side. Maybe his mother was conducting prayers for him.

Back downstairs Nirmalji and his wife were standing by the dining table, talking quietly. She was shaking her head.

Avtar said that he would bring the motorbike in now, if that was all right.

'Were you with him all night?' Nirmalji asked.

'Yes, sahib.'

'Did you take drugs also?'

His wife let out an anguished groan. Avtar didn't know what to say and in the end mumbled, 'I don't know.'

'How much is he stealing from the company?'

'I don't know, sahib.'

'So you do know he is stealing?'

'I don't know, sahib.' His voice getting quieter now.

He could feel the threat, because he knew the rich were the kind of people who find fault with the pet and not the leash.

'I've never cheated you, sahib. I do my job well.' Maybe Nirmalji was annoyed that the neighbours had all seen. 'I would have taken him to a hotel but you know how people talk. I thought you would want him home.'

'You did the right thing. Under the circumstances.' Then: 'Go. Leave the bike where it is.' He turned to his wife. 'Wake Satram.'

'I can walk, sahib.'

'You'll go in the car. Your parents must be worried. Have you called . . . ?' But he stopped, perhaps thinking they were too poor even to own a phone and he'd only be embarrassing the boy. In fact,

Avtar had called earlier in the evening and spoken to his mother and said that they'd had a puncture, it was late, and he'd be staying at Harbhajan's house tonight.

Avtar walked out the front door and into the garden and through the gates. He felt guilty and he wasn't sure what he'd done to feel guilty about. He kicked a stone hard and it went prancing off down the road. The car pulled up and the window wound down and a man with a droopy moustache and tired eyes told him to get in and shut up. Driving young bhanchod layabouts around in the middle of the night. As if he didn't have better things to do.

*

At work, he assumed driving duties with old Sreenath as his conductor. The wrinkled Brahmin seemed to know everyone and he'd sit there on his fold-down seat and welcome passengers in, exclaiming how nice it was to see Keshav again, and Rana Bhai, and – be still my heart – Namrata Devi, too? How is the hip these days, sister?

Avtar brought his knees up to the steering wheel, fingering absent-minded circles into the flaky window dirt. He wished he'd gone into Nirmalji's office when he'd had the chance yesterday and demanded to know if his job was in danger. All this not knowing was making him feel ill. He closed his eyes and heard Lakhpreet's voice from the night before, saying she was sorry for being mad that he couldn't come again this month, and that she loved him and would see him soon. Opening his eyes, Avtar felt suddenly certain everything would be all right.

As he was pulling into the depot that evening, he saw Harbhajan's motorbike, and then Harbhajan himself in the office, feet up and paging through a newspaper in a bored way. Avtar locked the wheels left and parked at the end of the line, making himself invisible. He couldn't afford to be friends with him any longer.

Sreenath flicked his toothpick to the floor. 'You are doing right. When father and son are firing bullets at each other, don't get caught in the crossfire.'

'I've not done anything wrong.'

'He's stealing from the workers' funds. Someone will have to pay.'

Avtar looked helplessly at the old man. 'But I've not done anything wrong.'

'Some drivers are saying they'll strike if the duffer doesn't do something. No one would have dared strike when I was young. Strange how times change.'

'It's not fair. He's just looking for someone else to blame.'

Sreenath twisted his hand, as if to say, Who knew? 'But it's your own fault. Plain mouths and rich food. Indigestion is inevitable, no?'

Harbhajan finally caught up with him as Avtar was exiting the rent-collector's house one morning. 'O-ho!' he shouted, pulling Avtar into a half-hug. His eyes looked heavy and he wore a black patka instead of his usual turban. Avtar guessed he'd not slept all night. Perhaps not been home, either.

'See how good my memory is? See how I remember which day you come here?'

Avtar shrugged him off. 'I need to get to work.'

'Tsk! Wait a minute, yaara. Where have you been hiding?'

'No one's hiding. You know where I live.'

Harbhajan ignored this. Maybe he felt too ashamed to meet Avtar's parents. 'How's old Sreenath?' He made his mouth gummy, mimicking: 'When the rainbow comes, the storm isn't far behind.'

Avtar frowned. 'I'll be late.'

'I'll drop you off.'

Avtar carried on walking. Harbhajan blocked him off.

'I'll drop you off in my car.' And he turned Avtar around and pointed to the gleaming red Honda City parked twenty yards up the road. Already, a couple of schoolboys had stopped to admire it. Avtar stormed off. Again, Harbhajan caught up.

'What's the matter, yaar? Did you see it? Let's go.'

He pushed Harbhajan in the chest. 'You stealing, sister-fucking bastard. I need my job. Do you understand? We can't live without my job.'

Harbhajan looked hurt. 'Why the filmi drama, friend? It's just fun. We're just having some fun.'

'Don't. Not with my life.'

Slowly the silence deflated and Harbhajan said, 'Let's go tonight. Wherever you want. Let's go see your girl. I'll drive you.' Before he'd even finished Avtar was walking away, shaking his head.

Four days later he asked Nirmalji when he might be able to take a day off and one week after that he was with Harbhajan on their way to Chandigarh in the red Honda City. He'd not wanted to go like this. When he'd got off the phone to Lakhpreet the previous week he'd looked in his wallet and calculated that after giving his parents enough to cover the rent and monthly gas bill he had just enough for the return bus fare and a day in Chandigarh: he'd have to walk instead of using the scooter for a few days, that was all. But then in the morning his mother said she was going to the temple. She wanted to make a donation in Navjoht's name and Avtar, as the boy's elder brother, had to contribute.

'But the exams are finished. You can't change the results now.'

'Don't make questions, beita. He's worked so hard.'

He handed over half of what he had and left for work. Twice over the next few days he'd nearly called Lakhpreet and said he couldn't come. In the end, he dialled Harbhajan. Don't tell anyone, he'd said on the phone, and this he now repeated as the smug-looking 'Welcome to Chandigarh' sign loomed fast towards them.

'Arré, relax. We're having a fun day out, that's all.'

Harbhajan beamed, his smile elastic under the wraparound shades, and they sped into the precisely gardened city, where the cars looked official, government-sanctioned, and the men and women on scooters wore small Sixties helmets.

They parked in the shallow forecourt of Mega Mall and Avtar stepped out into the soft sunshine. It was a white marblesque building with intimidating black doors, a row of potted yellow trees flanking both sides of the entrance.

'Is she here?' Harbhajan asked.

'We're early.'

'In that case,' Harbhajan said, opening the boot. He returned with a palmful of red worm-like things. 'Take some, na.'

The balloons came up crinkled and heart-shaped. Some had a picture of teddy bears. Avtar looked dubiously at Harbhajan, who passed him some string.

'To tie them to the car. I'll have my fun at Geri Route.'

Avtar didn't ask. It was enough that he wasn't going to be around when Lakhpreet arrived.

Through the automatic doors, he took the central escalator which fed him into a burger place. She wasn't there. He ordered a Thums Up and took a seat by the window so she might see him easily. There were only four or five others at this hour: a couple in office clothes holding hands over a briefcase, and a few other men dotted politely about, a bottle and straw at their lips. The ventilation whirred and stopped, whirred and stopped.

He saw her materializing layer by layer up the escalator. Her hair, her eyes, her mouth and neck, chest, hands, her legs. She looked anxious, winding the end of her green chunni in and out of her hands. Then she saw him, and smiled. She stroked his shoulder as she passed and took the seat opposite. He sat down too – when had he stood? – and turned his dark-brown hand palm up on the table. She placed her fairer hand in his.

They spoke of nothing for a while, or at least nothing that Avtar could later remember. He'd felt a little light-headed at seeing her again. They ordered two more drinks and Avtar asked for a burger each as well. She said to forget the burger – it was too expensive here – but that only made him more determined to have one. The food arrived.

'Where's your friend?' she asked.

'He's gone to Geri Route. With balloons.'

She gave a gorgeous little laugh. 'If he's gone to find girls, it's too early. The balloons will go to waste.'

'Oh, he'll find some way to have fun.'

She swivelled her Thums Up, the glass bottle dancing unpredictably on the table. 'This is a very boring city, janum. Old people and government types only. There is no fun. I miss doing things. Going to the cinema, boating on the river.' She smiled at him. 'And other things with you.'

He asked how her father was. She said nothing. Her mood changed. He wished he'd not mentioned it.

'He's given up. I don't know how long we can keep him.'

He said that God would find a way through and she frowned and said she hoped He'd find it soon.

'It's the crying. He cries so much. At night especially. And I know he can't help it but I just want to scream at him.'

'Your mamma? How is she?'

She shook her head. 'And Randeep's at college so it's just me and Mummy trying to stop him from doing anything crazy all night.'

As their tray was collected, she asked him when they could get married. Avtar coughed and waited for the waiter to leave. 'Where would we live? On my mamma–papa's balcony?'

'I wouldn't mind. It'd be fun. It'd be an adventure.'

'It wouldn't. And I want to be able to afford a small hut for us both at least.'

'By the lake, maybe.'

'With mountains in the background.'

'Ducks outside?'

'And a little pink pig.'

'Oh! To keep as a pet?'

'To eat.'

'No!' And she laughed hard, ponytail swishing side to side. 'You know, my friends think it's so romantic what we're doing. They're so jealous.'

'You've told your friends we're getting married?'

'Shouldn't I have done?'

He wasn't sure. 'I suppose we never agreed not to tell anyone.'

'Oh, but I want to tell the world!' She brought her thumbs together and rested her lovely dimpled chin on them. 'How long, janum?'

'I don't know, honestly. It's so tough right now. Papa's not doing well.'

She looked alarmed, in a slightly theatrical way. 'What's the matter?'

'I mean, the shop. Business is slow. Has been for a long time. Everywhere is slow right now.'

She sighed, nodded. 'So many boys are going abroad these days.'

'You want me to go abroad?'

She made a cute puck of her mouth. 'I don't know. How long for?'

'A year, maybe. I have thought about it. A lot.'

'And maybe then, if you earned enough, we could have a bigger wedding. With all our family and friends. And a bigger house to live in.'

'Maybe.'

'As long as you come back. Some boys never do.'

He said of course he'd come back. He needed to.

'And me? Don't I need you?' She leaned in, head to one side, eyes intent. He could see down her kameez, to her breasts. 'Don't you need me?'

They left the mall and Avtar used the last of his money to rent a cheap hotel room. An hour later she freed herself from his limbs and said she had better go. He pulled her back down, needing her mouth again, and it was a full hour more before she could finally reach for her clothes.

Harbhajan wasn't answering his phone. Forty minutes passed, fifty, one hour and then two. He should have known Harbhajan would do this. The mall chowkidar came by, swinging his lathi. He asked Avtar what he was up to.

'Waiting for my friend, sahib.'

'You can wait by the road. Business people come here. Foreign types.'

At the roadside, Avtar snapped off his denim jacket and sat on it with his arms square around his knees. Still no sign. The sun pressed down on his eyelids and soon he fell asleep. When he looked up again, blinking, the red Honda was there. Harbhajan was some feet away taking a piss into one of the potted trees. Avtar stood up.

'What happened to the balloons?' he asked, as his friend walked back, zipping up.

Harbhajan stared at his car. 'Oh yeah.'

There was a sort of empty pressure in his eyes. Avtar said he'd better drive but Harbhajan got in and started the engine, revved it. Avtar hadn't even closed the door and they were speeding off.

They jumped lights and joined the trunk road.

'Slow down,' Avtar said. Harbhajan stared ahead, top teeth biting his lip and arm straight at the wheel, as if in a brace. Cars dodged out of their way. 'Hari, slow down.'

'Does your father hate you, Avtar?'

'Don't think like that.'

'That's not what I asked.'

A green-and-red lorry came honking towards them. Harbhajan veered onto the dirtroad and they felt the car shake as the lorry rumbled past.

'Does your girl love you?'

'Hari.'

'Does life bring you joy?'

Avtar looked out of the window. The fields merged. He turned to the front and saw three cars barrelling down. Harbhajan let out a wild laugh and swerved left where a concrete stump seemed to jump out of the ground. The air filled with crushing metal and the car lurched, then stopped. Harbhajan sat there looking at the steering wheel. Avtar put a hand on his shoulder and a short while later the young man in the turban began to sob.

Night fell. Maybe the electronics weren't working because the chowkidar had to apply his back to the bars and push the gates open. Avtar drove slowly in. On the porch, under the security light, Nirmalji was waiting in a regal-looking shawl. He had his hands behind his back. Avtar got out of the car and made his sahib-salaams. He was helping Harbhajan to his feet when the driver who'd taken Avtar home that one time shoved him aside and near-carried Harbhajan indoors. Avtar watched his friend dragged into the house, the driver closing the door behind them. It was several seconds until he summoned the courage to turn and look at Nirmalji: only briefly, for Avtar's gaze dropped reflexively down and rested somewhere around his employer's knees.

'You got my message, sahib?'

Nirmalji said he had and that the doctor was inside so not to worry.

'I think it is a sprained knee only.'

'Did you know he bought the car with stolen money?'

'Some ice. My mamma would put some ice on it.'

'You knew he was stealing from the workers' funds. Everyone knows that is what he is doing. I have to take action.'

Avtar felt sick. He was determined not to cry. He carried on talking. 'The radiator, sahib. I had to keep filling it up.' He showed his blackened hands and wrists as if providing evidence.

'They're angry, the workers. And when workers are angry they do silly things like revolt.' His voice lost its soft edges. 'They need to know I won't tolerate that. You cannot be weak in this world. Do you understand?'

'Please, sahib, forgive my mista—'

'Chup! Don't embarrass yourself. Don't be weak.'

Avtar looked at the hard, thankless ground.

'I'll give you a month's pay. That is the best I will do.'

'Please, sahib,' and Avtar started the move onto his knees. Maybe he felt that was what he was expected to do.

'Get up immediately,' Nirmalji commanded. 'Do not ever bow down before a man. Not anyone. Is that understood?'

Avtar nodded, swallowed. He heard the older man sigh, saw his heavy gut rise and fall.

'I am doing you a favour, son. Go abroad. Follow the others. It's too hard for boys like you in this benighted country. Abroad you might stand a chance.'

Avtar said nothing. He kept looking down. At least there was no danger of tears.

Nirmalji walked him to the gates and handed him his wages, plus some. Avtar managed a faint thank you and with a subtle declination of the head Nirmalji conveyed that it was time for Avtar to leave.

At the brass tap behind Gardenia Villas, he washed the grime from his hands and wrists as best he could. Then he made the long climb to the flat and waited outside the front door. The moon was high and caged beyond the thickly tubed windows of the stairwell. He could hear the TV in Mr Lal's next door. He turned the handle and went inside. His mother was at the stove, fiercely stirring. On the sofa, his brother read from a loosely stapled pamphlet of some sort, in English. Their father listened, smiling but clearly not understanding.

'Tari's back,' his father said, sounding relieved. 'Where have you been? Your brother got his marks.'

'I'm making prasad,' his mother said.

'Top five per cent,' their father said. 'Top five!'

'God listened.'

Navjoht turned back to the front page. 'Shall I start again, Papa? Now bhaji's here?'

Their father hesitated. Avtar swept his hand through his brother's hair and sat gingerly on the precarious armrest of their sofa. He felt something behind his back and pulled round a brown parcel. It had the green stamp of his father's shop, above that in green ink his mother's name, and at some point it had also been tied with green string. Now it lay ripped open, and folded inside was a red and very beautiful Jamawar shawl, the kind that he knew took many weeks to make by hand. Months, if you only had an hour or two each night after the shop had closed. He put it aside and decided that, no, he wouldn't say anything tonight.

'Beita, can you get some barfi? Is he still open? I want to take it to the gurdwara tomorrow. Ask your papa for some money.'

Avtar stood and said Nadeem would be closed but he'd find some somewhere else. He stepped over the urine bucket.

'The money,' his mother said.

'I've enough,' and he closed the door and started down the stairs.

His father's postings meant the family moved around a lot. Chandigarh was the latest. It was the ninth city Randeep had lived in and in each city they'd changed residence at least once, so he must have had more than twenty different addresses by now. More than his age – seventeen. His early years were in the south and east of the country – Tiruchirappalli, Bangalore, Nellore, Bhubaneshwar – then, when his naniji was dying, his mother insisted they head closer to home: Delhi, Pathankot, Ludhiana, Amritsar and now Chandigarh. He'd liked Bhubaneshwar the most, and often remembered the six months on the outskirts of the city, in a compound of thatched white cottages, as the best years of his whole life. He'd been about twelve and for the first time made some friends – two boys from the neighbouring village – and they'd given the entire summer to playing cricket in the village grounds. One day, Randeep promised himself, he'd return.

The bell sounded – shrill, constant – and he packed away his unopened books and moved to the windows of the library, looking down. From all sides of the pillared quad students spilled out of the doors, chattering, filling the square until it was all pigtails and schoolish greys and blues. Jaytha was at the centre of her group of girlfriends, head thrown back, neck lushly exposed, laughing. He watched until she vanished out of the quad. Then he returned to his room to pick up his suitcase.

He went home every weekend. It was only an hour on the local Sutlej bus but by the time he alighted and dragged the wheels of his battered suitcase over the rocky ground, darkness had fallen like a shutter. He got into the nearest auto and asked for the government flats in Madhya Marg.

'DIT side?' the driver asked, turning the thing around.

'Sector side, please.'

At Building 3B on Santa Cruz Drive, the resident chowkidar in his old peacock hat saluted and opened the door. Randeep took the lift and outside flat 188 he removed his shoes because the sound of footsteps in the hall had once made his father panic terribly.

That night, as he was watching TV with Lakhpreet, she asked him if he knew any boys who'd gone abroad. How easy was it?

'How would I know?' he said.

'But is it expensive?'

He shrugged. 'Who wants to go abroad?'

She shook her head. 'No one. A friend.'

'Tell her it won't be all shopping and playing in the park.'

He flicked through to the news and then to a yoga class.

'Has Daddy done his exercises this week?'

She nodded.

'How's he been?'

'Same same.'

'I wish I was here more to help,' he said, but he knew he didn't mean it, and her silence told him that she knew it too.

On Saturdays, the twins had their classical dance lesson followed by violin practice – or maybe it was piano these days – so when Randeep emerged showered and dressed from the bathroom they were kissing their father goodbye and disappearing out of the door. Then Lakhpreet said she was going – off to meet friends. The door slammed to a close and it was just Randeep and his parents in the light-filled room. The only sound was the hum of the squat grey fridge.

'A long time you spent in the bathroom,' his father said, not looking up from the newspaper laid out flat on the coffee table. 'Avoiding us?'

'Of course not,' he said, and as if to prove this came and sat beside his father.

He was a long, thin man, made to appear even taller in his white kurta robes. People spoke of him as being noble, intelligent, with sharp, questioning eyes. Nothing got past Sanghera Sahib. He was starting to grey and, reading his paper with deliberate slowness, looked exactly how people expected a senior government manager to look on a lazy summer morning. He'd shaved, too, Randeep noticed, which was a good sign. Mrs Sanghera darted about the kitchen. Cleaning, wiping, washing the steel and plastic cutlery, wondering out loud why-oh-why they didn't have a maid. She asked Randeep if he preferred eggs or paratha and he said he'd have some Tiger Flakes later. Then she placed two chalky pink pills and a steel tumbler of water beside her husband's elbow and left for the bedroom.

'How's school?'

'College. Good. The board exams are soon.'

His father nodded. 'NIT would be good.'

'If I get the ranking.'

'Isn't that why we pay the fees?' His father closed the paper, folded it twice, then picked it up and slapped it back down on the table again. 'These right-wing loons are taking over the country.'

His mother reappeared, dressed hastily in a white-and-yellow salwaar kameez. Her eyes went to the pills, still untouched. Then: 'Will you come with me? You're expected.'

'Next time. Take Randeep.'

'But I want to stay with you,' Randeep said.

'You mean you're too scared to leave me on my own for a few hours?' He wiped his hand across the table, palming up the pills, and dropped them into his mouth. He drank the water. 'There. I feel better already. Don't I look better?'

Mrs Sanghera said she'd be back by lunchtime – it was an akhand paat – but he had their number and there were two vegetable patties in the fridge if they got hungry. Then she kissed Randeep's forehead and picked up a gold box of mithai from on top of the fridge.

Later, while his father napped, Randeep took a textbook into the shade of the balcony. He set aside his mother's plant pots and sat against the whitewashed wall and made a lectern of his lap. With a faint groan, he began to read – absent-mindedly, half-heartedly – and soon the benzene rings on the smudged paper of his chemistry textbook dissolved and reconstituted themselves into images of

Jaytha. He wondered what to say to her when they next met – on the way to morning assembly, most likely, as long as this time he remembered that she walked via the mural on Mondays. And he should definitely ask after her bhabhi. As if on the breeze, a feeling of shame came over him. He didn't know why he was like this. He wished he could be more easy-going about these things. Less calculating. Less like one of those crazed stalkies.

'Shall we go for a walk?'

Startled, Randeep looked up: his father, in trousers and clean half-sleeved shirt, hair combed. 'Daddy?'

'I feel like going for a walk.'

Randeep pocketed the apartment keys as they exited the lift. The old chowkidar saluted – 'Good morning, Sanghera Sahib' – and opened the big glass door for them. Beyond the compound gates, they started down the chunky pink pavement of Santa Cruz Drive. The road was measured in trees, one following the other, orange blossoming through the leafgreen.

'Are you sure you won't be cold?'

His father didn't reply, just kept on ahead, chin tilted up to the day.

They passed under the bramble archway of Zakir Garden, which was no more than a flat expanse of shrubs – mostly roses – with a fenced-off pond in the middle. North of the pond, at the sunken bandstand, some sort of trumpet group seemed to be rehearsing. Randeep suggested they go back but his father said not to be silly, that there was a lovely quiet enclosure right by the eastern gate.

Mr Sanghera was right. A short walk up the path, a gap in the hedgerow revealed a secluded little garden: primrose, thistle, yellow jacobinia, more roses, and, in large clay pots guarded by bees, virgin-white rajanigandha twined with ice plants of the most intimate pink. At the centre of it all was a cheap and bow-legged red plastic bench.

'Let's sit,' his father said.

Though the hedges were high, the sun had risen and Randeep removed his sandals and wriggled his toes in the warmth. They used to do this all the time. Spending hours together. They'd talk about music or God or the state of the country. Mostly, his father did the talking. He was a great fan of Urdu poetry and would recite lines from Bahu or Bulleh Shah, testing Randeep to see if he'd understood the meaning. No, the deeper meaning, son. Always search for the deeper meaning. There was one that Randeep had especially liked, about wafa and khata. Loyalty and error and how one followed the other. How did it go? He couldn't remember. Perhaps now would be a good time to ask.

'Your mother and I would come here. We'd listen to the Christian Harmony String Quartet playing Schubert at the bandstand and then we'd come here.'

'Explains our balcony. Mamma must be trying to replicate this garden.'

'I wonder if they're still playing.'

'The band?'

His father nodded. His legs were crossed at the knees, hands clasped loosely in his lap. 'How is school?'

'It's still college and you asked me that already.'

'I know I did. I'm not going mad. So this time give me a proper answer. Are we meeting anyone?'

'Daddy!'

'Uff, Randeep, you'll be eighteen soon. Be an adult.'

'But I thought I'd always be your little boy?'

'That's just something parents say when it suits us.'

Randeep smiled. 'There is someone. Jaytha.'

'Sounds Hindu.'

He said she was. 'And she's from the smaller castes.'

'Your mother would have a problem with that. But problems are a long way off yet. First – is she pretty?'

'Very much.'

'And how long?'

'Not long. A month. Bit less. We're still getting to know each other.'

He wished he could stop the words, these lies that came too easy. But however much he hated the untruths, he felt better for them, too. They seemed to allow a different version of himself to be presented to the world.

'Well, I wish you the best of luck.'

It was an oddly formal sentence, said with something like finality. Randeep looked down and retracted his feet from the warmth of the sun. Mr Sanghera laughed.

'Don't worry. I meant it. I'm not going mad. Many years ahead.' Then, more seriously, 'I will beat this. You will get your father back.'

Randeep extended his arm along the bench and cradled his father's shoulders, which were as narrow as his own.

But the trumpet band seemed to have neared, and Randeep grew alarmed. He ducked through the gap in the hedgerow: the musicians, in red-and-white, were circuiting the park.

'Shall we go?' he said, trying not to sound anxious.

'Slow down,' said his father. 'You worry too much. You always did.'

'It's only that Mamma will be back. I didn't even leave a message.'

'Call her, then.'

A couple dawdled towards them, sharing an ice cream. Randeep was veering left to avoid a collision when the woman called out, 'Sangheraji? Oh, I thought it was you. How wonderful!'

She unlinked elbows with her partner and came rushing up, waving a little hysterically, a sixty-something with a bob cut and a short summer dress.

'How are you?' she asked, with heavy concern. 'We missed you last week. The office wasn't the same.'

He saw his father force a smile, and the band rounding the corner.

'Dolan said you fell?'

'Nothing serious. A minor act.'

She smiled with excessive slowness, as if she knew he was lying. 'Is this your son? He's even taller than you! A chipped block, is he not?'

The band was closing in, the trumpets shrieking on the air.

Randeep looked down and saw his father's hand shaking in his pocket, his face emptying. The woman said something else, then turned to her partner and laughed. Mr Sanghera closed his eyes. He seemed to be struggling to breathe.

Randeep took hold of his father's elbow. 'Let's go, Daddy.'

The woman gave a smile of confusion as he tried to drag his father on, but now the band was marching past, the air full of brass, and Mr Sanghera clasped the side of his head and fell to his knees.

'Is everything OK?' the woman asked. 'Charlie's a physician.'

Back home, his father cried angry tears and turned chairs over, banging his fists on the walls. 'What is wrong with everyone?' he shouted. 'What is wrong with you all?'

Randeep crashed down blinds, shuttered windows. Mrs Sanghera followed her husband through the darkened flat with a glass of water and two more pills.

'Get away from me!' he flashed. 'You're trying to kill me. Don't think I can't see it. You're all trying to kill me.'

'How can you say that? I'm your wife!'

He picked up a fallen chair and launched it against the wall.

'Stop this! Please! You're behaving like a child!'

When the doorbell rang the flat was still in darkness. Mr Sanghera sat in his red armchair. Classical music played on the stereo, as advised by the doctors: *something he associates with a more peaceful state of mind*, they'd said. Snatching up her chunni, Mrs Sanghera answered the door. It was their neighbour. She said she'd heard crying and thought she'd check if everything was all right.

'Everything's fine. Thank you.'

In the kite-shaped hallway mirror Randeep saw the woman trying to look in, and his mother blocking her off.

'I was sure I heard . . . Are the children all right?'

'The children are wonderful. The girls are out for their dance classes.' He heard his mother sigh, then, with no great zeal, begin the battle. 'Did I tell you the twins got their kathak level fives? Can't be long until Lata achieves too, no? Two years she's been trying?'

'Three.'

'Ah, yes. Three. And Randeep's here this weekend. NIT next year, with God's will.'

The door closed and his mother returned, looking strangely drained. 'The things I do to make sure people say nice things about our family.' It seemed to Randeep that none of the women enjoyed these encounters. It was all part of a bigger wheel that the world wouldn't allow them to step off.

The girls arrived home together, excitedly, until the atmosphere in the flat chopped short their laughter. The twins made straight for their room, silver ankle-bells tinkling, and Lakhpreet took off her wrap and unbuckled the thin green belt around her dress. She lifted the dough from the fridge and slapped it onto the kitchen counter.

'I can't cook in this dark,' she said, but the only response she got seemed to come from the CD player, where the strings began to subside and with a mighty click the whole thing stopped.

*

Randeep finished unpacking the wretched suitcase and kicked it underneath his college bed. He sat on the tight cotton sheet, elbows on knees and fingertips to fingertips, looking through the circle of his hands at a burn on the carpet. He heard more doors shutting, more loud goodbyes – other students, other arrivals. He reached for his pillow and pushed his face into it.

It had turned cooler by the time Abhijeet arrived, yanking his enormous cricket bag off his shoulder.

Randeep sat up, rubbed his eyes. 'Hi.'

'Oh, hi. Thought you were asleep.' He was groping about on the floor for something. He seemed in a hurry.

'I'll switch the light on,' Randeep offered.

'Don't bother. I'm going straight out' – he found his runners. 'All the girls are in the lounge.'

'Oh,' and then, in a moment of daring: 'Which girls?'

'The usual. Shirenjoht, Mausam, Jaytha, Pups.' He turned round at the door, hesitating. 'Do you want to come?'

He was asking out of pity, that much was obvious. They'd never become friends, he and Abhijeet.

'Maybe later,' Randeep said. 'I want to finish this chapter.' He looked to his desk for a textbook with which to supplement the lie. Abhijeet was already on his way, the luminous green of his moon-boots zipping through the darkness.

Randeep made an eye in the window blinds. The day was darkening over, the yellow of the trees retreating. No, he wasn't going to go down. It was stupid. He felt ashamed, recalling how he'd engineered the meet in the quad the week before. He opened his ring binder and turned to his timetable, determined to prepare for his lectures. Ten minutes later – nothing written, nothing done – he closed the folder and looked round for his wallet.

The corridor was too narrow and carpeted an ugly brown, the dreariness compounded by a large black-and-white close-up of Albert Einstein hanging at one end. He took the stairwell down to the lounge and waited his turn at the vending machine, behind a boy in a white turban. What to choose? What to choose? He tried not to stare at her. She was sitting with friends on three squashy sofas, staring reverentially up at the television. He could see only her profile: the hair all loose and pulled forward over one shoulder, the knifish uptwitch of her thin smile, as if there was a tiny pulse at the very corner of her lips. He imagined lying beside her in a sunny park and every now and then getting up to bring her flowers. Someone called his name. It was Abhijeet, his arm around a girl at the other end of the room.

'You won't find no theorems here,' Abhijeet said.

And then Jaytha turned round. 'Randeep!' She beckoned him over. 'Come sit, come.'

He looked to Abhijeet, who was nodding at him, so Randeep closed his wallet and strode across.

'Hi, Jaytha. How are you this evening?' It sounded stupid now, though she didn't seem to notice.

'Here, sit with me,' and she tucked her feet underneath her bottom, making room.

He wavered, then slid in, jamming his hands into the crevice between his thighs. Her elbow jutted out and touched his own and that point seemed to be the epicentre for the wild buzz radiating through his body.

'How was your weekend with your bhabhiji?'

She smiled. 'That's what I love about you. You remember things. You're so thoughtful.'

Across the room, Abhijeet cheered. 'Good on you, man! You got through her fortress. And believe me, many have tried; many have failed.'

'Don't be so vulgar,' Jaytha said. 'Not everyone's a Neanderthal.'

There was a woollen blanket over her legs which she opened out and spread across both their laps. She nudged closer to him so that elbows, arms and shoulders all touched. It took a while for his heart to calm, and he didn't dare move. He just sat there with the others, watching some American TV comedy. The only interruption came when two girls entered the lounge and asked if they could change channels. They must have been scheduleds because some of the other girls pinched their nostrils together. He felt Jaytha tense up, her eyes hard on the TV. He sought out her hand under the blanket and squeezed and this she didn't seem to mind.

*

One morning, a week later, he was shaken awake by Abhi, looming groggily over him, saying something about a call.

Still in his pyjamas, Randeep went down to the stairwell where the receiver was gently bouncing on its blue coil. He put the phone to his ear.

'Hello.'

It was his mother, which meant it was his father. Yesterday, she said, he'd had a fight with someone at work. He'd broken furniture. She'd had to go in and calm him down. It had taken nearly an hour to get him up off the floor. She paused. 'They all saw him crying.'

'I'm coming, Mamma.'

As he arrived home it took a moment to recognize the self-satisfied voice carrying up the hall. Vakeelji, his father's lawyer. Randeep couldn't face seeing him right away, so he slipped out of his shoes and curled his head into the twins' room. They were sitting on the top bunk, in secret conversation.

'I'm here,' he said.

They stared at him, waiting. Eight years older, he felt he really didn't know them at all. Their world was just their bubble of two.

'How's things?'

'OK,' Ekam said.

'Yeah, OK,' Raji agreed.

'Where's Daddy?'

'In his room.'

'How is he?'

'It's a difficult stage,' Ekam said, and Raji sniggered.

He stepped across the landing and opened the door. His father was sitting on the other side of the bed, facing the window. Randeep shucked off his rucksack and went and sat beside him.

'Daddy, it's me. Randeep.'

Mr Sanghera nodded. 'You didn't need to come.'

'Vakeelji's here.'

'Come to look at the tamasha, no doubt.'

'What happened at work?'

'Please tell them I'm sorry.'

'Tell who?'

'And your mother, too.'

In the main room, Vakeelji took up all of the tall red chair, and not for the first time it struck Randeep that the lawyer's small pink lips surely belonged on the face of a little girl. He was sipping very daintily from the best china teacup. Mrs Sanghera sat on the two-seater and behind her Lakhpreet leaned against the wall. Randeep looked to his sister and saw the flicker, the slight tightening around her mouth that she'd always done to convey to him that she was all right. He touched the lawyer's feet.

'Bless you, son, bless you. How is college? NIT next year?'

'With your blessings.'

'Always, always.'

His mother explained Vakeelji's presence. The DTTP had been in touch. They were concerned about his father's application to his work. His ability to do his job. They were considering not formalizing his contract at the end of the trial period.

'Can you believe it?' Mrs Sanghera said. 'So many years he has given to the government and this two-bit offshoot wants to cut him off like that. Who gave them the right?'

'The chief minister, bhabhi.'

She was only fleetingly deflated. 'He could do all their jobs with his eyes closed.'

Vakeelji smiled into his chins and very delicately set his cup down in its saucer, as if to make any noise was to risk some sort of detonation. 'Bhabhi, we have to face the facts. Bhaji is not well. Inshallah, we all hope he reverts to his normal self soon but until then the department is naturally going to protect itself. In twelve months he will have his full government pension rights secured. Unless they are certain he is a viable long—'

'Viable!'

'Long-term associate, they will move to terminate before then.'

'Then you must stop them, Harchand. We rely on you in these matters.'

The lawyer showed his palms. 'I will do my best, but I fear . . .'

The silence seemed to frighten Mrs Sanghera into temporary submission. She rallied. 'So what do we do? For the first time in history are the women of this house to go and find work? Shall I start offering my services to clean my neighbours' latrines?' She thrust out her arms from under the pallu of her sari. 'Perhaps you think I should pawn my wedding bangles?'

'Oh, don't make so much drama, Mummy,' Lakhpreet said.

'I can find work,' Randeep said.

'They will still pay his school fees, yes?'

The lawyer shook his wide head. 'Given the ridiculous bureaucracy around our property laws, they will let you stay in this flat for one year until you move somewhere else. That is all. They will no longer pay for medicines, servants, transport, or, indeed, college fees.'

Mrs Sanghera didn't know where to look. 'Why do they make the children suffer?'

'I'll find work,' Randeep said. 'I can help.'

'You are staying in college.'

'I can do both.' He looked at her. 'Honestly, I can.'

She turned fiercely to the lawyer. 'You see how brave my son is? He would never see his mother lower herself.'

The lawyer sighed. 'Truly you are blessed, bhabhi.'

He found work quickly, doing weekend shifts for a British insurance firm who'd outsourced their call centre to Mirla Business and Technology Park. He enjoyed it. The office was bright, with potted-palm fronds down the aisle, and on the front wall hung a series of professional-looking world clocks: London, New York, Sydney. There was air conditioning, too, and he had his own piece of white desk space around which he'd made a fence of his textbooks.

It was near eleven at night when he'd reach his digs and show his pass to the security guard and enter the lounge. Usually, it would be empty, but occasionally Jaytha would happen to be there and they'd drink hot chocolate from chipped blue mugs and talk about their day. He wasn't at all certain how to coax their relationship forward, into a corner more intimate.

At midnight he'd move to the stairwell and wait for his mother to ring. He'd asked her if he might buy a mobile with his wages – his wages were wired directly to her account – but she'd thought it unnecessary. Who would pay the bills, for one thing? The phone would ring and he'd lean tiredly against the wall and listen to her battles with the Chandigarh higher-ups. They were trying to cheat his father, she said. *They are deliberately giving him impossible tasks to prove their point. I will not allow it. I will not let them make a fool out of him.* Sometimes Randeep sensed glee in his mother's voice, as though she were revelling in it all.

'Your mamma's probably glad to have someone to fight,' Jaytha said one evening. 'She sounds like a tough woman.'

Randeep said she was, though on reflection he wasn't sure, and she sounded far from tough the night she rang to tell him that the bastards had won. They'd forced his father out of his job.

'What will we do?' she cried.

'How's Daddy? What's he doing?'

'Nothing. Staring at the wall. He looks broken, beita.'

Randeep put his fist to the wall and pressed his forehead against it. 'Tell him I love him.'

'Hain?'

He shook his head. 'I'll find some more work. There are more shifts I can do.'

'We can't survive.' She was starting to sound hysterical. Randeep imagined her balanced on the lip of the sofa, hair wild, the twins hiding in their bedroom, Lakhpreet trying to hold it all together. 'Everyone will find out. We'll have to move. We have no money. Oh, Rabbah, what will we do? What will we do?'

'I'll sort it out, Mamma. I'll work. Listen to me. I'll work.'

He joined the processing shift, nine p.m. to five a.m. There were four of them and overnight they had to log the day's customer claim requests and vet them for 'completedness'. If information was missing they pulled up one of the three standard templates and printed off a letter. They worked in isolation, one in each corner of the room, the only sounds the snicker of keys, the gurgle of the water cooler, the march of the clock. 2.30. 2.35. 2.37. Sometimes Randeep fell asleep into his elbow, only waking when one of his colleagues flicked a rubber band at him. The night sky had paled by the time his shift ended. He collapsed onto his bed for one, maybe two hours before trudging off to morning labs.

'This is crazy,' Jaytha said, one month into his exhausting routine. 'You're killing yourself. And you're failing. When was the last time you failed a test?'

'It was a stupid test, yaar. It didn't even count.'

But the next one did, and when he failed that too the deputy principal called him into his office. It wasn't like him, he said. He was usually one of their finer students.

'We had you written down as a real contender for NIT this year, Master Sanghera.'

'Sorry, sir. I'll do better.'

'I hear your father has some issues at work?'

Randeep sighed. It was all so predictable, the speed with which gossip spread.

His mother called him daily, on the new mobile she'd finally permitted him to buy. Sometimes she accused him of not wiring all the money through. Mostly she just cried her complaints. That his father did nothing. That he just gazed at the wall listening to his stupid Schubert. They could all starve and he wouldn't care. What kind of a man was he?

'We've not been to the mall for two weeks. And how long before they ask us to leave this flat? I'm scared to answer the door. Every knock and my stomach falls away.'

'It'll get better. Uncle said we could stay in the flat for a year and then I'll go to NIT and get a good job and everything will be fine afterwards.'

One night, putting the phone down on his mother, he reached sourly into his claims tray. He was angry at her, at himself. She'd said that he wittingly stayed away from home. That they were struggling with his father and he never helped. He'd argued that he was working, working for them. But he knew there was truth in what she'd said, that exhaustion was easier than being at home, and it was this that angered him. He clamped his head in his palms and looked again at the claim. They'd not signed it. Stupid people. How could they expect them to assess their claim if they didn't even sign it? There was a telephone number scrawled at the bottom, in a shaky blue hand. Randeep punched the digits in so hard his finger blanched. He wanted to tell them how they'd made a mess of everything and that they'd have to fill in another form and send that in and why couldn't they have just done things properly the first time? As the phone rang and rang, his rage wilted and he looked at the London clock and wondered what the hell he was doing. He had to put the phone down.

'Hello?'

'Hello? Oh, sorry, sir, wrong number.'

'Who is that? John? Is that you again?'

'Sorry, sir, I didn't realize it was so late. I'll say goodbye to you.'

'Hang on, there.' There was a dead minute until the man

returned, his words now echoing. 'Better. Who did you say you were again?'

'Sorry, sir, I didn't know it was so late. It was simply a courtesy call. I'll bid you goodnight.'

'Where you from? You Scottish?'

'India, sir. I'm Indian.'

'Oh, Indian. I've known a few Indians in my time. We fought together, you see.'

'OK, sir. Thank you, sir. I'll let you repair to your slumber now.'

'In Burma. I was stationed with Balwant Singh, if memory serves. And it really doesn't, these days.'

He laughed, sadly, Randeep thought.

'Always took a bucket of water to the shitter with him, that one.' A chuckle. 'Must've had the cleanest arse in Arakan.'

Randeep switched the receiver to his other ear. He knew the battle. 'The 1944 campaign, sir? We really out-foxed the Japanese, I think.'

'Once we got Maungdaw, we knew we were in with a chance. As long as those tunnels stayed true.'

'The tunnels. Yes, the tunnels. You must admit the engineers were heroes, sir. The Indian Seventh Division put their lives on the line for your country. We studied it at school.'

'Balwant was one of those engineers. Couldn't have done it without him. Does he still like his Fairweather's?'

Randeep paused. 'I'm not sure, sir.'

'I was in the second West Yorkshires myself.'

'Brigadier Evans, sir!'

There was a croaky laugh on the line. 'I saw him pelting out of the station in just his underpants once, waving a pistol. We were about to come under attack, you see. A great man.'

An hour passed and still they were on the phone and still Randeep had a heap of claims to vet before his shift ended. He said he had to go.

'Oh, really? I was enjoying myself a fair bit.' The old man did sound disappointed.

He waited a week before calling the man again. No one

answered. He tried again the next night and it seemed to take the old man some time to remember him.

'And happy birthday, sir. For yesterday. Happy belated birthday.'

Randeep explained that through his father's former job he'd got access to the Historic War Archival Records Office and in there were details of Private Michael Sedgewick.

'Like your date of birth, sir.'

'I had no idea,' Michael said, apparently awed by the notion that bits of him should exist in stacked-up files in Indian offices.

They spoke about the Burma campaign and then about themselves. The difference between their ages seemed to allow this type of conversation. He said he was a widower. Janice had been dead ten years. Her lungs gave up on her, you see. All those Park Drives. Their children now had their own families and mighty proud of them he was too. Philip was some sort of hospital orderly and Janet senior secretary to a big director type. He had four grandchildren. He was eighty-seven and lived alone. There was a mixture of pride and sadness in Michael's voice which broke Randeep's heart a little. He promised to call at least once every week, though no such promise was asked for, and on each call they'd speak for at least forty-five minutes, never more than an hour, because calls over an hour long were checked the next morning by the day supervisor. Michael appreciated this, Randeep could tell. He said how good of him it was to care about an old man on the other side of the world. He said he'd understand if Randeep wanted to stop these conversations and spend time with people his own age. Randeep wouldn't hear of it.

'I don't have any money, you know,' Michael said.

'But I don't want money,' Randeep said, confused, hurt even. 'I just want to talk.'

*

Three weeks before his finals Randeep was granted a few days' leave. His mother and sisters were going to Anandpur Sahib to pray for his father and Randeep had been summoned to look after him until they returned. On the bus home his textbook lay open on his lap, the spine nestled between his thighs. None of it made sense. He'd missed too much, caught up on too little. He shoved the book back into his rucksack and stared out of the dark bus window.

The women left before daybreak. Mrs Sanghera said it was vital they make the morning puja, though Randeep suspected she just didn't want to be seen standing in line at the bus stop. He closed the door after them and went back to his father, who was sitting in his red chair, barefoot, eyes closed. He had grey stubble. His kurta pyjama was buttoned up to the neck.

'They've gone, Daddy.'

A nod, eyes still closed. Randeep, determined, moved to the cupboards. He found three eggs and some jam.

'Scrambled?'

Nothing.

'What about jammy toast?' He turned the sticky jar around. 'Gooseberry.'

He looked at his father. His hands were threaded across the small swell of his belly, as if he was only taking a short dreamy nap. And perhaps he was: the gentle rise and fall of his breathing suggested so. He looked peaceful. Randeep decided to cook his father brinjal later, and was thinking about the aubergines he'd seen in the fridge, when his father's eyes shot open and he bolted out of his seat, screaming, with arms outflung. He had hold of Randeep's throat and Randeep felt his head banging the cupboard.

'You're trying to poison me. You're like the rest of them.'

But his father was the weaker of the two now and Randeep prised the fingers from his neck. He held his father's hands down by his side until he stopped fighting, then led him back to his chair and sat him down. He fetched his pills and a glass of water and watched while he took his medication. For lunch Randeep cooked rice and vegetables and when his father refused even to look at the plate Randeep fed him forkfuls, as if his father were the child.

He seemed much improved the next day. When Randeep walked in he was reading at the table, his body washed in sunlight. 'Morning, son.'

Randeep moved to the sink and pointlessly shifted around a few of the dirty dishes.

'Looks like Farhan might just break the record after all.'

'Maybe,' Randeep said.

He heard his father crisply folding away the paper. 'Shall we have tea and toast? With some of that gooseberry jam?'

Over breakfast, his father asked him about school – 'College, Daddy!' – and his new job and that girl he'd mentioned last time. What was her name again?

'Jaytha.'

'Well, let's not tell your mother just yet, eh? There's only so much dying with shame a woman can do in one year.'

They played backgammon long into the afternoon, hunched over the thick old board, fists curled to their throats. The sun had moved, now buttering the wall, and a late-afternoon tiredness hung in the air. Randeep started setting up the pieces again.

'Five–four. I'm catching up.'

Mr Sanghera stretched, glancing at the oven timer. 'I thought you were making brinjal?'

'One more game.'

'Afterwards.'

'But—'

'Tsk! Do as you're told.'

Randeep stood, only pretending annoyance. He was glad to have been mildly rebuked, the way fathers should rebuke their sons. It had been such a good day. The best. He couldn't wait to tell Lakhpreet how well their father had been. He'd turned a corner, he was sure of it. He took the brinjals from the refrigerator, washed them, and found garlic and cumin and onions and ghee and salt. Soon the aubergines were stewing.

'Smells delicious,' Mr Sanghera said.

Randeep lifted the lid, the steam pushing up his nose. He coughed. 'Another twenty minutes.'

'And what's for dessert?'

Randeep paused. He hadn't thought of that. He looked in the

cupboard. There were some damp biscuits. A half-pot of cream. He knew there were apples in the cool box. 'I'll mix a fruit salad.'

Mr Sanghera made an incredulous face. 'That food deserves more than a fruit salad. Let's have custard. With bananas.'

A childhood favourite. 'But we don't have any powder. Or bananas.'

'Then I'll go to Stephen's and fetch some.' He bent down to look for his flip-flops.

'No,' Randeep said.

His father looked up.

'I mean, it's too far.'

'It's fifteen minutes.'

'And cold.'

'Randeep.'

Randeep turned away, still holding the cupboard open. 'I'll go. I'll be quicker.'

He went down Santa Cruz Drive, his walk blooming into a run every few metres. The leaves were shading to pink. He took the flower-planters' alley – a weedy strip of gravel – and cut across the commerce building gardens to get to the PCO, behind which was Father Stephen's All Items Store. They didn't have bananas so he settled on a chocolate roll to accompany the two jars of custard. He remembered they were running out of toothpaste and asked for some Pepsodent too. The thin, unsmiling boy put the items in a green bag, and it seemed to take him forever to tie a knot and push the bag across the counter to Randeep, who snatched it up and hurried out: round the PCO, across the gardens and up the alley. As he reached Santa Cruz Drive he tired, slowed, spun the clammy bag round and strangled the top of it into his fist. He looked up the long road to where their apartment block was. He patted his pocket but knew he'd left his phone behind. He could hear his footsteps beating the ground, the bag banging his thigh. He flung open the main door, not even waiting for the chowkidar, and took the stairs two, three at a time.

'Daddy!' He rattled the handle. 'Daddy! Please open the door!' He could hear the Schubert playing. 'Open the door!'

He banged and banged until a hand on his shoulder pushed him aside. It was one of their neighbours, a man whose name Randeep couldn't remember. He had a crowbar which he wedged into the door beside the lock. There was the sound of wood splintering and then the neighbour came at the door twice with his shoulder until it swung brokenly open. Randeep ran in. He could see his father's naked dark-brown feet dangling in the main room, a chair in place. His head was tilted to one side, as if in mid apprehension of something. There was a piece of flex around his neck. Randeep wrapped his arms around his father's feet as if to push him up, and the neighbour stood on the chair and untied the flex. The body slumped to the floor. Its eyes were wide and staring. Its lips opening and parting. It blinked, blinked again. Randeep knelt beside him. More neighbours gathered, puffing out their cheeks, saying how lucky he was. The music was still playing.

'It would have been better if he had died,' Mrs Sanghera said.

Four days had passed and she was coming back into the room from seeing off yet another concerned visitor.

'Mamma!' Lakhpreet said.

He heard his mother sigh, sit down. 'Oh, I know. It's . . . I don't know what to do any more.'

Randeep closed his father's door and joined him on the bed. Mr Sanghera lay propped against the cushioned headboard, chin on his chest. The plate of jammy toast sat untouched by his side.

'OK, Daddy, I'm going back to college now. I'll see you soon, acha?'

Perhaps there was a nod in response. He couldn't be sure.

The coach broke down and it was past midnight when he jiggled open the lock to his room. He waited a minute for the furniture to outline itself, then saw that Abhijeet wasn't around anyway, so he clicked the lamp and a triangle of silver light split the room. He was sitting on the floor when his phone vibrated and *Jaytha Hall* flashed up at him.

She arrived in a thick green duffel coat with fur-trimmed hood, removing it as she sat beside him on the bed. Her arms were brown and thin and beautiful. She smelled of almonds, and a few forgotten breadcrumbs stuck to the corner of her mouth. She must have rushed over here.

'You didn't have to come,' he said.

'Don't be silly.' She linked arms with him. 'We're friends. You sound like you've been crying.'

He told her about how his father had tried to strangle him and how he'd had to feed him forkfuls of rice like a baby. He told her that he'd been better the next day, they'd even played backgammon, but it must have all been a pretence, and that when he'd seen his feet hanging in the air like that he'd never felt so scared before in his whole life. He wasn't sure why but he didn't mention the helpful neighbour. He found himself saying that he'd untied the flex and lifted his father down.

'I really thought I'd lost him.' He felt her arms circle his waist. 'I was so scared.'

'I'm so sorry.'

She held him tighter and that felt good. To be wanted like that. He wanted her too. He put his arm around her back and kissed the top of her head. She didn't seem to mind.

'Thanks for coming.'

She held him tighter still. 'We're friends.'

He adjusted a little, kissed her forehead, and made the slow drive towards her lips. She responded, reaching up to meet his mouth. He'd never felt this kind of drowning sensation before. It was his first kiss. His first anything, and suddenly the world seemed like a less difficult place. Maybe things would turn out all right. His father would get better and he'd go to NIT and Jaytha would be welcomed into his family.

'You're the only one who understands,' he said, easing her down, her head on his pillow. A nervous look crossed her face, which she tried to smile away. They resumed kissing. Her hands roved around his back as if not sure what they should be doing. His were on her waist, then her bottom. She pushed against his shoulders, but when he insisted on kissing her neck she seemed willing to let him. He wanted to show her how much he loved her.

How much it meant to him that she understood. He pushed up her top and couldn't believe that under it were her breasts. Just there under this thin top. The pink-brown tips revealed. He heard her say something and try to move away but he knew she liked him and he held her arms and kissed her breasts. She was saying it louder now and the louder she said it the stronger his grip, the more fiercely he applied his mouth to her body. He felt her knees in his stomach, pushing him away. That didn't make sense. He rubbed his cock against her and she screamed but he was groaning himself and he bit her breasts and dug his fingers into the maddeningly soft flesh of her arms and pushed his weight down, down on her. He was telling her how much he really loved her when he felt a pair of arms around his waist yank him violently away. Randeep gasped, as if only now coming up for air. Abhijeet was telling him to get out. On the bed, Jaytha reached for her torn top, face turned away.

In an alleyway behind the art block, he ground his teeth and smacked his forehead against the wall, again and again, as if trying to knock all feeling out. Her frightened bedsunk face wouldn't stop floating into his mind.

He walked for hours. The streets were quiet, the only light coming from a top-floor dance studio where a girl was pirouetting, practising for the end-of-year ball. He passed the tennis courts and sports gym and saw another light on in the student study rooms. He thought Jaytha might be there. This close to the exams, maybe she'd forgotten what he'd done and was in there revising. He opened the door. 'Ja—' It was some other girl, head bent delicately over her books. She turned round.

'Sorry,' Randeep said, and withdrew to the street.

Across the road an auto applied its wheezy brakes and two males got out. They had a crate of alcohol with them, though they already seemed pretty drunk.

'Randeep,' one of them said. Harshly?

They were friends of Abhi's. 'Oh, hi.' He waited for them to do something, his stomach cowering. They must not have heard yet.

'There's a party. Wanna come?'

'Not tonight, yaar.'

'Sure? Plenty of . . .' The boy made a *V* with his fingers and ran his tongue inside it.

'Arré, sahib – paise?' the auto driver said, and the boys paid and told Randeep to come along later if he felt like it.

He stayed out all night, until he was sure Abhijeet would have left for lectures. As he re-entered the dormitory no one turned to stare. The few students were hunkered over desks, preparing for finals. He went up to his room and sat on the bed and scrolled down to Jaytha's number. No one answered. He untied his shoelaces and fell against the pillow. Her smell lingered. Briefly, he noticed a new cricket poster on the door, and then he closed his eyes and hoped he'd sleep through it all.

The sun forced him up, hitting his face. He reached for his phone but she hadn't called. Perhaps she'd left a note in his locker box. He used the kitchen stairwell, with its squeaky suggestions of guilt. There was no note from her. Only a card from the Senior Pastoral Care Warden ordering him to her office at four o'clock. Randeep read the card again. His hand started to shake. He thought he was going to cry.

Her office was on the sixth floor of the humanities block. He shared a lift with two teachers discussing their sons' prospects in Canada, and followed the signs to the warden's door. A battered plaque read Mrs Bimla Manapadhay, IPS. Randeep, head down, knocked.

Jaytha was already there, in a cushioned armchair at Mrs Manapadhay's side. Her hair was tied back. She was dressed normally: blue blouse, black skirt and shoes. Randeep smiled with relief. She was all right. She was alive. Mrs Manapadhay asked him to take a seat. She looked too young for a widow-white sari. Her hair, deliberately messy, had two chopsticks criss-crossed into it, and her single gold bangle kept clinking against the glass top of her desk. Randeep sat down. His eyes were fixed on the patch of carpet between his shoes. He felt Mrs Manapadhay leaning across. She had a surprisingly soft voice.

'Mr Sanghera, a complaint's been lodged against you.'

He nodded.

'It's in relation to your behaviour towards Jaytha. That you tried to force yourself upon her in a sexual way.'

He nodded again. But he felt confused. He'd not thought of it in those stark terms. He'd thought he was only guilty of loving her too much too soon. Stupid boy. He didn't dare look up.

'You admit that you did behave inappropriately towards Jaytha and tried to force yourself upon her in a sexual way?'

'I do,' he croaked.

She sighed. 'I should tell you that it was not Jaytha who made the complaint. It's my unfortunate experience that girls rarely say anything at all.'

He nodded.

'You're very lucky that she insists on not involving the police. She doesn't want to put her family through that.'

Again, he nodded. But he didn't know what this all meant. He wished his hands would stop their trembling.

'But we have our own internal procedures which Jaytha cannot influence and which we must adhere to. Even more so when there's a caste factor involved.' And she said that she was sorry but they had no choice other than to remove him from college and discredit all his examination results to date. This was with immediate effect. 'Do you understand, Mr Sanghera?'

He nodded.

'I'll complete the paperwork by the end of the day and the SEB will be notified in due course. I suggest you speak to the college careers adviser while you still can about the options now available to you. But as you live only in Chandigarh I'm expecting you to have vacated your lodgings by tomorrow. Let your college warden know if you require assistance arranging your travel.' She paused. 'Is that all clear?' she asked, not unkindly.

He nodded. 'It's just, madam, I have a job and have only two more shifts this week. I won't be paid if I don't do them. Can I stay until the end of the week, please?'

Mrs Manapadhay counselled against this – 'Students can be

cruel' – but Randeep said his family relied on him and Mrs Manapadhay said very well. As long as he stayed away from Jaytha, he could remain until the weekend.

It was a horrible week. He spent most of it in the library, avoiding everyone, entering his room only if Abhi was asleep. Word had spread. Students stared, some swore. One shoved him down the stairs.

He arranged his suitcase and bags into a pile by the door, topping it all off with his ceramic goose lamp, and left for work. It was his final shift. Tomorrow, he'd board the first bus home. He wondered how he was going to explain everything to his mother. He wondered whether to try and contact Jaytha. He wondered if he shouldn't just run away to Africa and start again.

'What's in Africa?' Michael said.

'Nothing. Exactly.'

'Better to face things out, young man. At least then you can see who's hurling the shit at you.'

Randeep smiled for perhaps the first time that week. At the end of his shift, the night manager settled his wages and he walked out of the grey cement block with a small sense of being freed. The streetlights were still on. Maybe he could go to Delhi. Or Bombay. Or back to Bhubaneshwar like he'd always wanted?

He turned into a wide passage that by day acted as a parking station for cyclists. The moon hung at the end of it. He felt edgy and walked quickly, but wasn't even halfway when three figures slid into the lane, coming towards him. Hands in pockets, faces in shifting moon shadow. Their footsteps made no sound. His heart pumped. They'll walk past, he told himself. Don't be scared. But they weren't talking to one another, and this frightened him. As they crossed, the one in the middle stared sidelong. He had an *Om* stud in his ear. It looked familiar. Randeep carried on, agitated. Then he knew: it was the boy who'd shoved him down the stairs. He looked over his shoulder. All three had stopped, turned.

'Kaiso ho?' the one with the ear stud asked.

Randeep nodded. 'I'm just going back to my room. I'm leaving in the morning.'

They didn't reply. He started walking again. He closed his eyes and said please God no, but no sooner had he opened them than he heard steps pounding behind him. He ran, shouting for help. At the end of the lane they tripped him up and covered his mouth with huge clothy hands. An *Om*-knuckled fist came driving down on his face and he heard himself groan, and then nothing.

He felt thick-headed as he started to stir, as if a deep mist shrouded his brain. Voices, laughter, hands applied to his body. He heard, 'Let's see how much the high-caste fucker likes being shat on.' He tried to speak, but clouded over again and the tiredness was too much.

When he next came round, he was so very thirsty. He swallowed, with difficulty, and realized there was something stringy blocking his mouth. He tried flexing his jaw but it didn't budge. He wondered what he was doing on his side. He tried to sit but couldn't. His ankles. Who'd tied them? And his wrists. Crossed and bound behind his back. He was deep in a well. His head throbbed. They'd left him to die. He twisted his neck in wild panic: there was a light, not far. A thin beam of light. A doorway, it looked like. He was naked. No, not quite. They'd let him keep his underwear, but it felt funny, wetly padded. He rolled onto his back and – one, two, three – straightened right up. As he did so his forehead hit his knees and he felt something strange and flaky come off his skin. He bent his head to his shoulder and smelled and retched. The bile came up the walls of his throat and trickled down his chin. He began to cry. Slowly, he moved onto his knees, his bound ankles beneath him, and wriggled to the door. There were voices. His eyes widened in fear. It was them. He listened some more. It was a teacher, teaching. Someone who would help. He wriggled closer, right up to the door. A class. Students. He looked about him, his mouth still gagged. Projectors, folders, boxes of pens. He'd been locked up in the stationery cupboard. He didn't know what to do.

He didn't have a choice. He banged his forehead to the door. Banging and banging. The teacher's voice halted. Footsteps got louder. A key turned, the door opened – light! – and with a screeching mewl Randeep collapsed into the lecture hall.

Avtar and Lakhpreet sat side by side in the waiting room. She paged through a dental magazine, of all things. He was set forward, elbows on thighs, one hand closed around the wrist of the other as if choking a small animal. He looked down at the frayed hems of his black trousers. At the candle-wax stain on his blazer that had refused to come out. Again he observed his reflection in the window and again he ran his palm over the slick side parting. The receptionist smiled into her keyboard.

'Stop that,' Lakhpreet whispered.

'It's not used to being combed like this.'

'Then you should've left it how it was.'

'Are you even sure he's coming?'

'Oh? Do you have somewhere else to be?'

He frowned, stood up.

'Sit down. Don't be nervous.'

'I'm not!' and he sat back down, nearly missing the chair.

Another hour passed before the door opened and Vakeelji came forward, his big bearish arms outstretched.

'Baby!'

'Uncle!' Lakhpreet said, rising.

They touched the lawyer's feet, and he showed them into his office, apologizing for the wait. There was a time when he could walk to the club and back and not be stopped by every two-bit Ramu in the book.

'But those days seem to have passed. Now even the criminals think they have a case!'

He moved around his impressive desk with its clever inlay, and his huge tan chair crackled to accommodate a fat man getting comfortable on hard leather. Avtar and Lakhpreet had to bring in their seats from the waiting room.

'And how is my friend?' Vakeelji asked.

'Same, uncle. He still can't leave his room.'

'Well, tell him to hurry up and get better. We need to get our squash games back on. I'm starting to put on weight.'

Lakhpreet gave a sad little smile and Vakeelji patted his desk, as if it were a proxy for her head.

'Give it time. And I'm here, aren't I? Jhub hum hain tho kya ghum hai? And a few more months and I'll have clean-fine licked that brother of yours into shape and onto a plane straight for America.'

Lakhpreet gestured towards Avtar, shifting in his chair, alert. 'Uncle, you remember I spoke to you about . . . If there's something you can do.'

The lawyer gazed at him and for the first time seemed to acknowledge this other presence in his office.

'It was at Lohri, uncle,' Lakhpreet said. 'You said he'd need to learn English.'

'And have you?'

'It's all he's done for the last six months.'

'When I'm not working with my papa,' Avtar said. He didn't want the lawyer to expect too much. 'But my younger brother helps me. He can speak it very well. And I went to an English medium school until plus two so I could speak it a bit already.'

'I see. And where do you want to go? Where did you have in mind? The south of France? The Gold Coast? Monaco, perhaps?'

'If that is where I can make the most money.'

Vakeelji seemed to allow himself a tiny smile and reached for a drawer down beside his knees. He presented Avtar with various dog-eared papers and used his gold fountain pen to point out specific clauses, options, fees. It felt as if he was going through the lawyerly motions, for Lakhpreet's sake; as if he'd taken one look at Avtar and decided this was a waste of his time. There are several visas you can opt for, he said, dully. Ultimately, it came down to the concept of risk and reward.

'And what I can afford,' Avtar said.

'Naturally.' The marriage route was usually the most expensive, but you could work legally and it more or less guaranteed full rights after one year. It could sometimes take some time to find the right girl. At the opposite end, holiday visas were cheaper, but you can't work and you have to come back. 'Many don't, of course. But then many don't find work either. So they starve in a shed at the bottom of some chacha's garden.' He could always get Avtar there illegally – there was a truck leaving UP only next week. Higher chance of getting caught on the way, but cheaper, and if you made it and found work you'd generally do well. If he were to get caught then the lawyer and agent fees, it went without saying, were non-refundable.

'He's not going illegally,' Lakhpreet said. 'They die on the way.'

'There have been many sad incidents, yes.'

'She mentioned a student visa,' Avtar said, meaning Lakhpreet.

'That is another option.' He turned the piece of paper over and directed Avtar towards the relevant section. 'Usually for one year but if you're good the institution will keep you on. I had one boy who went to a college in Wisconsin. Eight years now and he's a lecturer earning more than me. His whole family has moved there. American citizens all.'

Avtar nodded cautiously, fearful of being drawn into such wishful dreaming.

'Of course, most of our boys enrol on day one and start work on day two. Usually in one of those takeaway houses. And then they go into hiding. They don't think about the long view. Only concerned with what they can earn now.'

'It's hard not to be, uncle. When you've got a hungry family back home.'

At the end of the discussion Vakeelji walked them into the waiting room, where the receptionist quickly minimized her screen. The student visa form was secure in Avtar's hand, his hand pressed against his thigh. He kept rubbing his thumb along the edge of the folded paper. He thanked the lawyer, who was busy talking to Lakhpreet.

'Tell bhabhi I've not forgotten. I'm hoping for a suitable girl later this month. He's not getting off that easily, the rogue.'

'Thank you, uncle,' Lakhpreet said, and with the most girlish of movements tipped up onto her toes and left an elegant kiss on the lawyer's cheek.

The money the lawyer was asking: Avtar didn't know how he'd ever earn that much, even if they did remortgage the shop. And Navjoht's school fees were coming up. And the rent and bills. He reached a window in the stairwell, traffic glowing below. Nothing in their lives was working and the city lay there roaring its indifference. What a world.

Trudging up the final steps, he had to flatten himself against the wall so two men carrying a large TV could pass by. Avtar's neighbour, Mr Lal, stood at the top.

'I'll call my son. I'm sure there's been a mistake,' he said, voice quivering.

The men looked up from their squatting position. It was a big TV. 'Tell him to cough up or we'll be back for the rest.'

Avtar ventured up a few steps. 'Is everything all right, uncle?'

Mr Lal frowned, probably annoyed that Avtar had witnessed this, wondering who else in the building would find out. 'Fine,' he said, snapped, and disappeared into his flat.

During the evening, Avtar sat with his family around the small fold-out table, eating the plain rice and wet potatoes his mother had prepared. It was a pitiful meal.

'The lady with the red bangles came again,' his father said. 'I think soon she'll be placing a sizeable order. Didn't you think so?'

Afterwards, his father lay on the settee and Navjoht opened the English newspaper they bought at half price from a man who passed by the shop each evening. Avtar stepped through the shower curtain and onto the warm concrete of the balcony. He crossed his arms on the railing, his knee nosing familiarly into the fretwork. It was a greasy airless night. Crickets scratched in the hot spaces and leaves from the amrood tree hung drily by his face. He could hear Mr and Mrs Lal arguing next door. He reached up and closed his hand around a gnarled branch, right where branch met trunk, and ripped at it and ripped at it until all that was left was the white wound.

His mother called him to take the empty gas cylinder to Karthik's, and to make sure he got a fair price this time.

'Tell Navjoht.'

'He's emptying the bucket.'

Avtar pushed off the balcony, throwing the branch aside, and lifted the gas cylinder to his shoulder. When he got back, his brother still wasn't there.

'Downstairs. Teaching. Earning.'

'I thought I was his only student.'

'You were his first,' his mother said.

He told them he'd been to see a lawyer. A good one. An honest one who said he'd help. He explained about the student visa and when his father asked how much Avtar told him a figure that was less than half of what the lawyer had said.

His father looked concerned. 'We'll sell the shop.'

Avtar laughed. It was typical, reassuring even, of his father to go straight for the big and obvious answer. 'We could just take out a loan against it. And I'll start paying that back as soon as I find work over there.'

'A loan. Yes. So we can keep the shop?'

'Yes.'

'And do you think they will lend us that much?'

'I think so, Papa. I'll find out.'

'Yes. Find out.'

'Do you have to go? Can you not find work here?' It was his mother, speaking from the kitchen, her back to them.

'It's been over six months, Mamma. And I'll be back in a year. Maybe two. And then you can get me married and I can try again for work here. But at least we'll have money.'

'And Navjoht will be working by then,' his father said.

'How will you pay his college fees if you're paying for this loan-shoan?'

'I don't know. I'll do two jobs. Maybe he'll have to wait a year. But at least there's a chance it can work. There's nothing for me if I stay here.'

'There's us,' his mother said, turning sharply. Her sari had snagged on a nail in the counter and strained almost indecently across her body. 'There's your family.'

Avtar was silent. She turned back round and after a while her hand hovered over the two small mangoes ripening on the window-sill, wondering which to choose for a dessert.

He didn't know how he was going to earn the rest of the money. Each morning for two weeks he dressed in his blazer, shirt and trousers and took the bus round the city. He tried the same places he'd tried several times already this year – the rubber factory, the software firm, the rickshaw hiring company. The manager of Parvati Jewellery Emporium didn't even wait for Avtar to speak.

'Same as last time, yaara. Nothing.'

'But I can speak English now, sir. You said if I could speak English.'

'Sorry,' and the man went back to arranging his female busts.

The evenings he devoted to whatever new list of English phrases his brother had drawn up. *Where can I locate the train station? The weather today is very fine. Might I interest you in a cup of tea?* He'd lie on the balcony, list in hand, the stars encouraging while at his side a white candle burned steadily down to its little hot pocket of wax.

*

He was coming back from the mandi, blazer hooked over his shoulder, when Navjoht ran to meet him.

'They're being kicked out!' he exclaimed. 'Uncle and Aunty.'

A truck was parked outside Gardenia Villas, piled high with a florid sofa, a French-looking dining table, several cabinets, beds. A whole flatful of stuff. There were police, too, to oversee the exchange. Beyond the truck, the neighbours had gathered, Avtar's parents among them.

'What will they do?' Navjoht asked.

Mrs Lal was weeping onto the shoulder of her husband, who was, in turn, stroking her head.

'Their son. He wasn't earning much, after all.'

A man got out of the truck – the same man Avtar had seen removing the television – and clicked his fingers. Mr Lal handed over the keys. Then he took up the suitcase by his feet and led his wife away from the building. No one knew where they were going, though six months later the gaswallah would say he'd seen poor Mr and Mrs Lal rattling a can outside Harminder Sahib. For now, the old couple passed by Avtar and he reached out and touched Mr Lal's shoulder, but it was a faint touch, not enough to detain anyone.

*

He had to press the buzzer twice before the chowkidar appeared, yawning. He flicked his eyebrows at Avtar: what did he want?

'I'm here to see Harbhajan Sahib. I'm his friend.'

'What friend? Harbhajan Sahib has many, many friends. Friends who use his car. Friends who take his money. Which one are you?'

'Is Nirmalji here?'

The man spat at the ground. So, no one was in. He wouldn't have dared spit like that otherwise. Avtar asked when they'd be home but the chowkidar laughed and told him to go and piss on someone else's doorstep. He headed back down the avenue. Perhaps if he went straight to the bus depot Nirmalji would be there. A woman called to him. She held a watering can and wore a tatty brown sari. A maid. She stood on the other side of her gate and asked what Avtar knew of Nirmalji's situation. More specifically, his son's. Probably her madam had tasked her with finding out details, and probably each detail earned her a few extra rupees.

'About what?' Avtar asked.

'The shor-tamasha all night.' It seemed an ambulance had been called at about four in the morning and the son carried out on a stretcher. 'You should have seen the poor mother. I hear they've gone to that private one. Do you know?'

He whistled for a rickshaw, bribed the deskman with twenty rupees and followed his directions past the children's ward and up the thin stairwell. At the top, through a square window in the door, he saw Harbhajan. He looked asleep. A red drip sprouted from his hand and connected to the stand by his bed. The stand had four wheels, Avtar noticed. Beside Harbhajan was Nirmalji, wearing a face that expressed nothing more than stately forbearance.

It must have been five months since he'd last met his friend. That time, after another week of empty searching, he'd asked Harbhajan to speak to Nirmalji about giving him his old job back. Harbhajan had blankly refused, saying he wasn't going to do anything that involved asking a favour from his father. Angry, Avtar ignored all of Harbhajan's calls in the weeks that followed, and then the calls dwindled to the occasional message, and, later, Harbhajan stopped contacting him altogether.

Avtar applied the flat of his hand to the door and pushed it open. He said sat sri akal and waited about a metre from the bed, feet together and hands closed over his stomach, the heels of his palms touching as if he was standing in the gurdwara. Nirmalji sat motionless and Harbhajan lay between them, under a pale-green blanket. There were terrible marks down both his forearms. Avtar wondered what to say. He asked after Aunty.

'She's at the temple,' Nirmalji said.

'I'll ask Mamma to pray too.'

'Is the God that will help him different from the one who put him here?'

Avtar said nothing. Then: 'Shall I fetch you something to eat, uncle?'

'Someone's bringing something.'

'Some water?'

Nirmalji closed his eyes and for several minutes Avtar stood there wondering if he could go.

Back in the reception lobby, he waited until the deskman had dealt with the fidgety queue trying to force an appointment for that same day. When he did approach, the man looked up from his calculator, then back down. He had an ugly moustache, the bristles hanging unevenly over his top lip.

'Yes?' And the looking down, the practised indifference with which he said this single word, made clear that the earlier bribe was now meaningless, forgotten. Any future favours would cost Avtar again.

'I'm looking for work.'

'No openings,' he said, almost singsong.

'Any job will do. Cleaning. Carrying. Portering.'

The man shook out a form from a sheaf trapped under a Buddha-bust of a bookend. 'Fill this in and bring it back.'

'Nirmalji sent me,' he lied.

Now the man stopped his calculations and raised his head. 'How long for?'

'Kya?'

'Are you looking for a permanent position?'

Avtar hesitated, then said that yes he was. It was too late. The man smiled. He had horrid teeth.

*

Randeep reached out of the window and stroked the basket of English Lady apples being offered up to him. In the end, he disappointed the kid and opted for the cheaper Green Bharat ones, with their Shivji logo. He'd get the others on payday. He dropped the lumpen bag of fruit in his lap and loosened his tie and waited for the bus to move.

It had been half a year since the teacher unbound his arms and legs and he'd scrambled out of the lecture hall, humiliated, grunting, the students all standing to look. He'd written to Jaytha once since that day, a long letter in which he'd underlined his mobile number three times. He said he felt sick thinking of how he'd held her down. Those were the words he'd used. He couldn't quite say it any more strongly, even to himself. It was too adult a crime. Of course, he'd told his family nothing. He'd simply said college wasn't for him any more. That he missed his family. Wanted to be with Daddy.

Outside the flat he paused, cocked his ear. His mother was speaking in her special chiming voice. He wondered which guests they might have. She hadn't complained in advance about anyone coming over. He turned the key lightly and stepped inside. He recognized Vakeelji's red Panjabi brogues, but not the slim, sensible black shoes placed tidily next to them. Women's shoes. He closed his eyes. Will they never give up?

'Randeep? Is that you, my dear? Do come. Vakeel Uncle is here.'

His mother, addressing him in English? Whoever the girl was, she must have impressed. Randeep kicked off his shoes, a little petulantly, and padded down the hall, suddenly aware of the sweat patches flowering in the armpits of his white shirt. His mother sat on the edge of the settee, ankles crossed and feet aside; she'd set her hair differently, so the streak of white made a significant sweep up past her ear. Vakeelji more or less filled the space beside her. His pencil tie with its baby knot and psychedelic pattern made him look even broader, and a little silly. Later, Randeep would wonder if the tie had been an attempt to lend a more relaxed atmosphere to the meeting, given how terrifically badly the first few had gone. At the window, on the red armchair – on his father's red armchair – was a woman. The first thing he noticed was her small turban, the kind he sometimes saw women wear at the gurdwara. It was black and started halfway up her brow and smoothly covered her hair and head. Her chunni was a simple green unembroidered rectangle, overlaying her turban and pinned in the traditional manner, so it stayed in place down her shoulders and across her chest, the way few girls seemed to bother doing these days. A delicate steel band circled her wrist. No rings, no jewellery. Her small hands seemed calm in her lap and her eyes were bright and clever. She looked elegant, plain, kind. He pinned his arms to his sides – the sweat patches – and realized he was staring. He looked back to his mother. She indicated the bag.

'Apples. For Daddy.' He put them on the table. 'Sat sri akal, uncle.' He turned to her. 'Sat sri akal.'

'Sat sri akal.' She was the only one who'd said that. She'd even pronounced the t, which no one ever did. The others had all said *Hello*, or *Hi*. Maybe she wasn't from abroad. Maybe this wasn't at all what he thought it was.

'Well, sit down,' Mrs Sanghera said, and he balanced on the armrest beside her. 'This is my son. Randeep.'

The woman nodded.

'He's a well-educated, well-mannered young man. Respectful of elders and loving of those younger than him. He's handsome and enjoys to exercise.'

'Mamma!'

'What? Will you stop a mother from praising her son, her piece-of-the-moon?'

Vakeelji put his giant hands on his knees and pushed up onto his feet. 'Bhabhi, show me to bhai sahib. I miss our chats.'

Mrs Sanghera sighed grandly, for she wanted to make clear that she understood the subtext, and led the lawyer out, taking the apples with her. Randeep heard them enter his father's room, and the lawyer expressing exaggerated joy at seeing his old friend again. Then the door closed and Vakeelji's voice cut out and it was just Randeep in the room with this strange, quiet woman.

He rose a little off the armrest and slid down onto the settee proper. She was some feet away, and she was staring at him. Randeep had the uncomfortable feeling of being appraised, or even judged.

'Where are you from?' he asked.

'England.'

He nodded. 'I have a friend there. Michael. He's from Doncaster. Do you know it?'

'Sorry. I'm from London,' she said, as if that explained everything.

He nodded again. He noticed she didn't have a drink, but she said no, she was fine, that his mother had given her some Limca earlier. He nodded. The silence swelled. He noticed a hole in his sock, exposing his big square nail, and he rubbed his toes together until the hole dropped out of view and then he looked up and grinned, just in case. A job? He could ask about her job.

'Are you employed?'

'I teach a little at the gurdwara. That's all.'

'For the gurdwara?'

'For everyone.'

'My father works for the government.' He paused. 'Worked for the government. He's not very well these days. He doesn't leave his bedroom much. We don't really know what to do.' But probably Vakeelji had explained everything already, so he stopped there.

'God will guide us,' she said, firmly, and though he wasn't sure whether she meant He'd guide the world at large or just the two of them, sitting in this room about to weave their lives together, Randeep nodded and said that perhaps she was right, and then they remained sitting there and let the silence grow into something that didn't feel uncomfortable at all.

He thought about her that night. He flipped onto his stomach and sighed hotly into his thin pillow and wondered what it would be like to be married to her. He'd liked her laugh, the honest, open-faced shine of it. What had he said? Something about how the best Indian families were the ones big enough to get lost in. He should remember that line. Through the wall he could hear his mother's voice, muffled. Talking to his father. About the meeting, no doubt. He hadn't committed himself to anything. In fact, the woman had stepped into her sensible black shoes and left alongside Vakeelji without any talk of weddings or visas or money. It seemed like a magnificent thing to try and get away with. Enough had, if Vakeelji was to be believed. Which he should be, of course. And he needed to get away from all this. From his fear of being sent back to college. From the shame that made him want to smash every mirror. This girl seemed to offer a new start, another chance. He flipped onto his back again and held his fist to his forehead. He tried to remember what colour her eyes were.

Vakeelji came round again the next evening. It seemed to be a pre-planned visit, for Mrs Sanghera had the teapot ready on the table. Lakhpreet brought in a plate of apples, sliced and fried in cinnamon. Randeep was called in from his room and the lawyer got down to business.

'If you want to go ahead with it, bhabhi, we'll have to be quick. She's leaving in four days.'

'Four . . . ? How in God's name can we be ready in four days?'

The lawyer raised his hand, as if swearing an oath. 'All will be done. You just need to say yes to me now.'

Randeep sank into his seat, sinking further when his mother turned to face him.

'Well?' she said.

'I don't know.'

'It's simple. You either go back to college and complete or you do this.'

He felt the heat come into his face.

'Don't pull that face with me, Randeep. If you care about the long-term survival of this family, then you need to start making something of yourself. You're nineteen now. You're not a child.'

'But I am making something of myself.'

'In that electrical store?' She looked to Vakeelji. 'What dreams I had, Harchand. A husband high up in government. A son at NIT.'

'We can all work,' Lakhpreet said, resting a hand on Randeep's shoulder. 'You're not being fair to him.'

'And we will work. When we are all in England. With well-paid jobs worthy of a family like ours. What hope for that in this snake basket of a land?'

Vakeelji said, 'She's not asking for much money at all. And she's a good, God-fearing girl. Some of them have all sorts of tricks, demanding more at the last minute and whatnot. But I think you can trust her.'

'A very quiet, simple girl,' Mrs Sanghera said, approvingly. 'Jat Sikh, too. What more could we want? She's landed in our lap from above.'

'And you'd be her first transfer. When it gets to the second or third they start asking questions, but this should be straightforward.'

'You see how much effort Vakeelji has gone to for you?' his mother said.

Randeep nodded.

'Is that a yes?'

'What's her name?'

'Narinder. Narinder Kaur,' the lawyer said.

'A nice name,' Randeep said absently, and his mother hid her smile in a sip of her tea.

Vakeelji was right. It was all done in four days. They drove the next morning to a small, isolated gurdwara about thirty miles outside the city and were married in a short ceremony witnessed only by Randeep's family, the lawyer, his assistant, the priest, and a few locals who happened to have wandered in. Vakeelji's assistant brought along a sherwani for Randeep to wear, a long gold-and-maroon kaftan, a little scuffed-looking. Randeep guessed it had been the assistant's own wedding outfit and that this wasn't the first time it had been reused. The red turban Randeep wore had been his own grandfather's. When Narinder arrived, the lawyer took a wedding dupatta from the boot of his Ambassador. She accepted it with both hands, like a gift, and touched it to her eyes and forehead. Then she repaired to the outside toilets, emerging a few minutes later with the dupatta arranged and pinned over her head and chest and shoulders. She smiled at Randeep, who smiled back, and Mrs Sanghera led everyone into the temple, where the priest seemed to have a slight cold as he read from the book. Afterwards, the locals surrounded Mrs Sanghera, nagging her for their wedding gifts. She recoiled – the proximity of these chi-chi village folk was clearly too much. But it seemed Vakeelji had thought of this as well and his assistant proceeded to hand out boxes of sweetmeats. Randeep and Narinder stood apart from all this, looking on.

'Are you OK?' he asked.

'It was so easy,' she said. She sounded almost annoyed. 'I don't know why I didn't do it before.'

He didn't know what to say to this. 'Thank you.'

Vakeelji was calling them. It was time to be going. Narinder ducked into the car and the rest of them watched as the assistant double-clanged the boot shut and drove her off. It was a strange sight: a red bride sitting alone in the back of a black Ambassador.

'A good girl,' Mrs Sanghera said.

'Will we see her tomorrow?' Randeep asked.

'No need,' the lawyer said. 'We got all the photographs and computers will do the rest. I doubt you will ever have to see her again.'

The wedding cards arrived from the printer the following afternoon and in the evening the lawyer turned up with a photo album and video of the wedding, along with some 'love letters' dating back several months. He'd had copies made for the girl which he'd take over in the morning, but first he wanted to sit Randeep and his mother down and explain what would happen next. *So. The girl will go back to England in two days and file for a marriage visa for you. She'll need to provide savings slips and evidence that the marriage is real. Hence the wedding, the photographs, the letters. Once she has done that we'll apply for the marriage visa from here. Delhi will call you for an interview and, if successful, the visa will be granted and you will leave for England. Then after one year you will apply for your stamp, your indefinite right to remain. When you get that, you apply for divorce. A year after that you can get full citizenship status and call bhabhi and your sisters over.*

'Years,' Mrs Sanghera said, falling back against the settee.

'Not really, bhabhi. He'll be in England by September.'

'Only three months?' Randeep said.

'You're paying all this money. It should be quick.'

'About that, uncle. What about paying Narinderji?'

'Ji?' Lakhpreet exclaimed, from the red armchair. 'Careful, brother.'

Vakeelji said it was all no problem. 'We've given her partial payment now, as I agreed with your mother, so she has savings to show them. The rest she won't get until it all goes through. So once you are over there I will give you her address and each month you send her what we've agreed. But only if you can afford it. She was quite adamant about that.'

Randeep nodded. 'She's very kind.'

'Hmm,' the lawyer said. 'The money doesn't seem that important to her.'

He felt his mother's hand stroking his hair. 'Three months and you'll be leaving me. All alone in another country.' He wasn't sure if she meant his loneliness or her own.

The lawyer took one of the apples before him, speaking and eating at the same time. 'Actually, bhabhi, I have another visa case running at the moment. Nijjar Sahib. The Ambarsar shawl-wallah? He lived in the same block as you.'

'Shanti's husband? He is looking for work abroad? At his age?'

'His son. I forget his name.' He looked sidelong at Lakhpreet.

'She has two.'

'The oldest.'

Mrs Sanghera turned her face to the ceiling, willing the name into being, but then shrugged and gestured vaguely towards her head. 'The memory, it is going, Harchand.'

'I thought the two boys could go together. Four eyes are more likely to find work than two. Do you agree?'

She said she supposed she did. 'And it means Randeep will have someone with him.'

'Good. That's settled, then. I'll arrange things so.'

Lakhpreet stood and excused herself from the room.

*

It was a small, miserable place: steaming dirty towels stacked on the tottery coffee table, a torn blue sheet coming detached from its rail, a lamp in the form of a goldfish and beside that, strangely, disturbingly, the top half of a grandfather clock. The wooden bed was high and his bare feet dangled several inches above the grime of the chequered floor. He could hear the old woman singing to herself, and the clink and splash of metal objects being run under a tap.

'Won't be long, child!' she called.

Avtar tried to smile, failed. He mouthed a silent 'Waheguru.'

The woman pottered in, humming, carrying a gold-bottomed tray with large French handles. Various sharp-looking things were arranged on it. Very carefully, she placed it on the coffee table, beside the steaming towels.

'There. All cleany-cleany nicey-nicey.' She smiled a wide, loose smile, shoulders bunching up, as if he was a little boy and they were about to embark on a nice little adventure. A picnic, perhaps. The smile made her tiny black eyes disappear but brought the rest of her face out in a sudden storm of wrinkles. Her over-washed flower-print dress was cut roughly at the knee and shoulders and her hair was skinned back into a braided rat's tail. Her name was Nurse Gomes.

She explained that she was going to give him an injection now which would make him all sleepy because once he was asleep she could make a really long cut at the bottom of his ribs. She'd then tie up a few pernickety little tubes before removing the little moon-sock. And then she'd stitch it all back up, do a final clean, and that would be that. Not even one hour it would take. Easy, na? Not one jot thing to worry about.

'You get the best care with Nurse Gomes!'

At some point during the procedure his eyelids fluttered, making a veil of his lashes. There was pain. A long razoring pain which he couldn't locate. It seemed to be coming up from his legs. He could hear the old woman. Singing. The snickering of scissors. He tried to lift his head. Too heavy. He moved his lips but no sound came out. Then his eyes closed and he felt himself being taken under again.

When he did wake, blinking in the steady sunlight, the pain was very definitely coming from his stomach. His throat caught. He reeled up and moved his hand to where it hurt. The area was criss-crossed with furry white bandages. He looked around but the place was empty.

'Madam!'

She came hurrying in, bunny slippers shuffling on the floor. 'Lie back! Lie back!' She applied her hands to his shoulders and pushed him down. 'You must let it mourn. Your body is calling for its missing part. You must let it mourn.'

So he lay there, one hand tamping down the bandages. He lay there all afternoon staring at the damp ceiling. Breathing hard.

Gulping down the pain and starting to sweat. The tears slid from the corners of his eyes and pooled into his ears.

In the evening Nurse Gomes placed her shrivelled little hand on his brow and asked if the dear wanted to stay another night.

'What cost?' he managed with enormous difficulty.

'Normal, dear. Always normal.'

'Thank you, madam, but I'll be asking your leave if you don't mind.'

He hauled himself up, head hanging low. Sickness threatened. Sweat dripped from his nose and soaked into the wood. She went away, still singing, and came back with a fussy yellow envelope. He thanked her and secured the envelope into his shirt pocket. She explained that she'd deducted Mr Bhatia's cut. The hospital deskman. Avtar thanked her again, pushed off the bed, and, holding his numb left leg, hobbled out.

At the gurdwara, the beds were all gone. He'd have to find a hotel, the granthi said, but first he rested a while, marshalling his strength. When he tried to move on, he couldn't get up. The priest returned with two younger men who helped Avtar to his feet and pointed out a nearby guest house where he could try and rent a bed. But only mattresses were available there, no beds, so he chose the cheapest one – sheetless, springless, and yellow-stained. He spent two days and nights on the foul, damp thing until the pain began to dissolve. Till his body stopped mourning. Then he washed his face in the sarovar at the gurdwara, tidied his shirt into his trousers and did some calculations. The loan against the shop, plus what savings they had, combined with the operation money, and still he was short. He added it all up again, and then a third time. He looked over to the temple. Why was He making it so hard for them? He walked out of the gurdwara's gates and took the route across the flyover. Pocket Bhai had been right.

It was the hospital deskman with the bad teeth who'd first told him about Pocket Bhai. He'd said if Avtar needed serious money and quickly, he really only had two choices. Either give up some part of himself – a kidney, say – or go to Pocket Bhai. In some ways it didn't matter, the deskman went on, chuckling, because if things went wrong with Pocket Bhai both options resulted in the loss of an organ. Avtar ignored the man and had gone to the bank instead, to ask if they'd increase the loan against the business, and then, when they'd refused, he'd gone back the next day, to see if they'd change their mind. There was another week of unsuccessful job searching before he caved in.

Some said Pocket Bhai acquired the name in England during the Seventies – apparently, in that country, if you'd made lots of money you were said to have deep pockets. Others said it was because he always kept one hand stuffed inside the pocket of his kurta, even when eating. And fucking, some joked. He had the sinewy, tough body of a strict self-disciplinarian, and his face was as neat as a ball, with its nothing chin and absent earlobes, its extreme baldness. A small pot of raw orange lentils lay on the table before him. It wasn't clear what the shop sold. There were a few bits of furniture here and there. Avtar supposed it was all a front for the moneylending. He had already explained his situation on the phone to one of Pocket Bhai's people – about the student visa, about working in England – but had to go over it all again. He'd pay the money back as soon as possible.

'Name?'

Avtar told him.

'Address?'

He thought about lying, but had a feeling he'd only be found out.

'Come back tomorrow.'

He did, and the orange lentils were still there. Pocket Bhai threw down a stapled wad of notes next to them and Avtar felt himself take a pace backwards. It was bewildering to see that much money made available to him. Beside it Pocket Bhai placed a lemon-pale piece of paper detailing the repayment schedule.

'My nephews live in the UK. They'll collect the money every month in person. These are their numbers. As soon as you land you tell them where you're living. You understand? We give one month to find work and the next month you start paying. You understand?'

He was looking at the amounts he was expected to pay back. It would end up costing more than five times what he'd borrowed. 'Uncle, I can't afford that. Maybe lower the rate a bit?'

'And yet you can afford your brother's school fees?'

The man had done his checks. He wondered what else he'd learned. Avtar couldn't do it. It'd be impossible to repay that much on top of the loan against the shop, and who knew what these people would do to his family if he defaulted on his payments. He apologized and said he'd manage without. Pocket Bhai laughed. 'You'll come back. They always do.'

And now, not even a month since that visit, Avtar was indeed back, salaaming Pocket Bhai and taking a seat on the bench against the wall. He sat with his weight across his right hip, which dulled the pain slightly.

'Kidney?'

Avtar nodded. Pocket Bhai sighed.

'You silly boys. You silly desperate boys.'

When he walked through the door his mother and father were standing at the photo of Guru Nanak hanging on the wall. They'd been worried, they said. He'd been away so long. But was there work, like Nirmalji had promised him?

He nodded. 'Lots of work. That's why I stayed longer.' He took out the yellow envelope and the money from Pocket Bhai and handed it all to his father. 'I earned enough.' He sat on the settee. His parents looked at him. He looked at the floor. 'I'll see the lawyer about buying me that visa.'

The summer months passed, hot and fume-filled, the air ferrying around spicy waves of shit and diesel. Even the monsoon, when it finally came, gave little respite, and by September Randeep was still wearing his thinnest cotton shirts. He turned up the wall fan and went back to the clothes he'd laid out on his bed. There was a knock on the door behind him.

'We bought you something,' his mother said, moving to reveal it. A suitcase: brown, shiny, expensive-looking leather. A red bow around its middle. She put a hand to his damp back. The fan made her chunni all fluttery over her head. 'So tall you've got these days,' and then: 'Let's pack together.'

The next morning at Delhi International Airport Avtar spotted Lakhpreet in the departures terminal, standing around with her family. Though they spoke every Sunday, and had been on the phone last night for a full two hours, this was the first time he'd seen her since she took him to the lawyer. She seemed anxious, her gaze darting, trying not to look as if she were searching him out. They'd agreed not to meet each other's eyes today, and definitely not to talk: it was too risky, she'd said.

'But I talk to unmarried girls all the time,' he'd replied, joked, though neither of them felt like laughing.

Her brother, Randeep, was dressed much more smartly than him. Shirt, tie, trousers. Even the kid's suitcase had a fucking bow tie. Avtar adjusted his pen to conceal the fact that his shirt pocket was missing its button, then pointed out to his mother that Aunty was over there.

The two families met, the mothers embracing, commiserating, reassuring one another – and, therefore, themselves – that God willing all would work out well for the two boys. Again – because she had already made several phone calls over the summer – Avtar's mother pressed her thanks on Mrs Sanghera. It was so very, very kind of them to let Avtar stay with Randeep and his massiji in London.

'Please, pehnji, you are embarrassing me. And my sister's London house is very big. It is zero trouble for them.'

Avoiding Lakhpreet, Avtar moved to Randeep and extended his hand. 'I used to see you sometimes. In the block. Just hanging around looking lost,' Avtar added, laughing in what he hoped was a friendly way.

Randeep smiled miserably. Everything about his long, skinny frame – shoulders sloping in, feet crossed shyly – suggested an innocent view of the world.

'Have you been on a plane before?' Avtar asked.

Mrs Sanghera interjected. 'We used to fly all the time. With Randeep's father's postings. We even went to Colombo once. But Randeep was very small then. You probably don't remember, do you, beita?'

'It's my first time,' Avtar said. 'So you can help me, na?'

At this the boy smiled more openly, showing his large, straight teeth.

They checked in their luggage, anxiously showing their visas and passports to the sour-faced man behind the counter. At the security gates the guard advised that it was strictly passengers only beyond this point.

'Tell Papa not to worry,' Avtar said, embracing his tearful mother. 'It's all going to be fine. I promise.'

He looked across and saw Randeep stroking his sister's hair. She was crying against his shoulder. 'I love you, too,' he said, but still she wasn't letting go.

'Don't be silly, Baby,' Mrs Sanghera said, pulling her daughter away. 'This isn't like you.'

On the plane, whenever he closed his eyes, Avtar kept seeing Lakhpreet's face, tears rolling down. How helpless he'd felt standing there. He sighed. It was for the best, he reminded himself. Just think how much he'd make. Save. He'd save so much in a year. In fact, he'd have a savings pile, he decided, and add to it every month. Before he knew it, their lives would have turned round. He allowed himself a smile at the thought of Mrs Sanghera's face as he married her daughter. And Randeep's. Though Avtar doubted Lakhpreet's brother would be that bothered. He seemed pretty reserved, not at all like his sister, and it was hard to believe he was the elder, even if only by a year.

'So. You're a married man?' Avtar said.

There was a ripple of confusion down the boy's face, tiny movements that finished in a slight parting of his mouth. 'Yeah. I suppose so.'

'You don't sound so sure?' Avtar smiled.

'No, no. I am. A married man,' he repeated, almost to himself. Randeep felt a strange dissonance, how the bald fact of it made him instantly adult, and yet their handling of it all, of his life, was like a regression to childhood. He couldn't work it out. He felt too young to be married, though. He felt too young to be anything. 'She's a kind person.'

'Yeah. A real gutkawalli,' Avtar said, repeating Lakhpreet's description.

'Hmm? How do you know?'

'Your mother said. To mine,' and Avtar turned to the window, telling himself to be more careful next time.

At Heathrow, a short woman with a frazzled look approached them. Her salwaar kameez was a plain cranberry, and her widow-white chunni covered her full grey head.

Randeep took the lady in his arms. 'Massiji. Sat sri akal.'

'Welcome, beita.' She had a soft voice. She held his face and pulled it down to kiss his forehead. 'You had no trouble?'

'None. This is Avtar bhaji. My friend.'

Avtar touched her feet, but she seemed unused to this and mixed up her blessings.

'Where's Jimmy bhaji?' Randeep asked, looking around. 'I thought he was coming.'

'Oh, something came up. But he'll be at home. They're both looking forward to seeing their cousin.'

She lived in Ilford, in a small semi on the straight edge of a keyhole-shaped cul-de-sac. There was a mean black hatchback with a phat exhaust on the drive and behind this she parked her grey, spluttering metal bucket of a motor. Home, she said, as if amazed to have made it back in one piece. She held the front door open while they wheeled their cases over the step and found themselves immediately in the living room. Two lime leather sofas and a massive TV dwarfed the space. There were video consoles, too, and boxes of computer games, a clutch of keypads tangling about the carpet. An archway led to the kitchen and at the table sat a young man hunched over his bowl of cereal. Long shorts, gym vest. A buzz cut and a goatee. Glassy studs in both lobes.

'Jimmy bhaji! How are you?' Randeep paused at the table, waiting for Jimmy bhaji to jump to his feet at seeing his cousin after so many years. Jimmy remained sitting. He looked up and with his spoon still in his hand nodded at Randeep.

'Hey, man. Welcome to England. I forgot Mum said someone was visiting for a bit.'

Randeep smiled, a little chastened.

'This your first time? To England?'

'Ji.'

'Well, wrap up warm. You know what they say about England.'

A door closed somewhere above and from a staircase partially obscured by the archway a girl – a woman – entered the room. She wore denim shorts over thick black leggings, and an old grey T-shirt. Her vast frizz of crunchy-looking curls was mushroomed high up on her head, fountain-like, and earplugs emerged from her neckline to noodle about her chest.

She looked at Massiji and Avtar, and then at Randeep. 'Oh, hi.'

'Pehnji? I didn't recognize you.'

'It's Aki,' she said, with emphasis.

'Sorry.' He tried again: 'I can't believe it's been, how long, more than ten years since we were all together? Do you remember when we milked those cows and how it went all over us? We talk about that all the time.'

She gazed at him, then glanced at Jimmy and the two of them

exchanged smiles. Abruptly, she turned to Massiji. 'I'm going for a jog and then to Lauren's. I probably won't be back tonight.'

'Akaljot, we agreed. I told you.'

'Sorry, Mummy dearest. It's her birthday.' Then to Randeep: 'Enjoy your stay.'

She left via the back door, fixing her earplugs in as she went. Then Jimmy pushed his chair back, screeching it along the linoleum, and dumped his dishes into the sink. He patted the pockets of his shorts, checking for keys, said *laters* to Randeep and whoever the other freshie was and followed his sister out. The glass panel in the door rattled as it closed. Randeep turned to his massi and smiled in an effort to convey that he wasn't offended. But Massiji was looking out of the window, altogether embarrassed.

She tried to give them her room – the children have college, you see, they need their sleep, otherwise absolutely they would have given up their rooms for you – but the boys insisted they'd be fine on the settees in the front room. 'Please, Massiji, it's much more comfortable than we are used to.'

The next morning, rooting in his suitcase, Avtar found the manila folder of student stuff Vakeelji had given him. He recited a short prayer in front of the Guru Nanak calendar hanging in the kitchen and set off to enrol. In his hand he had an old Tube map Massiji had found and over which she'd penned in careful blue Panjabi a list of directions Avtar was to make sure he followed. She didn't want him getting lost in that big city.

Even so, it was long past two o'clock when he passed under the grey concrete frame of Edgware Station and looked around for some helpful street sign. He was exhausted, and late: the ticket-wallah on the Underground had sent him off towards Edgware Road, not Edgware, and hours seemed to pass before he found a Panjabi-looking man willing to explain that Avtar would have to buy another ticket because he needed to be in another part of London altogether. Thankfully, the friendly man demonstrated how to use the ticket machines, which saved Avtar having to queue at the counter again.

He walked straight on, towards what looked like a major road, and kept to the right-hand side of the pavement. He reminded himself to ask Massiji about changing up some money and to then give her some for letting him call home. They were fine, his parents had said. Pleased he'd arrived safely, his father added, a little formally. They weren't used to speaking to their son in this way – generally, without a real reason for the call – so it was a short conversation, the main thrust being that Avtar wasn't to worry about them. He was to concentrate on making something of himself in England now God had blessed him with this opportunity. To that end, Avtar allowed himself a little optimism. The trains had come when the electronic signs had said they would. The guard hadn't expected money to point him in the right direction. Cars were only driven on roads and only in nice long columns. Even the air was a clear and uniform blue. All the signs of a well-run country. A fair country. A country that helps its people. A country that might even help him.

A brown signboard read 'Coll. of NW London' and indicated the first left at the big grassy roundabout up ahead. He wondered how to cross the road. Grey railings lined the kerbside, and it was surely against the law to jump them. He tailed a woman with wheatish hair, hoping she'd show the way, but at the roundabout she followed the road as it curved off and Avtar was left behind. Cars flowed round as if in a deliberate rush to fill in any gaps. He returned to the railings. Perhaps they were low precisely so that people who needed to cross the road could do so. Maybe it wasn't illegal at all. He secured the folder into the back of his black trousers and, with one foot lifted to the top of the railing, jumped over. The cars were so close. Drivers glanced confusedly over and one or two pointed at the ground, mouthing words. He hoped that now he'd made clear his intention the traffic might stop, but there seemed to be no sign of that. He ventured a foot forward, then took it back as a white van came roaring down. He was breathing hard. He looked about again: nothing. No traffic lights. He had no chance. He waited. When the moment came he felt the cold of the railings leave his body and he was running as hard as he could. The road felt coarse under his thin soles. He could feel his folder coming loose from his trousers and as he reached behind to hold it in place a long brassy horn sounded. Avtar looked over his shoulder. The cars were coming. He wouldn't make it, and as he launched towards the central mound of the roundabout his foot gave and he felt one of his shoes slip off. All he could do was squeeze between the black-and-white arrow signs and clamber onto the grassy circle. Safe at last, he covered his ears. He felt stupid and angry and through the legs of the arrow signs saw his poor shoe being flipped about like a fish.

About an hour later, a beautiful yellow-haired girl smiled at Avtar as if she'd been waiting the whole day just for him to walk into the college registration office. She looked like one of those white girls that used to come on the television, selling Sunsilk or Amla Shampoo. He managed a weak smile and tentatively presented his folder. He hoped he'd removed all the grass stains.

'Welcome to North-West,' she said, unclipping the folder, going through his papers. 'Computing with Security Systems. I hear that's a good course.'

'Thank you,' Avtar said, just about understanding.

She asked him where he was from and he said India, and then she said they had him down as making his own accommodation arrangements, and he said that, yes, that was true.

'Not a long way, I hope?'

'Ilford?' He showed her the address Massiji had written down for him.

'Lots of early starts if you want to make your nine o'clocks, then!' She laughed, which permitted Avtar to laugh too.

She photostatted his visa and passport and Avtar watched her filing the copies into a metal cabinet. She handed him various things: maps, a student union application form, an events listing, his timetable, a pass with his name and picture on it – to give him access to the Mathematical Sciences building, she explained. All this he gathered into his folder, thanking her, keen to leave before they reneged and shipped him back home.

'There is a strong college Indian Students' Society, which does a lot of good work helping students adjust to – ' she struggled for the word. She seemed to want to avoid saying *England* – 'a new approach. They're still open. It's just down the corridor if you're interested.'

He thanked her again, inadvertently bowing his head a little, and turned to leave. He couldn't believe it had been so easy. No interview, no questioning, no police. At the exit, he thanked her once more, only to catch her staring at the cracked heels of his naked feet. He felt suddenly embarrassed and, clearly, so did she.

'It's just down the corridor,' she said again, pointing.

The corridor – an open-air walkway, really – was a low corrugated roof protecting a slabbed concrete floor. To his left were doors and classrooms, while the right opened onto a half-empty car park. There were several squat buildings: Materials and Metallurgy, Blocks 3F to 4B, the Tony Baker Building. So this was a real college. He imagined impossibly clever people in spectacles behind each of those doors, being groomed for a rich and employed future. And here he was, amongst them. If his parents could see him now. Behind him, a voice called out, 'Hello?' An apna, Avtar knew, before he'd even turned around. A plumpish middle-aged Indian, in fact, in woolly, dark-coloured clothes. His round glasses balanced on top of his shaved bald-grey head.

'Ji?' Avtar said.

'Foreign students should come see us.'

Avtar tracked back and followed the man into a classroom plastered floor to ceiling with detailed maps of India and huge images of students on elephants. Across the wall ran a banner: *NWL IndiSoc Back to Roots Annual*. The desks were arranged into a horseshoe, as if for a meeting. The man sat down and started pulling out great sheaves of paper from a nearby cabinet.

'First day? . . . Please sit.'

Avtar didn't.

'I'm Dr Amarjit Singh Cheema. General Secretary of the International Society here at NWL. Of which IndiSoc is one part. We offer foreign students support and guidance. Language courses. Visa advice. Accommodation tips. Pastoral care. Et cetera et cetera.'

Finally, the doctor seemed to find his papers and slapped them on the desk and looked up at Avtar.

'We have an excellent mentoring programme.'

Avtar nodded, smiled. He wanted to get out of here. This man was an Indian and a doctor to boot. He'd work out everything. 'I'll come tomorrow, thank you.'

There was a pause, and something like a question mark appeared in the man's face. Avtar could feel himself being studied, filleted.

'The annual fee is very reasonable,' the doctor said, but the tone of his voice seemed to convey something altogether different. 'Where are you from?' he asked, switching to Panjabi.

'Amritsar.'

'Your elders?'

'Nijjar.'

The man's face softened pleasantly. 'My mother's people are from there. So you're Doabi?'

Avtar nodded, said ji, Chachaji, and the doctor laughed.

'Nice, very nice.'

He put the lid on his pen and closed the door and told Avtar to sit, and this time he did.

'How much did it cost you?'

Avtar looked down to his knuckles.

'Listen, I'm Indian. I might have been born here but I'm Indian and I want the people of my country to prosper.'

So Avtar told him and the doctor nodded and asked Avtar what course he was doing and whether he intended on actually doing any of it or if he was just going to disappear like most of them did.

'I'm here to work.'

'But there is no work. It's drying up. *Pfft!*'

'I'll find something.'

'You kids . . .' He sighed, and, removing his glasses, rested his chin on interlocked hands. 'Work, by all means. But you'll be in a much stronger position if you also pass your first year. Then the college will protect you. But if you fail . . . Well, the college will kick you out and you'll have no choice but to disappear. And for how long can you really hide?' He advised Avtar to keep up with the course. He might not be able to make the lectures – he understood that – but he should definitely improve his English and get the textbooks from the library: 'They're free. Think of the long term, Nijjara. If you leave here with a diploma, just think what you could do back home. If you're lucky, you could even stay and bring your family over. You shouldn't waste this chance.'

They had a cup of tea – with cloves and fennel and elaichi – and the doctor listened as Avtar told him the story of how his grandparents had moved from tiny Nijjar to Amritsar city. Until recently, his papa used to take the family back there every summer. Avtar had always liked the bull races best.

'Do they still happen?' the doctor exclaimed. 'Ha! My mother still talks about them. You should come to our house. Mataji will light up when she knows someone from her village is here.'

'How often do you go back, sir?' Avtar asked.

'Me? Oh no, no, no. I've never been. I've always wanted to, but with one thing and another . . . And the kids weren't ever interested.'

'Life is busy here,' Avtar offered.

The doctor made an agreeable sound and his gaze shifted away from Avtar. For a long while he stared at the large bookcases beside the whiteboard, at the ordered ranks of books upon books upon books. A lifetime of them. He looked back at Avtar and smiled sadly.

Avtar received by post three waxy-paged and thickly dog-eared computing texts. Dr Cheema had also included books on learning English, with accompanying CDs. Attached to the package was a note saying that Avtar was to remember their chat and be sure to visit him and his family at their home once he was settled in. Avtar folded the note and slipped it into an elasticated pouch on the inside of his suitcase. He couldn't imagine someone being as helpful to a newcomer in his own country. He ran his hand over one of the textbooks, over the laminated image of lightning bolts forking wildly out from a computer screen. He was sitting at the kitchen table in Massiji's house. Randeep was sleeping a few feet away on the sofa. He opened to the first page and began to read.

He studied for two hours every morning, rarely getting further than a few paragraphs. By seven, Massiji would be downstairs preparing for her shift at the 24-hour supermarket. She'd make them a breakfast of paratha with achaar, and foil-wrap some more to keep them going for the day. Not long after, they tidied away their blankets and left the house too, before Jimmy bhaji and Aki pehnji woke up.

Doctor Cheema had been right: work really was drying up. In two weeks the closest they'd come to finding anything was a half-hearted promise from a Muslim cash-and-carry owner who said he'd keep them in mind for the Christmas rush. They'd already exhausted the streets of Ilford, Barnet and Poplar in their search, and following a tip from an aunty-type shopkeeper they'd even spent two days traipsing around Southall and Ealing, and then Hounslow, looking for some phantom gurdwara she said was being built.

'She must've misunderstood,' Avtar said, as they got off the bus at Ilford.

They waited on the concourse, on a bench, until they were certain Massiji would be home. Randeep seemed withdrawn. Avtar wondered if it was his cousins, and how they were always avoiding him. Or maybe it was his father. Last night, on the cheap mobile phone Massiji had bought them, Lakhpreet said that he'd had 'an episode'. Should he ask Randeep about it? It might help. In the event, Randeep got there first.

'Your father's quite old, isn't he? I remember him now. Total white hair. Very slow on the stairs.'

'That's him,' Avtar said, a little irked at the description.

'A nice man. He made the bus driver wait for me once because my suitcase was heavy.'

Avtar smiled into his jacket, imagining the scene. 'Yeah. He'd do that.'

Randeep turned, stared. 'You miss him,' he diagnosed.

'Oh, I miss everything. Why?' he went on, passing it over, 'Do you miss your father?'

Randeep looked away, blinking, and Avtar regretted the question.

The sun had almost set, and they watched as another busload set out from the concourse.

'Any paratha left?' Randeep asked.

Avtar showed him the foil balled up in his fist. 'Have you called those numbers Vakeel Sahib gave you?'

'There was only one,' Randeep said. 'It's too far.'

'Where?'

'He said Scotland.'

'How far's that?'

Randeep shrugged. Avtar walked over to the fag-holed timetable on the lamppost. *Birmingham. Bristol. Derby. Edinburgh. Glasgow. Gravesend. Leeds. Manchester. Newcastle. Wolverhampton.* But no Scotland.

'It's not on there,' he said, sitting back down.

'Because it's too far.'

'But if that's where the work is . . .'

They waited another half an hour and returned to the house. The daughter, Aki, was in the kitchen, pouring hot water from a kettle into a white plastic pot. It looked like noodles.

'We have noodles in India, too,' Randeep said.

She frowned, nodded, sat down to eat. Randeep wondered if it would be rude to ask if they might have some. Probably, yes, but not as rude as not offering some in the first place. Perhaps it was the effect of being brought up without a father. She glanced across to him and abruptly got to her feet and went upstairs, taking her noodle pot with her and muttering something about Pakis always fucking staring.

Massiji arrived late, with a paper bag of courgettes which she stewed into a quick sabzi for the boys. They ate two, three, four rotis, and for dessert a thickened-up bowl of milky semiya.

'All that walking around must make you hungry.'

'It tastes so good. Like home.'

'Better than home,' Avtar said.

'Bas karo. I'm happy simply to have children to cook this for.'

Jimmy came thundering down the stairs in his tan stud-rind boots and reached for his leather jacket.

'Are you going out, too?' his mother said, in a voice disappointed and exasperated.

'Just to the pub. Won't be long.'

'Your sister's already gone. Why don't you two spend some time with your cousin and Avtar? They look for work all day and have to sit here getting bored by me all night.'

Randeep protested – they weren't bored, Massiji, that wasn't . . .

'They're eating,' Jimmy said, as if they weren't sitting just across the room.

'They've finished,' Massiji said, and there was a strained look on Jimmy's face as he failed to summon a comeback.

Randeep and Avtar stood awkwardly at the bar, holding pints of cola up by their necks while Jimmy shot pool with his friends. Aki had been there too, but led her friends out as soon as she saw the boys enter. 'PMS,' Jimmy had said and Randeep had looked at Avtar, who'd shrugged.

Avtar wondered if this place was like that 1771 club in Jalandhar, with its secret upstairs gambling room. It didn't seem to be. He couldn't see any stairs, for one thing. Just lots of tables and around the tables lots of friends and couples of all different colours laughing and drinking. Women laughing and drinking. Indian women freely laughing and drinking. He imagined some impossible future in which he and Lakhpreet were settled with good jobs in Ilford and coming here together after a long week at work. The thought was funny. He sipped his drink.

'I'd never let my sisters come here,' Randeep said, because this was horrible. This was dirty and vulgar and he could feel the smoke sinking into his clothes. He was glad Jimmy had told him not to wear the tie.

A young black man appeared beside Randeep at the bar, waving a note to get the barman's attention. Kaleh, Massiji said, were everywhere in Ilford, and the first time the boys saw one walking towards them they'd fallen silent, until the man passed by and Randeep whispered how frightening they looked. But he'd never seen one up close, right here beside him, like now. Their skin was so smooth, he thought. Not a blemish, no variation in tone, as if a machine had played some part in it all. He wondered how it would feel to touch. And that hair too. Like it had been stitched onto his head with silver thread. The man turned towards Randeep, a hard look in his eye. Randeep smiled, tight-lipped, edging a little closer to Avtar. Secretly, he watched the black man pay for his drink and rejoin his black friends at another pool table.

'They're fast, hain na? All the good runners are kaleh. Do they have their own language? Like ours is Panjabi?'

Avtar said he didn't know, though they seemed to be speaking English.

'Look how smooth their skin is. Why is that?'

Jimmy left his game of pool to ask if they needed a top-up. 'Sure you don't want a knock?'

Randeep asked if he knew any kaleh and what they spoke and ate and why their skin was so smooth.

'Black don't crack. E-vo-loo-shun, innit. Thought Mum said you were clever?'

'What are they like?'

'Like?'

The black man bounded over, his eyes bulging monstrously. 'You got some beef with me, man?' He was pointing, his face inches away.

Randeep lurched back, shaking his head.

'You dotting me for time. Dot me to ma face.' He stepped closer. 'To ma fuckin' face.'

Avtar moved Randeep behind him, protecting the kid, and Jimmy placed a hand on the man's shoulder. 'He's fresh man, fresh. Lights out.'

'Nang that. This Simon sidepart simpleton . . . What, we taxed your fucking Co-op?'

'Allow it, nigger. He's learning. The rents were freshening up one day gone. Yours and mine. Same ends now, though, right? Same fucking drum. Right?'

A pause, then a chin-jut. 'Standard, standard.'

'Hectic,' Jimmy said, emphasizing the syllables. He turned his back to the man and slurped the foam from his beer. This seemed to be some sort of message because the black man nodded and he and Jimmy touched fists, which Randeep thought must be an agreement to fight later.

On the walk home, Randeep was still shaking, his lips trembling. 'I'm just cold.'

'I don't know why you freshies stare so much, man. Might be all right back home but it's proper rude here, you know? People get really offended.'

'Sorry, bhaji.'

'Allow it. And don't look so . . . so defensive all the time. It gives you guys away like shit in a shoe. The way you lot stand close to the edge of the platform, eyes fixed on where the train's coming from. The way you quickly take a look at everyone on the bus as you walk down the aisle. The way you stand so straight, as if your ankles are tied together. Spot you guys a mile off. Just chill,' he finished, drawing out the word.

The boys nodded, not really questioning why these were things they ought to be trying to hide. Avtar had thought it was his clothes, his hairstyle, his sockless feet that had given his foreignness away to Dr Cheema. But it seemed alongside the cosmetic changes there was a whole system of other things to correct.

All night he heard Randeep rustling about on the other settee: smacking his pillows, throwing his blankets on and off, sometimes facing the room, sometimes not.

'Arré, these things happen, yaar. Don't dwell. Go to sleep. And for God's sake let me sleep as well.'

'It's nothing to do with that. I'm hot–cold. I might not be well.'

Avtar sighed and brought the blanket over his head.

'I think I will ring that Scotland number tomorrow,' he heard Randeep say.

Somehow, Avtar kicked the blankets off at five o'clock for his two hours of study. He sat on a dining chair, the plastic clammy against his thighs, and set about untangling the wires of his headphones. He'd do an hour of Better English and then an hour of his course.

The sky was turning light grey and Avtar was still muttering along to his CD, as Aki came through the front door. He lifted away his headphones and let them hang around his neck. She'd been saying something to him.

'Hahn ji?'

There was a liquid look in her face, as if she was struggling to coordinate eyes, mouth and brain, and – Avtar now noticed – her feet seemed to be constantly adjusting themselves. He felt an immediate rush of disgust.

'I said, I suppose you think I'm bad.'

'Ji?'

'Bad. Do you think I'm bad? Do you think I'm nothing but a gorafied cow?'

Avtar said nothing. He'd probably not said five words to her in the time he'd been here. It wasn't his place.

'Well, fuck you. Fuck you, you freshic fucks.' She took a step forward, one steadying hand on the wall. Half her face was in shadow. 'Fuck you freeloaders. You come here expecting us to wait on you. What, because you're family?' She reeled back. 'Where the fuck was you when my dad died, hey? Where was "family" then?' She adopted a different voice. 'Oh, sorry, that's right. Because it's my mother, she has to deal with it on her own. Because it's a woman, she's not allowed to turn to her family. Well, fuck you.' She made shakily for the stairs, then stopped. 'I'll tell you who was here for us. My friends. They helped us. Were here for us. Got us back on our feet. The same people Mum wants me to stop hanging out with. Because she's got the same fucked-up idea of family that you've all got. But I tell her. I tell her, the next time we're on our knees it ain't gunna be the Indian lot that come to help. It'll be my friends again. Think of that. Think of that.' She snorted, looked away. 'You ain't got a fucking scooby,' she ended, quietly, and perhaps tearfully, though Avtar couldn't be sure. She climbed the stairs, creaking her way up, and seconds later a door slammed shut.

Avtar looked down at his inked-up hands, then across to the settee, where he knew Randeep was lying awake under the blanket.

At the newsagent's on the High Street they asked the Guju youth behind the counter to help them top up their phone. Then they found a bench down the side of Woolworths and Randeep folded out the blue chit with the Scottish number on it. He dialled and put the phone to his ear.

'What do I say?' he asked.

'Say you've just landed in England with a marriage visa and that Harchand Vakeel Sahib said they'd give you work. Don't tell them your name yet. Give a fake one.'

He half hoped no one would answer. But they did. 'Hello? Hello. Who is this? . . . My na—? . . . I've just landed with a marriage visa and Harchand Vakeelji Sahib said you'd give me work . . . Chandigarh, uncle . . . Amritsar . . . Yes, on marriage, uncle.' A slow grin spread across Randeep's face. 'Yes, ji, I'm Randeep Sanghera. That's me.'

It turned out that Vakeelji had already sent word of them to this Scottish uncle. He'd been waiting for them to call. In fact, he'd been saying to his wife only last night that he was going to call Harchand bhaji and say his men hadn't been in touch yet and did they actually make it over OK.

'But is there work?' Avtar cut in.

'He says so. He promised to call back later today.'

All afternoon he was checking the phone, or Avtar was asking him to check it. Then, as the high street filled with kids slouching home from school, the mobile rang and the Scottish uncle said there wasn't anything in Glasgow or Aberdeen or Newcastle, but they weren't to worry because there were plenty of other contacts he had to try. The main reason he was calling was to ask if they had National Insurance and City and Guilds cards, and if not, to make sure they had some passport-sized photographs handy, along with photocopies of their visas and passports. The boys went back to the house for their passports and visas and then back to the Guju youth in the newsagent's to ask where they could get photostats. He laughed and said, here, pass them to him and he'd photocopy them in the back. I mean, not as if you're faujis or anything, is it, he said with a wink. They found a photo booth in the chemist across the street, but didn't have enough pounds and decided to wait until tomorrow before exchanging what rupees they had left. They returned to Massiji's, Randeep excited at the prospect of work despite Avtar's warning that they shouldn't get their hopes up.

'What kind of work do you think it might be?' Randeep asked. The night had come round again, and they were under their blankets on the settees.

'You're the one who spoke to him, yaar.'

'I didn't ask. Sorry.'

Avtar frowned. He wished he'd stop saying sorry all the time. 'Shop work, maybe.'

Randeep nodded in the dark. That would be all right. He'd hoped for something better, something software- or consultancy-related, but at least shop work would be nice and clean and easy.

The mobile vibrated hard against the glass top of the table, scurrying towards the edge. Randeep lurched for it – 'It's him!' – and put it to his ear. 'Hello?' He listened for a long while. Avtar came and knelt beside him. 'Tomorrow?' Randeep said, and looked at Avtar, who nodded, urging Randeep to accept whatever the offer was, whenever it was. A little later Randeep said thank you, uncle, sat sri akal, and closed his phone.

'There's work?' Avtar asked, shaking Randeep's knee.

Randeep nodded. 'One of his relatives. He has work in a city called Sheffield.' Randeep paused. 'I've got to be there tomorrow at one o'clock.'

Avtar withdrew his hands into his lap. He understood. 'Oh.'

'He said there was only work for one. So you go. I'll find work here.'

'Don't be stupid. That fat lawyer gave you the contact.'

'But where will you stay?' he said, then tried to backtrack. 'Of course, Massiji won't mind—'

Avtar shook his head. 'I'll be fine.'

Avtar and Massiji came to St Pancras to see him off. He seemed quiet, as if thinking of what might lie ahead.

'Don't be worried,' Avtar said.

'I'm not, bhaji. I'll manage. This is the world we live in now. But I do wish you were coming with me. It's been really nice having someone to talk to.'

Avtar looked away, hiding his face because, overnight, he'd decided that this parting was actually a blessing in disguise. The boy relied too much on him. Exchanging money, approaching strangers, buying things – in all these it had somehow come to pass that Avtar would take the lead, even with his poorer English. Yes, it was definitely a blessing. It would force the boy to grow up. And Avtar could forget about him and concentrate on looking after himself. He only had six weeks before Pocket Bhai was expecting the first of the repayments. God willing, work would come.

'If I find work for you there will you come?' Randeep asked.

Avtar laughed. 'I'll come swimming in boiling waters if that's where the work is.'

Massiji passed Randeep a food parcel for the journey and some money, which he tried to resist. 'Just take it,' she said. 'And if there are any problems you come straight back, acha?'

He pushed against the turnstile and onto the platform, waving from the door then stepping up into the carriage, walking through, lugging his shiny leather suitcase behind him, and, as Jimmy bhaji had advised, not staring at any of the other passengers.

The train juddered out of the station and into the mechanical sprawl of London: cranes, pulleys, industrial lifts; then suburbs, the charmless wet platforms of one outpost after another. Only when they reached a station called Leicester did Randeep experience a change in his spirits. He was used to nice things, nice surroundings, and here were flat green fields, cows, palm-sized villages in the far distance. The view grew more beautiful still when, some two hours from London, the landscape changed again: hills, tumbling clouds, a church with a strangely twisted spire. He smiled. It was all so – he thought hard – so civilized. An image came to mind, of his father before the illness, still writing reports at his desk while the rest of the family slept. It was a time when he thought his father could withstand anything; an innocent time whose return he pined for. He put Massiji's food parcel aside and by the time the train pulled into Sheffield, thirty-five minutes late, he still hadn't touched it.

The station impressed him. It wasn't as draughty as the London ones, and seemed cleaner, airier. This Sheffield must be a good city. He wondered why he'd never heard of it. As he studied the electronic departure boards, he saw someone by the payphone, holding a piece of cardboard bearing Randeep's name. He was a short man with a goatee, receding spiked-up hair, and a busy, impatient look about him. Randeep took up his suitcase.

'Virender bhaji?'

The man stopped his whistling. 'Randeep?' He screwed up the cardboard and threw it over his shoulder. They shook hands. 'Good trip?'

'I'm really happy to be here. What a beautiful city you have.'

Virender looked surprised. 'Hold that thought.'

The van ride took them out of the city and onto elevated roads that wound through narrow, boarded-up, wretched-looking streets.

'Mostly clearance at the moment,' Virender was saying. 'Decluttering sites, blah de blah. But I've got my eye on a new contract soon. A hotel, fingers crossed.'

'I have a friend who came with me if you need more help.'

Virender bhaji ignored him. Perhaps he heard this a lot. 'You'll be all right digging up rocks and shit, yeah?' He reached over and shook Randeep's shoulder. 'Put some muscle on those bones! You're like a stick! Ronny the stick!'

They parked outside a large Victorian house with an overgrown, bushy front garden. The curtains were drawn haphazardly and giant cobwebs hammocked above the door. Virender knocked, twice, loudly.

'One of these days I'll remember my keys.' He kicked the door. 'Come on, you lazy chimps.'

The handle shook, and the door was at last opened by a sleepy, unshaven man with long, loose hair. His red mesh vest stretched tightly over his gut, which was as large as the belly of a heavily pregnant woman.

'Still asleep, Gurps?' Virender said, pushing past. 'Won't earn your millions like that, now, will you?'

Randeep nodded at the man and followed Virender into the front room. There were mattresses, grey sheets crumpled on them, and the wallpaper was torn in several places, revealing the pink underneath. It wasn't too bad, Randeep tried to tell himself, and wondered which bed was his.

'This is Gurpreet,' Virender said. The long-haired man raised an elbow to the doorframe. He looked older, unfriendly. Randeep said sat sri akal.

'Where's the others?' Virender asked.

'Asleep. Out,' Gurpreet said.

'Anyway – ' turning to Randeep – 'your room's upstairs. At the very top. You're lucky. You've got your own space. I've put a mattress and shit in there already.'

He said he'd call later about work tomorrow but in the meantime he needed Randeep to come back outside and sign some forms.

'You got your visa, yeah?'

'Ji.'

Gurpreet let out a forlorn little laugh. 'Everyone's got a visa.'

'Should've paid a bit more, then, shouldn't you?'

Randeep spent the rest of the afternoon in his room, up two flights and at the end of the landing. He wiped his suitcase down with dampened toilet paper and stored it on top of the single-door wardrobe. He moved the mattress to the wall, so the sun wouldn't wake him up in the morning, and aired the powder-blue blanket that had come with it. Then he stood at the window, texting

Narinderji his new address and details, looking out at this new world. He hadn't realized they were so high up. That there were so many hills.

He crept downstairs in the early evening, at the sound of voices and laughter. There were loads of them packed into the kitchen, more than he had expected. Eight, nine, ten . . . Where did they all sleep? Most ignored him. One or two asked where he was from, how he got here. Randeep explained that he'd been staying in London with his massi but had to come up here for work.

'My chacha's son was the same,' someone said. 'Went from Uzbekistan all the way to Hull until he found a job. He's back home now. Idiot got caught in a raid.'

Gurpreet's voice came over the top. 'He's got a visa, the boy has. Not a deadhead fauji like us lot.'

The background chatter sank as swiftly as water down a plughole. 'You a scooter?' someone asked.

'I'm on a marriage visa.'

There were whoops and cheers. His shoulders were rubbed. *You've hit the jackpot*, they said. *Lottery nikhel gey.* 'Arré, janaab, you don't even need to work. One year and all your dreams come true.'

Gurpreet thrust a plate into Randeep's hand. 'Welcome to England. Maybe you'll bring us all some luck.'

It took two of them to convey the steel vat of food into the front room and steady it on a three-legged stool. Gurpreet invited Randeep forward. You first, he said. Randeep thanked him, and smiled hard to conceal how revolting he found it all. The tomatoey streaks on his plate that hadn't been washed clean. The flies in the room. Even the tips of his cutlery were slick with some sort of green jam. He took up the large spoon and moved it through the grey mixture. He couldn't tell what it was. It looked like nothing he was used to. This was just a grey-yellow slurry, the odd carrot and pea. He shook a small amount onto his plate and held the spoon out to Gurpreet. But Gurpreet said he had to have more.

'Don't be shy. You're the guest today,' and Gurpreet hurled

down two huge ladlefuls of the stuff onto Randeep's plate and sent him away with a couple of chapattis.

He didn't want to appear ungrateful. He sat on the plastic trim of the mattress, plate balanced on his knees, and told himself he had to finish it. But he couldn't. The chapattis were like wet cardboard and the sabzi had a gritty, slimy, sludgy texture, and all this seemed somehow to connect with the notion that there were things crawling out from the carpet and up his ankles. He started to sweat. He looked across to Gurpreet who was smiling at him, encouraging. Randeep smiled back. He tried one more mouthful, forcing his lips to close around his fingers and take it all in. He managed a few seconds of chewing before he felt his insides contract, refuse. He clamped his hand over his mouth, but the vomit seeped between his fingers and down onto his lap.

*

The work was a few miles away in a place called Catcliffe. An old building had been demolished and the ground had to be prepared for a new one. They were split into groups. Some were dispatched with orders to find all the intact bricks and pile them to one side, so they could later be sold. Some had to work the JCBs and clear the rubble and topsoil. And some, like Randeep, had to gather the boulders and wheel them to the waiting yellow skips. He'd been given a pair of worn-looking boots, and thick gloves for handling the stones, but could still only manage one rock at a time, and it became almost comical how often he had to stop the barrow and turn the thing round. The rocks were so big they had to be rolled up a laddered plank leaning against the skip.

'My grandmother could go faster,' the guy who was rolling said.

'Sorry,' Randeep replied and trudged back with his barrow.

At the end of the week he got his wages from Vinny and went to the supermarket to buy a plate, a knife and fork and spoon, and a bar of soap. That evening, he came down into the kitchen holding his purchases by his side, hoping no one would notice. But Gurpreet was dishing out and as soon as he took hold of Randeep's clean white plate he looked up.

'I see. So what we have isn't good enough for you?'

'It's not that, bhaji. You saw how I was sick. My stomach is just very sensitive.'

'O-ho! He is just very sensitive! Did you hear that, faujio? And I suppose you think the rest of us are barbarians compared to you?'

'I'm sorry. I'll take it back. I'm sorry.'

'No, no. If the prince is sensitive, then we must respect that.' He shook the brown porridge from the spoon and onto the bright white centre of the plate and handed it back to Randeep. 'Enjoy.'

No one spoke to him during the meal. Afterwards, he cleaned his plate and spoon and went to lie on his mattress in his room. He called Avtar but it went to voicemail. He didn't know how he was going to survive a year. Maybe if he asked Vinnyji if there was somewhere else he could live? He could say he'd be happy to take a pay cut. He drifted off to sleep, still in his boots.

He did ask Vinnyji if there was alternative accommodation, catching him on his own before he drove off one morning.

'Look, I sympathize, mate. You like the finer things. My missus is the same. If it ain't Gucci I get no smoochy. Know what I'm saying? But – ' he shrugged – 'it's one in one out. The other house is full and, to be honest, it's best to have everyone in one place. Easier.'

Randeep listened miserably, but as he listened he remembered his friend Michael. 'Vinnyji, how far is Doncaster?'

'I ain't picking you up from fucking Doncaster.'

'Could I live there? I have a friend there. Could I live with him?'

Vinny sighed and said he supposed he could live on the fucking moon if he wanted as long as he arrived to work on time.

'So I can move there? With my friend?'

'Like I said, just be here on time, every time.'

Before dinner, he called Michael. He'd rung him so often Randeep could picture perfectly the telephone number printed below the address in the office filebook. Someone answered. 'Yes?'

'Michael? Is that you? It's me. Randeep. Your friend from India. I've just arrived in England. In Sheffield.'

He couldn't be quite clear how much the old man had understood. But definitely Randeep had said he'd like to come over tonight and definitely Michael had replied that he looked forward to seeing him.

He lifted his suitcase down from the cupboard and had made it as far as the front door when Gurpreet entered the hallway and asked where he thought he was sneaking off to.

'Nowhere, bhaji. My friend called and asked me to visit him.'

'So you're taking all your clothes?'

'It might be a little permanent.'

The taxi from the station dropped him off outside a pebble-dashed bungalow, at a flame-red gate almost hidden in its privet hedge. A light was on in the window. Randeep wheeled his suitcase to the door, ringing the bell, and had to wait a good few minutes before he heard the lock turn, and even then the door stayed on its chain.

'Yes?'

'Michael? Oh, it's good to meet you at last. This is great.'

He was seated on a comfy plaid armchair by a three-bar heater glowing blue. There were an oppressive number of family photographs on the walls and the window ledges, the side tables and mantelpiece. Black-and-white images of Michael in his uniform, of Michael and his late wife – Janice, Randeep remembered – and colour photos as well, of children slurping ice cream or grinning on their bicycles.

'I wasn't expecting visitors until you called,' Michael said, coming in from the kitchen with a glass of milk. He was a slightly hunched man with a silver comb-over, his face a network of deep wrinkles connecting the soft nodes that were his mouth, nose and ears. His left eye didn't open fully. Several times he had to ask Randeep to speak up.

'I said, I remember you telling me the story of you and Balwant Singh.'

'Oh, yes, Billy.' Michael made a sympathetic noise. 'He was a good one. An engineer, you know. He had a girl waiting to marry him back in the Punjab. Don't think he'd ever clapped eyes on her, mind. One of those arranged jobbies. Is that what you're here for?'

'No, sir. Too young for that. I'm here to work only.'

'Because there's plenty of them knocking about Donny. Your sort. And a young chappie like you won't have any trouble to start a-courting.'

'Sir, actually, I have a girlfriend back home waiting for me, too.'

'Have you seen her, though?'

Randeep asked if he might remove his jacket – *to get more comfortable, sir.* When he came back from the cloakroom, Michael was waiting at the frosted-glass cabinet, beckoning Randeep over.

'My grandchildren.' He went through their names, ages, how far they lived, what they were like. 'They all take after their nana, if you ask me. Bright as butterflies, the lot of them.'

Randeep suggested that he – Randeep – make them both something to eat. Michael said he'd eaten. 'But you help yourself.'

He found some sort of pie in the fridge and a tin of baked beans and he heated this all up in the microwave. As long as he kept making himself useful, Randeep thought, waiting for his food to cook. Maybe then Michael would let him stay. He hoped so. It would make all the difference, knowing he had a cosy home to come back to, that he'd never have to spend an evening with Gurpreet again. He could suggest a walk to the park one evening next week, or to the cinema, even, to watch an old wartime film.

He returned to the front room, hot plate in hand. Michael was rousing awake the television. He wanted to watch the news and for the next half an hour the two of them sat there quite companionably: Randeep, for once, enjoying his meal, while Michael wielded his remote at the screen and swore at the flaming Tories.

After the news came the weather, and the bearded man with the map said they expected a mild, dry day tomorrow, with only a small chance of showers.

'Maybe when I come back from work I can take you to the park. For some fresh air.'

'That's kind of you. I'd enjoy that.'

'And I also want to talk about rent. I insist. What sort of payment would you like for all this?'

'Rent? You staying?'

The front door opened and a man started backing into the room. 'Sorry, Dad, the pigeons took the arse-end of forever. I tried calling but you must've been fast on.' He wore a fluorescent raincoat, though it wasn't raining, and was dragging over the doorstep some sort of trolley covered in tartan. Only when he rested the trolley against the wall and turned round and pulled off his hood did he see Randeep sitting in the armchair.

'Oh, I'm sorry. I didn't know you had company.'

Randeep stood and offered his hand. He tried to sound assured. 'I'm Randeep Sanghera. A friend of Michael's. From India.'

The man – 'Philip,' he said, accepting the hand – looked to his father. 'I didn't know you had friends in India.'

'Many a thing that many a man knows not many about.'

Philip unzipped his raincoat, slowly, with an air of deliberation. His light-blond hair was so wispy that his pink scalp showed through, and when he spoke his whole face seemed taken over by the twin avalanches of his fleshy cheeks. 'Been in the country long? Holiday, is it?'

'No, sir, I'm here to work. I work in construction. Building.'

'Oh, nice. I'm in the medical profession myself. Thirty-two years this August just gone. We see a lot of you lot. Builders.' He turned to his father. 'How did you two become friends?'

'On the telephone, weren't it?'

Randeep confirmed that it was. 'I used to work as a claims officer in India and one day I called your father and we became very friendly. He's a very kind man. You're lucky,' he added.

'The telephone?' Philip said, confused, or maybe suspicious.

'I helped your father with his claim,' Randeep went on. 'I did my best.'

The man was staring at Randeep's suitcase, stowed neatly beside the cabinet. 'How long are you visiting Dad for?'

'Oh, Philip, that's no way to treat a guest in our country. He only landed today, the poor bugger.'

Randeep moved to collect the dishes. 'I'll clean all this up.' His hands were shaking.

'Is that my washing?' Michael asked brightly, nodding towards the trolley.

Randeep washed the dishes, including the pans and mugs collected in the sink from earlier in the day, then carried in Michael's clothes from the trolley and folded them into neat piles on the small Formica table. All the while, he could hear Michael's son asking what the hell was going on, Dad? *How could you be so gullible? . . . For the love of God, tell me you haven't given him your bank details? . . . Of course he can't stay here!*

Shyly, Randeep re-entered the room. 'Sir, please don't send me away. I understand your concern. Really, I do. But I want you to know that I mean your father no harm. I'll pay rent. I'm from a good family. My father works in government.'

'I'm sorry, Mr Singh. Truly, I am. But this just isn't on. I know in your culture guests can come and live willy-nilly, but that's just not how we do things. Perhaps that's all to the bad, but it is how it is. If you don't have a bed for tonight then by all means you're welcome to stay, but I'd be grateful if you'd respect my wishes and find somewhere else tomorrow.'

'Oh, Philip . . .'

'I'm sorry, Dad. He seems like a very nice boy but I couldn't forgive myself if something happened to you.'

Randeep said he understood. He took his jacket from the cupboard, picked up his suitcase and thanked Michael for the meal. He tried to give him a few pounds for the pie and beans, but neither Michael nor Philip would hear of it. Instead, Philip drove Randeep to the station and helped him catch the last train back to Sheffield.

*

'Why are you so bhanchod slow?' the guy at the skip said, as Randeep upturned another barrowload at the foot of the ladder. 'It'll take a whole other week like this.' His name was Rishi, a fair-skinned and good-looking boy from Srinagar. Perhaps five or six years older than Randeep, he had a reputation for causing trouble.

'They're heavy,' Randeep said. 'I'm all on my own.'

Rishi snorted, saying that wasn't his problem, and on the van ride home he told Gurpreet that Randeep had been complaining, that he said he was having to work harder than everyone else.

'I never said that,' Randeep said, shaking his head fast. 'I didn't.'

Gurpreet smiled. Randeep's fear seemed to be satisfaction enough.

He stayed in his room that evening, reassuring himself that one day he would be reunited with his family, his father; that the loneliness he was feeling would not be for ever. When he was sure everyone had gone to bed, he took his laundry to the bathroom, filled the tub with a few inches of tepid water, and started scrubbing the clothes with soap. He was on his knees, leaning over, and aching from the day's work. He was determined. Then a noise started up, a sound like an angry bull trapped beneath the bath. Randeep froze. It was getting louder, closer: the others would wake. Gurpreet would wake. Panicking, he pulled out the plug. The noise stopped, only for a green sewage to gurgle up from below. He watched it circulate and make a mess of everything. He called Avtar, who answered, sleepy-voiced, but confirmed that, no, he hadn't found any work, let alone work they could do together. And then it was five o'clock and his alarm was going and he was sure he'd rather have been dead.

One in one out, Randeep kept thinking, as he wheeled to and fro. That's what Vinny had said. One in one out. At lunchtime, with everyone else gathered by the van, sharing round the achaar, he approached the plank ladder propped against the skip. He loosened the knots around the middle two rungs. Not so loose that they fell on touch, but loose enough that they might collapse under pressure. Then he went round the back of the skip and continued on to the van to collect his own lunchbox. He wasn't sure what he was doing. He convinced himself he was helping a friend.

'You're getting faster,' Rishi said in his nasal voice.

It was the first barrowload after lunch. Randeep tipped out the rocks at the foot of the ladder and started back down the slope.

Maybe it wouldn't work. Please, God, don't let it work. He'd not made it halfway down – a significant crack, the sound of thick wood snapping, a scream. He turned around. The ladder and the rock had fallen away and Rishi had crumpled to the ground, thrashing his fists as his foot lay twisted oddly on itself. The others relinquished their spades and released their drills and ran to gather round, while Randeep stood there, shocked, almost wondering if he really had done it.

Later, when Vinny bhaji dropped them off at the house, Randeep hung back and asked what would happen to Rishi bhaji. He wanted to get in first – it wouldn't be long before everyone started advocating some brother or cousin or friend.

'Maybe he'll learn his lesson now, yeah? Maybe he'll spend less time pratting about and more paying attention to his job. Let that be a lesson to you all. Meantime, I'll get my cousin Manny to take a look at his foot. Didn't look pretty, though, did it?'

Randeep shook his head.

'Puts me in a bit of a posish though.'

Randeep waited.

'I'll need to find another one of you chumps. Smartish. Don't suppose you've got a cousin breaknecking it across the Channel as we speak, by any chance?'

Randeep told him that he had a bhaji, Avtar, who'd come with him, but he'd left him in Ilford because there was only work here for one of them.

'Visa?'

'Ji.'

'Marriage? Holiday?'

'Student.'

Vinny shook his head. 'Been burnt by enough scooters in my time. Lying, argumentative. Always quoting their fucking rights.'

'Bhaji, I promise. He will work very hard. You have my word.'

Avtar moved out of Massiji's house and walked towards the high street with no clue where to go next. He spent the afternoon going in and out of the Asian businesses, though no one had work or seemed to know where to find it, and as the day tapered to dusk he made his way to the gurdwara. He put his suitcase and rucksack at the foot of the nishaan sahib and said a short prayer with his forehead to the flagpole. Then he took a ramaal from the wire basket at the entrance, secured it over his head, and went into the food hall. They were serving a langar of roti, dhal and water. Afterwards, he put his dishes in the sink and carried his belongings up the stairs and into the darbar sahib. The rehraas was being read. He bowed his head to the guru granth and found a spot against the rear wall where he could sit in peace and close his eyes for a while. The gurdwara elders gave him a ledge inside the shoe room to sleep on, and in the morning, leaving for the college, he asked God to make this the day he found work.

He knocked on the open office door – Room 625F, it said – and peered inside. 'Sat sri akal, uncle.'

Dr Cheema was at his whiteboard, in the middle of drawing something. 'Avtar! I thought you had forgotten all about us.'

They spoke for only a short while – the doctor had a lunchtime tutorial to lead – but Avtar was to wait, and when the doctor returned to his office he handed him a decent wodge of papers.

'Handouts from your course. I just picked them up. I'll keep sending them to you once you give me your address.'

'Thank you, uncle.' And then, after a pause: 'I need a job. I'm running out of time.'

Dr Cheema sat down and picked up his pen and started to press the nib of it into his desk. 'Do you have somewhere to stay?'

He lived in a large detached house towards Harrow-on-the-Hill. As they came up the long, winding gravel drive, the doctor said he was sure they'd find Avtar work, that there must be lots of jobs for hard-working men like him.

'I don't mind what it is, uncle. Building, cleaning, delivering. Anything.'

'Don't worry,' Dr Cheema said, opening the front door. He fixed Avtar with a look. 'You're with your own people now.'

Everything in the front room was white or gold: the huge white leather sofas, the gold-trimmed coffee table with its glossy fan of magazines. A fashionably tarnished mirror hung above the fireplace, and on either side of this were . . . paintings? Slabs of colour layered one on top of another.

'Rachna?' the doctor called.

A tiny bird of a voice replied. 'Amo?'

The doctor strode into the next room – the massive kitchen – where a small baby of an old woman in a white salwaar kameez sat scowling at her reflection in the long table. There was a bowl of something in front of her. Dr Cheema helped her out of the chair and to the sofas in the front room. It seemed she was blind. 'Just there, Biji. Sit. That's it. Have you eaten?'

She made a face, nodded.

'Do you want something else?'

'What that witch gave is poison enough.'

Dr Cheema sighed. 'Biji, I wish you wouldn't.' He gestured for Avtar to come closer. 'I've brought someone with me. One of our students at the college. He's from Nijjar.'

The old woman leaned forward, jutting her chin up slightly. 'Who?'

'My name's Avtar Nijjar, Biji. Grandson of Jwala Singh Nijjar.'

She said the name sounded familiar and patted the space beside her. 'It's been so long. Did they live near the marsh?'

Dr Cheema sat on the sofa opposite, teasing out the stories, watching, listening, encouraging. He seemed desperate to hear, even at second hand, of this past of which he had no experience. An hour passed in this way, until there was the sound of a lock clicking, of heels on tiles. A magnificently tall woman in a business suit appeared in the doorway. The two halves of her sleek black hair met sharply, precisely, at her chin. Red lipstick, Avtar noticed.

'Oh, hello,' she said, seeing Avtar.

Avtar moved his head, a cross between a bow and a nod. 'Sat sri akal.'

'Why did you leave Biji alone?' Dr Cheema asked.

She stepped across the room, sliding her earrings off with two swipes of her hand and placing them on the mantelpiece. 'I had an emergency. I had to go. I paged you.' She sounded tired.

'You don't leave Biji alone like that. Anything could've happened. She could've hurt herself.'

'We live in hope.'

'What was the point in us deciding that you go part-time if this still happens?'

'Darling, I think you decided, not me. And I'm doing my best but I had no choice. I'm sorry. I made sure she had food and I came back as soon as I could.'

'Well, don't let it happen again,' he said, conceding a little.

She looked to the ceiling, shaking her head. 'My patient died, by the way. Thanks for asking.' And with that she left the room.

The Cheemas' son was off in America on something called a gap year, so Avtar was given his room.

'Uncle, this is too much. I'd be happy on the floor downstairs.'

'Let's just concentrate on finding you work. Sleep well. We start tomorrow.'

'Uncle?'

The doctor turned round.

'Thank you for all this. I don't know why you're doing it, but thank you.'

The doctor's mouth pursed up, then he said, 'I remember my father telling me that back in the day people would open their houses to young men like you. To help you get started on this new life. That's all I'm doing.' He paused. 'Something happened a few years ago that made it clear to me that I'm only ever going to be a guest in this country. That it didn't matter how many garden parties I threw for my neighbours, this would never be my real home. It's important that a man has a sense of a real home. A sense of his own ending.'

For over a week Dr Cheema drove Avtar around London – Harrow, Ealing, Southall, Hounslow, Grays, Brixton, Hackney, Uxbridge, Croydon, Enfield. They enquired in newsagents', fish-and-chip shops, market stalls, in gurdwaras and factories. They criss-crossed the capital following leads, acting on tips, pursuing half-chances. They left each day at a little after dawn, packed lunches in the boot, eager to miss the traffic, and when they arrived back at the house it was long past ten o'clock. But none of their efforts resulted in a job for Avtar and after the tenth day of this he collapsed onto the sofa and said he wasn't going to impose on Dr Cheema's family any longer. He'd leave the next day.

'Of course you can't leave. Where will you go?'

'But, uncle—'

'Let's give it a few more days, hain? We're so close. I can feel it.'

That night, Avtar came downstairs and into the kitchen, textbook in hand. He couldn't sleep. He had little money left and no job in sight. And now Pocket Bhai's nephew had got in touch. They wanted the first repayment.

'I still have a few weeks,' Avtar had said.

'Fair enough. A few weeks. I'll be in touch.'

That was already two days ago and still he didn't know what he was going to do. He heard footsteps on gravel and the kitchen door opened and Rachnaji stepped in with her briefcase. 'Oh, hi. Up late.'

'Studying,' he said, indicating his book.

'Good. Studying is good.'

She dumped the briefcase on one of the high stools and poured a glass of water from a hatch in the fridge. She drank deeply, then brought the glass down hard.

Avtar flinched. He took it as a sign of her frustration that he was still in their house. 'Thank you, aunty, for everything you and uncle are doing.'

'Huh? Oh, it's nothing. It's your uncle. Nothing to do with me.'

'But I think I will be leaving tomorrow. It's time.'

'And you think my husband will let you?'

He wasn't sure he understood. Was he held captive here?

Rachnaji slid out of her heels and sat a few chairs down from him at the table. Up close like this, he could see the powder-sheen of her face. The chalky grey at her temples. 'The last one he brought home was here for nearly three months. A girl. How the aunties tittered.'

'Ji?'

'I don't even pretend to know what it is. I used to think it was just nostalgia. Some attempt at connecting with his roots. Some regret at living the life he does. I don't know. All I know is that it's become much worse since he became president of that IndiSoc or whatever it is. He's become much concerned with "ideas of belonging",' she said, holding up fingers.

Avtar nodded. But, no, he didn't understand.

'It really is a pathetic thing. To mourn a past you never had. Don't you think?'

*

Lakhpreet called early one morning, so early it was dark outside. He was still half asleep and her voice sounded creamy in his ear, gently stirring his dreams away. *I wish you were here beside me,* he said, murmured, *so I could hold you, touch you . . .*

'Randeep's in trouble,' she said.

Frowning, Avtar sat up, wiping a crust of sleep from his eyes. She'd always had a leaning towards the dramatic interruption. 'What trouble?'

'I don't know, but he called yesterday and he sounded so down. I've never heard him like that. I'm really worried, janum. Have you spoken to him?'

'Once or twice. Briefly. He's just homesick.'

'Maybe. Do you know the men he's living with? What are they like?'

Avtar said he hadn't a clue.

'You just let him go? On his own? Without knowing anything about . . . anything?'

'I've got my own worries,' he said, a little peeved. 'And he's not a kid.'

'He is though, in some ways . . .' She trailed off.

'Jaan, is there something else?'

'No, no. I just . . . I guess Daddy being how he is, is making me more worried.'

'Randeep's not like your father.'

'I know, I know. But can't you just keep an eye on him? Stay in touch? Just keep making sure he's all right?'

Days passed, a week, and he still hadn't called Randeep. He was putting it off. He didn't want to discover that the boy really was in trouble. In which case, Avtar would have to do something. Wouldn't he? He was thinking of this, folding clothes into his suitcase, when Cheemaji knocked. It had taken Avtar a while to get used to this – people knocking – and he still wasn't sure whether to get up and open the door or tell them to come in from where he was sitting. On this occasion, Cheemaji walked right in. He was excited. He still had the cordless in his hand.

'That was the factory-wallah. From that clothes factory we went to last week. He has a job.'

They drove down to Southall, past kebab joints and sari shops and curry houses and travel agents promising the cheapest fares to Amritsar through Air Turkmenistan. The factory was towards the old gasworks, and a dark-skinned, full-lipped man in a green safari shirt came into the loading bay to greet them. He wore a gold watch, too.

'Avtar, you remember Mr Golwarasena?'

For half an hour it was very slowly and very tediously explained to Avtar that the job was 7 a.m. to 8 p.m., six days a week, with two thirty-minute breaks to be taken in turn by all the workers on the line. He would be paid at the standard level for the twenty-two hours per month his visa permitted him to work, with the rest of his hours paid at the reduced level. The fauji level, they called it. The contract, of course, would itemize the standard hours only.

'The job has many angles,' Mr Golwarasena went on in his strangely accented English. 'From patternation to executive stitching to industrial storage.' And he proceeded to detail exactly what the duties in each of those angles entailed.

'And the pay?' Dr Cheema asked, sounding exhausted already.

Mr Golwarasena's eyes became heavy-lidded, as if talk of money was beneath him. He gave the figures. Avtar tried not to let his delight show. It sounded like an obscene amount to earn.

On the drive back, Avtar asked why they hadn't just accepted the job. Instead they'd invited Mr Golwarasena over for dinner that night.

'Because he's the type who's impressed by a big house and shiny things. So we ask him to dinner, give him a few whiskies, he becomes a friend, and then he offers you more money. Good plan or what?'

The plan was never executed. As Avtar was pulling his best shirt out of the suitcase and wondering if it would be rude to ask for use of the iron, his phone rang.

'Randeep! You've called on a great day!'

'Bhaji? Is that you? I have good news.'

And Randeep launched into something about how they could now work together because someone had broken their foot and all he had to do was come up tomorrow and even accommodation was included and it'd be great and he couldn't wait for Avtar bhaji to join him because he was lonely and had no friends but it was all going to be all right now because he was going to come up too.

'There's a job? Working with you?'

'Yes, yes. So what time will you come? I'll meet you at the station.'

Avtar made Randeep go through it all again, slowly, calmly, explaining what the job was, the pay, how long-term.

'Very long-term. Vinny bhaji is always thinking of new projects.' The silence on the phone grew. 'Is something the matter? You will come, won't you?'

Avtar said he needed to think and that he'd call Randeep later – and what a horrible feeling it was, hearing the disappointment in the boy's voice as he came off the phone. Really, the choice should have been easy. The job here, in Southall, was better all round – better pay, better accommodation, better hours. He'd have to get a second job in this Sheffield place to come close to earning as much. And yet there was no choice. Lakhpreet was right. Something had sounded wrong, and because Randeep was her brother, and younger than him, weaker than him, and because they'd come across together and stayed with Randeep's aunt that first month – all this seemed to have conferred on Avtar an irritating and exaggerated sense of responsibility towards the boy. He smiled ruefully. Funny how God offers you everything you've asked for, only to force you to turn it away. He sat a few minutes in the silence of the room, then went downstairs to tell Cheemaji that the dinner wouldn't be necessary.

SPRING

5. ROUTINE VISITS

Behind Avtar, the yellow cranes did their noisy browsing: giant birds biting up great mouthfuls of earth, only to jerk their heads to the side and spit it all out. The racket was such that Langra John limped up with a box of noise-cancelling earphones, and Avtar had one set circled loosely around his neck. He was hunched over his college folder, going through handouts forwarded on by Cheemaji. Most of them were stamped 'College of North-West London'; underneath that, 'Preparing You For Your Future'. Around him the lunchtime talk was of the latest raids.

'Three last week,' Rishi said, his foot recently out of plaster. 'Two in Wolverhampton, one in Luton.'

'See,' Gurpreet said. 'It's always down there. Nothing for us to worry about.'

At this, several of them cringed and said a waheguru and threw some soil over their shoulders.

'My fuffer – the one who works in customs – he says they've even started checking the marriage ones. He said one brother was sent back because when they visited he couldn't speak English and his gori visa-wife couldn't speak Panjabi.'

'Arré, janaab, those pindu types are stupid. They give the rest of us a bad name. It's like they want to get caught.'

Randeep reattached the lid onto his lunchbox in a series of tiny clicks. 'How much time do they give before they visit?'

Langra John shouted at them to get back on it and so Avtar packed his folder away and re-secured the leather harness around his waist. He'd been paired with Gurpreet and together they had to climb the scaffolding and score off the lock-points between the planned executive rooms on floors ten through to fifteen. They were both complicatedly belted up and tethered to a double-chain rope that ran around the hotel perimeter, and the platform was wide enough to walk side by side. The ladders connecting the floors didn't sway once in the wind and drizzle. Despite all that, they'd only made it up one floor and were walking round with their spirit levels and pencils when Gurpreet stopped and folded onto his knees.

'What now?' Avtar said.

He held up his hand, as if to say he'd be fine in a minute. Ten minutes later they were still there, their backs to the main drop and facing the grey mesh curtain that hung all down the inside of the scaffolding.

'It's the height,' Gurpreet said.

'You must love living in Sheffield, then.'

He smiled faintly. 'It's not easy, this life, is it?'

Avtar jutted out, then immediately withdrew, his lower lip. A facial shrug. 'Who said it would be? But it'll get better. Hard work, that's all it takes.'

'Yeah, I used to be like you, too.'

'You're nothing like me.'

'I used to think I only had to work harder. Longer.' He shook his head. 'Bhanchod liars.'

'You should go home. Eleven years is a long time.'

Gurpreet laughed. 'Forget any ideas about going home. You'll still be here, still doing this, in eleven years' time as well.'

'Nah. If I don't pass my exams I'll go home with what I've earned.'

'That easy, is it?'

'It is for me.' The rain puttered against his yellow hat, dribbled down the back of his neck.

'So how much have you saved so far? With all your working?'

Avtar stared straight ahead.

'Thought so. I said the same. That I'd go home after one year with my money. You really are like me.'

'Fuck you.'

'You're me in eleven years.'

'I said fuck you.'

'Why? Scared? And it's only going to get harder. Now chamaars like him are coming over.'

Avtar dipped his gaze and saw Tochi far below, tiny, switching drills.

'It makes you only care for yourself.' Gurpreet spoke quietly. 'This life. It makes everything a competition. A fight. For work, for money. There's no peace. Ever. Just fighting for the next job. Fight fight fight. And it doesn't matter how much stronger than everyone else you are, there's always a fucking chamaar you have to share the work with, or a rich boy who can afford a wife.'

'You play the cards you're dealt,' Avtar said.

Gurpreet clucked his tongue. 'Or you tear up the game. You get rid of the players.'

Avtar checked his harness, his stay.

'It's not your time yet,' Gurpreet said. 'Don't worry.'

'I'm not the one who needs to be worried.'

'But I would do it, you know. If it helped me, I would throw you over. And, one day, you'll say the same.'

Tucking the orange uniform into his trousers, he ran across the road and into the Botanical Gardens. The grasses were starting to bud, the daisies closing for the night. He should ignore Gurpreet. Lazy and bitter, that's all he was. Kirsty was waiting outside the shop, in jeans and a T-shirt printed with four faces he didn't know.

'Late again?' he asked.

'I didn't know you came up that way. Wouldn't it be quicker through the wood?'

He couldn't remember where he'd told her he lived. 'I was visiting a friend.'

'Oh,' she said, sounding unconvinced.

She'd started nearly four months ago, in the new year, to save for university. She said she was taking Criminology. At first, this had alarmed Avtar and his desi co-workers. They'd even complained to Malkeet, their boss, who'd had to come down and explain that they were idiots, the lot of them, and of course it didn't mean she was going to tell the police. Her dark-blonde hair, when it wasn't pinned into an orange net, fell about her face and shoulders. She had flinty eyes and a handspan waist, fingers that stroked the counter each time she walked by, and a way of standing – hip stuck out – that seemed both careless and defiant. She lived with her mam and her mam's boyfriend, who wasn't her dad.

A black Mini swerved into the forecourt and braked abruptly, so close to Avtar and Kirsty that they both jumped back. A middle-aged woman in leggings and a fluffy white jumper scrambled out, jangling keys. Diamond-studded sunglasses sat on top of her glamorous mane like a second pair of eyes: insect eyes.

'I'm so sorry. So sorry. He goes away for two weeks and I can't even manage to open up on time.' They went to the entrance round the back. 'There you are,' she said, deactivating the alarm. 'It's all yours.'

Avtar went in, switching on lights, the fryers, the spit. Kirsty tied her apron round her waist.

Their boss's wife hovered at the door. 'All OK? Shall I leave you to it?'

'Unless you want to get the chicken on,' Kirsty said.

'It's fine, bhabhi,' Avtar said hastily. 'We'll look after it all from here.' He waited for the door to close, then gave Kirsty a look.

'Well,' she said, flapping a hand towards the window. 'She goes round kneecapping people like a trout in a Ferrari. It makes me want to vom.'

He got the potatoes through the peeler and into the hopper, and then straight into the fryers. Harkiran, who worked the same shift, entered through the back door, his over-gelled hair swept to the side, and Avtar took his turn on the small settee in the back, beside the door to the toilet. They did this whenever their boss wasn't around. It never got properly busy until around ten, so they'd have an hour each to try and catch up on some sleep. Only these days Avtar used the time to study. He set his chin in the palm of his hand and started on the first page: The Basics of Cryptography. He made it halfway down the sheet before he ceased taking anything in.

When Harkiran woke him, it was nearly 10.30: he'd been curled up asleep on the settee for almost three hours.

'You should've nudged me.'

'It's not busy, and I've got the morning off to sleep.'

Harkiran zipped up his suede jacket – he did the graveyard shift as a security guard – and said he'd be seeing Avtar tomorrow.

Avtar splashed cold water on his face and went through to the serving area.

'Everything OK?' he asked Kirsty.

'Quiet, but the numpties are starting so you might want to make yourself scarce.'

He nodded gravely and returned to the kitchen. When they'd first started, he and Harkiran had been warned that it was fine to go out front if it got busy early on, but to make sure they stayed out of sight once the pubs closed. Usually, this wouldn't be a problem. Malkeet bhaji tended to arrive at around ten to help with the Drunk Rush and such was his reputation and size that things never got more lairy than the occasional loudmouth who couldn't even stand up straight and had to be helped – thrown – out of the door. The last few days though, Kirsty had got the worst of it. They called her a slag when she refused to spade on extra chips, they asked her what she was like in bed, whether she took it up the shitter. Once, Avtar had come forward, hoping a male presence would hurry them on. It only made it worse.

Tonight, he was brushing around the trunk of the toilet when he heard Kirsty shouting at them to get out. He stopped with the broom and listened. Drunks.

'Temper, temper.'

'She's a feisty one.'

'Like a bit of sausage, do you, love? Battered?'

'I said get out. Now. We're closing.'

They didn't.

'I'll call the police.'

There was laughter. One of them told her to get her rat out and, predictably, they started singing: 'Get your rat out for the lads!' It was a chant Avtar had heard a few times on his way home past the pubs. He hated the aggressive sound of it, and hated it even more once he'd discovered what the words meant.

They sang it again and again, clapping in time. Avtar ventured out and spread his arms either side of the counter, trying to make himself appear bigger. The singing stopped, though the laughter on their faces remained. He must look clownish to them, this man in an orange hairnet.

'We need to close. Can you leave, please?'

'What were that? Speaka da English?'

'Kirsty, can you call the police, please?' It was a hollow threat. All the staff had been warned never to bring in the police.

'Oh, Kirsty, is it? Thirsty Kirsty?'

Avtar went through the counter flap and opened the door. 'Get out.'

'Or what?'

'Kirsty?'

She lifted the receiver. 'You've got five seconds or the pigs are here.'

One of them – light-brown curls cut close to his skull – moved to the door and spat right into Avtar's face. 'Cunt.'

They filed out, spitting in turn, and Avtar closed the door, locked it, dimmed the lights, and went back to the toilet to clean his face in the basin. He heard Kirsty behind him.

'I'm so sorry, Avtar.'

He nodded, though perhaps even worse than the spitting was the quietness in her voice, the sense of someone being embarrassed for him.

*

Narinder took the letter from the pocket of her cardigan. It had arrived for her at the gurdwara, over a week ago now, and it was from Karamjeet, her fiancé. She reread the brief, typed message for perhaps the twentieth time. He said he knew she was in Sheffield and that he wanted to meet. If she refused then she left him with no choice but to tell her father and brother where she was. He reminded her of his mobile number and signed off by saying that he hoped she agreed that he deserved an explanation at the very least. As she slipped the letter back into her pocket, there was a knock on the door.

———

'Sat sri akal,' Randeep said. 'The front door was open so I came straight up.'

She looked past him and down the stairs. 'I must've forgot.'

'I thought maybe someone had moved in. Into the flat. Downstairs.'

'Have they?'

'Sorry?'

'Who is it?'

'No one. I don't – sorry?'

She shook her head, apologizing – she seemed agitated – and moved aside to let him past. 'Please, sit down,' she said and poured tea with her back to him. She wore one of her usual plain salwaar kameez. A light-blue and white one, like a Panjabi girl's school uniform, which on some level Randeep was too anxious to reach for he found vaguely arousing.

'I hope you don't mind,' he said. 'I just thought it would be better if we discussed this face to face.'

'No, I'm sure you're right.'

They sipped their teas. She asked him how work was going, gesturing towards his hands. He looked at his rough palms.

'It's fine. Thank you for asking. Easier in this weather. Even if everything's so damp. I hated the snow. And for you? You're still enjoying living here?'

She smiled a so-so face. 'The weather doesn't really affect me.'

'Yes. The summer will be nice when it comes.'

'Let's not get our hopes up.'

He wondered whether a joke might be appropriate here, something about how British they were being, talking about the weather like this. She stood and returned with a piece of paper from a low kitchen drawer.

'They say the visit shouldn't last more than a couple of hours.'

It was a confirmatory note from Her Majesty's immigration people. As per the terms of the spousal visa, they intended to pay a routine visit which included interviews with both parties. The last line of the letter specified the date of the appointment and an injunction that Mr Sanghera and Ms Kaur make every effort to accommodate the visit, or to call them as soon as possible if this wasn't possible.

'It's good they gave a date. They don't usually do that.'

'How do you know?'

He smiled. She must think he did this kind of thing all the time. 'Someone told me.'

She closed her fingers around her tea. He could see her swallowing.

'Please don't be nervous,' he said. 'I'm here.'

'It's hard not to be.' Then: 'I suppose you'll take the day off work and come here in the morning?'

He placed the note back down, adjusting its position by minute degrees until its edge sat exactly parallel with the table's. 'I was talking to some of the guys and they said the things the inspection people look for are signs that we're definitely living together. For example, that I know my way around the flat. One couple was caught out because the inspectors asked the man if they could have a glass of water while they interviewed the wife. And the man didn't know which cupboard the glasses were in. They got suspicious and then it was all over for them both.'

'So shall I show you where everything is? It won't take long.'

Randeep tried again: 'Actually, Narinderji, my bhajis were saying I should spend some time living here before the inspectors come.'

She waited for him to go on.

'They said two weeks, at least.'

Her face betrayed no reaction. She put her mug down.

'I'll be at work most of the time. And then after the inspection, I'll be gone. I promise. As soon as they leave, I'll go too.'

'No. I'm not going to agree to that. Two weeks is a long time.'

He nodded that it was, it really was. 'I just don't want anything to go wrong during the visit, that's all. And I'd sleep on the settee, of course,' in case that was what was troubling her. She looked at him as if to say *where the hell else did he think he would be sleeping?*

He started on a routine of press-ups and crunches. Each morning, while he waited his turn in the bathroom, he leaned his mattress against the wall and did fifty of each, and the same again in the evening after work. When Avtar accused him of trying to impress Narinderji – 'What are you going do? Walk around with your top off?' – he laughed it off, saying that was only for those filmi hero types. On the evening of the move, he finished his press-ups, jumped to his feet and looked down at himself. His white vest seemed to hang on his frame as limply as ever. There was no discernible change in his soft biceps. No muscles showed through his stomach.

Avtar knocked, entered.

'I shouldn't have to do this, you know,' Randeep said. 'You'd think working on that building site all these months would've made some difference.'

'Ready?'

The crack in the mirror ran right over his mouth, so he had to bend slightly to check his teeth were clean. They were. And, yes, his shirt buttons were done up correctly, as was the zip on his black trousers. He turned round and picked up his suitcase.

'OK. I'm ready.'

They made a strange pair walking down Ecclesall Road. Tall, thin Randeep dressed as if for the office, rolling a suitcase behind him, and Avtar in his baked-bean orange. The neon of various restaurants struck out against the fresh damp evening, and queues were hedging up outside the more popular bars. Avtar read the signs out loud. Any chance to practise his English.

'Cubana. Prezzo. Mud Crab. Café Rouge.' He screwed up his face. 'Abuelo? Is that right?'

Randeep looked. 'That's right,' he said, not really knowing either way. 'You'll fly through the exams.'

'Arré, Baba, don't tempt the evil eye,' and Avtar palmed up some imaginary dust from the pavement and threw it over his shoulder. 'Was Vinny OK with all this?'

Randeep nodded. 'He said he'll pick me up from the station first and then do the rest of you.'

'Makes sense. And it's light when he picks us up now. You'll be fine.'

'Jashn-e-bahaar, bhaji.' He inhaled. 'My favourite time of year. Everything's so new.'

'Acha, acha, calm down. Don't get too excited about staying with her.' He sighed. 'You on the rota?'

'No. I checked.'

'Good. And I'll cover your milk run. I'll speak to Gurpreet.'

Randeep thanked him, and at the bus stop he waited with his case while Avtar continued on to work.

*

That evening, Tochi was stacking cans of lager in the chiller cabinet at the shop when Aunty called him upstairs, saying her husband was back and wanted to meet him. The cans immediately doubled in weight. He dumped the cardboard in the recycling bins and slowly made his way up the steps at the side of the counter. He'd never been into the flat. The stairs turned at the top, into a living room papered sunshine-yellow.

'Aajo, Tarlochan,' Aunty said. 'Come inside.'

She was sitting on one of two brown leather settees. On the other was her husband, a big, shaven-headed bloke with a scruffy goatee. From somewhere deeper in the flat came the sound of computer games.

The husband got up and extended his hand, as no one from back home would have done. So, one of those first-generation men: born here, married there. Tochi had nothing to worry about.

'Kaise ho?'

'Good, thank you,' Tochi said, shaking the hand. 'The work's good. Thank you.'

'More than good,' Aunty said. 'Not once has he been late or had time off. Everything is done quickly and cleanly. He even knows how to do the newspaper returns. You know how they hurt my back so.' She sounded eager for her husband's approval.

'OK, OK. You did good. Stay for roti?' he added, to Tochi, but

Tochi said he'd already eaten and should get going if there wasn't anything else.

Back at the house, he transferred his wages to a small metal box which he kept hidden in his room. He stroked the money rolls packed into the tin, like cigars in their expensive box. His savings really were mounting up. The shop work, the hotel work, plus what he'd earned in Southall. It was still early, but, who knows, by the end of the year he might even have enough to rent on his own.

Over the next week, the invitations upstairs became more and more frequent. At first it was to help move a cupboard from the living room into the bedroom, or to see if he could have a look at fixing the noise coming from the sink. Soon, he was asked to join them at the table, especially as Aunty was plating up anyway and the boys were heading out with their friends. 'I'll only be throwing it out,' she said. 'It's already two days old. Keep us company.' So Tochi asked to wash his hands and sat down tentatively. Uncle wondered if he'd join him in a whisky, and when Tochi declined, saying he didn't drink, he saw a smile spread into Aunty's face.

One evening, after using his clunky English to move on a couple of boys drinking outside the shop, Tochi was approached by Uncle who had a good long chat to him about his plans and hopes for the future. Did he intend on living illegally forever? Was he going to return home once he'd earned enough?

'I don't know.'

'Your aunty says you have no family back home?'

'Ji.'

'They passed away?'

'Ji.'

'Brothers, sisters?'

Tochi shook his head, once.

Uncle nodded thoughtfully. 'It's up to us to think of something for you, then.'

He was asked up to another dinner a few days later and that was when Aunty came right out and said that she had a beautiful niece who would be the perfect match for him.

Tochi stared, then said, 'No. Sorry.'

'Just think about it only.'

'No girls agree to marry boys like me from India.'

'Well, she's divorced and thirty-eight with a twelve-year-old boy, so obviously her choices in this life are limited. She needs to be realistic about who she can get.' Then: 'But she's lovely. Really, she is. She can cook and clean and she's such a respectful girl. She's had some real bad luck in life, that's all.'

After a short silence, Tochi said, 'Thank you, but I don't want to get married.'

She batted this nonsense away. 'You boys all say that. Your uncle was the same. But once the hot fresh rotis start coming you soon change your mind. Now,' she went on, tapping the table with a coin, 'obviously if your matah-pitah were still with us I'd speak to them, but is there anyone else, an elder, I can speak to?'

'I've said, marriage isn't for me. I'm not the right person.'

Uncle seemed to register some of Tochi's concern, and laid his hands flat on the table, warning them of the plain speaking to come. 'As usual, your aunty is getting too far ahead of herself. All we are saying is that the family is desperate to get Ruby married. The longer it goes on, the less chance there is, and you know the stigma of having unmarried girls sitting at home. Especially ones with children. Secondly, we think you're a hard-working young man. You're a good Jat Sikh boy. You've been with us for several months now and we've been very pleased with you and we trust you. We feel we know you. We don't think you'd run off and divorce her and get a normal bride once you got your stamp. So many boys do that these days and it's a real worry for us.'

'And she can still have more children!' Aunty exclaimed, as if that was the clincher. 'I know some of the girls you boys have to settle for can't, but she can. She's all there.'

'Mum,' her husband cautioned, and she withdrew, apologized. 'Tarlochan, all we're saying is why don't you and Ruby meet and if you decide to take it no further then that's fine. But if you do get on and things reach their natural conclusion, then, well, both

Ruby's problems and yours are solved, aren't they? And isn't that what we all want?'

They wouldn't stop talking about the girl, saying how perfect she was, that once he saw the photo he'd soon change his mind. They weren't listening, and, on the site, his frustration seemed to be powering the hammer drill all afternoon, until he saw Vinny parking the van. Very gently, Tochi released the drill brakes. He'd learned his lesson last time when he'd stopped drilling all at once and the shock of it had taken his feet from under him and the shooting pains in his shoulders lasted an entire week. Now, the metal growling calmed, died, and he shook each arm in turn until it felt normal again. He pawed at his face with the yellow plastic gloves and the oversized goggles slipped off. He tapped the chalk out of them. Forty metres, he guessed. Forty extra metres he'd drilled, all because some gora architect got the gas pipes on the plans in the wrong place. Vinny stepped out of the van. But it was too early to be picking them up. He had a tie on, too. Tochi watched him stride over to the foreman's cabin, knock, enter. He didn't look happy.

They teased him about the tie on the ride home. *Interview, Vinny Sahib? Take us with you!*

'I'd rather eat my own turds,' Vinny said, charmingly.

He seemed in a better mood now, but later, when someone asked why the electricians hadn't turned up yet, his eyes flicked to the rear-view mirror and he told them all to keep their bastard mouths shut.

More suits turned up over the next five days, some leaving with boxes of files under their arms, and John, Tochi noticed, was spending less time on the site, more on the phone in his cabin. He watched Vinny on the rides home; at the tense, shifty way he sometimes glanced about. If they really were on to him, it wouldn't be long before they found and raided the house. Maybe it was time to return to London. He could call Ardashir. Then, one evening, Vinny showed up at the shop. Tochi hid himself in the aisles. He didn't know why Vinny would've come here. Or how he knew this was where he worked. He'd been careful to not tell anyone the shop's name. Always checked no one from the house was following him.

'Del!' he heard Vinny say. 'How goes it?'

'Well, well, look who it is.'

They spoke for a while. The usual things. Family, football, work. Vinny said it was going well. That he had a big project – a hotel – in his portfolio and a couple more in the pipeline. 'Happy days. Just waiting for the funds to come through.'

So, he needed money.

'Well, if you need any more faujis,' Uncle said, 'I might know someone.'

And maybe he gestured or something because Vinny appeared at the top of Tochi's aisle. 'Him?'

Tochi came forward, nodding at Vinny. 'Uncle, shall I start sweeping up outside?'

He was ignored, while Vinny explained that Tochi was one of his men, that he'd picked him up from a restaurant in Southall.

'You didn't say you worked on the building side?' Uncle said.

'I didn't want to.'

'Oh, I bump into them everywhere,' Vinny said. 'Fuck knows where the pigs are looking, cos I can't go into a chippy without seeing one of my lot. You've got a good one here, though. Hard worker. Not the chattiest, mind.'

Uncle agreed. 'But he's stubborn. Maybe you can talk some sense into him. We want to get him set with my missus's niece. Marriage-wise. I don't know what's wrong with him. He just says no.'

Tochi stared at the floor, heat rising horribly up his neck. It was all going to come crashing down. Right here. Vinny looked from Tochi to Uncle and back again. 'That's great. That's really open-minded of you, Del.'

Tochi closed his eyes, waiting.

'He's a good lad,' Uncle said. 'He deserves a break.'

'Still. Good on you.'

Vinny left soon after, saying he'd come again another day. They watched the van reverse out.

'I was waiting for that,' Uncle said. 'He's been everywhere with his begging bowl. Lucky for me you were here.'

Tochi said nothing.

'He's a nice boy but they're on to him so if you've got any sense you'll cut your ties. Find another job. And if you're living in one of his houses, move.'

Tochi asked again if he should start sweeping up outside.

'And if you've got any real sense, you'll agree to meeting the girl.'

Tochi looked away.

'Uff, so what if she's divorced? Or is it her boy? Look, son, in your situation that's the best you're going to do. Most wouldn't think twice.'

'I'll get the broom,' Tochi said.

'Yes, yes. Fob me off. But don't think for a minute your aunty is going to be so easy.'

Alone in his room, Tochi made a call to Ardashir. There was nothing at the restaurant, he said – Tochi had been replaced by a fauji from Bangla.

'Let me know if that changes.'

'OK.'

'I'd need somewhere to live, too.'

'Was there something wrong with my floor?'

He went downstairs and sorted himself some water from the sink. He checked the rota. No, not his turn tomorrow. Beneath it, the naked girls calendar was still on March, a month out of date. The front door went and Avtar came in and walked straight past Tochi and to the cooker. He took two rotis out of their foil and spooned on some cold sabzi from the fridge. His rucksack hung squarely on his back, a textbook discernible through the thin material.

'Vinny's in trouble. We're going to be raided,' Tochi said.

'Move, then.'

'And jobs. We'll lose our jobs.'

Avtar looked across. 'How do you know?'

'What's it like where you are?'

'There's nothing.'

Tochi looked at him for a long while, then pushed off the counter and returned upstairs.

His eyelashes quivered, he wasn't sure; something, some furry dream-tail, was trying to lead him back to sleep. But that was his watch pipping, which meant – what? 5 a.m. already? He remained beneath the duvet and it took another minute for sleep to evaporate completely. He could hear the pale sounds of the gurbani coming from her bedroom. Before he'd even arrived, she'd cleared the shrine from its corner, saying he could use the vacated space for his suitcase and things. At ten past, he swung his feet to the carpet and padded softly to the bathroom. He showered in the evenings after work – and what a joyous feeling it was to once again have a shower, and a hot one at that – so all he had to do in the mornings was brush his teeth and wash his face and take a piss, which he aimed at the side of the bowl. He didn't want to disturb her praying. He dressed in his work clothes, reflector jacket over the top, folded the duvet to the end of the settee and at twenty-five past he started for work. It was a delicate and spotty light that greeted him these days.

He could have left the flat as late as six o'clock and still made it to the station in time to be picked up by Vinnyji. He just thought it was best to go as soon as possible – she seemed reluctant to come out from her room while he was there. No doubt she was afraid of walking in on him naked or something. She was a modest girl. Woman. A woman of mystery. He still didn't know who she was or what was driving her. It definitely wasn't the money. He wished she'd let him in. If she was in trouble, then, like any good husband, he wanted to help her.

Inevitably, the boys – at the site, in the van to and from work – wanted to know how it was going. Had he finally experienced his suhaag raat, his wedding night? Their questions and insinuations pained him, even more so as he deflected them, and when he was dropped off at the station in the evening he climbed down from the van and said, 'Enjoy your night,' as if suggesting that was exactly what he'd be doing.

Once he reached the flat they'd exchange a polite sat sri akal and Randeep would take some clothes from his suitcase and on into the bathroom. He'd shower and re-emerge barefoot in a white cotton kurta pyjama. They ate quietly opposite one another at the small round dining table, fresh daffodils in the vase.

One evening he asked her, 'If you could go anywhere in the world where would you go?'

She was making some sort of list. 'Pardon?'

'Next year I'm going to go to New York. I've decided. And then one day Australia. I want to fly everywhere. Don't you agree?'

'Agree?'

'Because the world is big! And we make life such a small thing. I want my life to be big, too.'

She went back to her list. 'I'm happy with wherever God leads me.'

His smile wavered. 'Of course. I didn't mean you weren't. I'm sorry if that's how it sounded.'

She nodded, not looking up, and Randeep turned again to the map on the wall.

The following afternoon, the first of his two Sundays, he rushed back from the station. It was starting to rain, true, the fine drizzle beginning to soup up, but that wasn't why he was running. He'd had an idea. When he got back, she was unpacking groceries. Raindrops beaded the edge of her chunni and a wet, peachy scent seemed to have swept in behind her. Going to the supermarket had been one thing he was going to suggest they do, like other couples, maybe tomorrow evening. But that could wait—

'Narinderji, let's go to the fair.'

She turned round, a jar of something in her hand. 'The fair?'

He took the flyer out of his pocket and thrust it at her.

'Oh, no. It's not for me.'

'It's for everyone! And it'll be fun. Please say yes.'

'Sorry. You go.'

'Oh, yes, I suppose I could.' But the whole point was that they do something together. Open up to each other a little. 'What about the gurdwara, then?'

'Excuse me?'

'The gurdwara.'

'This evening?'

'Just, with the visit next week, it might be good to get God's blessing. Make sure He's watching over us.'

She returned to her cupboards, her back to him. 'There's an akhand paat on. It'll be busy.'

'Is that a problem? Doesn't that only make it even more auspicious?'

'I don't like to go when it's busy. We can say a prayer here if you like. I have the rehraas on CD.'

'We wouldn't have to stay long.'

'I'm sorry.'

'I don't think you've been for a few days now.'

She said nothing.

'What about if—?'

'I said no,' she snapped. 'Why can't you understand?'

Silence fell, filled the room. Her shoulders slumped. She closed the cupboard and he watched her disappear into her bedroom.

*

A crow swooped down from the hotel roof and up into the blue wash of the sky. Clouds turned the colour of mercury, grumbled, and in the space of a breath the air greyed and the rain came. Tupperware boxes were shoved inside jackets and the men rushed under the plastic awning John had kicked them into building a few days ago, in preparation for a downpour like this. The rain drummed harder, pooling where the awning hadn't been pulled taut. Water slithered in streams, like eels making good their escape. They had only got an hour's work done and by lunchtime John had to relent and call Vinny to come and take them home. A few refused to go, fearing the loss of half a day's pay, but Vinny said he'd see them right and that they'd best get in the van now summat pronto, cos this pissing rain was fucking him right off.

She wasn't there when Randeep let himself in. He wondered where she could be. Most days she stayed in with the doors locked. He'd already taken his muddy boots off outside and these he placed on the newspaper he'd arranged beside the settee. He looked around. It was strange being alone in the flat, silent save for the rain. It was the first time it had happened. He took his towel and a fresh set of clothes and headed straight for the shower, resolutely avoiding even a glance at her bedroom door. Dressed, he found an onion and some potatoes in the fridge and started dicing them up. He'd surprise her with a sabzi. Alu muttar, maybe. He added butter to the pan, then the onions, and now the next stage, he remembered, was to wait for the onions to soften. So he waited. A minute passed. Two. He removed some imagined fluff from his shoulder, then quickly, so quickly that he almost tricked himself into thinking it accidental, raised his eyes to her bedroom. What harm would a peek do? And shouldn't he get to know all of the flat, anyway, in case the inspectors asked him something tomorrow? He gave the pan a quick stir, then before he had a chance to change his mind bounded straight into her room. Silence. No one shouted at him to get out, which he seemed to half expect. It smelled different from the rest of the flat. Nicer, somehow. Was it berries? He flicked on the light. The rail for her clothes was still there. The wardrobe was new but plain: it was all very bare. No photographs either side of the bed, just matching lampshades like mauve cubes. And the shrine, of course: images of the gurus placed all along the sill, a spent joss stick in the middle. The window itself seemed to be made of a million trembling raindrops. He opened the wardrobe. Perhaps a dozen salwaar kameez. All simple, drab even. Not a single item of western dress other than her cardigans and, on the bottom shelf, three pairs of near-identical black shoes. He moved to the bedside drawers and crouched to pull open the large bottom chamber. A pair of plain white knickers stared back at him. Underneath them, several more, all white, and a packet of ladies' pads. There were bras, too, and it was one of these – white again – that he lifted out and held in his hands, running his thumbs over the spot he imagined her nipples to be. He opened the shallower top drawer. Photos. Her mother and father, he guessed, a devout-looking couple, kirpans at their side and gazing seriously into the camera. A young turbaned man who had to be her brother, though the resemblance was more general than specific to any single feature. He returned them to their drawer, in the same order, and tidied away the bra, too. Then, feeling simultaneously satiated and ashamed, he resumed his work in the kitchen. It was only when he heard the downstairs door shut that he remembered the light in her room, and sprinted to switch it off before she made it up the stairs.

That night they hung up their wedding photos, and around the TV Narinder stood the holiday pictures Randeep had brought with him on one of his first visits. They littered the bathroom with more of his toiletries, incorporated his clothes into her wardrobe, and hid the suitcase under her bed. She'd bought a pack of gummed Post-it notes, too, which she wrote on and stuck to the fridge: *Back at 6 p.m. today. Can you put the rubbish out, please? Mummyji called.*

Throughout this, the rehraas sahib played in the background, so that His blessings might be with them tomorrow. They hardly touched their dinner, Narinder especially, and went to their separate beds on empty, nervous stomachs.

They agreed Randeep should go down and open the door. There were two of them: an older man with a neat grey parting and a wrinkled handsomeness about him, and a younger round-faced lady with cropped, shiny dark hair and smiling brown eyes. They reminded him of TV news couples. They confirmed who they were, displaying their ID wallets – David Mangold, Katie V. Lombardi. Randeep showed them up the stairs, where Narinder was waiting by the dining table.

'My wife,' he announced.

She smoothed down the back of her kameez and lowered into her chair. The inspectors took off their coats.

'We're really not inspectors,' the woman, Katie, said, sitting down too. 'We hear this a lot, but please rest assured this isn't an inspection by any means. We're immigration officers, and we really are just here to see how you're getting on and whether you need any support. With finding work or getting around or language skills. That kind of thing.'

'We're here to check in, basically,' David said, cutting across.

'So, how are things?' Katie asked. She pulled some papers from her briefcase. 'It's a lovely home you have here.'

Narinder and Randeep looked at each other. She spoke: 'It's going well, thank you. It's going well.'

Katie consulted her notes. 'You don't currently work, Ms Kaur, and you're in construction, yes?'

Randeep nodded. 'It's a very good job. I've been working there for nearly eight months now.'

'Eight?' repeated David.

'I think it's more like five,' Narinder said. 'We've only been here since the new year.'

'You were both living with your parents before then, of course,' Katie said. She went to her notes again. 'London. Croydon.'

'We moved here for Randeep's work.'

'There was no work in London?' David asked.

Randeep smiled, nodded, shook his head. Already, he could feel his temples starting to hurt.

'Would you like some tea?' Narinder asked.

'That'd be lovely. Would you mind getting it, Mr Sanghera, and we'll finish chatting to your wife here?'

He scraped his chair back and turned into the kitchen. Left cupboard for mugs, the drawer nearest to the sink for spoons.

They asked Narinder about her days, what she did, whether she missed her family. Yes, lots, she'd replied.

'But I suppose you'll be looking to build your own family soon,' David said, as Randeep arrived with the tea.

'One day, sir,' he said. 'We are still getting on our feet.'

'You're both very young but I can tell you'll make wonderful parents,' Katie said, taking her mug from Randeep.

'Oh, well, the first thing we need to do is save up enough to buy a house. With a garden. Instead of renting.'

'Who's the landlord?' David asked, quick-smart.

'Mr Greatrix,' Randeep said. 'I'm happy to give you his details.'

Katie seemed pleased. 'Where would you like to move to?'

'There are some very nice areas to the south of the city. Near the Peak District National Park. Those are good areas for schools, too. After that we can start thinking about children.'

'Wonderful. What would you like?'

'A boy and a girl. I think mixed families are best.' He glanced at Narinder, who really wasn't saying very much.

Katie smiled, taking in her colleague in a slightly superior way. 'You're so clearly very happy together. I can't tell you the number of times we meet couples – ' the word spoken with emphasis – 'who seem to be struggling to adjust.'

They asked Randeep some more questions about how he was getting on: did he use the support facilities available to new immigrants? Did he know where they were in town? What about the free language courses? Not that he needed them, of course, though there were the advanced classes which might prove useful.

'There really is a lot of support for you out there. You're not alone.' Katie placed some leaflets on the table, then shut her briefcase and checked her wristwatch. 'Not even an hour. One of our shortest visits.'

She looked to David, who seemed unsure about something. 'Could I use your bathroom?' he asked.

'Of course,' Randeep said. 'It's that door just there.'

'Sorry,' Katie mouthed.

Randeep and Narinder smiled thinly, waited. The toilet flushed, which seemed like a slightly embarrassing thing for everyone to hear, and David came out looking just as unsure as when he went in. Randeep walked them to the top of the stairs. Narinder remained a few feet behind.

'You haven't taken your husband's name?' David said, looking at Narinder.

'No.' Then: 'I didn't want to.'

'That's a little unusual, wouldn't you say? In your culture?'

Katie stepped forward. 'So lovely to meet you both. We hope you have a wonderful future together. One of us will be in touch in a few months – it's all routine, you know.'

The officers clomped down the stairs, she whispering something about regulation questions and the inappropriateness of his last remark, while he wearily held the door open for her. Randeep went to the window and watched them climb into their car, belt up.

'They've gone,' he said, as the car drove off. He turned round. 'We did it.'

She'd insisted he leave that very afternoon, though he'd patently not wanted to. At first he said they should celebrate, that he'd noticed a new Indian restaurant on the way to the station. She was tired, she'd replied. She had things to do. The disappointment on his face was obvious, but she wasn't going to indulge him. They settled for a celebratory ice cream. A van's jingle sounded outside and before she could stop him he was out the door, returning with two flaked cornets. She ate hers sitting at the table, with him several feet away on the settee.

'I've enjoyed living here,' he said, in an exploratory tone.

She nodded carefully. She didn't want him getting ideas.

'It's much nicer than the house.'

'You mentioned friends, though. Avtar?'

'It's still much nicer here. I feel relaxed.' He smiled at her.

'It was always going to be a temporary arrangement. We did agree.'

'I'll pay more. I don't mind.'

She said nothing for a while. Then: 'What was all that about children? Schools?'

'I wanted to sound convincing.'

'You do know that this isn't real, don't you? This is only until the end of the year.'

'Of course I do.' There was a briskness to his voice. 'I'm not stupid. I just thought we'd got on well these last two weeks.'

She took a deep breath. 'I think you should go.'

He delayed further, taking his time to repack his suitcase, a palpable sadness in his slow movements. He tidied away the blanket, pillow and duvet and insisted he clean the bathroom, seeing as most of it was his mess. Then he shucked on his tracksuit top and picked up his case. She followed him to the door, feeling a guilty sense of relief. He handed her that month's payment, smiling across at her.

'Honestly, Randeep, you'll be fine.' She felt as if she was sending a lamb into a cesspit full of snakes. But she wasn't going to budge. She wasn't. And she closed her eyes and started counting to ten, and had got to six when she heard the front door shut behind him.

All her energy seemed to have leaked in the last few hours. Still, she did have things to do. That wasn't a lie, she told herself, though the appeal to her honesty brought no comfort. Standing at the window, she saw a bus pass at the bottom of the hill, brake lights coming on, and thought she made out Randeep running to catch it. Randeep. A strange boy. Clearly, he was struggling with life in England. It was a mistake to have let him stay so long. She was certain he'd been in her room, too, on that thundery day. Her clothes had looked handled.

Sighing, she took Karamjeet's letter from her bag. It had been tugging away under everything these past two weeks. Once, when Randeep had asked to see 'the letter' again, she'd stared at him, her pulse surging. He'd looked baffled, as if wondering what he'd done wrong. He'd meant the letter about the inspectors' visit, of course.

She returned to her bedroom, Karamjeet's threat still in her hand. She'd have to meet him, she knew that. Maybe he'd tell her parents anyway, once he knew the full story. The police, even. It was a chance she'd have to take. She opened her phone and for nearly half an hour tried to compose a coherent text. She gave up, threw the phone aside. She'd do it tomorrow. Her mind might be clearer then, after a night away from Randeep and his inspectors.

6. *NARINDER: THE GIRL FROM GOD*

Narinder Kaur had been told the story so often she believed it must be her earliest memory: that she was four years old when she'd sprinted out of their Croydon semi and straight into the road. The car braked just in time. But the funny thing was that the car belonged to a reverend, on his way to open the church, and the reason Narinder had run out of the house in the first place was because her mother had said they needed to hurry, that God was waiting for them. In other words, God, sick of waiting, had come directly to Narinder. They'd been on their way to Panjab, to spend the entire summer in the service of their guru at Sri Anandpur Sahib, and on landing in India Narinder's mother told the story to the other volunteers and they all ran their hands over the girl's head and said she must be blessed and Waheguru really was watching over her.

It was Narinder's first time in Panjab. Her mother came every summer and Narinder had always stayed behind with her father, her dadiji, and brother, but now she was four her mother said she was old enough to start understanding the importance of seva, of service.

They were given a bed inside the Anandpur temple complex, in a hostel less than a mile from the hundreds of marble steps that led to the Gurdwara Takht Sri Keshgarh Sahib. The hostel was cold and the beds narrow and hard, and each morning Narinder woke with pink welts across her back. Her mother said she mustn't complain, that they were very lucky to be so close to the Takht and that most volunteers had to find accommodation in the villages beyond the city's five forts. Worse than the welts on her back was the heat. It was too hot to make a four-year-old climb all the way up to the Takht. Instead, each sunrise, Narinder was passed to an elderly woman, a pilgrim, who took her up in one of the rentable donkey carts that hung around the back of the gurdwara. Narinder would then wait in the shade at the top of the steps, watching her mother's prayerful ascent. She watched how deeply her mother would bend to touch each step with the tips of her fingers, and how she'd touch those fingers to her forehead and mouth a silent Waheguru. Only then did she place her foot on the step and in this way move up. It was an amazing sight for the young Narinder waiting at the top: the giant white expanse of the steps triangulating away from her, and, alone in the centre of it, as true as bread, her mother in quiet standing prayer, her chunni pinned over her turban so it wouldn't slip each time she bent down, her feet pressed together at the heels, as they should be. It took her nearly an hour in that crucifying heat to reach the shade at the top, yet to her daughter she didn't seem made at all hot or bothered by the effort. *Travelling to our guru is no great hardship,* her mother would say, adding, winking, *though it would be nice if he was a little more down to earth.*

Narinder's mother was called Bibi Jeet Kaur and she was in her late thirties when Narinder was born, seven years after her brother, Tejpal. It was a great blessing, relatives had said. God had listened. Everyone at Anandpur Sahib – and everyone back in England, for that matter – said Bibi Jeet Kaur was a model gursikh. She could read the gurmukhi script with fluency. When she wasn't running the gurdwara canteen or serving langar to the congregation or in the darbar sahib performing the kirtan, she was helping youngsters understand the importance of sikhi. She'd never cut her hair but swept it all up beneath a black turban, and over that turban she wore a long, wide chunni double-wrapped across her chest. Most importantly, she was bringing up her children as gursikhs, and by the time Narinder and Tejpal were eight they knew all of the sukhmani sahib and would be called down to perform a portion of it when relatives visited from Birmingham, Leicester or, once, from Vancouver.

During her third summer at Anandpur Sahib, when Narinder was six, she stood in front of the holy book and received the cloth from which she was to cut her first turban. It was of coarse orange cotton and Narinder's arms jerked down as the old granthi dropped the material into her hands. Bibi Jeet Kaur indicated for Narinder to touch the cloth to her forehead. The whole congregation then recited the ardaas, asking Guruji to bless this child who was going to give herself in service to Him and his alms.

At the hostel, her mother took the cloth and folded it into the suitcase. 'We'll get it cut in England.'

'Can't I wear it tomorrow?'

'What's the hurry? I promise He won't mind if you wait a week.'

'But I want to wear it tomorrow.'

In truth, she wanted to be like her mother, whom she'd never seen without her kesri. Bibi Jeet Kaur did get the cloth cut the next day and a week after that mother and daughter stepped into Heathrow's arrivals lounge sporting matching orange turbans. Narinder's father awaited them. Baba Tarsem Singh was a tall, strong, shoulders-back man with a long, foamy black-grey beard whose sideburns were combed up into his turban. He nodded courteously at his wife, who nodded just as courteously back, and then he gathered Narinder up into his arms.

'My beautiful little sikhni!'

She loved her turban. Her mother taught her how to wash it and keep it starched up, how to stretch it so it retained its shape on her head for the whole day, how to tie it up, remembering to make a slim pocket at the nape of her neck so that the thick pin needed to tuck away loose hairs could be hidden away.

Narinder and Tejpal were homeschooled, and each morning, after prayers, from seven through to eleven, her father went through their lessons. Afterwards, Narinder touched her forehead to the ground, said, 'Waheguru ji ka khalsa, waheguru ji ke fateh,' and accompanied her mother to the gurdwara, to spend the afternoon doing seva.

She pushed up the sleeves of her tunic and helped the women sift through the vast trays of lentils and beans and rice. They seemed to find her funny. *Why don't you go outside and play?* But Narinder said she'd rather help. That that was why her bibi and baba sent her here. Sometimes she performed the kirtan with her mother, and while Bibi Jeet Kaur played the harmonium, Narinder sat by her side, clapping the two tiny cymbals only when her mother gave the nod.

'Chatur disaa keeno bal apnaa sir oopar kar dhaario. Kripaa kattaakh avalokan keeno daas kaa dookh bidaario. Har jan raakhae gur govind. Kanth laae avagun sabh maettae daeaal purakh bakhsand rehaao. Jo maageh thaakur apunae tae soee soee devai.'

'In all four directions the Lord's might is extended upon my head. His hand protects me. His merciful eye beholds me, his servant. My pains are dispelled. I am saved by my Lord. In his embrace, by his compassion, my sins are erased. Whatever I ask of my Lord, that and more I am blessed with.'

It was Narinder's favourite hymn, this hymn of encouragement. Reaching the end, she'd open her young eyes and it was as if the world seemed brighter, greater.

*

One morning, at Anandpur Sahib, after Narinder had finished distributing the prasad, she asked her mother for a roti. She took the roti out to the yard behind the gurdwara and tore it into small pieces and cast these pieces around. The birds came at once. They'd got used to Narinder this last week, perhaps even come to expect her and her roti. One bird seemed to be limping and each time she – Narinder always assumed any animal in pain was female – got near a scrap of roti, another bird would snatch it away. Crouching, Narinder placed a few pieces of roti in front of the creature, but it seemed too weak to take them. It tried to flap its ragged wing. Its feathers were sparse, as if other birds had pecked at it, and it made a thin sound that Narinder took as a cry for help. Gently, she gathered the bird into her palms and held it to her chest and carried it inside to show her mother.

At the hostel, she made a little bed for it out of a box that had once contained rolls of masking tape. She lined the box with a warm tea towel and placed the bird inside it. Then she turned down the ceiling fan so it wouldn't get cold. She shook beads of water from a cartoon cup into its beak, even waking up to do this through the night. And all day Narinder softened roti in the same cup of water and fed the bird a few morsels, which seemed all it wanted to take. It didn't seem to be recovering. Its skin appeared to be turning yellow and its eyes were dulled.

'Bibi?' Narinder said.

'Did you pray?' Bibi Jeet Kaur asked.

Narinder nodded.

'Then it's in His hands now.'

The bird died on the fourth day and Narinder wouldn't stop crying. It wasn't the death so much, more the suffering that preceded it, that seemed so unfair.

Her mother promised her a bird table when they got back to England, and so one weekend in September Baba Tarsem Singh drove them to a garden centre thirty minutes away and Narinder chose a mahogany feeder topped with a small square house. She and her father started putting it up straight away. Bibi Jeet Kaur said she was going to lie down for a bit, that her back had been hurting all week. They finished erecting the bird table and Narinder said a waheguru and headed inside. She met her mother on the stairs.

'Fetch your baba, beiti,' Bibi Jeet Kaur said. She had a hand to her lower back. She looked to be in agony.

It was a blood clot, and in the drive to the hospital it travelled up her spine, causing a blockage which stopped oxygen to her brain. The funeral was very well attended. No one had ever seen a better one, people said. Baba Tarsem Singh stood up and pulled round the curtain and pressed the button which activated the belt and carried his wife into the furnace. Narinder was sitting with her dadiji near the back of the room. She was nine years old and it was the first time she'd had to wear a white turban.

There was hardly any furniture in the room and what little there was looked as if it had been set there for a long time. The single bed coming out from the chimney breast, the plain wood dressing table at its side and the straight chair tucked neatly underneath. There was no wardrobe – the bed contained two drawers for her clothes. The evening light was the colour of dark amber and came through the window in two wide beams. The beams ran in parallel, along the brown carpet, over the bed, and then along the floor again, stopping just short of Narinder standing in the doorway with her suitcase. She closed the door and went down the dark staircase and into the hall. Her father was in his room, rocking on his chair, praying quietly to himself. He was so engrossed he didn't seem to hear Narinder set down her case and enter.

'Baba?'

He opened his eyes, turned his head. He was sixty-five now, and a stroke two years ago had knocked the strength out of him. His beard was fully grey. 'Ah, is it time?'

'Tejpal's outside. He'll drive me.'

Baba Tarsem Singh stood and when she touched his feet he blessed her and held her for a long time. She could feel his old hands quivering against her back.

'I wish you would come,' she said.

'I know you'll do our name proud.'

Together they said, 'Waheguru ji ka khalsa, waheguru ji ke fateh,' and then Narinder took up her suitcase and went down the hall.

She was on her way to Sri Anandpur Sahib. It was the tenth anniversary of her mother's death and time to go back.

She arrived at dawn, the sky a concentrated orange, and she stood at the marble steps and looked up to the temple. Bending deeply, she touched her fingertips to the first step and began the climb. When she got to the top she turned round and the sky had turned a broad blue and it felt as if her mother was all around her. Be with me, she said, and before she'd even said it she heard Him there at her side.

The granthi was in the darbar sahib, flicking holy water through the hall. Narinder waited until he'd finished, then said she was Bibi Jeet Kaur's daughter and wanted to do a paat in her mother's name, so her soul might be at peace.

The granthi said this was a most excellent idea. 'So few do that these days, when it is more important than ever. I assume you'll be making a healthy donation, too, hmm?'

'Ji.'

'That is excellent. I'll ask the readers to get straight on it.'

'I'd like to do the reading, please,' Narinder said. 'All of it.'

'On your own?'

'If you will allow it.'

For three days and three nights she read the guru granth sahib from beginning to end, pausing only to sip water from a steel glass a pilgrim kept topped up at her side. Word got round that Bibi Jeet Kaur's daughter was in town, doing this, and many came to watch her read. They said she really was her mother's daughter.

At the end of it, Narinder was exhausted and slept for much of the next day in her room at the hostel. Then she started to volunteer at the gurdwara, mostly in the langar hall, sometimes in the darbar sahib, once in the villages. Every day, she worked from dawn until the evening, when she'd have a simple meal of roti-dhal and water. Before bed she visited one of the smallest gurdwaras in the town, Sisganj Sahib. It was her favourite place. During the day it filled with devotees, because, as the gold plaque put it, this was where Guru Tegh Bahadur's head was cremated, after he was decapitated by the Mughals for refusing to convert to Islam. In the evenings, however, the devotees dwindled to a weeping few, and Narinder could sit by the window and listen to the evening rehraas prayers while, outside, the river lapped onward.

One evening, a shadow appeared on the carpet. Narinder

looked round. It was a woman, at the open window. She had an elongated, V-shaped face, with severe rings of black around close-set eyes. Her salwaar kameez was an old-fashioned, over-washed thing, most of its sequins missing, though the fancy way she wore her chunni made Narinder think she'd spent some time looking in the mirror before leaving the house. The woman brought her hands together and said sat sri akal.

'Sat sri akal,' Narinder replied, hands together too.

'Are you the one from England?'

Narinder said she was.

'I heard you read through the speakers. You do it very well.'

'Thank you.'

'How old are you?'

'Nineteen, biji.'

'Do you live in London?'

'Ji.'

It seemed the woman was working up to ask something of Narinder. It wouldn't be unusual. She remembered people all the time asking for her mother's help. To send a message to a relative in England. To arrange a UK–India gurdwara tour. But now the granthi of the gurdwara appeared and told the woman to leave.

'You have no right!' the woman said. 'I can speak to whoever I like.'

'We don't want troublemakers here.' He took her by the elbow and forced her on her way.

'Call yourselves God's people!' she said.

Narinder didn't see the woman again for the rest of the trip and by the time she'd returned to England had forgotten about the encounter.

*

All year she longed for the summer, when she could return to Anandpur Sahib and to the bustle of India. The intervening months were dull, made long with winter. Breakfast was in silence – there was no TV – and then Tejpal would go up to his room while Narinder stayed down to read the granth with her father. They walked to the gurdwara for lunch and so that, later, Narinder could take her turn on the harmonium. The evenings were given to prayer and after dinner she washed the plates and asked if she might go to bed. Her father would smile at her from his armchair, looking up from his book, and wish her a good night. One evening that winter she remained in the doorway.

'Baba, might I ask you something?'

'Of course.'

'There was a poster in the gurdwara. About teaching Panjabi to some of the children after school. Do you think I might ask about it?'

'I don't think so, beiti. Do you need money?'

'No, Baba.'

'And in one or two years you'll be married – these are things you can discuss with your husband.'

'As you say, Baba. Goodnight.'

'Goodnight, daughter.'

In her room, she allowed herself to feel disappointed, though she knew he must be right. To make herself feel better, she put on one of her CDs. It was a shabad – hymns were all they had – but anything would have filled her mind with musical delight. As she sometimes did, she started floating around the room, slowly, describing little circles every few steps, and when Tejpal banged on her door telling her to keep it down, she simply ignored him until he went away.

*

In the summer, the gurdwara committee sent her out into the villages with some of the other Anandpur Sahib volunteers. She handed out clothes and kitchen utensils and blankets, and international offerings with labels that read: *Kindly donated by Mr and Mrs Prashant Singh, Portland, Oregon*, or *To our fellow Sikh brothers and sisters from attendees of Sri Singh Sabha Gurdwara, Darlington, UK*.

Narinder made a little niqab of her chunni and gripped it in the corner of her mouth. It might just keep the dust from her eyes. Then she shook the metal bolt on the gate and stepped back, holding the blankets out. A lock wrenched and squeaked and the gate pulled open, and a tall, dark woman with a large gold hoop in her nose stood gazing down on her.

'Waheguru ji ka khalsa, waheguru ji ke fateh. Please take a blanket for the cold nights.'

The woman stretched her elegant neck towards the woolly stack, then her eyes shifted all at once back up to the girl.

Narinder pressed the blankets forward once more. 'Please. May God keep his hand on you and your family always.'

'The valetheni's come to do her annual pilgrimage. Her donations to the poor.'

Maybe it was the voice – snippy, too ready to retaliate – but like balls rolling into place Narinder realized that this was the same woman who'd come to the window. Last summer. The one who'd been forced away.

'You needed help,' Narinder said, without thinking.

The woman rested her hip against the gate. 'You people don't help. You pity. That's what your gursikhi is. Go on, get away. We don't need your blankets here. I'd rather freeze.'

The gate closed with a reveberating clang and Narinder stood there in the stony alley still holding her blankets. Something was wrong. She could sense it. This woman did need help. She knocked and, again, heard the shuffle and scrape of slippers crossing the courtyard. The woman was muttering even as she reopened the gate: 'They don't let you live, they don't let you die . . . What is it now? I told you we don't need your blankets. Give them to your God. He can use them to warm that cold heart a little.'

'Please, massiji. If you tell me what the problem is maybe I can help.'

The woman stayed silent, staring.

'Please. Our gurus said we have to help one another.'

Inside, the weedy little courtyard was covered in trapezoid shadows cast by the trough, at which an old emaciated buffalo nosed mildly. Here and there were peaky slops of dark-green buffalo shit, and these Narinder worked hard to avoid as she tried to keep up. She was shown to a sticky leather settee in a dark, airless room.

'The electricity,' the woman said, both index fingers pointing to the sky. 'It is gone.'

Narinder placed the blankets on her tidy lap and her hands on top of the blankets. Her silver kara dug uncomfortably into her wrist. The woman crouched on the stone floor, knees flaring out indecently.

'You want to help?'

Narinder nodded. 'Please.'

'How old are you?'

'Twenty, with the guru's grace.'

'The same age my daughter was when she left here.'

Narinder lay on her bunk that night unable to sleep. In the bed underneath was a young sikhni from Fresno and her quiet sighs swept the room. The moon hung tiny in the far window. Narinder turned back to the ceiling. Everything was so peaceful, the night so heavy-lidded, that she half thought she had only to lie there as still as she could and she'd catch herself in the act of thinking. That she'd be able to observe herself thinking. It was something she'd often tried to do, and in some unexplainable but vital way it was an impulse linked to the idea that if she flicked her pupils quickly enough she'd be able to glimpse the side of her face, the part that was otherwise only visible to her when looked at in the mirror. Childish habits, for the child in her.

She'd left the woman's home promising to do her best and, God willing, find her daughter and tell her to contact her family. Narinder imagined the girl wandering lost in England. Asking for help and no one listening, no one caring. Strangely, sleepily, this feeling of loss opened out into a further memory. They'd been sitting together at the back of the Croydon gurdwara, Narinder playing with her mother's green rosary, when Bibi Jeet Kaur smiled and said that if she were to die now, by her twenty-first year Narinder wouldn't even be able to recall what her mother had looked like. Lying on her bunk, sadness washed over Narinder in a single large wave, for her mother had been right. Already her face was becoming nothing more than a warm smile surrounded by a faraway blur.

She told her father about the encounter with the woman and the missing daughter in England. He was at the dining table, going through his pension statements, and light from the standard lamp made his beard glow red.

He listened to Narinder without interrupting, then returned to his work. 'It's a police matter, beiti. Let's not get involved.'

'Ji,' Narinder said, nodding. She looked down, looked up. 'I'm sorry, Baba, but does she not need our help?'

'I agree she needs help. She should go to the police.' He looked across, smiled. 'You can't take on all the world's troubles. I'll say an ardaas for them both tomorrow. Theek?'

'Ji. It's just that I thought I could maybe—'

'Narinder? We're not getting involved, acha?'

She nodded. 'Yes, Baba.'

She regressed into the daily shuffling between the house and the gurdwara, to reading and tidying and heating up meals, to working at the langar hall and awaiting her turn on the harmonium. If a verse was unfamiliar, she brought the songsheets home and stood them on her dressing table, against the wall. She practised by imagining keys on the wood, eyes slightly scrunched in application, whispering the words. Time seemed to vanish and her father had to shout to get her attention.

'Ji?' she said, moving onto the landing and stretching over the banister.

'I said I'm going to the bank. I'll be back before lunch.'

She heard the door shut. She paused. She was still leaning over the banister. The house was silent. She returned to her dressing table and took the piece of paper from the drawer. It was the number of the agent in Ludhiana who'd arranged the missing girl's transit. She went down to the hallway and dialled the number. The agent answered and very happily gave Narinder 'full, all disclosure' details of the fabric factory the girl was headed to on reaching England. Encouraged by how easy that was, Narinder called the factory. Another man answered – gruff voice, thick Indian accent – and said he had no sister-fucking idea who she was talking about and to leave him the fuck alone. Shocked, Narinder put the phone down, her hand shaking on the receiver. She looked over her shoulder, though she knew the house was empty.

In August, Baba Tarsem Singh said he'd arranged for her to perform the kirtan during the gurdwara's morning service.

'It must get very boring for you to spend so much time in the house with me.'

'I'm not bored, Baba. I love you.'

'You're a kind daughter. Nevertheless, it will do you good.'

She loved these services, with their accompanying birdsong, and afterwards she had at least four hours before her father arrived to escort her back home. Usually she did some sort of seva, but one morning she buttoned up her duffel coat and caught the train to Newham and waited outside the factory boss's office. She was a girl to whom waiting came easily and when the man showed up he didn't seem able to turn her away. He pored through his battered tea-stained register and said that the girl had left some months ago. He did, however, have the girl's telephone number. Did Narinder want that? The next day, she called the number from the payphone in the gurdwara and it was several minutes before the old lady understood that this wasn't her granddaughter Anastasia calling. It transpired that she had had an Indian girl staying in her basement – 'lovely-looking thing she were, too' – but not any more.

'Said she was going to Poplar. God knows why.'

Narinder smiled into the phone at that.

It was almost September before she had sufficient opportunity to attend the Sri Guru Gobind gurdwara nearest to Poplar. The granthi, a snowy-bearded man with a wooden cane, sighed disappointedly and confirmed that it had been brought to his attention that they had a handful of daughters living illegally in the area, who needed the community's help. It was rumoured they lived in some sheds backing onto one of the alleys. He gave Narinder the address and, in the name of their gurus, asked her to help these sisters of hers.

'Third one along, pehnji. Look for the rubbers,' a brown girl with severely straightened hair directed, and at last Narinder walked up the alley, sidestepping the used, teaty condoms, the thrown-out sofas and TVs. She wasn't sure which of the wooden gates to knock on first and then, sooner than expected, found herself at the alley's end, facing a concrete wall sprayed with rude green graffiti. She frowned at herself. Be brave. Guruji is with you. She firm-stepped it to the first gate but hadn't even knocked when it was hauled open and a frightening Indian woman loomed above her. Chapped pink lipstick and emerald eyeshadow. Orange-henna hair frizzing back like an afro. All on a thick, angry face with a pronounced chin-wobble.

'What the fuck you spying up and down for?'

'I'm sorry. I'm looking for Savraj.' Then, more confidently: 'I have a message from her mother.'

The woman shifted her weight onto her other foot. 'What message?'

'Does Savraj live here?'

'I said what message?'

'Her mother's worried. She hasn't heard from her daughter in months. I promised I'd try to find her and see how she is. If she needs any help.'

'We all need help, sister,' the woman said, laughed. With some effort she turned herself around and padded up a wispy little path barely visible in all the overgrowth. 'She's in her room, I think.'

Her room, it turned out, was the shed at the bottom of the garden, a small wooden structure with a white net aslant across the only window. Narinder knocked with the back of her hand. No response. She tried again, and this time she heard movement – a mattress groaning – and footsteps. The door opened but remained on its flimsy chain. A high-boned face with sharp, darting eyes showed itself. Her mother's face.

It was a dispiriting little room: damp, cold, unloved and

unloving. Not quite enough height to stand up straight. The mattress lay on the floor, beside a dog-chewed armchair probably taken from the alley outside. No electricity. Narinder wondered how she cooked or went to the toilet. Perhaps the orange-haired woman let her use the house for things like that.

'Your mother asked me to tell you to call home. She's very worried.'

Savraj sat on the grey mattress and pulled her oversized woolly jumper over her knees and black leggings, so just her feet poked out. She must have cut her hair that short in England.

'You mean she's worried about not getting any money,' Savraj said.

It had occurred to Narinder that at no point had Savraj's mother expressed fear for her daughter's safety, or concern over her welfare. The message had simply been that they'd run out of money and Savraj was to stop messing about and call home without delay.

'If you could call her, I think that would help.'

Savraj looked up, cocked her head to the side. 'You got money? I've not eaten for two days.'

She refused to go to the gurdwara, so Narinder took her to a coffee shop she'd seen near the station. They perched on high stools by the window, overlooking some workmen drilling. Narinder sipped at her small sugarless tea. Savraj dipped cake into her hot chocolate.

When she'd worked out how to phrase the question, Narinder put down her cup and said, 'Pehnji, can I ask how many sisters are in the same situation as you?'

Savraj didn't answer straight away. She finished off her cake, licked her fingers. 'Honestly. Pehnji? You sound fresher than me.' She shrugged. 'A few. There's three patakeh sheds in my alley.'

Narinder didn't understand. 'You keep fireworks?'

'It's what the men call them.' A tiny smile, as if pleased at the shock she was about to deliver. 'We make their fireworks go off.'

Narinder gazed at Savraj and nodded slowly. She didn't blink.

Savraj looked annoyed. 'We have sex.'

Narinder nodded.

'They pay. For sex.'

'I understand. I'm sorry.'

And now it was Savraj's turn to gaze at Narinder, to scrutinize her. Then she threw her head back and a great laugh burst forth. 'Oh my God! You want to make me into one of your turbanwallis!'

Her shoulders were shaking, each breaking wave of laughter rapidly overtaken by another. People were starting to stare, but Savraj's laughter kept coming, so Narinder slipped down from the stool and tried not to look like she was rushing for the door.

For all of the next week, the last of the summer, her days fell back into place: morning chores, kirtan at the gurdwara, evenings of silence and prayer. She couldn't stop thinking of Savraj, though. How strong she'd seemed. How exciting Narinder had found it, going into the world and seeking her out.

'Don't think too hard,' her brother, Tejpal, warned.

He was chaperoning her home from the gurdwara. Since she'd turned eighteen her father had decided she was never to take the evening walk alone. For your safety, he had said.

'Or maybe he doesn't trust you,' Tejpal had later suggested. 'Maybe he's seen something in you that worries him.'

He was about a foot taller than she was, with a vast gym-trained chest that made his shoulders pop up.

'What do you mean, don't think too hard?'

'You're thinking. Don't. Girls shouldn't think.'

'Oh, shut up.'

'You'll get into tra-ble.'

She ignored him – there was no way he could have known about Savraj – and the following Monday she effected a return to the sheds of Poplar. Her gurujis wouldn't have just left it at that, she told herself. No one answered the door, so she waited beside the battered green gate, shielding her eyes from the low sun. A kid raced up on his bike, wheelied round at the wall, then just as quickly disappeared left out of the lane. Later, a postman emptied his sack of mail onto the rubbish tip. 'Fuck that!' he said, grinning at Narinder.

Savraj arrived, and, ignoring Narinder, unlocked the gate. Narinder followed her in, maintaining a distance.

'Pehnji—'

'Don't. I'm not your pehnji or your bhabhi or your didi. I don't want you babeh-brains near me.'

Narinder stopped at the shed door. She reached inside her pocket and held out the brown parcel. It was tied with orange thread. 'For you.'

'What is it? A gutka?' Savraj said, snatching at it. It was a velvet box inside which rolled a tube of red lipstick.

'Yours is running out. I noticed, last time I came.'

Narinder visited Savraj once, sometimes twice a week, leaving the gurdwara after her morning kirtan and always getting back before her baba arrived. Usually she'd take along a margarine tub filled with whatever sabzi they had at home. They'd give the tub to the landlady to put in her fridge and head to the coffee shop near the station. The workmen were still drilling outside.

'You should know I've started talking to my family again.'

'Oh, peh—! Savraj!' Narinder embraced her. 'I can't tell you how happy that makes me.'

'Calm down. Your turban'll fall off. I guess I'd just got sick of her always pestering me for money, like I'm earning millions. Like everyone in England must be earning millions. But I think she understands now. I'll only send what I can.'

'Oh, that's brilliant! It's so good that you help. I knew you would.'

'Did you? I don't see what's so good about helping others, though. If they only become reliant on you. Then you're just part of the problem.'

'But we have to help,' Narinder insisted. 'I couldn't live with myself if I just walked away. I don't know how people can do that.'

Savraj laughed a little. 'I've never met someone who talks like you.'

'There's nothing wrong with giving your life to His teachings. Our gurujis—'

'Oh, shut up. I've met worse fundos than you. I don't mean the things you say. I mean the way you say them. It's like you actually believe in your words.'

Narinder didn't know what was wrong with the way she spoke her words. Did she sound too serious? Was that it? 'I'm better when I'm singing.'

'You sing? A singing preacher?'

'It's true,' Narinder said, laughing. 'Come and hear me. I'm singing tomorrow morning.'

'To the gurdwara?' Savraj clucked her tongue. 'Not my scene. If a beardy's going to touch me up, he can pay for the privilege.'

'I'll be with you.' She reached out and placed her hand on Savraj's arm. 'You don't have to do what they make you do. We'll look after you. We look after each other.'

Finger by finger, Savraj released her arm from Narinder's hand. 'What who make me do?'

Narinder could tell from her voice, like a knife being unsheathed, that Savraj knew what she was driving at. Narinder said it anyway: 'The men.'

'Hmm. The men. What if I told you that some of those men are from the gurdwara?' Savraj leaned in. 'What if I told you that they don't make me do it? That I enjoy doing it?'

'Stop it. Please.'

Savraj laughed, mirthlessly, and Narinder looked away.

On the Tube she stood staring at her reflection in the knife-scratched windows. Two months now. For two whole months she'd tried to help this woman. Perhaps she wasn't strong enough. Good enough. Why hadn't she been made good enough? She exited at East Croydon and tunnelled through the press of humanity, surprising commuters with her turban, and walked home via the clock tower, whose advertised music library she thought she might one day visit. Outside her front door she straightened the chunni over her turban, and, stupidly, wiped a hand across her lips, as if she'd been the one wearing lipstick. She twisted the key and slipped inside, up the hallway, and was turning into their front room when a blow came crashing down on her face, sending her sprawling to the floor. She heaved, staggering up onto her hands, only for her brother to grip her at the neck and drag her across the carpet and into the centre of the room. She could hear her father rushing down the stairs, the thud-step thud-step of his cane.

'Tejpal! How dare you strike your sister!'

'If she's going to hang around with whores then we'll treat her like one.'

'Enough!' Baba Tarsem Singh said, struggling to kneel beside his daughter.

'Let her do more, you said. Let her do her singing. All day in the house is not good for her. What has it got us? What will people think?'

'I'm helping!' Narinder said. 'You can't stop me!'

'Watch me.'

'I'm not doing anything wrong!' she shouted, and launched the CD remote by her hand at her brother's face. It cracked against his forehead.

'You nasty little . . .'

But Baba Tarsem Singh banged his cane hard on the table. 'I said, enough!'

*

On the night of Diwali, Narinder covered their dining table with a hundred and one tiny clay dia lamps. She did this every year and it was always a ravishing display. Liquid shadows slid across the ceiling, and the shapes thrown against the wall were a dark vibrating mass. It made her feel as if she was underwater, submerged deep within His love. She drew out a chair, closed her eyes, and, quietly, began to sing. She felt weightless, like she was gliding. The words seemed to generate inside her a different heartbeat, and behind her interlocked lashes, sunlight squandered itself across the world. Swallows swooped over copper fields. And in the penance of song she could hear His breathing. At the end of the shabad, she opened her eyes and saw Savraj outside the window, staring with her forbidding brown eyes.

'I need money,' she said.

Narinder had shuffled her down the side of the house, away from Tejpal who was upstairs with his Khalistani friends. They huddled together for warmth, to whisper.

'You haven't come to see me in months,' Savraj went on.

'How'd you know where I live?'

'I asked. At the gurdwara. I was sure you'd be there tonight. What happened?'

'Nothing.'

'Your baba?'

Narinder was silent, then: 'I've never been so angry. When they said what I was doing was wrong, I just wanted to scream. I wanted to shout. I've never been like that.'

She looked across to Savraj, who seemed to be considering this, saying nothing.

'Your chunni,' Narinder said, and Savraj pulled her chunni – borrowed from the gurdwara, Narinder could tell – forward so it veiled her face completely, comically.

'Happy? Now all I need is a husband who doesn't mind me hiding my ugly face all day.'

'Shh! And you're not ugly. You're so beautiful.'

'Do you wish you were as beautiful as me?' Savraj said, lifting the chunni away.

Narinder was wounded. 'I'm fine how God has seen fit to make me.'

'You God people.' She reached for Narinder's hand. 'You're not even close to being ugly. Your eyebrows are a bit bushy and maybe some make-up once in a while, but other than that you're fine. I wish I had eyes so clear.'

Narinder didn't know what that meant. To have eyes so clear.

'Nin,' Savraj went on, more seriously, pressing Narinder's hand. 'You have to help me. You're my only friend. I don't know what'll happen if you don't.'

'You need to escape. Tell the police.'

'Police!'

'I'll speak to Baba. I'll make him understand.'

'Just this one time. Can't you help me just this one time?' She looked at her wristwatch – a digital thing with a white plastic strap. She was in a hurry.

'How much do you need?'

They cut through the adjacent avenue, and, under the glowing green cross of a pharmacy, Narinder handed over one hundred pounds, taken from a savings account her father had opened for her wedding. Savraj kissed her, thanked her, promised she'd pay it back soon, and then ran for the Tube, her borrowed chunni trailing around her neck.

Tejpal was waiting in the hall and it was clear he'd seen them.

'I've warned you,' he said. 'What'll Dad say?'

She looked at him, into his long, thin face on which a beard had only this year started to stake a claim. It gave him a harder look, the beard. Or maybe he was just hardening into a man, and the beard made no difference. And when did he stop calling their father Baba?

'Don't cause a drama, Tejpal. It's late. Have your friends gone?'

He stood firm. 'See her again and I'll really do something.'

'Tej! Should Guruji not have fed the hungry sadhus? Should he have walked past? Now come on, and shut the door – it's freezing.'

He yanked her back by the elbow. 'Your duty is to uphold our name. Mine is to protect it.' His face softened and his hand moved to her cheek. 'Don't force me into doing something I don't want to.'

Narinder laughed, nervous. 'Tej, you're scaring me.' She freed her elbow. 'Let's forget about it and go to sleep. We'll wake Baba up.'

A week passed, then two, and when Savraj still hadn't been in touch Narinder told her baba she was going to the community centre to use their new harmonium, and instead caught the train to Poplar. It didn't take her long to find the alley, despite the months since her last visit, and the green gate was, somehow, hanging on. Narinder knocked, twice, and twice again before she heard a door shut and the woman saying that she was coming for fuck's sake.

She still wore pink lipstick and emerald eyeshadow, and her hair was braided into thin lanes of orange cornrows.

'Hello,' Narinder said. 'You might not remember me. I—'

'I remember you.'

Narinder nodded. 'Could I see Savraj, please?'

The woman shrugged. 'It's a free country,' though she made no move to let Narinder pass.

'Could I come in, please?'

'Why?'

'To see Savraj. Is she not in? Can I leave a message?'

'Sure you can. But I won't be giving it to her.'

Narinder looked at her, confused. 'Has something happened?'

The woman bit into an apple that Narinder only now noticed had been in her hand the whole time. She spoke as she chewed. 'I don't know. Perhaps it has. She don't live here no more, does she. Hasn't done for months.'

'Oh, I see.'

'Did your friend not tell you?' the woman said, smiled.

'Do you have a forwarding address?'

She shrugged.

'Please?'

The woman, seemingly tired, seemingly bored, dropped her shoulders and looked away. 'Nothing for free, turban lady. Not in this life.' Then, with something of the full sadness of things: 'We all need help, now, don't we?'

Later, she stood outside the estate agent's – Randhir Chahal Lettings – and stared at the brown-framed windows of the flat above. It must be round the back, the stairwell. She walked for perhaps fifty metres, the street spawning buses, until a gap between two launderettes led to a partially concreted car park. She cut a diagonal towards the rear of the estate agent's, where a metal staircase led to a carrot-bright front door, a rose painted into the glass. Narinder knocked once and took a careful step back, mindful of the drop. The door opened.

'Sat sri akal,' Narinder said.

The young woman nodded, smiled.

'Is – I was told my friend lives here?' She didn't know whether to use Savraj's name, or if that would blow whatever cover she might have created for herself.

'Your friend?' the young woman said, just as Savraj walked into view behind her and Narinder lifted her hand to wave.

Savraj's room-mate brought Narinder orange squash in a china cup riven with cracks and asked her to take a seat. 'Please, sister.'

Savraj was quiet. She wore the same blue-grey apron as her friend – it said *Dashwood's* in a modern font along the hem – and sat on a straight wooden chair near the fan heater. The heater's clackety whirring was pretty much the only noise in that sparse room.

'You go,' Savraj said, and Narinder looked up, but no, it wasn't aimed at her. 'I'll follow.'

The friend asked Narinder to forgive her leaving – 'But I hope we meet again' – then grabbed her phone and went. They listened to her quick tread on the metal staircase.

'That's Karthika. We work together.'

'At Dashwood's,' Narinder said.

'It's owned by him downstairs. One of our former "customers". We clean offices.'

Narinder smiled, encouraging. 'That's good. That's so much better.'

Savraj frowned, as if unconvinced. The lines, Narinder thought. The two lines that widened down from her nostrils to the twin tips of her mouth. How much deeper they'd got. Furrows now. And her eyes. They seemed dimmed. Grey hairs, too. She hadn't noticed it last time. Perhaps it had been too dark. She'd aged so much in a few months. The winter, the work, the worry.

'I hope you're taking care of yourself,' Narinder said.

Savraj stood and went into a doorless room in which Narinder could see only the corner of a candy-striped mattress. She came back pulling a slim roll of notes from a maroon purse. 'I can give you the rest later. Next month. I'm sorry you had to come all this way.'

Narinder stood up too, so they faced each other. 'I didn't . . . I don't . . .' She shook her head. 'Please keep it.'

Savraj's arm fell to her side. She moved to the grubby white settee and perched on its edge. 'I need to ask for more money.'

Narinder sat beside her. 'What's the matter?'

She stayed silent, staring.

'Tell me, please. I want to help.'

Savraj rubbed together the notes in her hand, the crisp insect rustle of them. 'Mamma's not well. They say it's cancer.'

Narinder put an arm around her friend.

'We can't afford the treatment. That's why I came round. It doesn't matter how hard we try. We were hoping the rice would pay for it, but the land caught a disease and my brother doesn't know what else to do. None of us do.'

Narinder squeezed her friend's shoulder. 'Stay strong. God will find us a way.'

'There is no way,' Savraj flashed. She looked up to the ceiling as the tears coursed down.

No brother, no mother, no father. She sits with face turned, no turning known. These lines kept coming to Narinder. For several nights now, she'd lain awake in bed thinking of Savraj cold in that flat, face turned away from God, and the thought seemed to clot into a physical ache along Narinder's abdomen. Throwing back her duvet, she headed downstairs and into the kitchen. She put the japji sahib on a low volume and closed the kitchen door. She prayed for Savraj's family. Her lips moved in rapid silence, hands clasped in her lap, thumbs together and knuckles directed to heaven. She spoke to Him and He spoke back, the wingbeats of His presence changing the air around her. When the stereo clicked off, she raised her clasped hands to her face and finished her prayers. So deep had those prayers been that she hadn't heard her father come in and sit beside her. It was still dark outside.

'Your kesri?' Baba Tarsem Singh said.

'Upstairs.'

It was strange how unprotected, fearful even, she felt without her turban during the day, but how much closer to Him she felt without it at night. She didn't understand it.

She told her father about Savraj and the hardships she and her family were facing and how much she wanted to help them.

'I went yesterday and gave her food and a little more money. But I want to do more, Baba. Please don't be angry.'

'You've done what you can. She'll find her own way to Him. Let's just hope your brother hasn't found out.'

'You've always said we should help people find their way.'

'She's as loose as dust. The night will bark before she thinks of anyone but herself.'

Narinder looked away, at the night shadows along the wall. 'Her mother's dying,' she said flatly. A long silence followed. Then, something that had been bothering her: 'Baba, why does God make people suffer?'

'Hm?'

'I've asked Him. Maybe I'm not listening hard enough, but I don't know why some people have to suffer so much.'

Baba Tarsem Singh sighed. 'You do ask difficult questions, beiti. Must we know all the answers? Might not we trust Him?'

Narinder looked down at the table and pressed her thumbs together until the tips blushed.

'Our gurus suffered. They gave their lives for us. There's an answer of sorts there.'

'Yes.'

'Why would we do anything, feel anything, for anyone else? If there's no pain, how can there be love?'

'Yes,' she said again, and put her hand on his.

*

One spring evening, she brought Savraj kadi-chawl and munghi-di-dhal, food that could be preserved and eaten over several days. 'How is massiji? Have you spoken?'

Savraj nodded, ate, running her tongue over grey teeth. 'Same. Hopefully soon we'll have enough for the operation. My brother found a job.'

'See? I said God would show a way.'

Before she left, she reminded Savraj that, as normal, she'd be going to India in the summer. 'To Anandpur Sahib.'

'Oh good, out of this cold. Does it ever get warm?'

'Anything you want to send your mother?'

'You're going to visit?'

'Of course I'll visit. I'll even stay a few nights and help if I can.'

Narinder buttoned up her cardigan, her duffel coat. Savraj walked her out of the door, onto the metal landing, and said, 'Mamma will be so pleased you're coming.'

It was the hottest summer. Only ten o'clock, and the men were out of the fields and rushing indoors, to ceiling fans and chilled glasses of nimbu-pani. In the bazaar, shopkeepers lay asleep on their menjhe, not expecting any trade. A buffalo lay sprawled in the tree shade, blinking fatly each time a guava fell onto its wide head. Standing at the bottom of the marble steps, she took the metal pin from its neck pocket and scuttled it along the brim of her turban, and as the turban loosened the sweat oozed down her forehead. It felt nice. She heard her name and saw her mother at the top, holding a basket. Then they were together and the basket was piled high with slippers.

'It doesn't matter,' Bibi Jeet Kaur said. 'I'll do it myself.'

When Narinder woke, she lay still, recovering, gaze fixed on the three dazzling white blocks the sun had painted on the ceiling.

She couldn't remember the route to Savraj's house and all she had to help her was the family name. The teller at the grotty municipal bank waved her away, saying couldn't she see it was deposits this morning? Further on, outside the mandir, a man with pyramids of Spanish apples arranged on his cart accepted a ten-rupee note and directed her to an alleyway about twenty paces back.

She recognized the gate, the solid metal and slope of it. Even the wild spiderbush sprouting from the wall cast a shadow at her feet that seemed familiarly menacing. She knocked two, three times, pushing the tall hatch open.

'Massiji?'

There was no one in the courtyard, just the same buffalo that had been there the previous year. She stepped through the hatch, hitching up her salwaar so it didn't snag on the rivets. A television played in the back room, and maybe that was a foot dangling over the menjha. She started across the yard, head tilted, peering. Something shot down beside her.

'Bibi!' she called out, arms protecting her head. But it was a man, only a man. She looked up to the roof from which he'd jumped, then back at him.

He clapped the dust from his hands. He had the same sharp nose as Savraj and his white shirt was so full of sweat she could see the hair underneath. Narinder averted her eyes.

'Sorry,' they both said.

He laughed. She didn't.

'I'm Savraj's friend. From England. I've come to see massiji.'

'Oh, Narinderji?' He took a step towards her, so close she was forced to lean back slightly. 'Savi's always talking about you.'

Other than siblings and cousins, no boy had ever stood this near to her. She wished he'd move away, though he appeared to be enjoying her flutter of awkwardness.

'Mamma's just lying down.' He bowed, making a sweep of his arm. 'Please allow me to take you before her.'

'No, no, please don't wake her. Let her rest. I'll come back tomorrow.'

He had a languid, appraising smile. 'It'd be like turning away the Rani of England.'

Savraj's mother lay propped against the wall, a gold cylinder of a pillow squashed behind her. The TV showed a game show, similar to one Narinder thought they had in England. She slipped out of her chappals, her feet warm on the stone floor.

'Massiji?'

She said it twice more before the eyes opened and a greyer face than she remembered turned to look at her. Narinder spoke softly: 'How are you? Would you like some water? Did you get my messages?'

Massiji pulled herself up straight and blew the hair from her eyes. 'When I'm dead, then talk to me like I'm a baby. And even then I'd still wipe the floor with you, chikni, cancer or no.'

They talked. Narinder reassured the woman: Savraj was doing fine. Working, eating, living with friends. Nothing to worry about.

'Tell her we need double next month. The rent on the bike is due.'

'Any other message? How much you miss her?'

Massiji looked across, doubtful. 'I don't understand.'

Later, Narinder asked how the treatment was going – *they want to slice off my breasts,* Massiji said – and put forward her plan to stay around and help for a few days.

'You don't have to.'

'But I want to.'

The older woman snorted. 'I can imagine the look on everyone's face.'

'No one will mind. It's a form of seva, in my eyes.'

Savraj's brother returned with three glasses of pomegranate juice. He must have been to the bazaar to get it.

'Maybe you can sleep in Kavi's room,' Massiji said, laughing, and Narinder blushed.

She didn't stay, in the end. She didn't seem to be needed. And Savraj's brother unnerved her, with his smile and the way he'd whistled for a rickshaw even though she'd have preferred to walk. She passed the following week improving her harmonium skills: a renowned ragi was visiting from Bikaner and offered to help the young ones with their playing. It was a beautiful time, full of devotion and song. On the Sunday Narinder was chosen to play for the evening rehraas prayers and afterwards the famous ragi told her that her singing was like a balm for the troubled soul. Pleased with herself, she packed the instrument away into its wrinkled leather bag and heaved it to the metal cupboard in the adjoining room. Coming back through the alcove, she saw Savraj's brother – Kavi – lounging around with his friends at the back of the darbar sahib. A blue ramaal was tied around his head like a bandana and his feet were bare. He saw her too and pressed his hands together in respectful greeting. Narinder responded likewise, and then one of the granthis ushered the boys out, saying this was God's house, not one of their cricket grounds.

She started seeing him everywhere – in the market, near the hostel, eating at the dhaba she passed on her way home. She saw him one gruellingly hot afternoon in the langar kitchen, handing out cold lilac sweat towels to the women. And there he was the next day, too, praying with his head bowed. His kara was as it should be: chunky and clean on his wrist. And his hair, she noticed, wasn't slopping with smeary oil like that of his friends. It was blowier, the lengthier strands tidied away behind his ears.

'You have a lovely voice.'

He'd caught her in the tiny garden outside Sisganj Sahib, singing to herself, as she did sometimes of an evening. One of the best things – perhaps the very best thing – about coming to India was being able to roam, to breathe. She drew her chunni onto her head. 'Sat sri akal, ji.'

By rights, she should have addressed him as bhaji, as brother. That would have set the proper and chaste tone for their encounter. But she hadn't. She didn't know why. And of course he'd picked up on it. Look at him smiling.

'How's massiji? I keep meaning to visit.'

'I thought maybe you were avoiding us.'

'Of course not.'

'Avoiding me, then.'

Her mouth moved, until: 'The seva this year is more than usual.'

He plunged his fists into his pockets and sighed deeply. Irritatedly? His top two buttons were undone. He had long eyebrows. She could feel something at base start to unstitch, releasing into her feelings she'd not experienced before.

'When do you go back?' he asked.

'In two weeks. If you have a message for Savraj I'd be happy to deliver it for you. I'm sure she'd want to receive a message from her brother.'

'Don't you think we have phones?'

Narinder felt herself redden. 'Of course. I didn't mean to say—'

He was laughing at her, and almost but not quite tweaked her elbow. 'I'm only joking, Narinderji.' He emphasized the 'ji', which made her feel threatened. 'So you're telling me I've got two weeks to convince you to give me a kiss?'

She didn't know what to say. She looked around but no one was paying them the least attention. She stepped away – 'I have to go' – and concentrated on the sound of her footsteps on the stone path, which seemed to be flaunting her exit.

A week before her flight home, it was time for the blanket distribution, and she wrote her name against the three sub-district villages to the west of the city.

It was the festering, sticky end of the afternoon when she got to Savraj's house. The spiderbush plant had bloomed horrendously well, conquering both sides of the metal gate and most of the sandy wall. Blankets against her chest, Narinder opened the gate hatch and stepped over the gutter and into the courtyard. To her right, a small cardboard box kept crashing against the wall, the feet of a cockerel padding underneath. Narinder lifted the box off the poor thing and the bird squawked away in a flap.

'Massiji?' she said, turning back to the courtyard.

She could hear noises from the back room. The TV, probably: Massiji watching one of her game shows. Narinder wandered across the yard, ducking neatly under the washing line. She stopped at the door. It wasn't the TV, and she knew she should turn right round and leave. She pushed the door open, silently, smoothly. On the menjha Kavi was lying on top of a girl, both of them naked. Narinder watched, fascinated, feeling pangs of shame and excitement. The girl smiled and tapped Kavi's shoulder. He twisted round and Narinder said sorry and hurried back across the courtyard and out of the gate, the blankets still clutched to her chest.

She could not shift from her mind the image of him locked against the girl, the look of pleasure on the girl's face. She went to bed feeling wretched. She wasn't jealous. Either of the girl or of what they were doing. She'd never so much as touched a boy – she'd never so much as seen two people kissing, with her own eyes – and she had no intention to start. It was more that she felt inadequate. She felt like a child. No. She felt that the world made her feel like a child. Because she had no conception, let alone experience, of the thing that it thought was the most adult act of all. She moved onto her back and placed a hand under the blanket, on her abdomen. All evening, a warm glow had been spreading out from her stomach and down towards her thighs. She slid her hand beneath her navel, then further down, and clenched her buttocks and pressed them hard into the mattress. The metal springs resisted. From below she heard this year's room-mate lift her head, then, perhaps a full minute later, put it back down.

Narinder collected her ironing from the dhobi. The ironing board at their hostel had gone missing a few days earlier.

'I hear you're leaving soon,' the dhobi said.

Narinder said she was.

'Arré, then why so glum? There's always next year.'

Narinder paid the man and made her way back through the bazaar. It was true. She did feel glum and she wasn't sure exactly why. She forced her clothes into the overstuffed suitcase and with renewed determination zipped it closed. Because this moping was ridiculous. She was twenty-one, for God's sake.

She was on kitchen duty that afternoon, chopping coriander mainly, when she saw him through the doorway. He was taking off his shoes, tying a ramaal around his head. Surely he wouldn't dare come and talk to her. In front of all these people. But that was exactly what he seemed to be doing, smiling with each step. Narinder tried to concentrate on her chopping.

'I'd like to give my sister a message.'

She looked up, wrong-footed. 'Oh. Of course. I'd be happy to.' She waited for him to go on.

'It's a private message. Can I talk to you later?'

She frowned, resumed chopping. 'I'm sorry. I'm leaving soon. No time.'

A silence, then he said, 'I'll be outside after rehraas. I'll see you there.'

'I said I don't—' But he'd moved away already.

He was waiting for her at the bottom of the marble steps, his back to the gurdwara. His cuffs were folded to midway up his forearms, thumbs hooked into his rear jeans pockets. Narinder's sandals clacked loud on the marble, louder still in her ears. He turned round and waited for her to complete the descent.

'Shall I take those?' he asked.

She gave him a couple of the blankets from the stack in her hands. 'If anyone asks, we're talking about tomorrow's donations.'

'You've thought of everything.'

'I'm busy, bhaji,' she said combatively. 'Please tell me the message and I promise to deliver it as soon as I return.'

For a long time he looked off to the side, where a handful of boys were getting caught up in the sunset. Still looking away, he said, 'Mamma doesn't have cancer.'

Narinder blinked, confused, but then thought she understood and her arms loosened across her chest, her hardness dissolving. 'But that's the best news! Oh Waheguru! How long have you known? Does Savraj know? I have to call her!'

Kavi raised his hand, speaking over her in a clear voice: 'She never had cancer. We thought she did but they got it wrong. There's nothing wrong with her.'

Time halted. Narinder didn't move.

'I think when Savi first borrowed money from you, she wasn't lying. But then they wanted to keep you thinking she had it.'

'Your mother and sister.'

'So you'd help us.'

'Help you?'

'Help me get a visa.'

Visa. Cancer. Lies. It all floated around Narinder's head, dots she wasn't able to connect. Kavi made an impatient noise.

'I was meant to get you to like me so you'd agree to being my visa-wife. So I could come to England and earn enough to pay for the cancer treatment.'

'But there was no cancer.'

He shook his head again impatiently, as if he needed to get beyond this. 'But after meeting you in the garden that time I told Mamma I wasn't going to do it that way.' He paused. 'I don't know why.'

'Because you have a girlfriend,' Narinder supplied, not really thinking straight.

'What? Oh – ' he made a swatting motion with his hand – 'she's just one of the chamaars. She gets passed round. I'd never treat one of our own girls like that,' he added, apparently keen that she understood this fact about him.

She said she had to go. She wanted to get away from him. From him and his cruel, lying family.

'Wait.'

She ignored him.

'Please.'

The desperation in his voice stalled her. He came closer. She could smell his aftershave, like old leather.

'I'm an honest man, believe it or not, so I wanted to ask you honestly. Not through deceit. Savi said you're a very caring girl, so if you could see it in your heart to help us I'd be forever in your debt.'

'Help you how?' she said, her voice rising until she could hear the pain in it.

She saw him swallow. 'We've saved and sold enough to cover the visa permit. Of course, when I start working in England I'd pay you every month. I promise you that.'

'You want me to marry you?' The question came as a shriek.

His finger leapt to his lips. 'It would only be for one year. You'd be free again after.'

Narinder said she was going. He blocked her off.

'Let me go. You're being crazy.'

'We can't make anything of ourselves here. Land rents keep going up. Rates are going down. Nothing's growing. It's impossible. I'd be forever in your debt.'

She believed him. She was sure she did. But before she could allow herself to be even halfway persuaded, she looked away, away from him and his aftershave. Darkness had fallen in the sudden way that happened here in summer. She said he could keep the blankets, seeing as she'd not left them with any last time.

She couldn't go to India the following year; she had to stay at home and meet potential suitors. There was another one coming tonight. From Surrey, Narinder thought, as she stepped into the bath and under the shower.

It would be the fifth family so far this year. Three had been rejected for not being sufficiently gursikh, and the one family who had seemed suitable was discovered to have an older daughter who'd married out of caste. The boy's parents hadn't mentioned it during the initial meeting, and it only came out when Tejpal asked some relatives in India to dig into the family's background.

Narinder turned the shower off and pulled her long rope of hair, as thick as her wrist, forward over her shoulder, wringing the water out. She hoped this match would be suitable, if only for Baba's sake. Tongues would start to wag if they kept turning boys away. She dressed in a simple chocolate salwaar kameez and chose her saffron turban from the cupboard. When she was halfway down the stairs, Tejpal said they were here, parking up. Narinder returned to her room and sat on the bed, waiting to be called. She'd spent hours here these past few months while prospective families were entertained downstairs. It gave her time to think. She was certain there were women out there who'd view her with pity, women who'd implore her to live her own life and thought all marriages of this design were the product of some sinister family pressure. She wondered what that meant: living your own life, as if your life was a thing closed unto itself. Did these women not understand that duty, that obligation, could be a form of love? That the pressure she felt was the pressure of her love? It might not be their kind of romantic love, but maybe it was all the purer for that. Sometimes she wanted to ask these women to imagine some manure on the side of the road, with all their friends and family circled around it. Now imagine leading your parents to the manure and burying their faces deep in it, in front of all of their friends and all of their family. She wondered how many of them would actually do that, in the drive to live their own life. There was an uncle when Narinder was young who'd cut a razor blade across his wrists because his daughter had run off with a Muslim boy. That, obviously, was an extreme case. Most parents whose daughters had strayed lived with their aura of shame, and everyone else gave them a wide berth, as if they really did stink of shit.

She couldn't hear a thing – usually there'd be laughter or some sort of exaggerated exclamation as they discovered an acquaintance in common. But there was nothing. Perhaps they'd gone already. Maybe the boy had rocked up puffing smoke into Tejpal's face and been straight away sent packing. The thought made Narinder smile. She stepped across to the window and held aside the net. The car was still there. A black estate-type thing.

When Baba Tarsem Singh did come up he held Narinder by her shoulders and said he thought this might be it.

'They seem like a decent family.' He kissed her forehead.

Eyes lowered, she followed her father into the room and sat next to Tejpal. Her chunni hung far forward, like a veil. They could probably only see her mouth, her lips. Through the crêpe of her chunni she counted seven maple-cream biscuits, brought over by some massi in Calgary. There were half-empty cups of tea, too, and samosas arranged into a squat pyramid. Beyond the table was the boy and his parents, or their knees, at least. His must be the middle pair of legs, in trousers a delicate shade of green. The parents continued chatting as if she hadn't even entered the room. What plans did they have for vaisakhi next year? Do they go to the nagar kirtan? And then the boy's mother asked if the girl might be shown and Narinder felt her father's hand on her elbow. She raised her head and pulled back the chunni a few inches. Still, her eyes were cast down, fixed on a woody knot in the coffee table. This was always the worst bit. Wondering what they'd make of her face. It never seemed to get any easier. 'Beautiful,' the boy's mother said, like all the boys' mothers have to say.

'Karamjeet said he'd like to talk to the girl alone,' the boy's mother went on. 'If you don't mind?'

Perhaps her father looked to Tejpal, because after a pause it was her brother who spoke. 'What's there to mind? We're as modern as anyone else.'

They left – 'I'll show you the conservatory' – in a rustle of salwaars and closing doors.

Alone with him, Narinder looked up. His turban was a deep royal blue and maybe a touch big for his round face. His beard was nice and full – no trim-singh, he – and a neat little kandha hung on the chain around his neck. Just like the one she wore.

'Hey,' he said. 'You as nervous as me?'

'I thought I was going to be sick.'

He nodded – he knew the feeling. 'I'm Karam, in case no one's thought to tell you.'

'They did,' she said, relieved he had a sense of humour. 'And your age, job, education, height and complexion. Always complexion.'

'You practically know me inside out, then. Let's get married.'

A silence formed, which Narinder tried to find words to dispel. She settled for an inadequate smile.

'Sorry,' he said. 'Nerves. You nervous, too?' A shake of his head. 'Sorry. You answered that already.' A sigh. 'I'm making a hash of this, aren't I? I was aiming for funny-but-sincere.'

Narinder took hold of the situation. 'Did you have any questions? They'll be back soon.'

'Oh. OK. Well, I think your father said you go to Anandpur Sahib every year?'

'I try to. I enjoy the seva there. And I fully intend to carry on even after my marriage.' She said this with conviction, ready to argue her case, though he didn't seem to have been listening.

'To be honest, I just wanted to make sure you weren't being forced or anything. I'm five years older than you and . . . Well, you hear stories, don't you?'

She assured him no one was forcing her to do anything.

'And you'd be happy living in Surrey?'

'I don't see what difference that makes.'

He seemed like a good person. They'd spoken on the phone a few times this last month and often she'd found herself smiling into the receiver. He was kind and honest and had twice now said how happy he was and how lucky he felt that she'd agreed to become his wife.

Narinder felt a hand on her shoulder, making her start. It was her baba, come to walk her home.

'I was calling you.'

'Oh, sorry, Baba. Is it time?'

'What is this?'

He gestured to the posters on the gurdwara notice board, of Panjabi men and women who'd died trying to cross into the UK.

'It's very sad,' Baba Tarsem Singh said.

She hadn't really been reading them. The posters had been on the board for many months now. 'Yes. I'll pray for the families.'

'Is that what's been on your mind?'

'Nothing's been on my mind.'

'You've been lost in your thoughts a lot recently.'

'I'm sorry, Baba.'

'You've been very quiet.'

She smiled. 'I'm always quiet.'

He tried a different approach. 'Is it the wedding? You are happy with the match?'

'Yes, Baba.'

'It's a good family.'

She nodded.

'It's natural to be nervous.'

'I'm fine. Really.'

'And excited. Nervous excitement, they call it.'

She wondered whether to tell him that she didn't feel excited. Not at all. But she couldn't. Instead, they linked arms. 'Why don't you take the evening off?'

'Oh?'

'Yes. I'll escort you,' she finished, emphasizing the pronouns.

*

During dinner one evening she received a text message: *call me. urgent. Savi di.* Narinder slid the phone under her thigh. That 'di', she knew, had been calculated to remind Narinder that she was the younger of the two, the one who should obey.

'Still enjoying your new phone?' Baba Tarsem Singh said, reaching for the pot of raita.

'Who was it?' Tejpal asked.

'No one. A friend.'

'You don't have any friends.'

'And how would you know?' Narinder said.

He really was getting insufferable these days. With his collection of Khalistan turbans and Puffa waistcoats. Only last week he'd had a go at Narinder for not bathing before evening prayers.

She deleted the message. They'd not spoken once in the last year. Probably she needed money. Probably she was only going to feed Narinder more lies. A week later another text arrived, Savraj threatening to turn up at Narinder's house if she didn't agree to meet.

'I don't want to meet you or any of your family,' Narinder said, on the phone. 'You're all liars.'

'Meet me for Kavi's sake.' Before Narinder could work out how to respond, Savraj said, 'The gurdwara at six? Today. For Kavi's sake.'

They met in the langar hall and sat cross-legged on one of the runners. Opposite them, two young girls raced to finish their bowls of rice pudding. She'd changed her hair, Narinder noticed. Even shorter, with streaks of cheap copper. She'd given up her cleaning job and gone back to the sheds.

'More money for less time,' she said, pulling a few notes from her gold lamé purse. 'What I owe you.'

'Is that it? Is that why you wanted to see me? Can I go now?'

She made to get up. Savraj stayed her with a hand to the knee. 'Do it for us.'

'Do what?'

'What Kavi asked of you.'

It was so ridiculous she nearly laughed. 'I'm leaving.'

'They can't survive. Kavi's even talking about selling his organs.'

'Lies. More lies.'

'Do you think we'd have lied if we weren't desperate? Do you think I wanted to go back to the sheds?'

Narinder turned her face away; she wished Savraj would stop.

'It would be one year only. And no one would have to know. Not even your family. I thought if when you're over there this summer you could go with Kavi to see the agent, then it could all be taken care of before you have to come back.'

All the time Narinder was shaking her head. 'It's illegal. It's against the law. People could go to prison.'

'Think of the number of people you'll be helping. Not just us. But our children, and their children. We'll love you till we die.'

'No one has to die,' Narinder said, facing Savraj full on. 'Come to the gurdwara. We'll get advice. We'll help Kavi find a job. In India. A good job.'

'There are no jobs. There is only corruption. Or if there are jobs they go to the fucking chamaars with these government quotas.' Savraj reached for Narinder's hand. 'Please. Help us.'

Narinder shook her head, said sorry, that she couldn't take the risk, couldn't do it to her family, her father, and she kept shaking her head and saying sorry until Savraj gave up and left the langar hall for the dingy evening outside.

She told her father what had happened. Baba Tarsem Singh had been marking out passages in his gutka when Narinder appeared in the doorway and asked if she might interrupt him.

'It's not enough that they trick you, they also have to make you feel guilty,' he said afterwards.

'I'm scared they'll do something dangerous.'

'You've tried harder to help them than anyone else ever has. It's between them and God now.'

'What if her brother comes to harm?'

'Let's pray that doesn't happen.'

She knew he was right. And yet: 'I'm worried I should be doing more. That I'm not doing enough.'

'There is nothing more you can do, beita. It's in God's hands. You're getting married. Did you tell her that?'

Narinder hesitated.

'Narinder?'

That evening she was summoned down from her bedroom. In the rocking chair sat her father, a guilty look on his face. Her brother stood with his back to the portrait of their mother. His arms were folded across his chest, hands arranged in a way that cupped each elbow, and his beard shone blue in the mix of lights playing through the different windows. He'd set his turban on the sideboard, so his topknot flopped like a loose apple. When they were children, he used to let Narinder pull on this funny-looking hairball.

'Are you happy with this match?'

She'd been prepared for this. 'Of course. It all seems fine to me.'

'You're sure? Certain?'

'Get off my case, Tejpal.'

'Don't be too hard on her,' Baba Tarsem Singh said.

Tejpal raised his hand and their father withdrew into the chair.

'If you're not happy tell me now. While I can still do something about it. Because if you leave it any longer I won't be able to do anything. And I won't let you shame us. I won't let you make it impossible for Dad to walk into the gurdwara with his head held high.'

He approached, the blue light falling abruptly from his beard to his feet.

'Well?'

She could feel herself glaring at him, at the idea that she would ever do anything – had ever done anything – to shame their father. 'I've told you. Get off my case.'

*

Every so often she'd try calling India or Savraj. She wanted to know that the family was OK. That they'd not been ensnared by the kinds of agents she'd read up on recently. The ones who took all your money in exchange for a shoddy visa that wouldn't even gain you entrance to the airport. But the information from India was sketchy – the PCO she called didn't really know the family she was asking after – and Savraj never returned her messages. In time, winter broke to spring, and then summer, and somewhere along the way Narinder gave up trying to contact them. She was getting married in December and she needed to start coming to terms with that fact.

She'd seen Karamjeet twice since their introduction. Once when he'd come with all his relatives to drape a phulkari chunni over her head and officially claim her into the family. They'd not spoken that day. She wasn't absolutely certain she even remembered having seen him. The second time, they met secretly in Hyde Park on a Friday afternoon in late May. He brought along a small hamper full of posh vegetarian bits and pieces and they'd found a bench by the Serpentine, the basket of food balanced awkwardly between them.

'More juice?'

She said no, thank you.

He put the carton back. 'You're not going to Anandpur Sahib this summer?'

'There's too much to do. For the wedding.'

'Well, maybe we can go next year. Together. It's a while since I've done some proper seva.'

She nodded. 'That'd be nice.'

He nodded, too. Seconds ticked.

'So, have you thought any more about where you'd like to go? After our wedding?'

'I don't mind. Hemkund Sahib sounds nice. Isn't it only open in the summer?'

'June to October. But I have contacts. It is a lot of walking, though. I wouldn't want you to be bored.'

'It'll be worth it.'

'Maybe we can ask them to read an ardaas. For us. For our future together.'

'That would be nice.'

Nice, nice, nice. She wished she could think of something else to say.

'It's funny we both wore the same colour,' he went on. Their turbans, camel-brown. 'Maybe it's a sign. We think similarly.' He was smiling determinedly through his beard.

'It's good that we have shared interests,' she said, relieved to have landed on something positive.

'Yes. Though I think shared attitudes is more important. And I think we have that as well. Don't you?'

'Yes. I do. You definitely need that because otherwise things can be very . . . very . . .' She didn't know how to end the sentence.

'Not nice?'

On their way to the Tube at South Kensington, past the Science Museum, he spoke more about his job teaching physics in a secondary school, the joys and frustrations of it. As she listened, she realized that she was fond of him. He was gentle. He was patient. He made allowances for her nerves and understood how much bigger a step this was for her. He had so many sweet qualities that surely it didn't matter that she felt no . . . No what? Sometimes she remembered the moment Kavi had nearly touched her elbow. That flare of desire. She felt none of that walking beside Karamjeet. Instead, the thought of lying next to him one day soon came trailing a strong undertow of disappointment.

He followed her through the barriers before calling her back. 'Mine's the District.'

'Oh, OK.' She smiled. 'I guess I'll see you at the wedding.'

He was looking at her. He seemed on the brink of something. Then he stumbled in for a kiss, his eyes open and intense. She recoiled, and perhaps even made some sort of sound.

'I'm sorry,' he said.

'No, I just . . . You surprised me.'

'I know. Anyway – ' he shook his hamper pointlessly – 'I'll telephone you?'

'I'd like that.'

He nodded – he didn't seem to believe her – and headed for the escalator. Narinder watched him descend, his turban last to disappear. He looked crestfallen and she felt terrible.

For the wedding everything had been more or less decided. It would be a simple occasion, with none of the ostentation that most families engaged in these days.

'I hope you don't mind not having a reception,' Karamjeet said. 'The sooner we get you home the better. Only six months to go,' he added, laughing anxiously.

She closed her phone and felt better, lighter, their conversation set aside for another three days. She was fond of him, though, she reminded herself, as the front door opened and Tejpal came hurtling towards her.

'She's here.'

'What? Who?'

'Your friend. The whore. I can't believe Dad let her in the house.'

Savraj was sitting on the sofa, fingers threaded around a mug of tea. Her black PVC coat was several sizes too small, straining at the armpits, and her white chunni had fallen off her head. Baba Tarsem Singh sat beside her.

'Savraj,' Narinder said. The white chunni. 'What's happened?'

She couldn't speak. Tears ran haltingly down her cheeks. Narinder looked to her father, who explained that the brother had died. He'd tried to make it across in a coach. Hiding in a gap cut into the ceiling. It seems they suffocated. Three of them.

'They found the bodies in Russia,' Savraj said. 'They just dumped them in the snow.'

Narinder groped behind her for a table or chair to lean on. 'That can't be true.' She spoke as if to herself.

'I don't know how we're going to survive. Mamma's on her own.'

Narinder saw her father nod at Tejpal, and perhaps Savraj did too because she suddenly tugged her coat about herself and said she should go. That she'd bothered them enough with her grief.

'I just didn't know what else to do. I'm sorry.'

Tejpal left the room briefly, returning with a small wad of notes which he passed to his father. He in turn pressed it into Savraj's hand. 'Take care of yourself, beiti.'

Savraj touched his feet, then tipped the money into her pocket and walked straight past Narinder and out of the door.

She couldn't sleep and at first light she left the house and walked fast to the gurdwara. It was locked. She banged on the door and a sleepy-eyed granthi in white robes let her in. She raced up the steps, dragging her chunni on over her turban, and entered the darbar sahib, brought up short by the silence of it, as if she'd expected to find Kavi there. There was no one save for a second granthi, sitting with the holy book. Narinder fell to her knees and muttered prayers, rocking to and fro, speaking to Him.

When she returned home, her father called her into the front room. 'It's true. I made some phone calls and she's not lying.'

It hadn't occurred to her that Savraj might have been making it all up. She stood in the doorway, agitated, unsure where to put her face.

'You mustn't blame yourself,' Baba Tarsem Singh said, coming to her. And the voicing of this possibility, that she could have averted this death, arrived as both relief and accusation, and Narinder slid down the doorframe and covered her face with her hands.

One night, a week later, her father came into her room and she felt his weight on the end of her bed, heard the slight rattle of his cane.

'It wasn't your fault, daughter. You couldn't have known.'

'But I did know. I knew they'd try something like this. And still I did nothing.' She pressed her knees together to stop their shaking. Her bedside clock ticked gamely on.

'You're not sleeping. You're not eating. Look how dark your eyes have become. From all this worry.'

'I destroyed a family, Baba. My actions killed someone and I don't know how I'll ever forgive myself.'

'God will forgive you. He knows your heart.'

'But why did He let it happen? Is He teaching me a lesson?'

'Narinder, we've spoken about this. We have to trust Him. I promise you it will all make sense in the end.'

She turned round. She needed to see his face. 'Does it make sense that my mother died?'

He looked away, with clear difficulty. 'If it pleases Him.'

It was a frightening thought, that God might be pleased by their suffering.

In the morning, hoping it might help, she went to the gurdwara. There was a poster on the way in reminding the sangat to make time for next summer's trip to Anandpur Sahib. When she'd volunteered last time she'd felt a great sense of goodness, that she was on the side of goodness. But real goodness, she now understood, wasn't chopping vegetables in the canteen or distributing blankets. It was what her gurus had all done. It was putting yourself at risk for other people. It was doing the things that others wouldn't do. It was sacrifice. And she'd never done that. The opposite was true. The one time she'd been tested, the one time someone had asked her to take a risk, to make a sacrifice, she'd walked away.

She stared ahead, mouth open, as if the granthi's words were sliding right down her throat. Maybe it wasn't such a ridiculous idea. Maybe she could do it. It seemed to be something that had been in the dark suspension of her mind ever since Kavi first asked her, but only last night had it poured over her brain, like a ramallah lain over the granth. It would be a risk, and that was the point. It wouldn't help Kavi but it would help someone like him, someone who was struggling to survive. Maybe it would help her, too. Because how could she stand by and do nothing? Knowing what she now did? The wedding could wait. Karamjeet could wait. It was only for one year and then she'd come back and get married and life could carry on as expected. One year of her privileged life. One year. That's all it was. As she thought these things, the guilt seemed to lift a little and for the first time in weeks she felt a smile come to her face, a smile in which could be seen a curl of excitement, in which the wedding was so happily, so boringly far away.

*

She was in Amritsar, showing the man her diary and indicating the number. She'd been coming here every day for the last week, at more or less the same time, and still the man asked if it was a UK call. He dialled the number from his side of the counter, and when the phone in the booth started to ring he pointed to the receiver. Baba Tarsem Singh was on the line.

Ringing home every day had been one of her father's conditions. She'd said she needed to spend some time doing seva, to gather her strength before the wedding. Tejpal had been hard against it. Barely six months from the wedding. How would they explain it to Karamjeet's parents? Baba Tarsem Singh talked him round and it was agreed that she could go for two weeks only and that, other than to call home every day, she wasn't to leave the grounds of Anandpur Sahib. Narinder hadn't set out to go against their wishes. The whole idea of marrying someone to help them come to England had begun to seem slightly mad; though that was before she pulled her white chunni from her suitcase and headed out to see Savraj's mother. The gate was repeatedly padlocked and there was no sign of the animals. A woman on the neighbouring roof shouted that they'd gone. She didn't know where. Maybe the city? They couldn't pay the rent, you see. Did Narinder know the son had died trying to get to valeyat? Narinder tried to find a lawyer, but the closest the town had was a local man who dealt primarily with village disputes. He advised her to go to Amritsar, which was two hours away.

She told her father that, yes, she was still in Anandpur Sahib, then replaced the receiver on the prongs of the phone and paid the man. It was a five-minute walk up the Jallianwallah Bagh road to her lodgings inside the Golden Temple. Dusk was falling, and a passing cyclist switched on his flashing red headlight. She walked through the channel of water at the entrance to the temple and went in through the eastern gate. She loved the view from here, especially at this time of day, when the evening-red sun dipped behind the temple and the lake became a wet pasture of liquid gold, and the whole world seemed but a reflection of His glory. She'd prayed that morning, asking Him what to do, and had received direction. It was only for one year. She thought of three young boys lying dead in the Russian snow and knew she was doing the right thing.

'There's a good supply of lawyers near the furniture market, madam. In Hall Bazaar,' the auto driver added, early the next morning.

The streets were already steamy with traffic and the bazaar was impossibly clogged. She'd walked and with some loose directions from the driver picked her way through the rickshaws and golguppe sellers, the scooters and carts and students on their way to college. Huge banners hung between rooftops, images of a bespectacled man who reminded Narinder of a distant uncle.

The lane widened out and she took the rightmost fork in the road and then the left turn immediately after the big wedding-card emporium. A little further on was the tatty white-and-blue board of R. K. Santoshi Advocate. She peered in. It seemed busy. At least three people were fanning themselves in the waiting room. With an internal waheguru she pushed open the glass door and waited for the receptionist to look up from her huge white box of a computer. She had heat-frizzed hair and – now she looked up – a strikingly beautiful face.

'I'd like to speak to a lawyer, please,' Narinder said.

The woman plucked a form from her in-tray. 'Fill this in. The next available appointment is in two months.'

'But I need to speak to him today.' She took the form. 'I don't mind waiting. It's only that I'm not here for very long.'

'Two months,' the woman said, returning to her keyboard.

By the early afternoon, Lawyers4u was the fifth office she'd tried, though the first to offer her an appointment for that same day. It looked shabby – a second-floor operation with peeling beige paint and a giant plant starting to brown. There was no receptionist, just a man in a khaki two-piece handing out numbered green chits. Narinder took her ticket – 00183 – and a young man in a white lunghi offered her his chair. The chit-man called out, 'Ticket number 155.'

Four hours later, her turn came. The lawyer's office was tiny, the size of their bathroom at home, and far too small for the huge oak desk he seemed to insist on. He was older than she'd expected – it had looked like the outfit of someone at the beginning of their career, not that of a slight, elderly, grey-haired man like this. A brass prism on his desk read D. S. Yadav LLB, and on the wall hung a certificate confirming his membership of the Amritsar Bar Association. There was nowhere for her to sit.

'And how can I help you, miss?'

Narinder cleared her throat. 'I'm looking for a husband.'

It took a few minutes for the details to be straightened out. She wanted to help someone who needed to come to England. It was important that this person really needed the help. Money wasn't a consideration – she'd need a little for when she arrived back in England, but that was all. The important thing was that the person must really need her help.

Mr Yadav called for a chair – 'Forgive me, but if I let everyone sit down they'd never leave' – and he leaned back, fingers making a steeple beneath his chin.

'I hoped you might be able to assist me?' Narinder said, taking her seat.

'People have such strange ideas, madam. They think we break the law, not uphold it.' He must have seen the alarm in Narinder's face because he flung out his arms. 'But how could I not help a daughter of God, hain?'

He made several phone calls, one call seeming to link to the next, and by the time it sounded like he was getting somewhere the window behind him had darkened.

'I heard there were a few desperate for visa-wives at the club last month,' he said, dialling again. 'It seems our Mr Harchand might be one of them.' Someone must have answered. 'Dinesh Yadav Advocate. Call for Vakeel Sahib, please – I see. Is he coming back tonight? – That will be all. Thank you.' He reached for a letterheaded pad and spoke to Narinder as he scribbled. 'Take this with you. Go to the Circular Road Basant Avenue crossing. I'll ask Bilal to flag an auto. There you'll see H. S. Dokhlia Law Association. Give him this.' He tore the page off and held it out. 'He'll help you.'

Narinder looked at the paper, at the darkness outside.

'What was I thinking?' Mr Yadav said, and crumpled the paper into a ball, letting it fall where it landed. He stood and removed his lawyer's cloak from the back of his chair. 'Come, madam. Let's find you your husband.'

They took an auto across the city, over misshapen concrete roundabouts and past a grand-looking cinema that Narinder somehow recognized. At the lawyer's office, the receptionist rose to explain that Mr Dokhlia wasn't back yet but would they please take a seat in the waiting room and she'd bring them some tea-coffee.

Narinder sat down. She slipped her hand into her bag and touched the picture of her mother she'd packed that morning. Beside her, Mr Yadav was flicking through a waiting-room magazine. It had an X-ray of someone's teeth on the cover. She should thank him for all this, she thought, and was just opening her mouth when the door buzzed and an obese man in a lawyer's white collar entered.

'Harchand!' Mr Yadav exclaimed, striding over, arms wide. 'How long you make us wait, to experience the pleasure of your date.'

'Arré, Poet Sahib, what can I say? It's sangraand, no? And when Mother insists, Mother insists.'

They embraced casually and Mr Yadav took this other lawyer by the elbow and steered him into a corner. She caught bits – spouse-visa, England – and every now and then this Mr Harchand looked over. They seemed to finish by agreeing Mr Yadav's cut – percentages were mentioned – and then the new lawyer started making his way across the grey carpet, smiling at her. Narinder stood up – do the right thing, she kept telling herself – and readied herself to greet him.

7. JOB PROTECTION

Late spring, and the shell of the hotel was finished, a modern cuboid touching the sky. The ceilings were next, and they worked into their lunch break to get the first one in and levelled off, girders fixed at the mortise points. Afterwards, they swung down from the scaffold, took off their yellow hats and reached for their flasks. It was always water now; getting too warm for tea.

'I think we should drill the holes in first,' Randeep said. 'It's hard holding them up like that. My shoulders kill.'

'Can do,' Avtar said. 'But if the grooves go wrong it'll be coming out of our bhanchod wages.'

'What do you think?' Randeep asked Tochi.

'What you asking him for?' Avtar said.

Tochi tore his roti in two. 'Nothing's coming out of my wages.'

They ate in tired silence, hard hats upturned in their laps to dry the sweat out.

'Where is that limpy bhanchod, anyway?' Gurpreet asked.

'In his cabin,' Randeep said. 'All day on the phone.'

Gurpreet sent someone to find out what was the matter and the envoy returned saying that there'd been a delay on the drainage system and the engineers would come tomorrow. In the meantime, they should get on with the work they were being paid to do.

The drainage system didn't arrive the next day. Neither did the crane drivers, nor the electricians, who were meant to have started wiring up the site nearly a month ago. One other team of migrant labour hadn't turned up either. Mid morning, they all gathered around John's Portakabin, demanding to know what was going on.

'There's a few problems with the council that need ironing out,' John said. He had a defeated air about him.

'Where is everyone?' Avtar asked.

'They're not happy with the financial accounts for this project. They say some things aren't adding up.'

They stared at him, not at all sure what this meant for them.

'I'll give your lad Vinny a call. No point in standing around here. Too nice a day for that,' he added, closing the cabin door on them.

'Vinny bhaji will sort it all out,' Randeep said, as they waited.

'He better,' Avtar said, throwing him a tennis ball. He looked over to Tochi, sitting alone by the windbreak. 'Because I don't trust your room-mate one bit.'

It was late and the light patchy when the van parked up. They grabbed their backpacks and ran towards it, shouting.

'It's just a few glitches,' Vinny said, raising his hands in a calming gesture. 'Big project like this, it's inevitable.'

'What does that mean?' Avtar asked.

'It means this greedy cunt's been taking a bigger cut than he should've,' Gurpreet said.

'It means,' Vinny said, drawing out the word, 'you get a few days off while I sort it all out. Enjoy the sunshine. 'S not often we get weather like this. Make the most of it.'

'But what about our money?' Avtar asked.

'You live rent-fucking-free,' Vinny said, suddenly sharp. 'What more do you scrats want?'

Gurpreet and a few of the others took a bat and a ball and a crate of beer from the fridge and swaggered off to the park. Avtar, meanwhile, made for his room and split what money he had into the usual four piles. Then he made his four piles into two. He wouldn't eat. He'd tell his parents he couldn't help with the household bills this month. Still he was short for the loan. He had to make a decision. If he didn't pay the mortgage the bank would seize the shop: that wasn't an option. So his only choice was to ask Pocket Bhai's men if he could make up the deficit next month. It was a risk. They'd slap him again, but perhaps this one time – he turned his eyes to God – they'd stay away from his family.

Later, Randeep knocked and poked his head into the room. Avtar was sitting cross-legged on his mattress, a computing textbook in front of him and his hands hovering over the open pages as if for warmth. He was gazing towards the window, at the brick wall beyond, and seemed not to have heard Randeep enter.

'Studying?'

'Hm?' Avtar nodded, winced. 'Not really.'

'When are your exams?'

He closed the textbook, hard. 'Two weeks. I'm not going, though. I've decided.'

'What do you mean, you're not going? Of course you are.'

'I can't risk leaving my job. Not now.'

Randeep dropped to the mattress, beside Avtar. There was an excited gleam in Randeep's eyes. 'So you're going to go fauji?'

If he went, even if he didn't pass – as long as he showed up – then Dr Cheema said his visa would almost certainly be extended for another year, and he could carry on without any fear of being deported. As long as no one found out about him working. If he didn't even show up then his visa would be revoked, and the police would come to find him. He'd be worse off than those who snuck in illegally, because at least no one knew who those young men were. Therefore, not showing up would be, at least according to the doctor, a really stupid decision.

'Fryers off?' Malkeet asked. He was a big, chesty dump truck of a man, topknot showing through his American baseball cap, sweat patches in the pits of his T-shirt.

'Ji, boss.'

They locked the back door and walked round to the forecourt, where Avtar helped pull down the shutters.

'You not got a home to get to?' Malkeet said.

Avtar passed him the padlock. 'Actually, bhaji, I was wondering—'

'Here it comes.'

'—if there were any extra shifts I could do?'

'Nope. Ask me in September. When the gori's gone.'

Avtar nodded. 'Would it be OK to get an advance on next month's pay, then?'

'What do you think?'

'It's only that the building work seems over and I owe—'

Malkeet flung out his arm, palm raised, as if to stop an onrushing vehicle. 'Don't. Don't tell me. I don't want to know what you are or who you owe. I don't need to know your problems. Now, was there anything else?'

Avtar asked if he'd still have his job when he came back from London.

'Why?'

'Please promise me I'll still have my job.'

'Is someone coming for it?'

'They might.'

'Well, that'll be for me to decide then, won't it?'

'I've worked hard for you. Can't you promise me my job?'

Malkeet took his car keys from their apron pouch and de-alarmed the old estate; he left the Mini to his wife. 'Do you think I'd have got anywhere in this country if I made promises like that?'

*

Tochi ate his evening meal early, then washed and shaved. He returned to his room, locked the door, and, in his underwear, sat facing the cracked swivel-mirror propped against the window. He draped a towel over his shoulders and twanged the tortoiseshell comb – several of its teeth missing – and combed his wet hair forward so it clung together in thick slats over his eyes. Because he was now trusted to work on the till, Aunty had told him always to come looking – he grasped for the English word she'd used – 'presentable'. He patted his hand around the sill, docking on the scissors, and began to snip.

There were noises downstairs: doors shutting, laughter. A plate smashing, maybe. Tochi cut about two inches off his fringe, the hair falling into a child's red potty gripped between his feet. He rinsed the scissors and the potty and returned them to the bathroom, where a quick head-bath dealt with the fussy little filings of hair stuck to his neck. Back in the room, he unfolded the letter. The handwriting was untidy, loopy, with great curling tails and circles drawn above certain letters. Or perhaps the circles were letters in themselves. There were crossings-out, too, probably where she'd decided against a word or simply misspelled it. In any case, it all made no sense to him. Maybe he should have accepted Aunty's offer of translation. But he hadn't wanted to give her false hope. He looked at the photo again: a pretty, shy, nervously smiling face. A fullish body, nicely curved, wrapped in an orange-and-brown salwaar kameez. The doorknob rattled, followed by a knock. He stashed the letter and photo under his mattress, then dressed. As he opened the door, Randeep was standing up from the keyhole.

'Gurpreet's back. Drunk again,' he said, passing inside, speaking quickly – caught out. 'I threw my dinner down as quick as I could. They'll be drinking all night now.'

Tochi reached for his boots and forced them on, leaving the laces untied for now.

'You going to work?'

'Looks like it.'

'Some of the guys are saying that Vinny bhaji's finished. That it's dangerous to stay here.'

'It is. You should find somewhere else.'

Randeep placed his cutlery on the windowsill. He noticed a few hairs stuck to the mirror. 'What about you?'

'London.'

'Really?' He turned round. 'Have you found work there?'

'Not yet.'

'But when you do, you'll go?'

Outside, a bus rasped up the hill.

Tochi stuffed his hand under the mattress and brought out a sheet of light-blue paper. 'Read this for me.'

'What is it? Is it from home?'

'Just read it.'

It was a short letter, which Randeep read to himself first and then translated sentence by sentence: *Hello and sasrikal, Bhuaji asked me to say a little about myself. Well, I'm Ruby. I'm 37 and I have a little boy who's 12. His name's Santokh (which probably tells you how strict my in-laws were! Bhuaji said she's spoken to you regarding my divorce so I won't go into that here but I'm happy to talk about it if you want to meet.) I'm a homely girl and like being with my family. I work part-time in a supermarket. I'd prefer to stay in the area after marriage as I don't want to disrupt Santokh's schooling again, but if that's a problem I'm happy to talk about it. I don't mind that you're illegal but if things do move onto the next stage then I'd like to do things properly (i.e. get proper visas from India and live here by the law). I've included a photograph of myself. Thank you and best regards, Ruby.*

Above the salutation Randeep discerned, vigorously crossed out, 'Bhuaji says you're very good-looking!' She must have decided that was a bit too much informality.

'So where's the photo?' Randeep asked.

'They don't listen,' Tochi said heatedly. 'I'll have to find another job.'

Randeep understood. 'You lied.'

'I had to.'

He passed the letter back to Tochi. He felt quite moved that Tochi had asked him to read it, that he'd trusted him. 'You know, there's a flat sitting empty underneath Narinderji's. We could go there: you, me, Avtar bhaji.'

Tochi was standing at the window, looking out.

'You've never mentioned your family,' Randeep said, pushing a little further.

'I'm not going to start.'

'I'm here because my daddy isn't well. He tried to kill himself.'

Tochi nodded, slowly. 'Be happy yours is still alive.'

At the shop, they seemed to have heard everything.

'I don't think he'll get away this time,' Uncle said, about Vinny. 'They know too much.'

'Poor boy. He's only trying to help. What his family must be going through.' Aunty double-kissed the air, sympathizing. 'What about you? How are you surviving now?'

'Fine,' Tochi said.

'Do you want any extra shifts?'

'I wouldn't say no.'

Uncle asked him to do an hour on the till because Aunty would be cooking upstairs and he needed to complete next week's cash-and-carry order. She came down at ten o'clock, the ends of her fingers yellow with turmeric, and started to cash up. Tochi seized his jacket.

'Staying for dinner?' she asked.

Tochi said he wasn't.

'I spoke to Ruby today. And I know you keep saying no, but she's so keen to meet you. She's a great girl.'

'I'm sorry, aunty.'

'But I don't understand. It could be everything you've dreamed of. None of this hiding or lying or worrying about the police. A passport. A British passport. Isn't that what all you boys want?'

'I'm sorry,' he said again, and nodded at her husband on his way out.

He could smell the saag as he arrived back at the house. He made for the stairs – he wasn't hungry – but froze when Gurpreet called his name.

'I hear congratulations are in order! You're getting married!' Others joined in, laughing. 'You're reaching beyond your dreams, Bihari!'

Tochi bolted up the stairs and into the room. Randeep followed, running. 'I'm sorry! They overheard. I was only telling Avtar bhaji. I thought he might be able to help. With work.'

Tochi pushed him to the wall and held him there. Fear sprang to Randeep's face.

'You're the same. You think I'm just someone for you to laugh about.'

He shoved him again, then let go, and Randeep stood there gasping, a hand to his throat.

They'd tied coloured ribbons to the cabinets and scattered confetti over the kitchen counter. He could hear them still laughing behind the door to the TV room. Tochi filled a glass with water. He downed it, one hand on the tap, filled it again, drank half and chucked the rest.

Avtar came through the beads and leaned against the fridge, running a hand down his tired face. He hadn't changed out of his uniform.

'Randeep told me what happened. He's sorry.'

'Right.'

'Maybe you should apologize, too.'

'He should learn to keep his mouth shut.'

'It was an accident. He was trying to help you.'

'I don't need anybody's help.'

'He's a kid. He's the youngest here.'

'About time he learned.'

Avtar pushed off the fridge, sighing resignedly. 'Whatever. Just don't let it happen again.'

'Right.'

'I mean it. I'm giving you a chance now. Next time, pick on someone who'll fight back.'

Tochi turned his face, sharply, as if someone had pressed a button in his neck. 'Like you?'

'If it happens again, or if you steal my job, I'll wrap your head around that fucking wall.'

Tochi put his glass in the sink.

'I'm not scared of you,' Avtar said. 'You act like some man of mystery, some tough guy. It doesn't scare me.'

'Maybe it should.'

'There's only one person I'm scared of.' He pointed up.

'Good for you.'

'Meaning?'

'Meaning your God's a bastard.'

'I think you should take that back.'

Tochi came into the centre of the room. 'Is this all you can do? Talk?'

They circled round, fists raised loosely. Tochi aimed one to the stomach, which Avtar dodged. 'Nearly,' Avtar said, and crunched a blow across Tochi's cheek, cutting it. Tochi reeled back, then flicked in and caught Avtar twice: chest, side. Avtar doubled up, heaving. Sick came lurching up his throat. He forced it back down and with an almighty roar launched himself at Tochi, throwing him back onto the counter and sending all their Tupperware boxes whirling about. They grappled, cussing and punching, and were still kicking out when the guys from the TV room rushed in and split them apart.

Two evenings later, Tochi shouldered the final sack of potatoes from the storeroom and carried them into the shop proper. He took a knife from his back pocket to slice the bag open and was counting out the first few when a gold saloon parked up, half on the kerb. The driver wore an oversized turban and had an impressively floury beard. Two women got out as well, and all three walked past the window to the metal stairs at the side of the shop. It was the girl from the photo, and her parents, no doubt. Aunty came round from the counter.

'It's only a meeting. There's no harm in you two saying hello.'

'I can't. I won't.'

She started fussing over his cuts, touching his face. 'Better. Now wait down here and I'll call you when the time's right.'

He stared at her, at the tremendous glee in her eyes.

'Oh, you'll thank me in the end,' and she disappeared behind the sliding panel and up the stairs.

He could run. He should run. They didn't know where he lived. But he hadn't had his wages – he wasn't working for nothing – and back at the house they were still laughing about it all. It filled his ears. The man had a big turban: obviously Indian-born, raised. It was reckless, asking for trouble. But he wasn't going to run. Not any more.

Aunty led him upstairs, where the girl – woman – was sitting on the settee, clearly anxious. Her mother sat beside her, and sunk into an armchair was the girl's father, legs crossed at the knees, thumbs drumming the mahogany whorls of the armrests. His sky-blue turban gave him at least an extra foot in height, and it came to too precise a point at the tip, as if it could be used to prise Tochi open. Uncle invited Tochi to come and sit next to him, on the settee opposite the girl.

'How are you, beita?'

He looked up. It was the girl's mother. She had a kind smile, an understanding voice. Tochi nodded.

Aunty came back into the room – she'd closed the shop for half an hour, she said – and handed round plates of snacks, which Tochi declined with a single shake of his head. No one said very much.

'Maybe we should give Tarlochan and Ruby some time alone?' Aunty suggested.

'We haven't even heard the boy speak yet,' the girl's father said. 'He looks like he's been in a fight.'

'Twelve, fifteen boys in a house,' Aunty pointed out. 'Tell me where there won't be scuffles?'

'How long have you been here, son?' the mother asked.

He took care to speak in flat, accentless Panjabi. 'Nearly two years.'

'Two years and already a chance of a passport. You must think you've won the lottery,' the father said.

'It's kismet, isn't it?' Aunty retaliated. 'It's God's plan.'

'What's your pichla?' the mother went on.

Tochi said nothing. Aunty spoke: 'I told you. His matah-pitah are no more. He was an only child.'

'What? No taih-chacheh, no land, no anything back home? Everything he has is here?' The father moved his hands, as if displaying the air in front of him; as if by 'here' he really meant 'nothing'.

'He's here – ' the word said with force – 'trying to make a better life. He works on a building site all day and for us in the evening. What more do you want from him?' Aunty turned to the girl's mother. 'Bhabhi, you understand? I don't know why my brother is always looking for badness.'

'This is about my daughter's future. It's my job to look for badness.'

'Tell me about your pind,' the mother asked.

'It's Mojoram,' Aunty said.

'The one close to Jalandhar?' the father asked.

Tochi nodded.

'And how long had your people been there?'

A pause. 'Forever.'

'I thought most families there settled after the troubles?'

'Some, not all.'

The father nodded. 'So what happened to your family land?'

'I sold it to come here.'

He tilted his turban towards the ceiling, peering down the length of his nose. He uncrossed his legs and crossed them the other way, and there was something ominous in the way he did this. 'You must've had buffalo?'

Tochi nodded slowly.

'Remind me – it's been so long – what's that knot called our people use to tie the buffalo?'

Aunty made a face. 'Keep your nostalgia for another day. We're here to discuss these two and their marriage.'

'How many kanal make a khet?'

Tochi said nothing.

'And how many marleh go into a kanal?'

'Bhaji,' Uncle said, in a firm tone that kept its inflection of good cheer. 'I think nerves are getting the better of us all!'

'I just want answers,' he said. 'Answers that our people would know in their bones.'

They all turned to Tochi, whose eyes hadn't moved from the carpet.

'And I don't know any of our people, especially if he's a doabi like he claims, who would say "sold" in the way he did.'

Vho bikhegiya instead of eh bichhdah.

'What nonsense,' Aunty said. 'And enough of this. It's time we gave these two some space alone.'

The father stood up, turban inches from the ceiling. 'I think we four should talk, too, because something here smells very wrong to me,' and they vanished into a bedroom, leaving Tochi and the girl sitting opposite one another on the hard brown settees.

'I'm sorry about my dad,' she said. 'He's overprotective. After everything that's happened.'

She was trussed up in scarlet clothes and gold jewellery, chunni twisted vine-like across her throat. Only her eyes gave away her age – some fourteen years on Tochi.

'Do you want to get married?' she asked.

'I don't think your father's going to let that happen.'

'It's my decision.'

Tochi nodded.

'Your Panjabi's different.'

He nodded again.

'It doesn't bother me, you know. If you're not Jat Sikh. Been there, done that.' She added, 'T-shirt so wasn't worth the effort.'

What a ridiculous situation. Sitting here with this middle-aged woman who had to dress for the part of a virgin bride. He supposed it was the same for her as it was for him, that she too felt the grand impossibility of trying to recast her life. He could hear their voices through the door, the father's especially.

'He sounds angry,' she said. 'Maybe you should go.'

He stayed where he was. He'd see it through to the end.

It wasn't the father, though, it was Aunty who flung open the door and charged towards him. 'Is he right? What are you?'

'I am a man,' Tochi said.

'Don't get clever. You a chamaar?'

Tochi stood up. 'I've told you what I am. Now give me what you owe me.'

And this – this demand – seemed to enrage her further, and her eyes widened horribly. 'You bhanchod cunt! You dirty beast! What do you think you are?'

'Davinder,' her husband said, a hand on her shoulder. But she wouldn't be restrained.

'To think we trusted you. To think we let you into our home. Marry my niece? Go back to cleaning shit, you dirty sister-fucking cunt.' She spat at his feet. 'Go on. Get out of my home. I said get out!'

Uncle passed him a few notes and Tochi turned to leave.

'Get out!' she screamed. 'You people stink the whole world up!'

He didn't return to the house immediately. He walked for what seemed like miles: back along Ecclesall Road and down into the city, pausing at the train station to study its map of the area, then through Attercliffe and into Brightside. The houses narrowed, the streets darkened. He'd only ever seen the address typed on the inside of the kid's diary. Perhaps that was why it felt a little magical to see the street name for real, nailed to the real red brick of someone's real house. He started the climb up the hill, stopping a few doors from the flat and crossing the road to get a better look. A light was on upstairs. There was maybe even the shadow of someone pacing the room. Downstairs, though, nothing. He went back across the road and slipped down the gennel and over the wall. He peered through the window. A cooker stood stranded in the middle of the room. The cupboards were smashed in. There was evidence of mice – a nibbled loaf, saucers of poison. But it was empty. When the time came – when he got that big-mouth Avtar's job – it was somewhere he could live alone.

*

There'd still been no word from Vinny. Avtar tried to get hold of him, but his phone just rang out.

'Does anyone know where he lives?'

No one did. Rumours sprouted. Customs people. Tax office. One of the boys said he'd heard from his cousin-brother in Halifax that Vinny had run away to Panjab. A couple of the boys packed their bags to take their chances on the streets. The rest of them decided to sit it out.

'If there was going to be a raid, it would've happened by now,' Gurpreet said, forehead to the net curtain. He turned round. 'But we should pool all our money together. Until work starts again.'

No one said anything.

'What are you waiting for? We still need to buy food. We'll get more this way.'

He held his hand out. It was trembling.

'Give it me. I'll sort it.'

Shaking his head, Avtar kicked aside the milk crate and left the room. One by one, the others followed.

He switched SIM cards and called Lakhpreet that night. Her voice was sleepy – 'It's not even five o'clock, janum' – and she complained how hot it was. The air conditioning was down and she'd been up twice already to take a cold shower. He wouldn't believe how breathless and horrible everything was again. It was like living in an oven. He was lucky to be away from it all and even luckier to be going to London tomorrow. How she wished that was her!

'I'm missing you,' he said, cutting in.

He could hear her smile. 'Me, too,' but the words fell lightly and didn't provide the warmth he needed. Perhaps it was the distance. Still, he half wished he'd not called. Too often these days he felt closer to the stars out of the window than to anything Lakhpreet said.

Randeep walked with him to the station the next day. He even offered to buy the ticket, but Avtar said he'd hide in the toilets or something. And barriers could always be jumped.

'You just don't tell anyone where I've gone, OK? Especially your room-mate. You do understand?'

'Yes! I understood the first time. And the time after that.'

Avtar stroked the swelling around his eye. It hadn't quite gone down. 'I know that bhanchod'll try something.'

'He's not that bad. I shouldn't have said anything.'

'He didn't even take off his rings.'

'I don't think he wears rings.'

Avtar gave him a look, as if to ask whose side was he on? 'We've tried to be friendly, but he's ungrateful. I hate that. Have you ever even seen him smile? No. Exactly.'

As the train pulled in, he again reminded Randeep not to tell anyone where he'd gone.

'If someone asks, say I'm at work. I'll be back in a week.'

He nudged his rucksack into the centre of his back and climbed on board. Randeep waited on the platform, watching Avtar find a seat. He must be having money problems, he thought. Or worse money problems than the rest of them. It wasn't something he ever spoke about. Randeep gave him a thumbs up, and then the train began to move and Avtar's worried face slid slowly up the track.

It only took two days. Randeep had returned from delivering Narinderji her monthly payment – she'd barely let him through the front door – and was in the kitchen pouring himself some cereal. It was all they had in the cupboard. Tochi was sitting at the table, hunched over his roti-dhal. He hadn't said a word to Randeep since he'd told everyone about the girl's letter, and Randeep was beginning to wonder if he'd ever be forgiven. The beads were slapped aside and Gurpreet came in. He found a couple of empties in the bin and managed to shake a few drops into his mouth. Then he threw them back down.

'Pour me some,' he said to Randeep.

'There's no milk, though.'

Gurpreet nodded, wiping his perpetually runny nose with the back of his hand. Randeep handed him a bowl and they ate standing against the counter.

'Where's your friend?' Gurpreet asked Randeep.

'Work.'

'Not seen him for a few days.'

'He's busy.'

'He used to talk about his exams. When are they again?'

Randeep chewed his cereal, playing for time. 'I'm not sure.'

Gurpreet nodded. 'Is he still at the chip shop?' And there was something about the way he said this. Less an enquiry, more a confirmation.

Randeep looked to Tochi. 'He's still at the chip shop.'

Tochi raked back his chair, harshly, and hurried into his jacket. Gurpreet threw his bowl into the sink, charging forward, grabbing Tochi by the collar and yanking him back.

'Bhanchod chamaar. It's time you learned your place.'

He took Gurpreet's legs from under him and slammed him onto the table, pinning him there with a forearm to the throat. Gurpreet thrashed. He made strangulated sounds. A knife appeared in Tochi's hand, held high above his shoulder. He trained it on the space below Gurpreet's turban.

'Say that again and I'll slice your fucking eyes open.'

At the chips-and-chicken joint, a girl with hair the colour of hay looked up from behind the counter. She asked Tochi something in English.

'Foreman. Please,' he added, as if remembering.

She stared for a few seconds, her brow contracting, then sloped off into the kitchen and said something in English again. A man appeared, big, with strong, fat arms that he was wiping down. He nodded up at Tochi. 'Ki?'

'I need work.'

'My name's Malkeet. Bhaji to shits like you.'

Tochi adjusted: 'I need work, bhaji.'

'Welcome to the world. Nothing here.'

'Wait. Please.'

Malkeet waited.

'I'll work for less than the one that's gone to London.'

He seemed amused by this. 'That takes guts.'

A customer entered and Malkeet told Tochi to go outside and come round the back. When he made it round, Malkeet was already in the doorway, pointedly keeping Tochi standing outside. Blue plastic crates were stacked against the wall to Tochi's left, watery blood pooled across their bottoms. Chicken, he made out, from the pictures if not the words.

'What's your status?'

'Fauji.'

'How long?'

'Long enough.'

'Now, now.'

'Two years.'

Malkeet thought on this. 'Well, I suppose it is true: you are cheaper than scooters. Always wanting time off for this or that exam.' He said this loudly, airily, and the desi guy in the kitchen banged his fryer against the rim and flounced off into the shop. Malkeet chortled.

'You'll make enemies.'

Tochi said that was nothing new.

Randeep paced the room, mattress to wardrobe, wardrobe to mattress. Sometimes he paused at the window, but it was getting too dark to see much down the road. He put his head to the wardrobe. He might not have. He might not have stolen the job. The boss might not even have given it to him. Anyway, he had nothing to feel bad about. Even if he had wanted to make it up to Tochi, he hadn't said anything he shouldn't have. Had he? Outside, the gate opened, hinges screeching. Randeep went to the window – it was him – and rushed out of the door, meeting Tochi halfway down the stairs.

'You didn't?'

Tochi pushed past, carrying on into their room.

'I've told bhaji. I've called him.'

'Good.' He took his holdall from the wardrobe and began to stuff it with his clothes.

'What are you doing? Where you going?'

'To the flat.'

'The empty one?'

Tochi nodded. It was time to leave. He zipped up the holdall and slung it on. 'If your friend asks, tell him. I don't want him to think I ran away.'

'You can't do this,' Randeep said, following him onto the landing. Then: 'I saw your scars.'

Tochi halted. He didn't turn round. Then he went down the stairs and out the front door.

Some students got up and left the hall long before the invigilator instructed everyone to put down their pens. Avtar never did. It would only draw attention, especially as he sat near the front and the exit was right at the back. He waited, listening to the giant clock, seeing shapes in the tiles of the parquet floor. Once or twice he paged through the booklet again. It made no difference. It was all beyond him.

Today was his fourth exam – two more to go. Head down, folder to his chest, he burrowed through the hordes of students comparing answers in the corridor. Usually he went to Cheemaji's office. Not this time. He cut across the car park, past the library and out of the college grounds. He went under the roundabout that had once so confounded him and used Cheemaji's travelcard to take the Tube to Kings Cross. It had been deliberate, suggesting somewhere public, and this was the only place in London he really knew.

He waited near the ticket office and when the other two showed up they all moved to an empty table outside a coffee shop. The nephews took teas. Avtar shook his head.

'Sure?' Bal said.

'I'm sure.'

'Fair enough. 'S good of you to meet us here,' he went on. 'Saves us a trip up north for once.'

'I was here anyway.'

'For your exams. You said.'

Avtar reached into his shoes and pushed across the table a small roll of notes. 'It's not enough.'

'I can see that.'

'I'll make it up next month.'

The teas arrived. The waiter left.

'Is that why you wanted to meet here?' The nephews looked at each other, smiled. 'Did you think we'd play nasty?'

'I've said I'll make it up next month.'

'Let's go for a walk.'

Avtar didn't move.

Bal swiped up the money and put it in his pocket. 'Get up. We don't have long.'

They took him into the toilets where Bal covered Avtar's face with a hood and held his mouth under a running tap. The other nephew kept watch.

'Stop taking the fucking piss,' Bal said, whacking up the water pressure. 'If you take the money – if you accept the money – then pay it the fuck back, yeah? Isn't rocket science, is it?'

Avtar beat his fists against the basin, clawing at it. He couldn't breathe. He couldn't see. He thought he was going to drown. Black and silver strings vibrated behind his eyelids.

'If it happens again we're clearing your family out. Do. You. Understand?'

He let go of Avtar's neck and removed the hood and Avtar collapsed to the floor, on his hands and knees, gasping.

It was late when he got back to the doctor's house, though the sun was still taking its time to set. He went in through the garden and found Rachnaji, the doctor's wife, the proper doctor, balanced on the squashy lip of the sofa, slicing a carrot on the coffee table. Her hair was tied into a Spanish net and shelved to one side.

'Is uncle around, aunty?'

'He's at the gurdwara,' she said, and chopped the head off the carrot. 'He's always at the bloody gurdwara.' She turned her face to Avtar. 'I found him weeping a few weeks ago. He said he didn't know what he was for. That he felt empty.'

Avtar thought it best to stay in his room after that, emerging only when he heard Cheemaji's car outside, the gravel spraying under the wheels. He needed to ask about that Sri Lankan factory job from before. There was nothing keeping him in Sheffield, not now that cheat had stolen his job. He took a breath. He needed to keep his mind straight. He needed to find a job.

The doctor was mixing a whisky-soda from the cabinet. The lights were low and there was no one else about. Avtar coughed.

'Ah, you're still up. Revising?'

'Ji,' Avtar lied.

'Good, good.'

He tilted his glass towards Avtar, who said no, thank you.

'Probably best,' Cheemaji said, and necked his drink in one. He exhaled. 'That hit the spot.'

The front door opened and Neil, their son, came through in an oversized NFL sweatshirt. He went upstairs and slammed the door shut.

'Everyone's a little upset with me,' Cheemaji said. 'You've no doubt noticed.' He refilled his drink. 'They don't understand. We don't belong here. It's not our home.' He raised his glass to Avtar. 'You've helped me realize that. People like you.'

'Me?'

'We're like flies trapped in a web. Well, I don't intend on waiting for the spider.' He took a sip this time. 'I said that to Rachna. Do you know what she said? She said I seemed to have forgotten that for the fly, once webbed, it's already over.'

Avtar returned to his room without asking about the job. He sat on the bed and gave in to his anger. What decadence this belonging rubbish was, what time the rich must have if they could sit around and weave great worries out of such threadbare things.

He couldn't sleep that night, and when he called Lakhpreet, she didn't answer.

*

Randeep locked the door and turned back into his room. He hoped Avtar bhaji would agree to moving in. He'd got used to having a room-mate and didn't like being alone, not now the house was beginning to empty. For the first time, the rooms felt too big. He pulled his bag free from behind a panel in the wardrobe and counted his money. He had enough to cover another month's payment to

Narinderji, maybe even two, and if he only sent home half of what he normally did he should be fine for food as well. By then surely they'd have found work. He wondered what he'd tell his mother. Going by the pearls in her last photo, she'd got used to the cash. There was a big click and the lights went out. Randeep clutched his money harder, until his eyes adjusted and the darkness settled into something less confrontational. He folded the notes into the bag and returned it behind the wardrobe panel. Then he unlocked the door and stepped onto the landing. The whole house was black. One or two others came out from their rooms as well.

'What happened?' Randeep asked.

'The meter, probably,' someone said sleepily, smokily.

Randeep tiptoed down the two flights of stairs, a hand on the painted white globe at the end of the banister. He could hear voices up the hall, in the kitchen. Gurpreet, threatening someone to put money in the meter or else.

'It's your bhanchod turn,' the other guy said. 'Look at the sheet.'

There was the sound of someone being pushed hard against the fridge and slapped. Gurpreet's voice: 'Bhanchod, who taught you to talk back?'

Very quietly, on the balls of his feet, Randeep turned around and went back up to his room. He locked the door and reached for his blanket. At least Avtar bhaji was back tomorrow.

SUMMER

8. THREATS AND PROMISES

She'd suggested meeting at Leicester Station. It was more or less halfway for them both and, she'd thought, feeling a little ridiculous even as she'd thought it, she could shout for help if he tried anything. She waited for him under the departure boards. Her hands were buried inside the wide pockets of her cardigan and pulled round to the front, thumbs touching through the material. She looked to the floor and said a faint waheguru. She told herself to calm down. Her shoulder bag slipped and yawned down her arm and a few things fell to the floor. Her phone, a pack of tissues. She crouched to pick them up – a green biro, bus tickets, fingers shaking. She went to the toilets again and sat on the closed lid behind a locked door. She breathed. When she re-emerged onto the concourse he was standing where she had been. He looked exactly the same.

He took her in, up and down, as if surprised that she too wasn't someone entirely different. 'Were you waiting to see if I was on my own?'

'I was—' She indicated the toilets, then looked beyond him. 'Is someone with you?'

'I'm alone,' he confirmed. He cast his gaze a little above her head. 'Some of us still keep our promises.'

They walked to the gurdwara near the city centre, a temple they both knew from one wedding or another. They paid their respects, then came down to the langar hall and sat around one corner of a long steel table. A sevadarni brought tea in white styrofoam cups.

'You live alone?' he asked.

She nodded.

'You sure?'

'Karamjeet, please.'

He paused. 'Have you been in Sheffield the whole time?'

'Yes.'

'Why?'

She looked up, a question on her face.

'Why Sheffield?'

'I can't say. I'm sorry. But please believe that I'm trying to do a good thing. God would not judge me harshly.'

He nodded. 'I understand. You wanted to get away from me.'

She said nothing, but her face must have shown that there was some truth in what he'd said; when she glanced across she saw that a part of him newly hated her.

On the train down she'd considered telling him everything. There was a chance he'd understand and not inform on her, on them all. She now realized she couldn't say a word. It wasn't her risk to take.

'How's Baba?' she asked quietly.

'How do you think?'

'And Tejpal?'

'Angry. Violent. He's looking for you everywhere.'

'Will you tell him?'

'I should.'

She paused. 'Will you?'

'Damn you, Narinder! Damn you! Why'd you have to go and ruin everything?' He kicked the chair beside him, and it wobbled, fell.

The woman in the canteen kitchen looked over. 'Sab kuch theek hai?'

'Ji,' Narinder said.

'I'm sorry,' Karamjeet said, and the woman, displeased, returned to her work.

There was a crackle of static as the gurbani started upstairs in the darbar sahib, reaching them through the speakers in each corner of the canteen.

'I'm sorry,' he said again, to Narinder this time. 'But it hurts all over. All of it. The humiliation. How could you?'

She saw that the corners of his eyes were wet. He looked away. 'I won't tell them. I said I wouldn't and I won't.'

A feeling of shame came over her. She couldn't look him in the eye. 'Thank you. And I promise it's only until the end of the year.'

'And then? We'll get married then?'

'If you'll still have me as your wife.'

She heard him sigh, half exasperated, half grateful, and he brought his elbows up onto the steel table. 'We promised God. We promised our parents. We have a duty to honour them both. Of course I'll still take you as my wife.'

She nodded. 'Thank you,' she said again, and they both sat there wondering what else there was to say.

Arriving back in Sheffield that night, she left the station and headed away from her flat. She didn't know where she was going, and had only a vague apprehension that she needed space, clarity, air. The route took her through suburbs in the south of the city – Nether Edge, Millhouses, Totley – full of brooding Victorian houses under a thin summer moon. Near a church, she stopped and looked across the green depth of the country, at the vast spirit of those giant hills. Is that where He was hiding? Help me, she said. Someone help me. He wasn't there and she didn't know why He'd gone. In the past, every leaf, every light in every window, every brick in every wall confirmed His presence beside her, inside her. Tonight, she felt so horrifically alone. She dialled home, but cut off before anyone answered. She resumed walking. Three identical lorries thundered past, shaking the leaves on the trees and whipping her chunni across her face.

*

Coming down the stairs one morning, she noticed blades of grass pressed into the pile of the hallway carpet. Crushed, as if they'd been brought in underfoot. She checked the underside of her own shoes, then descended the last few steps, slowly, her face turned towards the empty flat. Outside, she tried to peer through the window, but the curtain had been drawn right to the edge. Squatters, most likely. She went to the shop to get some meter tokens.

Later, lying in bed, she was woken by the sound of metal being scraped, prodded, a door opening. She sat up. She could feel the fear in her chest. Maybe Karamjeet had told her family. No. She closed her eyes. It was only a squatter, only a squatter, and to prove this, to banish all doubt, she stayed awake the following night. She positioned one of the dining chairs at the window and sat down, lights off. She just wanted to see who it was. The shape of him. Or her. Maybe it was Savraj, she thought, suddenly convinced that it was, then just as suddenly appreciating that it almost definitely wasn't. She finished her yoghurt and walked over to the bin. It was nearing midnight. She'd give it another hour.

She was fighting sleep when she saw someone coming up the hill. It was a man, and his orange shirt blazed against the night. She inclined her face to try and see his. If only he'd stop looking at the ground. And maybe this wasn't him anyway. He might only be cutting across the top of the hill to get to the estate beyond. But then he stopped outside her flat and Narinder recoiled from the window. When she looked again, he was staring up at her. A brown face. Did she know him? She lifted her hand to wave, but he hurried out of sight and she heard those metallic sounds again, of a lock being tripped. God, oh God: she ran to the door – it was already bolted – and scouted round for her phone. She could hear him charging up the stairs. She whirled round, desperate. She found the mobile on her bed and stood there staring at it, thumbs poised over the keypad, willing a name, any name, to enter her head. There were knocks on the door. Her stomach fell away. More knocks.

'Police nu mutth bulaiyio,' he said. *Don't call the police.* 'Please.'

She hardly saw him. She heard him, coming back at night – *Crunchy Fried Chicken*, his uniform had read – and sometimes she saw his polystyrene food boxes in the bin outside, but that was all. She hadn't recognized the accent. Maybe it belonged to one of those southern regions of Panjab she'd never visited. She hadn't even asked his name. He'd just said he knew Randeep and was going to stay downstairs for a while. He wouldn't disturb her. She'd nodded, shut the door, bolted it, and listened to his footsteps retreating down the stairs. She'd nearly called Randeep, but the thought of talking to him exhausted her, and he'd be here soon enough anyway, to make his monthly payment. She'd ask him then, if this downstairs-man was still around, that is.

*

At work, Tochi was on his own. Harkiran had brusquely shown him where the potatoes, fish and chicken were kept, how high to fill the hopper and the chipper, when to add the Dry White and in what order to double-fry the fritters, but since then he'd left Tochi to it. He refused to talk to him, even when it came to translating requests from Kirsty. Tochi didn't care. He was earning good money and had his own place. He answered to no one.

He was on his knees mopping up spilled chicken juice when he saw Avtar in the doorway. His jeans, Tochi noticed, were about an inch too short, white socks showing.

'Stand up,' Avtar said, and hurled himself forward, and Tochi stood there taking the blows to his chest, to his face, until Malkeet lifted Avtar off his feet and threw him outside.

He sent Tochi home early that night, saying it might be best if he changed his route. Tochi ignored him.

Outside the flat, he snapped a twig in half and tried to sharpen one end against the other. He'd forgotten his screwdriver and had no other way of tripping the lock. He crouched down, eye to the keyhole, and threaded the twig in, rolling it between finger and thumb. It was useless. The end broke off in the lock and now he'd have to somehow dig it out. The light came on upstairs and he heard footsteps. The door opened.

'Everything OK?' she asked, arms folded over her black cardigan.

He stepped past her and into the hall, to his front door. 'Can I have your pin?'

He jammed it into the lock and rolled it a quarter-turn to the right.

'Your face,' she said. 'It's bleeding.'

The lock caught and he handed back the pin and disappeared into his flat.

Avtar and Randeep left the house on the hunt for work. They'd been doing this every long day for the last two weeks and so far all they had to show for it were a couple of faint leads – people who said they had friends who might know of building work in the Nottingham area. Avtar left them his number, though he wasn't optimistic.

'Nottingham wouldn't be too far, would it?' Randeep asked, as they came back in through the kitchen. They split between them the last of some flat orangeade left out on the side, then Randeep went upstairs, saying he was going to check his diary for any contacts they might have missed. Avtar carried on into the front room and slumped into one of the garden chairs. He tapped his phone against his teeth. There must be others. But it was hard to concentrate; all day his stomach had been flexing, and his thoughts started to soften, drift away. When he opened his eyes, Gurpreet was at the windowsill, lifting the net curtain, letting it drop back down. Looking for money. He was in black shorts and a white vest, revealing baggy knees, hairy shoulders, and a topknot many times rubber-banded at the root. Avtar sat forward, Gurpreet turned round and immediately the anxiety in his face converted into something tougher.

'I thought you were asleep.' Then: 'We should kill that chamaar.'

Avtar stood up.

'Listen,' Gurpreet said, as Avtar was leaving. 'Lend me some money. Only till tomorrow. I'm waiting. On a job. I'll definitely get it. So. I'll pay you back then. Acha?' He spoke as if the words in his head were so jumpy he could gather up only a few at a time. His fingers were twitching, Avtar noticed, and a sallow yellow pushed through the skin under his eyes.

'Sorry,' Avtar said, and as he climbed the stairs he realized the vents in his jacket had been inside-outed. Fortunately, he kept no money in them.

He used a tablecloth to lift the pan and pour the boiled water into their iron bucket, adding a small amount of cold from the tap. He took the bucket and the letter up to his room. He'd been expecting the letter: Cheemaji had already rung to say he'd forwarded it on. He sat in a straight chair, rolled his jeans up past his knees and slowly, wincing, let his blistered feet sink into the steaming water. The bucket was a narrow one, forcing his knees tight together, and as the water rose up past his calves it spilled over.

One corner of the envelope bore the shield of the college, and the London address on the sticky label had been crossed out with two decisive red lines and replaced with this Sheffield one. Avtar turned the envelope over, then back again. He ran his fingernail along the seam and jiggled out the folded white sheet of paper. A column of Fs. Below it, a short paragraph confirmed he'd failed his first year. If he wanted to continue at the college, the letter went on, then his only option was to retake all the modules. If he wanted to exercise this option a form was enclosed. Please could he fill it in, along with an indication of how he intended to pay the fees: in a single lump sum before term began, or in regular monthly instalments.

He rang his father, waking him up, and told him his visa had been renewed for another year.

'So you passed?'

Avtar hesitated. 'Yes.'

His father roused Avtar's mother, and she said she'd go to the temple tomorrow and distribute some mithai.

He had a few pounds left on his phonecard and knew he ought to call Lakhpreet and tell her the good news too. The dialling tone seemed to stretch time: a beep, a long pause, another beep. She answered: 'Hello?'

They couldn't speak for long, and afterwards he sat looking at the yellow screen of his phone. She was out at the cinema with her friends. Enjoying herself.

'Can I call you tomorrow?' she whispered.

'Fine.'

'Jaan? I'll definitely call you tomorrow, OK?'

'I'm doing this for you, you know. You and my family and all our futures. Do you even think of me while you're out enjoying yourself? Think of me living here – ' he drew his finger along the side of the chair and brought up thick dirt – 'living here in this squalor?'

He wished he'd not been so angry. He mustn't start hating her. He mustn't let this life change him. He groaned and, with what energy he had left, dredged his feet out of the bucket of cooling water.

*

She was quick to open the door, which Randeep took as a positive sign. Ever since the inspectors' visit she'd not once invited him in. Maybe this month would be different.

He was still panting a little from the climb. 'For you.'

She took the envelope, thanked him. 'I was starting to worry. He comes tomorrow to collect it.'

'I'm only three days late.'

'I know. I didn't mean anything by it.'

'And I did send you a message.'

'I know. Thank you.'

He smiled, hopeful, not sure what to say next. He'd planned on telling her about their job troubles, but there seemed no point. She didn't even care enough to ask him up. He worried he was making a fool of himself.

'Well, see you next month,' he said.

'Aren't you going to see if your friend's in?'

So he was here. Randeep had already tried looking in through the window – it had been too dark. 'He's not my friend.'

'Oh.'

'He's not a good person. He stole Avtar bhaji's job. It's his fault we're struggling.'

'How can you steal someone else's job? Isn't that up to the boss?'

'He did.'

He could tell she thought he was making it up, or making it sound worse than it was.

'He's a chamaar.' It sounded like he'd said it to clinch the argument, though he wasn't sure he'd meant it like that. He wasn't sure why he'd said it at all. Did he think she'd like him the more for it? And now she was withdrawing, saying goodbye, that she'd see him again next month.

He didn't know why she was being so cruel, always shutting him out. Had he offended her in some way? She couldn't still be annoyed about the inspectors. He slipped his shirt onto its hanger and hung it in the wardrobe. Then he moved to the swivel-mirror and inspected his armpit hair – it seemed thicker nowadays – and flexed his biceps. There was definitely some thickening there as well, he told himself, if he looked at it in the right way. The door opened and Gurpreet came in.

'You're meant to knock,' Randeep said.

'You on your own? Where's your friend?'

'Out.'

Gurpreet glanced around the room, at Tochi's mattress, sheetless and laid on its edge, as if awaiting removal. 'I thought you two were going to buddy up in here?'

'No,' Randeep said, though he had asked Avtar. He'd said something about Randeep needing to be more independent, which had hurt.

'Right. Anyway, I've just been tipped off about a job. You want to come?'

'You've got a job?' He sounded incredulous.

'You coming or what? Or do you have to ask your friend?'

After walking for some twenty minutes, Randeep found himself in a loveless part of town he wasn't sure he recognized.

'There isn't a job, is there?'

Since leaving the house, Gurpreet hadn't answered any of

Randeep's questions. A woman, prostitute, is that who he was going to meet?

'I want to go back,' Randeep said, halting, just as a pub appeared, a mouldy green thing squatting on the corner.

'There it is. How much you got on you?'

It was a rundown place, all chipped mahogany, powder-pink booths and John Smith's beermats. On the walls were hemispheres of frosted glass, and inside each glowed a dense yellow orb. They took their drinks – a whisky, neat; a lemonade – and made for the corner seat furthest from the bar.

'We shouldn't stay long,' Randeep said.

'Give it a rest,' Gurpreet mumbled, and brought the glass to his lips, eyes widening.

They drank in silence. Then Gurpreet pulled a knife out of his pocket and laid it across his lap.

'Why do you carry that everywhere?' Randeep asked, looking around. The half a dozen or so customers seemed busy drinking, smoking.

'Hm?'

'Have you ever used it?'

He seemed to consider this. 'Once or twice.'

'When?'

Gurpreet laughed, almost into his shoulder. 'When people don't do as I say. When I'm with a woman.' He looked across. 'You're shocked.'

Randeep moved his head, carefully, side to side.

'We all need love, little prince. And we all love differently. Some women like it.' He picked up the knife and turned the blade over. 'Some women like it when I hold it against their throat, ever, ever so lightly. You know?'

Randeep nodded, like someone trying to follow a complicated argument.

Gurpreet took a long sip of his whisky, savouring it. 'But, yeah, I've killed. Sometimes you have to.'

He didn't think he believed him. 'How many?'

'In England?'

Suddenly, Randeep felt conscious of how he was sitting, of his half-sleeved goose-pimpled arms just hanging there at his sides. He gathered them up in a fold across his chest.

'It gets easier,' Gurpeet said. He seemed to be enjoying himself and extended his arm across the back of the seat. 'Especially when things get desperate and people won't tell you where they hide their money.' He met Randeep's gaze. 'Where do you keep your money, little prince?'

'I want to go.'

'Do you know the way?'

Randeep said nothing.

Again, Gurpreet laughed. 'Another?'

'I'd like to go.'

'Another.'

They had enough for one more whisky and Gurpreet seemed to take twice as long drinking it. Amber beads attached wetly to the ends of his moustache, and perhaps it was looking at these that was bringing about the queasy feeling in Randeep's stomach. At last they got up to leave. The pavement ran uphill and the streetlights had come on, and as they walked in and out of these grim pools of yellow light it seemed to Randeep that they were going at an achingly slow pace. Each time he quickened up, Gurpreet would ask what the hurry was.

'It's getting late.'

At the Botanical Gardens, Gurpreet stopped at the locked gates.

'Through here, then, yeah?'

Randeep wavered. The darkness there seemed of a stronger concentration, turning the trees black, the rest invisible.

'Come on. Thought you were in a hurry?' Gurpreet lifted one foot to the padlock, heaved over the metal gatepost and jumped down on the other side. 'Easy.'

'Maybe I should just meet you at home.'

'Oh, for the sake of your sister's cunt. Fine.'

Though he knew he shouldn't fall for it, he could see Gurpreet in the morning, telling the others what a wimp he'd been. He could see Avtar frowning. He started pulling himself up, hand over hand.

'Good,' Gurpreet said when Randeep landed at his side, and they took the path between two hedges.

The rose bushes looked strange in the summer night, like many-eyed creatures watching them pass. There was only the crunch of gravel underfoot and the gentle zooms of city traffic.

Gurpreet pointed. 'Let's go down here a second.' It was a short dirt path that seemed to lead nowhere.

'But home's this way.'

'I need a piss.'

Randeep went down a little of the way, then turned round and waited. A branch hung low in front of his eyes, quivering with the work of some animal up above. He heard Gurpreet unzipping, then the strong thrum of piss striking soil. He looked up the path, trying to work out where the main exit was, how long it would take. It couldn't be far, surely. Then he jumped. Gurpreet, hand clapped on Randeep's shoulder. Whisky on his breath.

'Why so jittery?' he laughed.

Randeep tried to laugh, too. 'You just surprised me.'

Miraculously, one by one the streetlights came into view, and the gate appeared, almost haloed in dingy orange. Randeep breathed out. 'The gate.'

'So where's your money hidden, little prince?'

Randeep looked – Gurpreet was reaching for his knife – and pelted for the gates, yelling, 'Help! Help!' while Gurpreet jogged, laughing, on behind.

They were at the house in minutes, Randeep turning the key and letting them in. He flicked on the hallway light.

'OK, my friend. Enough joking for one day. Till tomorrow,' Gurpreet finished, and disappeared into the lounge, shutting the door. Randeep sank back against the wall. The house was quiet. There were probably only a handful of them here now, dotted about the three floors. He supposed it could be true and Gurpreet had killed in the past. Still, it was embarrassing to think how scared he'd been. *Help! Help!* He cringed and went up to his room and fell face down onto the mattress.

Narinder tried a different plug socket, even a different CD. Still the stereo wouldn't play. It had been the same the previous evening, but, as was her habit in matters technical, she'd hoped the thing would've sorted itself out overnight. She looked at her watch. 7.30. The whole long day stretched ahead, silent and flat. The only person she'd spoken to in the last week had been Mr Greatrix. She took her cereal bowl to the sink, washed it, came back, saw a green-beaked pigeon waddling along the window. 7.32. She took her chunni from the back of the chair and her coat from the table.

She hadn't set off with the intention of going to the gurdwara – or going anywhere else – but she seemed to just end up here, sitting in the langar hall while the morning service crackled through the speakers. A woman arrived with tea. She was young, perhaps the same age as Narinder, with a wide, pleasant face on a frame that was stout without being fat. Her red bindi was a little off-centre and her bridal bangles thick. She was from Panjab, clearly.

'Sab theek hai, pehnji?' she asked.

'Ji?'

'You look like there's a lot on your mind. Is everything all right at home?'

'Ji. Thank you.'

Narinder recognized the woman – she'd seen her once or twice working in the canteen – and now she noticed the low-slung swell of the woman's stomach.

'Please sit down,' Narinder said. 'You should rest.'

The woman eased onto the chair opposite, arranging her shawl over the bump. 'I've not seen you for a while.'

'No. I've not done much seva recently. I'm sorry.' Since Karamjeet's letter she'd avoided the place. It was less risky to stay indoors.

'Well, I'm glad to see you again. Someone my own age. Are your people from Sheffield?'

'I don't know anyone in Sheffield,' Narinder replied, in a quiet voice that made her sound grave.

With some clumsiness, the woman reached across and touched Narinder's hand. 'Me neither.'

Her name was Vidya and she was here with her husband. They were illegals from Haryana – not Panjab – and had married and got quickly pregnant in the belief that a child born in this country would guarantee a stamp for them all.

'But it's not true,' Vidya said. 'The rules changed years ago. I could kill him.'

'So what will you do?' Narinder asked.

'I don't know.'

'Where will you have the baby?'

Vidya threw her hand in the air and kept it there, as if waiting for a ball to drop into it. 'He can sort it out,' though whether she meant God or her husband Narinder wasn't certain.

By their third meeting they were sharing more, though both women seemed to sense that much was being left unsaid, and had to be. Narinder liked her. She was funny, often at the expense of the stern old women who thought they owned the canteen. 'Enough hair on her lip to weave a menjha,' Vidya would say, as Narinder tried not to laugh. Soon and more than anything else she looked forward to the mornings Vidya would be there.

'You should get a job,' Vidya said.

Narinder took the thaals from her and started hosing them down at the sink.

'I said you should get a job.'

'I know. I'm thinking. I've never had a job.'

'All day alone in that flat isn't good for you.'

'I don't have any qualifications.'

'Not all jobs need qualifications.'

Narinder squeezed the giant bottle of washing-up liquid until her fingers touched through the plastic. All she got was bubbles and farts.

'Well?'

'I'll think about it.'

Vidya collected and returned with more dirty dishes. 'You're very strange.'

'That I am,' Narinder agreed.

'You're brave enough to come and live in a strange city on your own. But you're too scared to do anything else.'

Narinder had never thought herself brave. She only did things when called upon, when He told her a great injustice was occurring right in front of her face.

'Our gurujis led me here. I wasn't being brave.'

*

The curve in the roof of the bus shelter forced Avtar to kneel with ankles crossed. Climbing had never been difficult for him. As a conductor he'd often monkeyed up onto the roof to confront fare-dodgers. From here he could see all the way to the yard of the chip shop and its white back door, beside which was the stack of empty chicken crates. He looked at his phone. It was twelve minutes past. Maybe the shop had got busy. But then the door opened and Harkiran emerged, briefly, and dropped into the top crate a bulging carrier bag. Avtar gave a small fist-pump. Now all he needed was the miss-call from his friend to confirm everyone was out of the way. And here it was, his phone buzzing happily in his hand. He threw himself to the ground and sprinted up the road and down the side of the shop, skidding to avoid being seen in the window. He snatched up the bag without really even looking at it and fleetingly thought of Dhano the film horse as he pivoted and set off again.

'Isn't that stealing?' Randeep said, in the kitchen.

Avtar flattened the bag into a circle around the chicken and then, with both hands, and with something approaching reverence, lifted the meat out and onto the wooden chopping board. It was large and fleshy and plump-legged and kingly. Yes. It looked majestic.

'So you stole it?' Randeep said again.

'Shall we just starve, then? That bhanchod gave my job away.'

'Still,' Randeep said, though he had to admit the chicken looked like the best chicken ever. He could hear the saliva in his mouth.

'Do you know how to take the bits out?' Avtar asked.

'The bits?'

'You know.' He flicked his eyebrows to the right, as if indicating someone over there.

'They have bits?' Randeep said.

'Of course they have bits. What did you think they had?'

'But aren't they taken out before . . . before they get to us?'

Avtar looked at the chicken. 'Do you think so?'

'I'm not sure. Where would they be?'

They turned the chicken over so it rolled slightly to one side, and peered in, nostrils doing the opposite of flaring.

The chicken – chopped and curried – provided two meals a day for three days, for all of them. At the end of the third day, Gurpreet slurped up the last of the gravy, licking his spoon clean in a predictably vulgar manner.

'Good work, Nijjara. You got the next one ordered?'

'No,' Randeep said and looked to Avtar for confirmation. But Avtar had a guilty touch about him. 'Bhaji, think of the risk!'

Chuckling, Gurpreet rested his hands on his turban. 'Not even a year and stealing like an old hand. You're on your way.'

They didn't steal a chicken, in the end. They stole a whole crate of them. The night before, Avtar lay awake calculating how many chickens he could sell and at what price. Each crate contained twenty, he remembered, and at least ten crates arrived every morning. Malkeet wouldn't miss the one. He wouldn't even notice. And Avtar figured he could get maybe five pounds for a whole chicken.

'Two hundred pounds a day?' Randeep cried, as they watched for the delivery truck.

'Shh! And it's one hundred. And I'll have to give Hari something.'

'Wow. That was nearly a whole week on the hotel. But what if we're caught?'

'Drop the chickens and run,' Avtar said, and they looked at each other and laughed.

When the truck came past – *Northern Foods Ltd* – Avtar shimmied up onto the bus shelter and watched it reverse onto the forecourt, obscuring his view of the shop. The delivery guy got out – a friendly Scot called Gordon, Avtar recalled – and the flaps of the truck opened with a squeal.

'What's happened?' Randeep asked him.

The crates were levered onto a pallet and wheeled to Hari. Then Gordon saluted – 'OK, boss,' he used to say – and less than a minute later the truck was on the road again.

'It's gone,' Randeep said.

'Yeah,' Avtar said, still watching.

Tochi came out and carried one of the crates indoors. It would take him at least five minutes to unwrap twenty chickens and perhaps another five to arrange them in that massive fridge of theirs. He saw what must've been Hari's hand gently closing the door, and then his phone glowed.

'Go!' Avtar said, jumping down, running.

They slowed at the corner, making certain the door was still closed, then rushed forward again. Avtar unclipped the catches, detaching the crate from its stack, and gestured urgently for Randeep to grab the other end. And though they started off with it lifted up to their chests, by the time they shuffled past the bus stop their arms were at full stretch and the crate like a swing between their thighs. The chickens were heavy.

All the chickens were sold by the following morning. Avtar sent a text round to every single fauji and scooter he knew, saying he had twenty chickens, each one enough to feed five men two meals a day for three days. *Only 5pd. Jaldi!* Their last sale was to a cheeky scrote of a Bangla who bought three chickens, intending to eat one and sell the other two at a profit.

'Right. The next lot I'm pricing at eight pounds,' Avtar said, coming back into the kitchen. 'But in the meantime . . .' He grinned and handed Randeep his share. 'Money! We've got money! Can you believe it?'

'We're rich!' Randeep said, circling the money around Avtar's head, as if he was a groom. 'We're rich!' and they did a little bhangra around the kitchen table, arms aloft, laughing, making up the tune as they went along.

Randeep passed Narinder the envelope, feeling a little smug. 'Early this month.'

She smiled, which surprised him. She never smiled at him. 'Thanks, Randeep. I'll see you soon.'

'We're making good money now,' he blurted out, keen for her to stay.

'Oh, that is good news. Are you still at the hotel?'

'No, no, that ended – ' he counted out loud – 'nearly two months ago now. We've gone into business.' He waited for her to be impressed.

'Business?' she said, though she wasn't really listening any more, distracted by Tochi coming up the road.

Randeep could feel his face filling with a meld of embarrassment and jealousy. Didn't she know how humiliating it was for him to be seen standing on her doorstep like this?

Without looking at them, without a word, Tochi sidled past and disappeared into his flat.

'Sorry. What were you saying?'

'Doesn't matter,' he said, deflated. 'I should go.'

'Me too. I have plans.'

'Oh?' Was she doing something with him? 'Are you going somewhere?'

'I am, yes.' She smiled again, wider. 'I'm going swimming!'

It had, of course, been Vidya's idea. At first Narinder pleaded that she'd never been swimming and didn't even own a swimming costume. Then, once a suitable costume had been sourced, she said she couldn't be in a pool with naked men. The thought of it seemed outrageous. A week later Vidya announced that she'd found a pool that offered once-a-week ladies-only sessions. 'We're going. No more excuses.'

Narinder emerged from the changing rooms in a neck-high elbow-to-knee number. 'Why are you trying so hard not to laugh?' she said to Vidya.

'I'm not! You look great.'

'I look like a seal.'

There were only three other women in the pool, all brown, and the whole place was thick with the smell of chlorine. At the shallow end, Vidya climbed in first, then waded out, her arms in a circle above the water.

'Is it good for the baby?' Narinder said.

'Just get in, you chicken!'

She clutched the chrome rail and touched her foot to the water. Cold. But not too cold. She put her foot in again and this time left it there. She looked at it, at the water and light rippling over her toes. She lowered herself in, the water coming up over her shins, her knees, all the way up to her thighs. It didn't stop. It felt like she was being taken over. Shivering, she turned round to face Vidya.

'Come over here,' Vidya said. 'You'll be fine once you start moving.'

So she started pushing through the water, arms in an X over her chest. The shivering ceased.

'Isn't that better?' Vidya said.

'It's still cold.'

'You need to get your face wet.'

'What?'

Vidya cupped her palms under the water and splashed Narinder's face.

'Pehnji!'

'Now do this,' and she pinched her nostrils together and dunked under the water. When she rose back up, her face was glistening, hair drenched. 'Your turn.'

'I'm not sure.'

'Just do it!'

She placed a palm over her face, covering her mouth and nose, and bent to meet the water, not going down vertically like Vidya, but forwards, as if she was bowing for prayer.

Afterwards, Narinder rubbed her hair dry and retied her turban and they stepped back out into the shallow heat of the day.

'Let's come again next week,' she said.

'You enjoyed it, then?'

They returned to the gurdwara and from there Vidya said she had to head home. Her husband would need his roti before he went to work. 'But why don't you come over later?'

'To yours?'

'I'll cook. And you'll be doing me a favour. It can get a bit scary when he's away at night.'

She said her prayers, fully if not carefully, then raced home. The day was only getting better. Is this what it felt like, she wondered, to be part of the world, to have the world take you in its arms? She knelt in front of her image of Nanakji and thanked Him for all He was doing for her. Then she chose a mustard salwaar kameez with a white trim, tied on a matching mustard turban, and caught the bus to Vidya's.

They lived in an unpainted room in a shared semi to the north of the city. The bed took up most of the space. Under the window was a writing desk, too narrow for the three large oval doilies it was dressed in, and the curtains were a lurid red. Narinder helped bring the food up from the kitchen.

'You've made so much. And it smells so good.'

'I thought you could take some with you. It's all freezable.'

They ate side by side on the bed, a little inelegantly as the mattress was high and the desk didn't quite come to their knees. Bhangra tunes blasted from the room next door and several tenants seemed to be arguing. Children screamed.

'It's all apneh,' Vidya said. 'Faujis.'

'Does the council own the house?'

Vidya clucked her tongue. 'A Panjabi. A proper gurdwara sardar type.'

'Really?'

'To look at him you'd think he shat pearls. You won't believe how much rent he charges.'

'That's horrible. I'm so sorry.'

'Why's it your fault? Our own people are the worst at bleeding us dry.'

The door opened and a man came in, stopping when he saw Narinder. Short, thin, dark. He had stained teeth and ringworm on his hands. He looked as tired a man as Narinder had ever seen.

'What happened?' Vidya said.

'We were sent home.'

'Why? What happened?'

He nodded at Narinder. 'Sat sri akal, pehnji.'

She'd already pulled her chunni over her turban and now she brought her hands together under her chin. 'Sat sri akal, veerji,' she said, seeing as they were Haryana folk.

He looked at the spread of food on the desk. 'Heat me some up, will you. I'll wash my hands.' He left for the bathroom.

Vidya sighed and, one hand to her belly, slid off the bed. 'Because of course using a microwave is beneath him. I won't be long.'

Narinder sat in the dim room feeling that she should leave soon. She heard the toilet flush and through the seam of light where door met wall saw the husband cross the landing and go down the stairs. After maybe a minute, with no sign of either of them, Narinder opened the door and leaned over the top rail. The husband was speaking.

'Are we that rich that we can waste food on strangers?'

'Oh, janum, don't be like that. She's a friend.'

'Let her family feed her.'

'She's not got anyone here. I feel sorry for her. She lives alone.'

Maybe the husband made some sort of face.

'Arré, you do know she's sikhni. You can see that much?'

'I know exactly what kind of unmarried girls live alone in this country.'

Narinder retrieved her bag from the room and slipped downstairs. They met her in the hallway, the husband's hand on Vidya's shoulder, as if warning her.

'It's late,' Narinder said. 'I should go.'

'You don't have—' Vidya began.

'I'm sorry if you heard me,' the husband said. 'But please don't come to our house or speak to my wife again. We can't afford to become involved in other people's problems.'

Avtar was in the kitchen negotiating a sale when he heard Randeep returning from his visa-wife's. He shut the door and stomped upstairs. Perhaps it hadn't gone so well, Avtar thought. He turned back to the sale, to this young fauji who'd bussed it over from Hillsborough.

'Seven pounds,' Avtar said. 'And that's better than I've done for anyone else.'

'Come on, bhaji. You know what work's like these days.' He shook his pocket out onto the counter. 'Five. That's all I've got.'

'And how much do you keep in your socks?'

The young man smiled. They agreed on six pounds per chicken and the fauji left with two, one tucked under each arm. As Avtar folded the notes into his wallet, he heard Randeep hurrying back down.

'What the hell?' he said, swatting the beads aside.

'I've just sold another two.'

'Why are there chickens hanging all over my room?'

'Oh,' Avtar said, looking up. 'Oh, yeah.'

'They're in my wardrobe!'

'I ran out of room in the fridge. And your room gets less sun than mine. What else should I have done?'

'It stinks! I can't believe . . . How am I meant to sleep in that?'

'It's not that bad.'

'Do you want to swap?' Randeep asked, petulantly.

'Look, I've got more buyers coming over tonight and in the morning. The chickens, they'll be gone by tomorrow.'

Hari advised them to wait a week before attempting their next crate snatch, until that chamaar was back on the late shifts and out of the way. In the interim Bal drove up and Avtar thudded into his hand a nice thick tube of notes. So keep away from my family, he'd said. The next day he wired his parents enough money to cover the remortgage, and the day after that they headed on down to the chip shop.

'I told you to wear a belt,' Avtar said. It was the second time Randeep had stopped to pull his jeans up. 'You'll slow us down again.'

'I don't have one, yaar. My clothes actually used to fit me.'

They waited at the bus stop, and soon the truck came past, bang on time, and deposited the chickens. As it left, Avtar told Randeep to get ready. There was no miss-call from Harkiran, though. Two minutes passed. Five.

'Shall we call him?' Randeep said.

'I don't know.'

Then – relief! – the call came and they hurtled towards the shop and round the back, where the beautiful chickens were waiting. Avtar went to flick the catches up but they didn't snap loose. He tried again. They were stuck. Like they'd been glued. Run, he was about to shout, when a hand closed around his collar: 'So that's why my invoices weren't adding up!'

Malkeet didn't demand his money back – if anything, it had seemed to Avtar that he half admired their guts – but he did say that if they pulled any stunts like that again he'd be on to the police quicker than they could say detention centre.

'As if he could ever call the police,' Avtar seethed, kicking the bus stop so hard the green panel dented. 'With everything he does!'

9. UNDER ONE ROOF

She continued with the swimming, visiting the leisure centre on her own now. At first she'd gone in the hope of bumping into Vidya, whom she'd not seen at the gurdwara since the night her husband told Narinder to stay away. But Vidya was never at the pool and now Narinder went simply because she enjoyed it, which felt like a scandalous and perhaps even a shameful thing to admit. Sometimes, during the silent unoccupied evenings, she wondered if some change had taken place inside her, or, disturbingly, was taking place inside her, imperceptibly, in the way that the night gives way to dawn. Even if her father and brother had permitted it, she couldn't ever have imagined herself in a pool with other half-naked people. She supposed it was living on her own that had done it. And now here she was, this afternoon, trying to make roti-dhal for the strange man downstairs. She peeled the roti off the tava and gave the dhal a stir. If her family could see her now! She'd even considered getting a job, and last week had made it all the way to the job centre before talking herself out of it, because who would want to employ someone for – what was it? – five months? When she'd have to return home and marry Karamjeet. And stay married to Karamjeet. Forever. There was a chance that this roti-making for the man downstairs was as much to do with resisting her fate as it was a desire to help, but this thought was too wild to get any sort of purchase on.

The dhal tasted good, though the rotis, which she'd always struggled with, were a little crisp. She hoped he wouldn't be offended and put it all on a tray and carried it down the stairs. She knew he was in because she'd heard him moving about, pots banging, but when after three knocks he still hadn't answered she left the food by the door and returned upstairs. She showered and prayed and began work on a five-hundred-piece jigsaw she'd bought the previous week on her way home from the leisure centre.

Once complete it promised a tantalizing sea view, the sky impossibly wide, the ocean sun-dappled. A few birds. No people. After two hours she'd perhaps managed only a couple of pieces when the meter started to tick. She fished out a token from her tin beneath the sink and opened the door. The tray of food lay at her feet, untouched.

*

At last Avtar found some work. Harkiran had to head down to Barking for a three-day family wedding and called in case he wanted to cover the security-guard night shift.

'Of course I do!' Avtar said, rising from his mattress.

The job was at a copper-pipe factory on Leadbridge Industrial Estate in Attercliffe, and all Avtar had to do was keep watch from his plasticized cabin outside the estate entrance and once an hour patrol the grounds. It was the easiest money he had ever earned. The cabin was small, stuffy with the day's warmth, and warmed even further by an electric radiator mounted low on the wall. He'd tried to switch the radiator off but it seemed stuck on its high setting. The only furniture was five narrow, armless blue swivel chairs arranged in a row against the window.

'I'll do a walk round,' Avtar said.

Randeep reached for his jacket.

'Stay. You don't have to follow me everywhere.'

He hadn't meant to snap, and if Avtar had bothered to look no doubt he'd have seen Randeep gawping glumly after him. But Avtar hadn't looked. He'd opened the door and walked straight out. He'd told him that this was a one-man job, that he couldn't afford to split the money. Randeep had said he didn't care about the money. He just wanted to come.

'I don't want to be on my own with Gurpreet.'

'Don't be such a wimp,' Avtar had replied. 'You won't get anywhere like that.'

He rounded the last grey block of the factory and ambled towards the perimeter fence. Something about being alone in the night air tended to create a space for compassion, for feeling ashamed. He didn't know what was happening to his mood lately. He should apologize to Randeep. It wasn't his fault he was so different from his sister, that he had so little of her fight. Perhaps it was time to tell him about their relationship. It would be good to get him on side before the big confrontation with Mrs Sanghera. But no. He was still too much of a kid in the way he thought of himself. Maybe in a little while, when he seemed a bit more stable. At the perimeter fence, he called Lakhpreet and felt relief when it went straight to voicemail. He wasn't sure he had anything to say to her: anything she'd understand. He remained at the fence for a while, staring through to the city lights beyond. Where was the work? He was promised work. He had a sudden memory of a disused factory, a staircase, a bell tower. It all seemed so long ago. Everything was moving away from him. Further and further away. At least he could keep Pocket Bhai's men away from his family for another month. He ran his hand down the wire mesh, his thoughts somehow following, and returned to the cabin.

Their shift finished at six, when Mr Shah, the fur-hatted factory owner, turned up in his second-hand Bentley, and by seven they were back in the house, starving. Avtar checked the boxes of cereal, then the freezer. Gurpreet came through the beads on bare feet.

'Have you had all the bread?' Avtar said, shutting the fridge.

'There wasn't any atta.'

'Great.' He opened one of the top cupboards, looking for a clean cereal bowl. 'Want some?' he said to Randeep.

'I'm leaving next week,' Gurpreet said.

Avtar looked across. 'Oh?'

'To Southampton.'

'Where's that?'

'Past London.'

'There's work there?'

'Maybe.'

'But you're not sure?'

'Who can be?'

Avtar lost interest and shook the cereal into two bowls. 'Enough to feed a couple of small birds,' he said, banging the side of the box, getting it to cough out all the crumbs.

'Lend me some money,' Gurpreet said.

'Don't have any.'

'You're working.'

'Still don't have any.'

'I'm not asking for much,' he said, in a tone laced with desperation.

Avtar said nothing and Gurpreet, furious, punched the doorframe on his way out.

'Idiot,' Avtar said, reopening the fridge. He made an exasperated noise and slammed it shut. 'I bought a whole carton yesterday.'

He looked to Randeep, who was staring at the beads, still swinging. 'Did you see how much he was shaking?'

'Gurpreet?' Avtar picked up his bowl of dry cereal. 'What's new?'

Mr Shah paid Avtar for the three nights' work and agreed to take his number in case of any more shifts in the future.

'I'll do any work, janaab,' Avtar said, dialling up his Urdu. 'Aap jho fermiyeh.' *Whatever you ask*. And then, because he'd heard this Mr Shah liked his poetry, and apropos of nothing at all: 'Zindagi tho pal bar ka tamasha hai.' *Life is but a spectacle of moments*, which had Mr Shah parting his lips a little worriedly.

They left – 'Khuda hafiz' – breaking off at the Londis for some bread before making a right onto their road.

'Zindagi tho . . . ?' Randeep said. He hadn't stopped laughing. 'Wah, bhai, Mirza Sahib!'

'Yeah, yeah.' Avtar popped his collar. 'You won't be saying that when he makes me boss of his empire. Lottery, here I come!'

A mellowness had filled the air these last few mornings. The soft clouds had hatched and a pleasant warmth broke across their faces and arms. They were halfway up their road when Avtar stuck his arm out, stalling Randeep.

'What?' Randeep asked, his first thought that they'd left something at the factory.

A crowd had formed up ahead.

'Wait here,' Avtar said, and passed Randeep the bread and his rucksack. They took their belongings everywhere these days, now that stealing had become so common in the house.

He thought it was only kids fighting, because most of the crowd looked to be teenagers on their bikes, but then he saw the van and the policewoman standing guard at the gate. The rear doors of the van swung open, though the angle was too oblique to see inside. Head down, he moved right, into the road, and looked again. Two of their housemates were in there, hands cuffed in their laps. One was staring at the roof of the van. There was shaving foam down the side of his face.

'Walk. Now,' Avtar said, returning to Randeep, taking his rucksack back.

They turned the corner, feet eating up the pavement. 'Police?' Randeep asked.

Avtar nodded. 'Raid. Keep walking.'

They were so wired, they were almost running around the city. They kept turning their faces to the sky, thanking God, saying that He really must be smiling down on them. How lucky they'd been! By the evening, however, the adrenalin had gone, and neither felt like laughing much.

'We've got nowhere to go,' Avtar said, dropping onto a bench outside the station.

'The gurdwara?' Randeep suggested.

'Too risky, yaar.'

'We could just eat and leave.'

Avtar brought his rucksack up to the bench and pulled out the loaf of bread. 'You go if you want. Your visa's fine. They take one look at mine and it's over.'

They shared what food they had, including a bag of peanuts Avtar had bought, and found a warm spot between two large green recycling bins.

'This isn't too bad,' Avtar said, arranging his rucksack.

'I need to pee.'

'I told you to go at the station.'

'I didn't need one then, did I?'

Randeep got up and walked to a bush further down the road. When he came back Avtar was already asleep.

In the morning Avtar retrieved his ringing mobile from the bottom of his rucksack.

'It's Gurpreet,' he said.

'He wasn't in the van, was he?'

'He must've got away.'

They met him at the station, which was where Gurpreet said he'd spent the night. His white vest was ripped across the stomach. He'd jumped the fence, he said. He saw the van coming up the road and had hurdled – 'Hurdled!' Randeep repeated – at least three gardens before hiding in one of the gennels.

'I saw you two walking past,' he finished.

'You saw us?' Avtar said. 'You saw us and let us carry on walking up? Did you want us to get caught?'

Gurpreet smiled, spat at the ground. 'Bygones. You got any money? I'm fucking starving.'

They bought a burger each from the station kiosk and gulped water from the taps in the toilets. Even if they could have shaken Gurpreet off, there was more chance of finding work if they stuck together.

'Maybe we should go see your Narinderji,' Gurpreet said.

'I thought you were going to Southampton?' Randeep said.

'You paying for my ticket? I can't hide for six hours.'

'She won't let us stay.' The idea of turning up at her flat appalled him. And it would appal her. He wouldn't put her in that predicament. 'No. We can't. It wouldn't be fair to her. She won't like it. She won't even let us through the front door.'

'She might.' It was Avtar, turning round from the departure boards. 'She might. If she's so into helping others.'

Avtar and Gurpreet promised to wait down the road and out of sight while he went upstairs to speak to her.

She answered the door in one of her usual cardigans. 'Randeep? So soon?'

He asked if he might come inside, that it was important.

She turned side-on. 'Is everything OK? Are we in trouble?'

'There was a raid,' he said, sitting down. 'Luckily I managed to get us all out in time.'

'Oh my God!' A hand went to her mouth. 'So, the police? They're on their way?'

'No, no. Please don't worry. That's what I mean – we got away. We're fine. But, obviously, we can't go back there and – well – Avtar bhaji wondered if we could stay here for a bit.'

'Here?'

'I said it's not fair and that you won't like it, but they made me come and ask.'

'Is it the two of you?'

'Three,' he said, and felt a rush of hope that she might like him enough to agree.

'There's no room. And I'm not going to have three men living here. It's not right. It's not what we said.'

'I understand.' He got up to leave. He was her husband, in name if nothing else, and it was humiliating to have had to lower himself in front of her like this.

She walked him to the top of the stairs. 'You do have somewhere else to go?'

'We'll be fine. Like I said, please don't worry.'

He rejoined the others, shaking his head as he approached.

'What?' Avtar said, shocked. 'She said no?'

'Of course she said no. Any decent girl would.'

'Put your foot down,' Gurpreet said.

'Did you tell her we've got nowhere else to go? That we're homeless?'

Randeep let his silence give its own impression.

'Who does she think she is?' Avtar said. 'Walking round with her turban in the sky.' He marched up the hill and rang the buzzer even as Randeep tried to pull him away.

The door opened only a few degrees. 'Ji?'

'Call yourself a daughter of God? How can you look in the mirror when you've just left us to die on the streets?'

Randeep remained with Narinder at the doorway, his suitcase on the floor in front of him. Avtar was plugging in his phone charger. Gurpreet had his head in the fridge.

'Thank you,' Randeep said. 'I know this isn't easy for you.'

'I should move my things,' she said, indicating the shrine.

'I'll make sure we're not here long. I promise.'

'How long?'

'A week. I'm certain bhaji will have found somewhere else for us by then.'

'OK. A week. But no longer, please. Someone might see,' she added.

He nodded. He understood. She was worried her family would hear she was living in a house full of men. 'I promise I'll do my best.'

'We'll be out looking for work during the day,' Avtar said, joining them. 'You won't see us.'

'This where I'm sleeping, then?'

They turned round. Her bedroom door had been opened and Gurpreet stood inside.

'Looks comfy.'

She charged forward and told him to get out, shutting the door hard behind him. 'Stay away from my room. Is that understood?'

They moved the settee away from the window and laid two blankets, folded lengthways, in the space created. Avtar and Randeep took these. Gurpreet lay snoring on the couch.

'What you doing?' Randeep asked Avtar. He was messaging on his phone, had been for some half an hour.

'Nothing,' he said, drawing the mobile closer to his chest, though not before Randeep thought he'd glimpsed . . . something. His sister's name? He must have misread. He must be missing his family, seeing their names everywhere. And, of course, there were a million Lakhpreets out there. So many. It all became too much even to think about. He blew the hair from his forehead – it needed a cut – and stared at the tiny fissures in the ceiling. There were noises outside, footsteps brushing the pavement. He moved onto his knees at the window and saw Tochi in his uniform, counting his money as he walked.

'Him?' Avtar asked.

Randeep nodded.

'What's he doing?'

Randeep lay back down, closed his eyes. 'Nothing.'

They tried every convenience store and off-licence and takeaway joint; they asked the man picking litter off the streets and the woman wiping tables in Burger King; they asked construction workers cordoning off a part of the road.

'You're idiots!' Gurpreet said. He was several metres behind, stopping for a pull on his half-bottle of whisky. 'There is no work!'

'Where'd he get the money for that?' Avtar said. 'Were you short this morning?'

'A bit.'

'I've told you. Keep it safe.'

At the end of the week, Randeep knocked on Narinder's bedroom door and she came out to meet them.

'We're sorry,' he said, 'but could we stay here a little longer?'

'Randeep!' she said, despairing.

'I'm sorry. I hate having to ask you. But we'll definitely find work next week. Won't we?'

Avtar said nothing. He seemed completely embarrassed to be standing there.

'And then I can pay you as well,' Randeep said. 'I'd have enough for this month, but I need to send Mamma—'

'It's not about that.'

Randeep nodded. 'Of course.'

'OK. But just one more week. Please?'

'Thank you.'

Narinder began to retreat into her room.

'One more thing?' Randeep said.

She waited for him to go on, but he went to the window first, to check Gurpreet was still outside with his cigarette. Then he plucked a healthy roll of notes from the inside of his sock and held it out to her.

'It's not safe having money here. With Gurpreet bhaji. We wondered if you'd mind keeping it locked in one of your cupboards for us?'

She took the money from him, and then Avtar crouched down too. His was a much thinner roll than Randeep's. It seemed to Narinder a pitiful amount for someone to be left with, after nearly a year in this country, and as the money passed between them she looked up and saw his embarrassment only deepen.

*

Narinder reread the letter she'd composed the previous evening. It contained nothing she hadn't already told them – that she was fine and would be back soon. On the other side of the door, Randeep and Avtar were talking. Something about a track and Hari's roommate and it being only a one-man job. And then the door closed. She rose a little off the end of her bed and saw Avtar jogging down the hill, rucksack bumping against his shoulder. Only three days left, she reminded herself. Then they'll be gone. She set the letter underneath her pillow and went out into the main room. Randeep looked up, miserably, his mouth dismaying her with its self-pity.

'Bhaji's got a job.'

'Oh. But that's great, isn't it?'

He looked back at his phone. 'I guess. I've got to stay here and go through our contacts again.'

Gurpreet was still asleep, an empty bottle held lovingly to his chest.

'I keep asking him not to drink here,' she said.

'I'm sorry,' he said, and she wished she'd not mentioned it.

She took a cloth and some polish from under the sink and returned to her room. He could hear the spray can. Housework. It was the least he could do, so when she came to make a start on the kitchen he took the can from her.

'You don't have to,' she said.

'I'd like to.'

'Well, OK, but why don't you go pick up some meter tokens? We're running out. The shop's—'

'I know the shop.' He looked at her. 'You forget I got you your first tokens. The pink ones, remember? Not the white ones.'

'I do. You were very kind to me. You even cleaned the whole place. Thank you.' She glanced to the floor as she said this, as if she'd not always been as kind to him.

He checked that Gurpreet was still asleep, then smiled unconvincingly at Narinder. 'I won't be long.' She heard him running down the stairs.

She picked up the can and sprayed a line across the kitchen table. She'd just finished polishing the table legs – was she the only person in the world who did that, she wondered – when she saw Gurpreet staring at her.

'You're awake,' she said, standing up, suddenly self-conscious.

He sat up, the settee succumbing with a groan, the empty bottle still in his hand. 'Sorry, sister. But carry on. It's so nice watching you put the shine on those legs.'

She moved away to the worktop, applying polish to the counter at roughly equal intervals. She heard him put the bottle on the coffee table.

'You should get a telly,' he said. 'You won't be so bored, then.'

'I have enough to occupy my time.'

'Hmm. Well, there are other ways I can stop you from getting bored.'

She turned round, twisting her body. 'You have no right to speak to me like that.'

'Why don't you tell me about my rights, sexy sister? Come here and tell me everything.'

'Stop. You either stop, or leave.' She realized her hands were trembling.

'All calm and godly on the outside. But there's a proper little fire going on – ' his eyes moved to a point past her waist – 'down there.'

'I said, stop it!'

He was grinning as he stood up and she thought she was going to yell when Randeep walked in. He had milk and a loaf of bread in one hand, keys in the other, and put all three things on the dining table.

'The tokens are in. And I thought we'd have toast,' he added, looking from Narinder to Gurpreet, back to Narinder. 'Everything all right, Narinderji?'

Very calmly, she put down the cloth, then the spray can, and went into her room.

'What did you do?' Randeep asked, and Gurpreet pitched up his shoulders and threw his arms in the air, as if to say, *Women!*

She re-emerged in her coat. 'I've got a letter to post and then I'm going to the gurdwara. I'll be back by the evening. I don't think he should be here when I return.'

'And who's going to throw me out? Your chamcha here? Just remember, one phone call from me and your little game is over.'

'Shut up!' Randeep said.

She took her lilac chunni from the hook. Randeep waited until he heard the front door close.

'Did you touch her?'

'Maybe. Maybe she's angry because she let me.'

'She wouldn't go near you.'

'Give me the change,' Gurpreet said, palm out.

'There wasn't any.'

'Get me some money, then.'

Randeep ignored him and put the milk and bread in the fridge. Behind him, Gurpreet entered Narinder's room.

'What are you doing?' Randeep said, coming to the doorway.

'What's it look like?' and, half clothed, he got into her bed. 'That bhanchod settee. Narrow as a cat's tongue.'

'She told you to get out.'

But Gurpreet only turned over, his head vanishing under one of the soft pillows.

Randeep ate his toast, dry. He should have thought to buy some butter, maybe jam too. Then he sat down and sent perhaps four or five half-hearted messages before he felt his eyes going and promised himself it'd only be a very short nap. He was woken by a clattering sound from the other side of Narinder's door.

'You up?' Randeep said, walking in.

Gurpreet was kneeling at the foot of her wardrobe, the drawers all tipped open, her clothes crashed to the floor on their coat hangers. The bedside cabinets lay upended, ransacked.

'Are you crazy!' Randeep yelled.

'She's got to keep her money somewhere.' He was shaking again, wiping his runny nose along his arm. He shoved past Randeep and into the kitchen.

'Just get out!' Randeep shouted, as he started righting her cabinets, picking the lamps off the floor. Her shrine would have to be rebuilt. 'You're going to ruin it for all of us!'

He could hear him in the kitchen, opening and slamming cupboards, cussing, crockery rattling. And then, silence. Randeep listened. Perhaps he had found the money? But no, because here was Gurpreet's voice, loud with an intimation of controlled hilarity, as if he was reciting: '*A beautiful flat for a beautiful person. And a new start for us both . . .*'

Randeep ran into the room.

'*I am at your service day and night.* And night, eh?'

'Give it here.'

Gurpreet held the note high and away.

'It's mine,' Randeep said, stretching, but Gurpreet moved the thing behind his back.

'I'm sure dearest Narinderji would love to see this.'

'She probably already has, OK? So just hand it over.'

'What's it worth?'

'I'm not giving you money.'

'Oh, I think you will. Because think how embarrassed you'll be when she sees it. When Avtar sees it. They'll think you're an even bigger loser than they already do.' He turned, walking away, sashaying his hips, and brought the note up to his face. 'If I may be of any assistance . . .'

Randeep ran at his back and sent Gurpreet tripping to the

ground. There was the dull crack of his head hitting the coffee table. Randeep stepped back, swallowing. Gurpreet lumbered to his feet, a trail of blood near his left eye.

'You're dead.'

'I'm sorry,' Randeep said, and raised his hands.

One punch to the side of his face threw Randeep to the floor, onto his hands and knees. The shock made it hard to breathe. He could feel a red throbbing somewhere. Everything seemed tilted on its axis.

'I'm sick of rich cunts like you having it so cosy all the time.' He heard Gurpreet's voice, distant. His hand seemed to be on the back of Randeep's neck. He had a faint revelation that that was why he couldn't breathe.

'Where you keeping it?' Gurpreet said, squeezing.

'I can't . . .'

There was something else, a sound, something being hacked at, looped around his neck. A rope. A lead. A belt. It was pulled tight. Randeep reared up, fingers clawing at his neck.

'Where?' Gurpreet said, yanking, coiling the lead into his fist.

He couldn't speak. Could only look. He felt his eyes straining to leave his face. On the carpet. Gurpreet's flick knife. Open. He launched his hand towards it.

Avtar hoped Hari's room-mate had been genuine when he said he'd call him again. The work at the track hadn't been bad and he'd seemed honest enough, though that was getting harder to judge. He climbed the stairs to the flat, tired, made even more so by the thought of a workless afternoon ahead. The door opened and Randeep stood there. He looked frightened, panicked even.

'He won't let me call an ambulance.'

'What's happened?' Avtar said, shutting the door.

'We need to call an ambulance.'

Gurpreet lay slumped behind the settee, his head thrown back to the windowsill. His Adam's apple was pulsing hard, and his mouth hung sloppily open, as if at any moment it might slip right off his face. His hand, gripping his side, was covered in blood.

'God.'

'I put a bandage round,' Randeep said.

'You did this?'

Gurpreet spoke, breathing out each syllable. 'No. Am. Bu. Lan.'

Avtar crouched beside him. Gurpreet slid his eyeballs across.

'They might not send you back,' Avtar said.

'No. Am. Bu . . .' He couldn't go on.

'Is there anyone we can call? Do you know anyone who can sort this out?'

Gurpreet turned his face to the ceiling and closed his eyes.

'Let's get an ambulance, bhaji. Please. He's not thinking straight. What if he dies?'

With a hand on the windowsill, Avtar pushed up onto his feet, slowly, thinking. 'Where's your Narinderji?'

'Out. She could be back any minute.'

'Call her. Make up a reason. Find out how long she's going to be.'

'Why?'

'Just do it.'

A door shut downstairs and he saw Tochi heading towards the bus stop. 'He's on lates, isn't he?'

'Who?'

Avtar took a knife from the cutlery drawer.

'Shall I still call her?'

'No,' he said, and hurried down to the lower flat.

Tripping the lock was easy, and, inside, it seemed as if Tochi only ever used the front room and maybe the kitchen. The bathroom had been gutted, wood everywhere. In the shower tray sat the white-bottomed trunk of a toilet. He cleared a space by the door and vaulted back up the stairs.

'We'll have to put him down there until it gets dark.'

'But what if he dies?'

'He won't die,' he said, uncertainly.

Carefully, they folded him into one of their blankets so that he wouldn't trail blood, and with even greater care carried him down.

They laid him curled to the bathroom door. Avtar took a closer look at the bandage and bound it tighter – 'We'll get you help' – while Randeep went back up to fetch a glass of water.

They washed the knife and Randeep zipped up his tracksuit top to cover the bruise on his neck. There were a few bloody handprints on the wall and a large stain absorbed into the carpet where Gurpreet had been lying. The handprints mostly washed away, but the stain didn't, so Avtar cut the carpet out and said they'd have to move the settee back and hide the hole. Then they sorted the mess in Narinder's room. Throughout all this Avtar kept making Randeep go over what had happened.

'I don't know what's wrong with me,' Randeep said, when he'd finished. He sounded close to tears.

'He was killing you. You didn't have a choice.'

'But he might die!'

'Do you want to go to prison?' Avtar said, raising his voice. 'Because I'm not being sent back because of this bhanchod, do you understand? OK? So let's try and stay calm. It's too light now but we'll get him out before that chamaar comes back.'

They checked on him two or three times every hour – the level of his water, the quality of his breathing – and when Narinder returned at dusk they stared at her, waiting for her to speak, notice.

'Has he really gone?' she said from the kitchen table.

'You told him to leave,' Avtar said, almost accusatory.

'I know. I know. But where will he go?'

Avtar paused. 'He'll find somewhere.'

'I was angry,' she said, fingers closing around a rung of the chair. 'I hope he's not on the streets.'

'Like I said, he'll find somewhere.'

They had a dinner of roti-dhal, eaten mostly in silence. Randeep's spoon kept clinking the side of his bowl.

'Your hand's shaking,' Narinder observed.

'I wanted to ask you where the doctor's is,' Avtar said swiftly. 'My stomach's playing up.'

'There's a surgery at the top. Past the shop and left down one of the roads. There's a big blue sign outside. You'll have to register as a patient first, though.'

Avtar said he'd wash up, hoping that might hurry her to bed, but she put a load in the washing machine and then sat doing her jigsaw puzzle at the kitchen table. Randeep and Avtar kept glancing at each other and at the clock, and it was nearly ten when she pushed back her chair and said goodnight.

They could hear her reciting the rehraas, then a switch being flicked, extinguishing the beam of light at the foot of her door. They waited an hour, not saying much, then trod down the stairs. Gurpreet hadn't moved. He seemed weaker now, and the blood on his hands and vest had congealed and blackened. They wrapped him in the blanket again and Avtar wiped the tiles clean and scrubbed the pinkish handprints from the door.

'When's he back?' Randeep asked.

'Twelve. One. Depends.'

'We should take him to the hospital, bhaji.'

'Too far.'

'But—'

'I said it's too far.'

They shouldered him up to his feet and in this way supported him down the hall and out into the night. They followed Narinder's directions, except that they circled around the shops to avoid being seen, and laid Gurpreet in the doorway to the surgery. They arranged the blanket so that it cocooned him. He was whimpering, shaking his head. There was blood all in his beard. Randeep took a step back and clasped his hands together up by his mouth, praying.

They wanted to leave that night but didn't know how to explain it to Narinder. So they returned to the floor, exhausted yet wary of sleep. Neither had wanted to take the settee. A car horn made Randeep flinch.

'Yaar,' Avtar said.

'I know.'

'He'll be fine. His breathing was getting better. They'll take him to the hospital and put him on a plane home. He'll soon be with his family.'

'I know,' Randeep said again, and turned over.

The buzzer rang the next morning. It wasn't even eight o'clock.

'Who's that?' Randeep said.

Avtar moved onto his knees and scuttled to the window. He could see the car but not who was at the door. Narinder came out of her bedroom.

'You expecting someone?' Avtar asked.

'The only person who comes is the landlord. But it's too soon for him.'

The buzzer rang again.

'It's the police,' Randeep said.

'It's not the police,' Avtar said, giving him a heavy look.

'I should go,' Narinder said and, grabbing her chunni on the way, headed downstairs.

Avtar and Randeep listened from the open door of the flat. It was a male voice, a white voice. Randeep's face tightened.

'What?'

'Immigration,' Randeep said.

Avtar snatched his rucksack from the settee and raced to the window, trying to force it up. But there was no time and he let go and turned round as Narinder walked in with the man.

'It's David,' she said, quietly, moving round the kitchen table, as if to place a safety barrier between them.

'Ah, Mr Sanghera, good to meet you again.'

He extended his hand, which Randeep took.

'As I was saying to your wife, I realized I don't have your phone numbers on file. And that's no good at all.'

'You should have written to us only,' Randeep said.

David smiled. 'I was in the area.'

His charcoal trench coat hung open, revealing a smart suit of a paler shade. The hair, grey, was swept back. He moved to Avtar.

'I don't think we've met. David Mangold.' Again he held out his hand.

'Hello, sir.'

'Your name?'

'Hmm?'

'Name?'

'Gurpreet.'

'Off out?' He nodded at the rucksack, or maybe the window.

'No,' Avtar said, reflexively, defensively, then wished he'd said yes and stolen the opportunity to get out of there.

'Are you staying with Mr and Mrs Sanghera? Sorry – ' a smile over his shoulder at the couple – 'Mr Sanghera and Ms Kaur.'

'No. Visiting only.'

'Oh. I thought that would've explained all this,' he said, looking at the pillows and blankets.

'Visiting for a few days.'

'Two blankets?'

'It gets cold.'

'Ah. Of course.'

He smiled that fake, flat smile again, and his gaze moved slowly around the room.

'I see you've removed all your photos.' He turned to Randeep. 'I hope all is well in the matrimonial abode?'

'We're fine. Thank you. We're redecorating.'

'And this suitcase? My, what expensive-looking leather. I'm assuming that's not yours, Mr Sanghera? Why would you keep a suitcase full of your things in your own living room?'

'No.'

'So it's . . . ?'

'My friend's,' Randeep said, nodding at Avtar. 'Sir, did you come to interrogate us or for our contact numbers?'

'Very true. I've taken up quite enough of your time,' and he scribbled down Randeep's and Narinder's mobile numbers and wished them all a pleasant rest-of-the-morning.

They heard the downstairs door shut and Narinder sank onto a kitchen chair. 'They know.'

'It'll be all right,' Randeep said.

'He can't prove anything,' Avtar said. 'Don't panic.' He unzipped his rucksack and crushed into it a T-shirt he'd left drying on the radiator.

'What are you doing?' Randeep asked.

'He might come back.'

'We're going?'

'I am.'

'I'm coming with you.'

Avtar swung the rucksack on. 'And if he comes back?'

'I'll say he's working. I'll call you,' Narinder said, turning to Randeep. 'And I'll probably handle it better on my own. But you can't stay here.'

They returned to the surgery before heading to the bus stop – Randeep had insisted. He wanted to make sure Gurpreet was all right. He wasn't there. They must have taken him to the hospital.

'You sure?' Randeep said.

'If anything had happened to him there would have been police everywhere.'

Randeep nodded and let his head fall back against the bus stop. He turned his face away from Avtar and the tears that fell were ones of relief.

*

Gobind's was an Indian supermarket that seemed to sell things in bulk: six-packs of lychee juice, giant mesh sacks of purple onions, sticky gold tins of rapeseed oil – *Food For Functions*, the sign outside the shop read. Hari's room-mate had told them about it. They had been sleeping in the station, their second night away from Narinder's, when Avtar got the call saying that there was definitely work going in Derby, in a place called Normanton. A gurdwara uncle on his way back from the cash-and-carry had given them a lift as far as Chesterfield and from there they'd hidden on a train.

Walking into the supermarket, Avtar was ambushed by the spices: cloves, coriander, ginger. There was another smell that reminded him more of home but which he couldn't place until he turned and saw the brown powder spilled across the floor; piled up beside it, the split boxes of malati. He marched on, climbing out of whatever mood he was in danger of sinking into. The woman behind the counter looked old enough to be their grandmother, though the gold eye make-up seemed to warn against addressing her as a biji. She had very long, very straight hair in a fat clip at the nape of her neck and her green cardigan was buttoned singly at the throat, over her darker-green kameez.

'Sat sri akal,' Avtar said.

She exhaled in apparent dismay – 'Mera ghar e tuhanu labda a?' – and moved onto her tiptoes, looking over Avtar's shoulder. 'Arré, ji? Another one!'

The job wasn't with them.

'Too much checking in this area now,' she said, shaking her head as if at an increase in crime. 'We only dare keep one. Not that he's much good,' she added and rolled her eyes at the young man come to sweep up the liquorice powder.

'So where is the work?' Avtar asked.

'No need to sound so desperate,' the woman said. 'The van's coming tomorrow. In the car park.'

'Whose van?'

'He has a few businesses in the area. A local man. Don't worry, he's apna. Just make sure you're there tomorrow. Early.'

The car park was too cold to sleep in so they returned to the shop and were given directions to the nearest gurdwara, where they ate and shat and climbed the stairs to spend the night in the darbar sahib.

'We'll find a room somewhere tomorrow. And work,' Avtar said, coming back with some prasad. He gave half to Randeep, who ate it in one and then seemed disappointed not to have made it last.

'I never thought it would be like this,' Randeep said.

'Have faith.'

Avtar's phone buzzed – a message from Bal, demanding the next payment, and a warning: *wanna c ur ma beggin on da street?*

'Work?' Randeep asked.

Avtar plugged his phone in to charge. 'No,' and he left it at that. If he told him it might get to Lakhpreet, and maybe even to his parents. He'd got his family into this mess and he had to get them out. He had to earn, and more than he was earning now.

Randeep turned to face the wall. Avtar lay down and asked God to keep His hand on their heads, before turning round and trying to sleep himself.

They were at the small, ragged car park behind Gobind's by six. Already five others were there, lined against the wall with their different rucksacks.

'Join the queue,' they said, though everyone knew that once the van turned up any queue would explode.

'Whoever gets in helps the other,' Randeep said.

More kept on arriving and by mid morning there must have been at least thirty waiting in the car park. They were from all over Panjab: Phagwara, Patiala, Hoshiarpur. The first thing anyone asked was what pind you were from. *Which is your village? Who are your people?* Some had been here more than ten years. One or two less than a week.

Someone ran in from the road and shouted that there was work in a biscuit factory on the other side of the city. The ones new to England slung on their bags and chased after the man, who said he'd show them which bus to catch.

'That was my cousin,' the man beside Avtar said, grinning. 'Bhanchods, why didn't more of you fall for that?'

The van – an old red Bedford – arrived late in the afternoon and a brusque round-bellied man in a quick-wrap saffron turban stepped out. His beard was neat and evenly black, the work of some dye, though his eyebrows were as white as butter. The boys assembled around the back of the van, Avtar elbowing his way to the front. The van man spoke.

'I'll only take men with National Insurance. If you don't even have a fake one, don't bother getting in the van.'

'What's the work?' Avtar asked.

'Cleaning.'

'Cleaning what?'

'Underground cleaning.'

A few made faces and detached themselves from the group. Perhaps they could afford to wait for something better.

'I only need ten,' the man said. 'I'll count you in.'

Avtar felt them pressing behind him, fighting into position.

'What's the money?' Avtar asked.

'Whatever I say it'll be.'

'But where will we live?'

The man looked at him. 'Shall I wipe your arse too?'

The van man put his hand on the door lever. Already they were shoving one another. Avtar turned round and nodded at Randeep, who looked nervous. The man smiled, as if enjoying his power. Then he opened the door and there was a huge animal noise and Avtar elbowed the guy next to him as hard as he could and clambered into the back. He spun round, looking for Randeep. His suitcase was making it difficult and others were easily slapping him back.

'Bhaji!' Randeep said, holding out his hand.

Avtar was looking at Randeep, looking at Randeep's hand, looking at Randeep holding out his hand.

'Bhaji! Bhaji, please!'

Avtar looked away. The door slammed shut.

'That's it,' he heard the man say.

10. INSIDE LOOKING OUT

A palmful of dank yellowing leaves held fast to the window and the low sun meant she had to squint to see Mr Greatrix on the path below. She wondered why he hadn't come up the stairs. She slipped into her cardigan and checked her phone in case Randeep had called in the last five minutes and she'd somehow missed it. It had been exactly two weeks since they'd left the flat and she couldn't believe he'd not returned by now to pay the rent.

'Sorry, I left my set at home,' Mr Greatrix said.

Narinder kept hold of the doorknob. 'Are you here for the rent?'

'It is the first day of the month, is it not?'

'So Randeep's not paid you directly?'

He pushed out his lower lip, a display of tender blue veins glazed in saliva. 'And, pray tell, he would be whom when he's at home?'

He sounded much older than he looked. Perhaps he thought he needed to speak like this to be taken seriously.

'My husband,' she said.

'No. I can't say your husband has been in touch.' His voice changed. 'Is this your roundabout way of telling me you don't have this month's rent?'

'I'm sorry.' There was fear in her voice. Surely he couldn't just kick her out? 'I'll speak to my husband.'

He flipped his notebook shut, a notebook Narinder hadn't even noticed until now, and placed his hands behind his back. 'Mrs Kaur, as this is the first time you've defaulted on a payment, please take this as your first and last warning. I'll expect you to make up your arrears in full next month. Otherwise I'll be forced to initiate proceedings. Is that clear?'

'I'm sure it's just a misunderstanding.'

'Be that as it may, you'll receive written confirmation in the post of what we've just agreed.'

He huffed irritatedly and turned round. There was some sort of lotion on the bony cartilage of his ears, the tips of which were burning red. He'd mentioned something about spending August on holiday. Florida, perhaps. He got into his car, checked his mirrors a little imperiously, as if he knew Narinder was still there, and nosed out.

Back in her room, she tried calling Randeep for perhaps the fourth time that day. Again it went straight to voicemail. She went to the window, as if expecting to see him coming up the road, and then she hurried downstairs and knocked on her neighbour's door. No answer. She tried again.

'Hello? Ji? Are you in, please? It's me from upstairs.'

She waited on the bottom step for a while, then, defeated, returned to her flat. She drew the curtains and lowered herself onto the settee, one hand on the armrest as if she desperately needed its support. She didn't feel like eating. She got nowhere with her puzzle. By seven she was in bed, though the day was still yellow and the light made a perfect unit of itself around the closed curtains of her window.

Later, past midnight, she got up and knocked on his door again. She knew he was in. She'd heard him. She knocked once more, harder, and listened for footsteps. None. Then the door was open and he stood there with his hand high on the frame, forcing his shoulder up by his ear. Behind him, all she could see was the dark strip of a hallway and a wire hanging without its bulb. He was in his orange uniform. He didn't say hello.

'I need to speak to Randeep. He's not answering his phone.'

'Nothing to do with me.'

'But do you know where I can find him?'

'Sorry.' He made to shut the door.

'Just – I was expecting to hear from him. It's very important.'

'Sorry.'

'Well, can you at least give me Avtar's number? I really need to speak to them. It's not like Randeep to not get in touch.'

He shook his head.

'But I thought you all lived together?'

He said nothing.

'Aren't you even worried? You said you were a friend.'

'I said I knew him.' He shut the door.

At the bank she withdrew all her savings. She had enough to cover the rent. Enough to keep him happy for another month, that was all. She tried Randeep again – 'You've reached the voi—' then pushed the phone deep into her bag and walked the half-mile to the job centre.

She'd decided she had no choice. She'd already tried the gurdwara, hoping the women would help her find some paid work, but they'd turned on her, demanding to know why she needed a job all of a sudden. She only prayed that coming into a place like this, a job centre, giving details they'd store away in their computers, wouldn't get her and Randeep into any trouble.

'So you don't have any previous work experience?'

A little green first-aid flag taped to the hard drive read 'Carolyn' and a whole gallery of silver-framed family shots fashioned a fortress around her desk. She was an older lady – fifties, maybe – with large, auburn hair so insistently sprayed it appeared frosted over. The whole effect seemed designed to provide her ears with a pair of giant brackets. Square red-framed spectacles hung on a chain around her neck and she lifted these to the bridge of her nose.

'I'm sure you must have done something?'

'I haven't. Sorry. Only my father and brother worked.'

'How very enlightened.'

Carolyn flipped to the back of the four-page form Narinder had had to complete before being called to the desk.

'I notice you've left the key skills section blank as well.'

'I don't have any.'

Removing her glasses, Carolyn slid the form to one side. 'Now. We're not going to get very far with that attitude, are we? You're twenty-one. Why don't you tell me what you've been doing since your schooling stopped at – ' she glanced across to the form – 'at sixteen.'

'Helping at the gurdwara, mostly. I did that nearly every day.'

'Volunteering?'

She'd never thought of it like that, as if it was an optional thing. It was just – had been just – part of what it meant to be alive. 'I was doing my duty.'

'And what kind of duties are we talking about?'

'One of my main duties was giving out food. Making sure no one goes hungry.'

'And did you do that alone or in a group?'

'In a group.'

'Excellent. Teamwork. A key transferable skill.'

She was writing all this down in a shorthand Narinder couldn't decode.

'What else?'

By the day's end Carolyn had two interviews arranged. The first was for a cleaning job in a city centre bar, which Narinder said she couldn't do.

'I'm sorry,' she said on the phone.

'You won't be serving alcohol. I understand your position on that. This'd be in the mornings when no one else is there.'

'But it's under the same roof. I'm not allowed.'

She did agree to attend the second interview, for a role in the womenswear section of a large department store. She'd never been interviewed and was so nervous she didn't eat. But she thought it had gone well. Two interviewers – a man and a woman – and they'd poured her a glass of water and said they were going to keep things informal by just going through her CV and asking a few competency-based questions. Nothing too taxing, they'd said. She'd left riding a wave of relief and pleasure and as she walked out of the store and into the new world she allowed herself some optimism.

'Lack of retail experience,' Carolyn said, when she called to explain why Narinder hadn't got the role.

'OK. Thank you.'

'Don't sound so despondent. Rome wasn't built in a day. Christ, it takes my Mal five weeks just to put a shelf up. And I've got two more lined up already. One tomorrow and one for a week on Monday.'

She didn't get those either. Both jobs were in supermarkets and both, again, cited a lack of experience. Narinder thanked Carolyn for letting her know, then switched off her phone and held it in her lap. No one wanted her. She couldn't see a way out. She walked to the doorway of her bedroom and gazed at the photos of her gurus, at the shrine, expecting some sort of solace. She could feel none. For the first time, it just looked like pictures of old men. She forced the thought away and took up her gutka and sat down and started to read, out loud, filling her mind with as many words as she could.

When Carolyn next called, she said she had something that was right up Narinder's street.

'It's at one of the smaller libraries. Part-time assistant. As soon as it came on the board I thought of you.'

'Thank you. That sounds good.'

'Oh dear. I hope you sound less like a miserable Marjorie in the interview.'

Narinder smiled. 'I'm sorry. It sounds great.'

'That's better. Now,' Carolyn said, her voice offering total discretion, 'what were you planning on wearing?'

She didn't take Carolyn's advice, that maybe she should replace her headwear with something less 'statementy' – *A headscarf does the same job, surely?* – and might she also consider trousers on this occasion? She wore a plain sky-blue salwaar kameez with a chunni of a deeper blue, and she topped it all off with a black turban.

The library was a bus ride away, in Dore, on the other side of the city, and abutted a doctor's surgery. She was buzzed through and saw that, in the children's aisle, some sort of mother-and-baby group was in progress.

'Narinder, is it?' a woman said, splitting from the group.

Her long, flowery skirt was elasticated at the waist, and her blouse as white as her hair. A gold brooch, like a fat sun with short rays, was pinned at the neck.

'Ji. Yes. I'm Narinder. I'm sorry if I'm late.'

'I'm Jessica,' the woman said, bringing her hands together in a clap. 'And I could not be more delighted to meet you.'

They sat in the staff kitchen, drinking tea and discussing things Narinder would later struggle to recall. They'd spoken about India, and Jessica's time there in the Sixties, and there'd been something about some modifications she was having made to her bungalow. Narinder sat there listening, nodding, waiting for the interview to begin. But then an hour had passed and Jessica said she had to get things ready for the afternoon sessions. So when could Narinder start?

'Oh!' Narinder said, her hand leaping to her mouth. 'You mean – I've got the job?'

'I think you'd be perfect.'

'Oh, thank you. Thank you so much!'

'There's no need to thank me, dear. I need to get the paperwork through, so shall we say two weeks from Monday?'

'Yes. Yes. That's – I don't know what to say. Thank you.'

Jessica squeezed Narinder's hand and left the room, telling her to take as long as she needed. Tears had come to Narinder's eyes. It felt as if for the first time in years some joy had entered her life.

She was desperate for the two weeks to be over. She cleaned the flat, she went for long walks, she read the gutka; anything that might urge the hours on and stop this grim staring at the walls. She was proud of herself, and it didn't matter that pride was one of the feelings she shouldn't submit to. She couldn't help it. She had a job. A real job. And she'd done it all by herself. She wanted to tell someone, anyone, but the only person who presented himself was Mr Greatrix, looking at her over his clipboard.

'I trust you got the written notification of your first warning?'

'Yes. Thank you.' She handed over what she'd withdrawn from the bank. 'I think that brings us up to date.'

He looked surprised, suspicious, even. He counted it. 'Yes. Well.

That seems all in order. Of course the warning still stands. If you miss any future payments—'

'I won't.' She could feel herself about to say it: 'I've got a job.'

She washed the clothes and turbans she wanted to wear during her first week and set them to dry across the radiator and on the rungs of the dining chairs. Then she stood by the window. It was a clear afternoon, a suddenly eloquent sky. Two girls in blazers were coming up the hill – school must have started again – and beyond them, rounding the corner, her downstairs neighbour. Bizarrely, he was rolling a large rubber tyre up the hill. She watched him for a while, then moved away from the window in case he might see her.

She made plain roti, which turned out far too doughy, and ate this with a sabzi of chickpeas. Then she went to the shop and bought milk and electric tokens. Her clothes had dried by now, so she ironed and put them away. Her first-day suit she hung on the back of her bedroom door, giving it a final brush and shake, ready for a week's time. It was eight o'clock. With nothing more to do, she brushed her teeth and went to bed.

Maybe minutes passed, maybe hours. She wasn't sure. The clock flashed 12:00. She checked her phone: 02:21. She was sure she'd heard something. A banging, maybe. A rumbling. It might just be him downstairs. She slipped out from under her duvet and peered through the long slit where the curtains met. The angle was too straight. She could hear voices, indistinct, but could see nothing. Neighbours? She went through to the front room and to the window there. She folded the curtain aside and looked down, then immediately leaned back, stupidly letting go so the fabric flapped a little. It was Tejpal. Others, too. She put a hand to her chest, as if they might hear its thudding, and inched forward again, peeling the curtain back by increments. They were looking up at her. She flattened herself against the wall. And now she could hear him, shouting.

He wanted to talk, he said. They'd all been so worried and they just wanted to make sure she was OK. She listened from the dark of her room. 'Narinder! Come on!' he said, as if she was being adolescent, unreasonable; as if all he was asking for was a lift to the cinema.

She waited for them to go, and when their voices withdrew down the hill, she reached for the settee, shaking. Tomorrow, she'd leave. She'd pack a suitcase now and tomorrow she'd go to a hotel. She tried to think if she could call the police, or whether that would get Randeep into trouble. She wasn't sure. Her thoughts kept disappearing into dark water. She didn't think she could do it. She didn't think she could call the police on her family. Then, suddenly, the silence was exploded by a horrific scissoring sound. She rushed to the window. They were doing something at the door. Hacking at it. Kicking it. She ran into her room and picked up her phone. They were thundering up the stairs, banging on her door.

'Nin – open up. Cos I swear I'll break this bastard door down.'

'Go away!'

He kicked the door.

'No!'

She undid the locks and chain and he barged past her and into the room. 'What the fuck!'

'Tejpal, leave. Or I'll call the police.'

'I'll leave all right. But you're coming with me.'

He looked fatter than she remembered, his beard thicker, bushier. His black waistcoat was all large padded squares and down the inside of his left arm a tattoo: Jatt Khalastani. The other two remained at the doorway. Distant cousins of hers, she recognized. From Dagenham. They looked, if not nervous, then slightly unsure of their role.

'Pack your bag,' Tejpal said.

'I'm not going anywhere. I'll come when I'm ready.'

He rounded on her. She'd never seen such clarity of hatred in someone's face. 'Do you have any idea what you've done? Do you know what you've put Dad through?'

'You don't know anything. Now get out.'

'I'm the one who hears Dad crying at night. Do you know he can't face going to the gurdwara any more? Because people start pointing him out? Do you know how ashamed he feels? He doesn't leave the house. Because of you. All because of you. You did this to him.'

Narinder's face gave a slight vibration. It was painful to imagine her baba like that. 'He'll understand. When I explain it to him. I know he will. I'll be back in a few months and it'll be fine. I'm doing a good thing here. You don't understand!'

'OK, then. Tell me what you're doing.' He sat on the settee. 'Come on. I'm waiting. Tell me why you're doing this.'

She looked away. 'I can't.'

'Right. Well, I'll tell you what you're doing. You're doing what you've always done. What's good for you. What makes you feel good. He's done everything for you. You've always been his favourite and now you're the one who's killing him.'

'I'm making a sacrifice so—'

'You don't know what sacrifice is!'

He rushed out of his seat and gripped her under the shoulder, pulling her along. She felt herself gasp. She couldn't breathe.

'Tejpal, don't do this. Let me go. Please let me go.'

'Pack your bags. You're coming home.'

'I can't! You don't understand.'

They struggled. The cousins didn't seem to want to get involved, as if this was going beyond their remit. Probably they'd only come in case there'd been men to fight. Narinder bit down on her brother's arm, hard, tasting blood, and all at once he screamed and pushed her with such force she fell into the dining chairs. She twisted round. He was crying.

'I hate you so much,' he said. 'I'll never forgive you. Never.'

In the rusted oven tray, Tochi arranged the squares of rubber into a small mound. He carried it into the main room and eventually got a little fire going, opening a kitchen window for the smoke. Then he sat on the semicircle of tyre that remained and warmed his hands. He'd stolen the tyre from a school playground and it was the only piece of furniture in the room. A black sheet with a border of orange lozenges lay in the corner furthest from the window. His holdall acted as pillow. He heard the man shouting on the pavement outside. He couldn't understand what he was saying. A family dispute, it sounded like. He made out 'sister'. Nothing to do with him. He tried to ignore it, but then they started crashing through the door and charging up the stairs, to the girl. He grabbed his bag, ready to run, waiting to hear sirens. Nothing happened, though. They were upstairs, still shouting, and a little later they came back down. He went to the window. A van was driven up and the bearded guy opened the side door and the other two forced the girl in, throwing her suitcases after her. Tochi turned away from the window and forced the image of Palvinder from his mind.

AUTUMN

11. WHAT PRICE FREEDOM

A man in a fashionably Pakistani kurta pyjama rose from behind his tabla set and walked the long diagonal towards Randeep. His kirpan was slung low across his body, and his royal-blue turban identified him as one of the junior granthis, perhaps only a few years older than him.

'You've been coming here several nights now, haven't you?' he said, kneeling beside Randeep.

He had a friendly voice, or seemed to be making an effort to appear friendly.

'I only need somewhere to stay a while,' Randeep said. 'Until my friend comes back. I won't be here long.'

'You're welcome at all times. This is God's house and you're his child. Where are you from?'

'Sheffield. Panjab.'

The young granthi nodded and kissed the air in Indian sympathy. 'There are no jobs, are there?'

'We looked everywhere.'

'I know you did. And you're not alone. There's so many of you boys about. Even here in Derby.'

'Can you help me?' Randeep asked.

There was a silence, the only sound that of the book being read in a sibilant hush. The granthi smiled in his serene way, and when he spoke it was as if he picked his words one by one, laying them next to each other with great deliberation. 'It's important to feel supported. To be with like-minded souls. It helps one cope. That's why I'm going to mention that most of the young men like you come together under the old railway bridge near the city. The one on the river, by the new flats. Do you know it?'

Randeep shook his head, not really following.

'We take food to them. And blankets. We try to help.'

'Do you think they might help me?'

'I'm sure they will. Maybe you should go there now.'

'You want me to leave?' Randeep exclaimed. Some of the congregation looked over. 'But you can't! This is God's house.'

'We have to think of everyone who uses the gurdwara. Try to understand.'

'But my father worked in government. You can't kick me out.'

The young granthi asked him not to see it like that, in those terms. 'You're always welcome, but maybe it would be better if you were with people in the same difficulties as you.'

He stood in the car park, suitcase in hand, and heard the gurdwara doors shut behind him. Three times he'd been shunned: Narinderji, Avtar and now God. He walked to the station and dropped down behind the car park, following the river into the city. The mornings were crisper now, with a breeze that made the leaves twitch and forced him into his jacket.

He found no bridge in that direction, only waterside bars and restaurants, and so he turned around and retraced his steps and carried on past the station and the flats, out towards the gasworks and factories. There weren't any joggers around here, just the odd fisherman thickly hidden. He walked on, convinced he'd gone too far, or that it had been a ruse to get him out of the gurdwara. Then he saw it: a wide, bottle-green bridge, beautiful in its way. Underneath it, three figures, all in shadow. Their chatter echoed coarsely.

They were slumped against the wall in their sleeping bags and blankets.

'Kidhaan?' one of them said.

Randeep nodded, and the man brought his hand out of his sleeping bag and gestured for Randeep to join him along the wall.

By the evening, there were eight of them under the bridge. A small twiggy fire had been started and someone came back from the gurdwara with a sloppy bucket of roti-dhal.

'They take it in turns, the gurdwaras.' It was the same fellow who'd first spoken to Randeep, a Panjabi with a rapid-fire way of talking while not looking up from his food. His name was Prabjoht.

An Ambarsariya, judging by his accent. 'It's their way of keeping us out here. Keeping us happy.'

'You went to the gurdwara, too?' Randeep asked.

'We all did. But the people, they complain. They say we're unclean. That we smell. Which we do. So let us come and use the shower once a day, right?'

'Don't you have family?'

'Don't you?' Prabjoht said tetchily. Then: 'Maybe my papa's bhua's derani's something. No one close. It wouldn't make any difference.' He indicated someone asleep a few beds away. 'His own chacha kicked him out. Said the kids weren't happy with him living there.' He shrugged. 'It was different in the old times. They say people used to take you in, help you on your feet, feed you. Times change.'

Randeep moved his suitcase against the wet wall. He took out his blanket and wondered how to arrange it, whether to use half of it as a sleeping mat or not.

'That's fine for now,' Prabjoht said. 'But you'll need something more soon. The cold's coming.'

'How can the cold be coming? When was the heat? Did summer even happen?'

He lay down and wondered what Avtar would be doing, what sort of job he might have found. He'll call soon, Randeep thought, and turned onto his side and watched the river.

*

They called it a plant, this flat-roofed building with its single, strikingly tall chimney. Inside, the pipes were running and the industrial hoses hung against the steam-stained walls like colossal gold jalebis. They wriggled into their white boiler suits and six of them loaded the van with hoses and drove off with Jagdish to other sites around the West Midlands. The four that remained split into their usual pairs, Avtar partnering Romy. Skinny, with bad skin and a raptor's beak, Romy had a student visa too, for an art college in Birmingham. He'd been in the country less than a month.

'We'll take S1,' Avtar said, and the second pair took their hose and rubber boots and moved to the north of the plant.

Avtar threw Romy their torch – the defunct lamps on their helmets had never been replaced – and they wound tape around the tops of their boots so too much of the thicker shit wouldn't find its way in. The manhole cover was already off. Avtar plugged the hose into the nearest jet, using both hands to secure the plastic nut, and climbed down into the sewer. The nozzle of the hose peeked out from his armpit like a little green pet, and, as he landed, one foot at a time, the dark water came to his knees. Things bobbed on the surface – ribbons of tissue, air-filled condoms that looked like silver fish floating dumbly towards the light. A furry layer of moss waved back and forth across the curve of the brickwork. Everything seemed bathed in a gelatinous gleam. Romy landed beside him and took the torch out of his mouth.

'I don't think I'll ever get used to the smell.'

'It's not so bad,' Avtar said.

'How long do we have left here?'

'He said his contract's for a month.'

'And then we can go?'

'Point the torch.'

They moved cautiously, hunched over as if anticipating an oncoming attack. The torch rippled discs over the water. Behind Avtar, the hose was unspooling, slapping itself into the stream. They came to a fork of two narrow tunnels.

'Did we do the left one yesterday?' Romy asked.

'The right.'

'You sure?'

'Of course I'm fucking sure.'

Avtar went first, stepping down to a slick ledge and into the dark cave.

'It's fine,' he called, echoed. 'Enough room to stand.'

Romy came forward, baby-stepping, trying to feel with his toes how far down the ledge was.

'I can't see you,' he said.

'I'm here,' Avtar said.

Romy panned the torch left, full in Avtar's face.

'Easy,' Avtar said, looking away.

Romy waded over, the water now at his thighs. The tunnel was probably only two arm-widths across.

'This is the worst,' Romy said.

'Over there. I think I can smell it.'

The light hit what looked like a writhing ten-foot maggot stuck to the side of the tunnel.

'Bhanchod,' Avtar said, with something like awe in his voice. 'The biggest yet.'

'It's moving.'

'Rats.'

Romy looked down, breathed hard. Avtar hoped the boy wouldn't be sick again, though he could feel his own stomach recoiling. The smell. Damp, lush, prickly. Marshy with faecal matter and eggs.

'Keep that torch straight,' Avtar said. He moved forward, pointing the jet at the globe of fat. It was so big it blocked off half the tunnel. 'Shall I go for the middle?'

'It's moving,' Romy said again.

'Hopefully it'll collapse.'

Romy stayed back, shining the torch while Avtar arranged his hands along the hose, keeping it steady, aiming up. He squeezed the chrome trigger and water came out at an astonishing speed, crashing into the fatberg. The sound was glorious, and with the amber torchlight and the fact of being underground, it felt to Avtar like they were in some computer game, battling their way past beasts.

He released the trigger and the jet of water flopped to nothing.

'How much?' Avtar said, and Romy shone the beam on the water. There were only a few plates of fat glistening here and there, detached from the main ball.

'I'll have to break it up,' Avtar said. He handed the hose to Romy and took the axe from his belt and splashed forward. 'Light!'

'Sorry,' Romy said, struggling with the weight of the hose.

With a hand over his mouth, Avtar raised his arm high and

started to hack. Bits plopped into the water. There were black-high scurrying sounds. Spitting, he returned to Romy.

'Bhanchod fucking shit-smelling dirty gora cunts.' He spat again, shivered. 'Here,' and he took back the hose. 'Where did I cut?'

'At the belly,' Romy said.

Avtar pulled the trigger and shook the hose about, making the thick rope of water dance. 'I think we've got it,' he shouted.

The globe of fat started to detach from the side of the tunnel, reaching, resisting, stretching like chewing gum peeled off the underside of a shoe.

'Back, Randeep! Get back!'

'Who?' Romy said, but it was too late. The fatberg crashed into the water, exploding against the sewer bed, and there was the terrible noise of frenzied black rats. Romy panicked and the beam plunged. The rats were everywhere, rushing between their legs, hissing through the water and the dark.

Avtar accepted the deck – it was his turn to deal. Stuck in the shed, there wasn't much else to do in the evenings. Their boss, with the dyed black beard and white eyebrows, lived with his family in the house while Avtar and the boys slept here. His name was Jagdish Singh – the side-panel of his van read *Jagdish Singh Dhindsa & Sons* – and he insisted they call him sahib. 'I pay you, I feed you, I put a roof over your heads. If after all that you can't respect me, then get out now.' That was on the drive up from Gobind's to this red-brick semi in Wolverhampton, and he'd repeated it nearly every day since.

'He thinks he's some big tycoon,' Avtar said, shuffling the pack.

'Count me out,' Romy said. 'Bed.'

'Take the mattress.'

'It's your turn.'

'Just take it.'

He dealt the cards. There were three of them playing, under the soft glare of a battery-powered lamp.

'Tough day?' asked Sony, a Malveyah.

Avtar nodded, finished dealing. 'You know, if there's a hell for boys like us, I think we've found it.'

'Tsk, come on, yaar. Play. This is meant to be our fun time. You're miserable enough during the day.'

It was Biju – Baljinder, maybe, though he'd never said. He was a fat little joker from a village near Gurgaon. His middle was so perfectly round, it seemed blown up like a beachball.

'I've been letting you all win so far,' Biju went on. 'Now watch how I make you all my bhabhi.'

'How many did you do today?' Avtar asked.

'Seven,' Sony said. 'You?'

Avtar frowned, played his highest club. 'Four.'

'He knows you work hard.'

'Yeah. Maybe.'

Biju went with a low heart, forcing Avtar to risk the ace.

'This'll cheer you up,' Sony said. 'I heard there's a pataka shed a few streets down. What do you think? Next pay day?'

'Can't,' Avtar said. 'Need to—'

'Pay my loans and send some home,' they finished for him, yawning comically.

'Have some fun,' Sony said. 'Make up for it next month.'

'Do you have a job for next month?' Avtar asked, genuinely.

'Something'll come up.' He sounded cagey, like he probably did have one ready. Avtar didn't blame him for not disclosing it. He'd have done the same.

'Oh, you goat-fucking Malveyah!' Biju said after Sony very gleefully turned over his pair of twos.

Avtar threw his cards into the centre. 'Whose deal?'

In the van, Avtar asked what was going to happen to them next week.

'Next week?' Jagdish said.

'You said the contract's finished next week.'

'It is.'

Avtar waited. All the boys were listening. 'Do you—?'

'I've not decided what I'm going to do with you yet.'

'So you might find work for us? Another contract?'

They could see him smiling in the mirror. 'There is work. But not for all of you. Some of you I'll have to kick out. Let's see who performs best, yes?'

On the last day, as they hosed off their suits and changed into their clothes, Jagdish approached. 'How many?'

'Four,' Avtar said. There was no point lying – they had cameras to double-check.

'Is that all? Four? Do I look like your chachi's cunt that you can come to me with a straight face and tell me you only did four all day?'

'Sorry, sahib.'

'Saala, bhanchod. Is it him? Is he holding you back?'

Romy stood a little way off, grimacing into the van's wing mirror as he pulled strips of slime out of his hair. Avtar said nothing, and Jagdish nodded and put a cross beside Romy's name.

They'd not been home an hour when five of them were ordered to grab their stuff and get back in the van. He'd drop them where he'd found them, and from there they could return to whichever rathole they'd sprung from. Romy collapsed onto his knees, then his belly, and pressed his forehead to Jagdish's grey loafers.

'Please, sahib, let me stay.'

'Get away,' Jagdish said, though he seemed to be enjoying this little moment. 'I've made my decision. It is final.'

'No, sahib. It can't be.'

'Sahib?' Avtar said, tentative. 'Please let him stay.'

'Do I look stupid? He's never been a worker.'

'I will, sahib,' Romy said. 'Please let me stay.'

'Get in the bhanchod van. Enough drama.'

'Please, sahib,' Avtar tried again. 'I'll make sure he works.'

'How about I keep you both and pay for one. You happy with that? Half each? Agreed?'

Romy looked at Avtar. 'Bhaji'll agree to that,' he said. 'That's OK, isn't it? We'll carry on working together.'

'Well?' Jagdish said.

Avtar shook his head and moved away from the van.

'Thought so,' Jagdish said. 'Not so high-horse now, eh?'

They returned to the shed: Avtar, Biju, Sony and two others.

'Surprised he kept you, fattyman,' Sony said.

'I raise the standard of the group,' Biju replied.

Jagdish appeared at the door. 'Before I forget, I need your passports and papers. For the next job.'

'You took copies already,' Sony said.

'Hurry up. Or do you want to get in the van?'

They handed over their documents and heard the key turn.

'Why's he locked it?' Biju asked, switching on the lamp.

'At least we get a mattress each now,' Sony said. He drew the deck of cards from his trouser pocket. 'Everyone in?'

Avtar sat down, forcing dust out of the mattress. He rubbed the space between his eyebrows and, as if the two things were connected, a picture of Randeep materialized: standing with his case in the car park, getting smaller.

'All right?' Biju asked.

'Why wouldn't I be?'

'No reason. Some people might feel a little guilty.'

'Luckily for me, guilt's a luxury I can't afford.'

'Hmm. Maybe.'

Avtar frowned. He felt disturbed by his attitude, though he was sure he'd had no choice, either with Randeep or Romy. 'Come on. Hey, Sony – deal us in.'

*

Her right foot rose off the seat of the chair as she reached up. She held the plastic collar, unscrewed the dead bulb, and replaced it with a new one she unfurled from the knot in her chunni. She tried the switch and the bulb glowed, palely bright against the window. There was nothing more to do. The room was clean, her bed made. And yet they were still here. She moved to the landing, where the sun ran thinly down the stairs. She'd not even been back a week and this must be the fifth family to visit, to congratulate Baba.

'But why did she go?' she heard the aunty ask.

'She's not said much,' Baba Tarsem Singh said. 'I think the wedding scared her. For so long it's only been us three. She's a good girl, really.'

'Don't make excuses for her.'

'Tejpal's right,' the aunty said. 'She rubbed your face in the shit, in front of everybody. She humiliated you. What kind of good daughter does that?'

'I know my Narinder. She has a good heart. And I know she won't do it again.'

'I won't let her do it again. I'll kill her first. She's getting married, and then she's someone else's problem.'

'Tejpal, please. You should support your sister.'

'I love her, Dad, but what she did was wrong. She put a knife through this family.'

'She's naive.'

'Stop making excuses for her,' he said again, louder this time. 'You've always made excuses for her. Oh, she's young. Oh, she's innocent. She's not any of those things. She knows exactly what she's doing.'

'I'm only saying it's not been easy for her. Growing up without a mother.'

A silence. Then: 'And I suppose it was a cakewalk for me? But I've only ever lived my life by the rules. By your rules.'

'Tejpal—'

Narinder shrank back before her brother could see her. She heard him take up his keys from the glass table in the hall and the front door slam.

They ate late that night, waiting for Tejpal, and when he did return he said he wasn't hungry and went straight up to his room. Narinder reheated the food and sat down to eat with her baba. The night pressed against the window. There was the choppy grind of a helicopter passing overhead. The lamp turned her father's yellow turban copper and cast on the wall a huge shadow of his cane.

'I'm sorry I embarrassed you, Baba.'

She'd been desperate to say this and as the words left her mouth a channel seemed to open up between them.

'I know you are, beiti. As I keep telling everyone, I know my daughter and even if she can't tell me her reasons they must be noble ones.'

'I think they were.'

'But you say it is all over now?'

She nodded. She still hadn't heard from Randeep. If he didn't get in touch by the end of the year she'd contact Vakeel Sahib herself and ask him to get the divorce done with. He'd said it would take a month or two only. For now she'd remain here, with her father. Next June she'd marry Karamjeet and spend the rest of her life with him and his family.

'Your chunni,' her father said.

'Hm?'

'It's fallen, beiti.'

'Oh, sorry,' and she reached behind her neck and lifted it up and over her turban.

'So, you lived alone? In Sheffield?'

'Yes, Baba.'

'You were never lonely?'

'No more so than here,' she heard herself say.

Her father paused mid bite, nodded. 'No friends?'

'No.'

'Neighbours?'

She hesitated. 'No. No one.'

She waited a few minutes so her father might not make a connection.

'Baba, in India, did you ever meet chamaars?'

'Every village has them. Why?'

'They spoke about them in the gurdwara yesterday. Are they treated very badly?'

'Chamaars? Better now than they used to be.'

'How did they use to be treated?'

He finished his mouthful. 'There was a boy working on our farm. We used to call them achhuts back then. Not chamaars. But he was only ever allowed to eat our leftovers. And not on plates, either. Your dadi would use a rag to scrape it all into his hands like this – ' he cupped his palms together in front of his beard – 'and I remember the dhal would be dripping between his knuckles and the vegetables would still have our teeth marks. And he'd walk off, stuffing it all inside his mouth.' Baba Tarsem Singh sipped water, perhaps to get the taste of the memory out of his own mouth. 'I've seen it still happen today.'

She'd stopped eating. She was looking down at her food. 'That's so cruel,' she said, quietly.

A pause. 'Why do you look so sad?'

She could hear the suspicion in his voice.

'Was he one of them? Who you went to Sheffield for?'

She imagined saying yes and seeing the terror on his face. 'I was on my own. Please believe me.'

'You promise me?'

She nodded and he seemed to accept this, though the concern remained in his voice. 'Of course. What was I thinking? But you were lucky. A girl your age living alone in a strange city. Anything could have happened.'

'It was exciting as well.'

Another worried look, a slight compression of the brow. Silent minutes passed.

'I forgot to tell Tejpal to change the bulbs in your room. Remind me in the morning.'

'I did them all earlier.'

He looked up from his spoon. 'You can change lights now?'

'It's not hard, Baba.'

'No, I guess not. What else can you do?'

'Fuses. And electricity meters. I can work them.'

Afterwards, she started piling the dishes into a small stack which she could carry in a single trip to the kitchen. Her father struggled to his feet, his hand tensing until it docked on the safety of his cane.

'Baba,' Narinder began. 'I wanted to ask how you'd feel about me getting a job.'

He said nothing at first, only stared. 'My pension does this family fine.'

'I nearly had a job in Sheffield. I think I'd enjoy it.'

He was looking at her strangely, eyes darting over her face, as if trying to follow where this was all going to end. 'We've spoken about this before. You agreed.'

She put the final plate on the pile and looked across. 'Maybe I've changed.'

She wasn't allowed to look for a job. Tejpal came charging into her room and told her that once she was married she could speak to her husband about it, but while she was under this roof things were going to stay as they were. 'You've done enough damage. Spare us any more shame.'

As Tejpal left, her father shuffled to the doorway. 'I'm sorry, beita. I did try. But you know what he's like. He'll never change.'

'Will you? Change? Or do you still expect me to follow your rules?'

He looked to the floor, sheepish, then reached for the doorknob and closed the door. She crashed her fists down on the bed, letting out a frustrated growl. They might never change, but she knew she had. She knew this wasn't how things used to look, that it was as if a filter now stood between her and the life she left, and what had at one time seemed clear was now a confusing grey.

She went to the gurdwara with her father that evening and sat behind the palki beside her fellow brothers and sisters. She thought it might help. She thought it might lend her mind some peace. Midway through the rehraas she opened her eyes. The others were still reciting, beautifully, tunefully; their faces lifted and ardent. She knew what they were feeling and knew she no longer felt it herself. Something had gone wrong. She found her baba at the back of the hall.

'Can we go, please?'

'You look like something's scared you.'

'No. Nothing. Please. I'd like to go home.'

—

She continued going to the gurdwara, every evening, with her baba. If she spent enough time in His presence she was certain these strange bottomless feelings would go away. The alternative was to parse her anxieties and discover what was wrong. She'd tried that, one morning at the window of her room. She looked out and saw Tochi being forced to eat some blank-faced master's leftovers and tried to connect that image with some idea she'd always held of His goodness. She couldn't do it. And then her whole being seemed to react in opposition to what she was in danger of glimpsing. Frightened, shaking, she stepped back from whatever thought lay on the other side of the sky.

In a roundabout sort of way, she asked Karamjeet about it on the afternoon of his visit. He'd been talking about whether they still had time to visit Hemkund Sahib after the wedding, and asked if she'd seen the news on DD, about the pilgrims who'd died trying to climb there out of season.

'Three of them. All young jawans. They thought they'd be fine.'

'Obviously they thought they'd be fine,' Narinder said.

'Pardon?'

'Why did they have to die?'

'Because it was out of se—'

'Why did God let them die? They were His people, coming to see Him.'

'I'm sorry, I don't understand. I don't think God killed them. He let them choose. They knew the risks.'

Her gaze dropped to the plain black leather of her shoes. If it pleases Him, she thought.

'Narinder, is everything OK?'

She nodded, looked up. 'I suppose it has to be.'

She didn't know why she was being so difficult – perhaps she just wanted reassurance – but it was unfair to take it out on him. He'd been so nice, defending her to his parents, not once bringing up the subject of her time away.

'I'm so glad to be marrying you, Narinder. I hope you're looking forward to the wedding as much as I am.'

They were sitting at opposite ends of the long settee, bodies angled towards the centre of the room so they were never quite looking at each other. She could think of no reply and reached for the prissy white teapot and refilled their cups.

When Karamjeet got up to leave, Tejpal escorted him to the door. Narinder stayed in the room, collecting the tea things onto a silver-plated tray. She could hear them in the hall.

'Thanks, Karamjeet. I don't know what to say. I don't know how Dad would've coped if you'd broken it off.'

'Stop apologizing. It feels like that's all you've done for the last nine months. We all make mistakes.'

'But she made a big one. Not many families would forgive and . . . Anyway, you've made it possible for Dad to show his face to the world again.'

She carried the tray to the kitchen, teacups rattling, and shut the door and stood with her back flat against it.

*

They'd been at the warehouse job for two weeks when, on the evening drive home, Avtar accused Jagdish of robbing them blind.

'Less than one pound an hour you're paying us.' He took a crumpled blue paper from his rear pocket – a cash-and-carry invoice – and pointed to the calculations on the back of it. 'I worked it out. Less than one pound an hour.'

'I'm getting less and therefore you're getting less. Simple economics.'

'But I can't live on this. I can't pay back anything earning this.' Bal would be calling soon. Perhaps as soon as next week. He didn't know what he'd say to him. 'I'm leaving. I'll find better work.'

'Arré, yaar . . .' Sony said, as if Avtar was going too far.

'Where do you think you'll go without your papers?' Jagdish said. 'You should be thankful I provide a roof over your heads.'

'You lock us in your shed.'

'It's an outhouse.'

The van stopped. They must have arrived. It was hard to tell from the back. As they filed into the shed, Avtar turned round. 'I mean it. I want to go. Give me my passport.' But Jagdish just laughed, as if Avtar had made a very pleasing joke, and locked the door.

Whenever a phone rang, he flinched. He prayed nothing was happening to his family. He needed to earn more. He needed to get out. Then, round the side of the cash-and-carry, in a grassy trough that had become a sump for several waste pipes, he found a pole, a short lilac metal one with flattened ends. It looked as if it might have once belonged on a girl's bicycle. He put it in his bag, and, that night, hid it in the gap between his mattress and the wall.

A week passed while he waited for his chance. The evenings darkened and a stiff wind blew in through the bottom of the shed door. Avtar pulled out one of his jumpers, which lay on him sloppily, as if on a coathanger, which, he supposed, he was.

'It's starting to get cold at night,' he said to Jagdish. They were on their way home. 'We need a heater.'

'Put some more clothes on.' Then, perhaps feeling guilty: 'Maybe I can get an extension lead.'

He told them there wasn't any work tomorrow. They could have the day off. His treat.

'Why?' asked Avtar.

'I'm busy. So you'll have to stay in. You'll get your food.'

'Will we still get paid?'

He saw Jagdish staring at him via the rear-view mirror. 'I'll think about it.'

In the shed, Avtar pressed himself against the door, his stomach to the iron and arms raised, as if someone had a gun to his back. He wanted to know what was happening tomorrow, but all he could hear was a car running, indistinct laughter, maybe a football being kicked against a wall. He rejoined their card circle, squeezing in between Biju and Sony.

'At least he might pay us,' Biju said.

'He won't,' Avtar said. 'He's just saying that so we're still here when he comes back.'

'Where would we go?' Sony asked, chuckling drily, and he accidentally flipped a card over while dealing and had to gather them all up and shuffle again.

The door opening woke them all up. Sudden, unfriendly light. Avtar wanted only to remain in his dream, but he could smell popcorn, fresh, and yawned and removed his arm from his eyes. It was a woman. He sat up – they all did. He'd seen her sometimes at the kitchen window, a scrunchie in her hair. Today, her hair was down and wet and pulled forward over one shoulder. She looked like she was from India, an impression given by her make-up, perhaps: a thickly applied bright pink to go with her salwaar kameez. She was holding a red beach bucket and placed this on the wood floor. A steel plate covered the top, to which she added a foil-wrapped bundle.

'Dhal-roti,' she said, simply, kindly. 'I'll collect it later.'

'Eating out of a bucket?' Avtar said, disgusted.

'It's what Papaji said.'

'Tell your father-in-law we're not his pets.'

'Won't the dhal be cold by lunchtime?' Biju asked. 'I don't think I can eat cold dhal.'

'I'm sorry,' she said. 'I wish I could reheat it.'

'Why can't you reheat it?' Avtar asked.

She looked worried, as if she'd said too much already, and backed out of the shed and turned the key. They heard her soft tread on the grass.

'Did she look dressed up to you?' Avtar asked. 'Like they were going to a wedding? What day is it?'

'Friday,' Biju said.

'Sunday,' Sony corrected him.

'They'll be gone all day,' Avtar said.

'Did she smell of popcorn to anyone?' Biju said, trying to find an opening into the roti bundle.

Avtar listened at the door, until he heard voices hurrying each other on and car doors shutting. Then, nothing.

'They've gone.'

'What are you going to do?' Sony asked, sceptical.

He took the pole from the side of his mattress and drove it into the gap above the doorjamb.

'You'll ruin it for the rest of us,' Sony said.

'Just let him go,' Biju said. 'More work for us.'

Avtar yanked the pole out and drove it back in, until finally it stuck, slipping far enough through to act as a lever. He left it hanging there, half out of the door, while he recovered. Then he secured his feet and pushed hard against it. He could feel himself grimacing – 'You look like you're having the world's biggest shit,' Biju said – and at times it seemed as if the pole might snap, but then, and without the explosion of noise Avtar had prepared himself for, the lock retracted and the door clattered open. He stumbled to the ground, it had happened so unexpectedly.

'It's open,' he said, turning round, as if anticipating applause.

He went back for his rucksack, then down the garden, the pole reassuring in his hand.

The drive was empty and when he pressed his forehead to the window he could see no one inside. The kitchen door held a glass panel which he smashed with the pole, snaking in his arm to reach the lock. As soon as he stepped inside, a siren sounded, a careening wail of blue noise. Desperately Avtar rifled through some post on the counter, hoping to find his papers there. Nothing.

Sony and Biju and the others came hurtling past with their bags.

'You fucking bhanchod cunt!' Sony said.

He wanted to look upstairs, in Jagdish's bedroom. He was sure his passport would be there. But the siren. It was blaring murderously. He picked up the pole – 'Fingerprints,' his mind said – and ran. He ran round the corner of the house and up the drive. There were fields far off to the left and Sony seemed to be making for them, Biju many metres behind. Avtar went right, sprinting towards the main road.

*

Halfway up the stairs, Narinder heard her phone. It never rang these days. Maybe it was Randeep. She scrambled across the landing and into her room, finding the thing on her dressing table. She didn't know the number. She answered anyway. *Hello? Randeep?*

'Hello. Is that Narinder Kaur?'

He sounded familiar. 'Yes. Hello. I'm Narinder Kaur.'

'Oh good. It's David Mangold here. From the immigration office. Remember me?'

He said they were due their second and final insp— meeting. *Meeting*, he repeated. But the office hadn't received a reply to either of their letters over the last month.

'I trust everything continues to go well for you and your husband?'

'There's another meeting?' she asked, closing her bedroom door.

'Routine, of course. So we can cross you off our list, so to speak. Are you still in the same place? I can easily pop over again. Some time next week, say?'

She held on to her dressing table. She sat down. 'Could I ask my husband to call you?'

'I took the liberty of contacting your landlord and he said you left quite unexpectedly. Apparently, the front door sustained some damage. It all sounded very dramatic.'

Narinder hunted madly through her mind for something to say.

'I'm sure it was nothing to do with you.'

'No,' she said, glad of the out.

'As I thought. So, next week, then?'

Her hand went to her throat. Her mouth felt dry. 'I'll get my husband to call you.'

'Is he not there?'

'He's working.'

'Do you have a work number?'

She winced. 'No, sorry.'

'And you are?'

'Pardon?' He knew who she was.

'And you are where, if you're no longer at the flat?'

'I'm at home,' she said carefully.

'Right.' She heard his voice change. 'You do know that, under the terms of the visa, you're required to notify us of any amendment to your personal details?'

'Yes. I'm sorry. It won't happen again.'

'I'm sure it won't. I'll just take down your new address and we can update our systems. Fire away.'

She didn't know what to say. She felt herself being ground down.

'Ms Kaur?' he said, with deep insincerity.

'Yes. My husband will call you and he'll explain.'

A pause, as if he was thinking things through. She waited for him to say he was sending the police round this very minute.

'Right you are. But do make it soon. According to our database the second inspection needs to take place by the end of this month. Otherwise the wheels start turning and warnings get automatically dispatched and things can get a bit messy.'

She nodded. She just wanted to get off the phone. 'Yes. Yes. That's fine. Thank you. Thank you.'

All afternoon she tried to get hold of Randeep. She even dialled Vakeel Sahib's office in India, but they hadn't heard from him either.

The evening meal was small, quiet. Occasionally, Baba Tarsem Singh and Tejpal exchanged a few words. She wasn't listening. She said she was going to her room and would be down to wash up later.

'But you've hardly eaten,' her father said.

'I'll have it,' and Tejpal stretched for Narinder's plate.

She started up the stairs, fretfully, a sick feeling in her stomach.

'Wedding nerves,' she heard Tejpal say.

She took the suitcase from where it stood against her dressing table and opened the drawers built into the side of her bed. She put her clothes in the suitcase, zipped it up, and put the suitcase in the drawer and shut it. Still kneeling on the carpet, she placed her cheek on the cold duvet and hoped her father might one day forgive her.

She wrote a letter and propped it against her pillow and moved to the door. She listened: they sounded asleep. She closed her hand around the doorknob, finger by finger, and twisted her wrist to the left. It swung open without noise, and she picked up her suitcase and stepped onto the landing. The darkness was total, until her eyes adapted and shapes appeared: the shallow, square well at the top of the stairs; the ceramic bluebirds in the window, silently aghast. Tejpal's door was closed, but her father's was open. She could hear him breathing, deep and long, and in her mind's eye she could see him too, lying, as ever, on the right-hand side of the bed, his birdlike hands locked gently over his stomach. He looked so vulnerable. She picked up her suitcase and returned to her room. She couldn't do it to him again, not like this. She felt too old to be running away.

Two days later, Tejpal went out and said he wouldn't be back until the evening. Her father was in the front room, napping. A plate of carrots, chopped in half and then into sticks, lay on the table before him.

'Baba?' she said.

'Hm?' he said, not opening his eyes.

She waited and he lifted his face to her.

'Ki?'

'Baba, I need to talk to you.'

She sat on the other settee, at a right angle to him, and said she'd received a phone call, a few days ago now, which meant she had to go back to Sheffield. People would get into trouble if she didn't. Would he please give his permission for her to go?

He looked down at the gutka in his lap, and several long moments passed before he picked the book up and set it on the table, beside the carrots. 'What kind of trouble?'

'With the police.' Her eyes were on the carpet a few feet in front of her. She felt too embarrassed to look at him.

'Why can't you tell me what it is? Maybe we can help.'

'You can't, Baba. I've just – ' she covered her face in her hands – 'I've just got myself into such a mess. I'm so sorry. But I can't let people's lives be ruined because of me. I can't.'

His face quivered with frustration, as if he'd thought they'd moved on from this. 'Narinder, you ask too much. Too, too much.'

'I know I've not given you any reason to trust me, but I promise if you let me go I'll be back soon.'

'When?'

'By the end of the year.'

'And what do we tell Karamjeet's parents?'

'I'll be back in plenty of time for the wedding. I won't let you down.'

'And Tejpal? Should your brother not have a say in this?'

'Do you think he'd agree?'

'Be sensible.'

'Do you think he'd come after me?'

'He's your brother. You're more alike than you think.' Though he reached for his cane, he didn't stand up. 'And you've never let me down, but you're asking me to put this family's honour at your feet. I can't risk that, daughter.'

'Baba, I've got to go.'

'Narinder.'

'I'm going, Baba,' she said. 'I won't let you stop me.' She felt the words rushing up her throat. 'Why can't you give me this? All I wanted was one year. A few months now. Why can't you give me that? I've given my whole life to you. For you. I've thrown my life aside so you can walk with your head held high and you can't even give me this? How is that right? How is that fair?'

It was the first time she'd ever raised her voice to her father. He gazed at her, neither of them blinking. Then he stood and left the room for many minutes. She could hear him in the kitchen. When he came back, he was holding some money in his free hand.

'Take it.' And she did, thanking him.

Then he did an extraordinary thing. He put his cane aside and with both hands removed his turban from his head and bent and placed it at her feet.

'Baba!' she said, dropping to the floor so they were both kneeling, his trembling hands in hers.

She'd never seen him without his turban. She'd never seen his grey-black hair in its tight ball on top of his head, seen the small, private, brown comb he used to keep it in check. It felt completely wrong to be seeing it now.

A tear rolled down his cheek. 'A Sikh's honour lies in his children and in the pugri on his head. Don't step on my honour, beita.'

*

The settee in the back was only big enough for a small child to sleep on. As Tochi uncurled, sitting up, he felt his spine click in several places. He fetched his holdall from underneath and, as always, checked his money was still there. He used the toilet opposite, brushed his teeth in the avocado basin, then switched on the lights and the fryers. This wasn't a sustainable long-term arrangement. Malkeet, the bastard, was taking half his wages in rent.

He'd been here ever since the gora knocked on his door. Some tall, tie-wearing guy with a clipboard, bubbles of foam at the corners of his lips, gesturing at the smashed door and demanding – as far as Tochi could make out – an explanation. Tochi had gone back for his bag, then shoved past the man and never returned.

He heaved a large white sack of potatoes to the chipper and slashed it open with a knife. It occurred to him that the gash looked like some kind of demented smile. Malkeet arrived, then Harkiran, and Tochi spent the morning in the kitchen, working steadily. He knew his way around by now.

That night, the shop closed, he tightened his bootlaces, grabbed his holdall and set off up the road. Everything was shut. The yellow Buddha in its restaurant window looked sinister and on the other side of the road a man shouted at a cashpoint. He noticed a red light blinking in the distance, under a streaky moon. He thought it was a plane, then realized it was the same iron TV mast he'd see during the day. How much more beautiful it was at night. He walked all the way to the end of Ecclesall Road, until shops disappeared and roads became lanes and the hills seemed close enough to touch. He carried on through the small wood and climbed the steps onto a bridge over the river. For a long while he stared at the black water.

He'd crouched beside a river like this and offered their ashes, four years ago tonight.

He'd spent a week in hospital, which Babuji paid for, then he'd discharged himself. His parents' bodies were with the old man – they'd been left in the auto. Tochi returned alone to the bend in the track, the bend where he'd told Dalbir and Palvinder to get out and run. It looked different in daylight. The sun on the fields. A gentle mist. He made for the trees and didn't have to search for very long.

The next day, towards the end of the lunchtime rush, Malkeet came through to the kitchen and said some Nanaki was asking about him out front. 'You going all fundo on us?'

Tochi peeled off his gloves, drew away his hairnet.

'Ask if she wants a job. Could do with replacing Kirsty.'

He lifted the counter flap and walked straight past Harkiran at the till and her waiting under the TV, and carried on to the forecourt. She followed him outside. She looked anxious, like she was lost. Her suitcase was with her.

'I need to speak to Randeep. We're in trouble. You need to tell me where he is.'

'Who's in your flat?'

'What?'

'Is it empty?'

'What? No. I don't know. It's not mine. I'm looking for Randeep.'

'You rented,' he said, to himself.

'I can't go back there. My brother . . .'

He made a face: her family issues were of no concern. 'I've got work to do,' he said and made to leave.

'Can't you at least give me his old address? It's the only place I can think of. Please? I'm desperate.'

He gave directions: through the gardens, up the main road, take one of the roads left, after the pub. It's up there. A green-and-blue door.

She looked pained – it was too much to absorb. 'You'll have to take me.'

He turned to go back inside.

'I'll pay you.'

She returned at night, after his double shift had ended, and he took the money and told her to follow him. The gates to the gardens were locked, so they walked the long way round. It was a cool night. Leaves were falling into measly piles. She noticed his things in the holdall across his back.

'Do you still live downstairs?'

'It doesn't matter where I live.'

The house was in deep shadow. He went up the path, crouching to listen at the letter box, then through the flimsy side gate and round to the back door. He tripped the lock with his screwdriver and stepped into the kitchen. The lights didn't work but he could make out the blue flour barrel, and the rota, and the calendar beneath that. The beads tinkled as if nautch girls lay in wait. He shut the back door.

'Is Randeep here?'

He heard fear in her voice. Perhaps she thought he'd tricked her into something. Into coming to this empty place.

'No one's here. They've all gone.'

He inspected all three floors. The TV was still there, and so were the Union Jack chairs and upturned blue milk crates, and the settee, and the pack of eight joss sticks, unused on the windowsill. In his old room, his mattress lay on its side, against the wall. Randeep's too. He turned round.

'Your friend's run away. I can't help you any more.'

She didn't seem to follow. 'So what do I do? How do I find him?'

'I don't know.'

'But don't you understand? I need to find him. We could be in trouble.'

'Get out.'

'What?' She sounded surprised. 'But I've nowhere to go.'

'Ask your God for help.'

She looked away, stung. 'Do you think he'll come back here?'

'I want to live alone.'

She nodded. 'It would only be until I can get in touch with him. I really do have nowhere else to go.'

He seemed to think about this. 'You only paid me to bring you here. Not to stay.'

She looked up, her gaze long, as if only now understanding the blunt terms of this world she had penetrated. She brought her bag round to her stomach. 'How much?'

He awoke before sunup, the water lapping the riverbank and his lips numb with cold. Already some of the men were sliding on their rucksacks and heading off for the day. He brushed his teeth, spitting red foam into the river, and as he dipped his toothbrush the sevadarni from the gurdwara arrived, a young woman in a kesri. She handed out roti and went down the line collecting any clothes that needed washing.

'Nothing today, bhaji?'

Randeep shook his head.

She left a small battery-pack generator, three sockets either side, so they could charge their phones, and said she'd collect it tonight when she came back with their laundry.

He was the last man under the bridge. It was always this way. A family of ducks squawked past, the babies fighting viciously. He folded the blanket lengthways, rolled it up so it fitted into his suitcase, and set off towards the city, its chalky greys and limes.

He walked through the Eagle Shopping Centre and past the Playhouse, on to the park. The pedalos were all chained to the railings. Every now and then some couple or other would arrive and the pimply student at the park kiosk would unchain one of the pedalos and roll it to the lake. Randeep watched them for a while, then carried on to the park cafe, put his suitcase down and read the menu on the blackboard outside. He had enough for jammy toast, which he ate with tea. Then he picked up his suitcase and walked out of the park, counting his steps from the cafe to the gate, wondering if the number would be different from yesterday's.

He reached a heavy junction jammed with black taxis and white double-decker buses, crossed when the green man told him he could, and carried on past the library and art museum, towards the hospital. At some point he turned left down an alleyway, which led to a tall, thin gate made of planks painted black. He walked in.

Straight ahead was the back end of the shop – Bhalla Textiles – and to his right was the shed. He knocked on the door. The same woman answered: much older than him, hair loose and cut coarsely at the shoulder, rouge smeared beyond her lips.

'Ah, you! I knew you'd be back! Come in, come in. You're not going to run away before we even start this time, are you?' He didn't move. She kissed the air, took him in her arms. 'Come to me, my baby. Come here and let Anita love you, my darling, darling boy.'

Afterwards, he leaned against the gate thinking he might vomit. He didn't. He looked up. The air had taken on a grainier feel, the day beginning to close in. He should go back to the river. Instead, he carried on towards the hospital, which went on for several streets, and on each street there was some sort of ward he had to circle round. Soon, he didn't know where he was. He didn't know these roads. They weren't full of shoppers. They were grubbier, most of the windows painted over. Signs. Chaddesden. Mickleover. Burton-upon-Trent. His heart was thick in his chest. He didn't know where he was going. He didn't know this place. He didn't know this country. He spotted a payphone and dialled his mamma. He couldn't get through. He tried four, five times. He bang-banged the receiver down and looked up. Their faces were in the glass. Jaytha. Rishi. Gurpreet. What he'd done to them. He'd done. He looked down at himself as if for the first time seeing the violence inside him. He was terrified. He didn't mean to do it. He thought of his father. He folded to the ground, as if the glass box itself was caving in on him.

'So you didn't jump? You fell?'

It was Prabjoht, passing Randeep tea from the flask. They were back under the bridge.

Randeep nodded, shivering wet under the blanket. 'I think so. I didn't see it.'

'It's a fucking river!'

He could feel all their eyes on him. He was sure he'd fallen and not jumped, though he couldn't be certain. All he remembered was staggering along the towpath, suitcase heavy in his hand, seeing their faces. And then someone was pulling him out.

Above, fireworks flared, dressing the night in sequins. Someone shouted that it was time to eat, and, as sometimes happened, there was a good amount of food that evening. There was mithai from Prabjoht, whose job involved assembling boxes of the stuff, and fish pakoras from a boy whose massi gave him food parcels every week. A new arrival passed around fried chicken drumsticks. He was a heavy Panjabi with fingerless gloves. He looked like Gurpreet. Gurpreet. Randeep shut his eyes.

Hours later he woke up, still shivering. At least the gurdwara would be delivering more blankets tomorrow – one extra for everyone. They needed them now the freeze had begun. He sat up, rubbing his arms. The night wind had picked up too, and as he looked down the line of sleeping bodies, he saw that they had disappeared under a fugitive covering of dead brown leaves.

12. CABIN FEVER

On Mondays she left the money on the kitchen table, the notes weighed down under the belly of a spoon. The money would be gone the next morning. She never saw him. He left before she came down, and she'd be in bed, the hour long past midnight, when she heard him return. There'd be the sound of a lighter being clicked, a pan being encouraged to boil.

Her room was at the rear of the house, on the first floor. His on the second. He'd told her to stick to her room, the kitchen and bathroom, and always to use the back door. They avoided the lounge and kept it unlit. She noticed one day that he'd removed all the light bulbs from any room with a window that looked out onto the street.

She was used to being alone in a house. The silence didn't bother her. The emptiness did. The clean sweep of the walls, the dark consistency of the rooms. It was as if wherever she went she was confronted by herself, ridiculed. She spent much of the day by her bed, whispering to God – to keep her strong, not to abandon her.

One night she heard voices downstairs. She'd been kneeling on the ground and she stood and moved to the landing. She leaned over the banister, then quietly descended and watched from the entrance to the kitchen, holding the beads aside. He had his back to her and the garden door was open and she could see three men trying to look in. Indians, all.

'We heard this had been empty for weeks. Months,' one of them said.

'Like I said, I live here,' Tochi said.

'You live here with her?' the man said.

One of the others guffawed. Tochi said nothing.

'Is he telling the truth?' the man asked her. 'Do you live here together?'

Narinder nodded.

'You both in this big house?'

'You'll have to find somewhere else,' Tochi said.

The men seemed to accept this.

'Can you spare any food, friend?'

'No.'

'I've some dhal,' Narinder said, coming into the kitchen a little. 'You can have that.'

They came in – 'Obliged, sister' – and sat shivering around the table while she heated the dhal in the microwave. Once finished, they thanked her and said they'd be on their way. Tochi followed them through the side gate and watched them disappear down the road. When he came back she was still there.

'Will they be all right?' she asked.

He returned to his food on the cooker. 'Don't do that again.'

'They were hungry. Would you let them starve?'

He said nothing and she went back through the beads and up the stairs.

She found the library again easily enough, and the lady's name clicked into place the moment Narinder opened the door and saw her standing behind the reception desk. Jessica. It was, she later thought, a name well suited to white-haired ladies with bright blue eyes. Smiling, anxious, Narinder approached. She wanted to apologize, that was true. She had also wanted to get out of that house.

'Narinder,' Jessica said. 'Well, better late than never, I say.'

'I'm sorry. I'm so sorry for letting you down.'

Jessica showed her to the staff kitchen, where the interview had taken place. 'I'm a firm believer in the power of a good, strong brew.' She plucked a box of camomile from the high cupboard. 'I'm assuming you've come back because you still want the job?'

'Oh, I'd love to . . .'

'You don't sound very sure?'

'You see, I'm only here for two or three months. Then I've got to go back home.'

'That's fine with me. It's always busier in the winter. Unless you have better things to do?'

'No, no. Definitely not. I don't have anything to do. It's just—' She struggled to know how to say it. 'I don't want anyone to find me.'

Jessica filled the mugs with boiling water. 'In that case, let's just keep it all very informal, shall we?'

She loved the job. It was basic admin and filing and only for two or three days a week, but it rescued her from the accusatory silence of the house. She found she liked being around other people, kind people. It was its own peculiar balm. Only when she left the library and started for home did she fully remember that the immigration man was on to them and that Randeep still hadn't been in touch. She'd tried calling him every day. At first his phone had gone straight to voicemail, as if it was switched off, but now it didn't even do that, and all she got was a long dead note, flatlining. She couldn't believe he'd run away, not this close to getting his stamp.

As she turned onto Ecclesall Road, she saw Tochi up ahead: she recognized his jacket, the ribbed collar arranged around his neck. There was something about the way he walked that had become familiar to her, something to do with the way he kept his elbows pressed to his sides. She expected him to take a left after the pub, then pass the school and climb to their road. He walked straight on. Perhaps he knew a shortcut, but when she got to the house he wasn't there. Thirty minutes later he came in, and, without acknowledging her, went to his room.

She'd not been to the gurdwara for nearly a month now, not once since she'd been in the house. She knew she was avoiding it, was scared of it, scared of everyone taking one look at her and seeing how she was failing Him. It was easier to stay in her room, where she could convince herself that these feelings weren't real, or were temporary and more to do with her situation than any change inside her. On Gurpurab, however, the pull was too great and she felt she had to go and pay her respects. She caught the bus after work, and, head bowed, went up to the darbar sahib and remained there until the end of the rehraas. Afterwards, she entered the langar hall, to share in the food. She saw her old friend Vidya coming towards her. She'd had her baby.

'You should go,' Vidya said, ushering Narinder out of the queue.

For a sickening moment, Narinder thought they really had seen inside her and were throwing her out.

'Some men were here looking for you. Showing your photo to everyone.'

'Oh.'

'Yes. Oh. So it's better if you stay away.'

'That's my brother. He—'

'I don't need to know. It's not safe here.'

She prayed that night. She took out from her suitcase the photo of Guru Nanak, stood it on the windowsill, and sat cross-legged before it. *Waheguru is my ship and He will bear me safely across.* It was one of her favourite lines. The words would surround the edge of her world in glimmering halo and she'd feel reassured. Not tonight. She repeated the words again and again but there came no halo, and there came no ship. There was only a frightening and oceanic darkness.

For two days she didn't eat. She couldn't. She felt hollowed out, as if some instrument had scooped away all appetite. On the third evening she forced herself to boil a quarter-cup of rice, which she sat at the table and ate with a glass of milk. She washed her plate and dried it with tissue-paper and set it aside. Then she returned the carton of milk to the fridge. As she closed the fridge door, she noticed on the upper shelf a second carton, opened. They wouldn't get through both. Half would be wasted. She felt suddenly angry and left a note, in Panjabi, asking him to please check in the fridge before buying milk as there was no point in wasting it, and that he was welcome to use any milk she bought. She didn't know why she did this, wrote this note. Because if He really had gone, then she couldn't understand what the force was that drove her to try and do good. So maybe He hadn't gone after all, maybe He was still there, watching undetected, another pair of eyes trying to catch her out.

She wrote a second note when two days later the same thing happened. She left it on the kitchen table, along with her weekly payment, and when she returned from work that evening both were gone. She opened the fridge. Another pointless new carton. She buried her face in her hands.

Jessica handed Narinder an envelope – her wages in cash. 'I do hope you're enjoying it with us?'

'I am. I really am,' and she meant it. She never felt more part of the world than when she was working.

She walked home with her coat buttoned up and a hand at her throat, scrunching her collar closed. Again, she saw Tochi up ahead, going past their turn-off. She still didn't know why he did that. Once she was in the kitchen, she went through the beads and up to her room, taking off her coat as she went. She splashed some water on her face from the basin in the bathroom and returned downstairs. She chopped an onion and set it to stew on the stove, adding a cube of the garlic-ginger mixture she'd learned to make in bulk and keep chilled in ice trays. Then she wiped the counters down with a new disinfectant she'd bought, hoping this one might at last rid the surfaces of their black streaky skin.

She heard the scrape of the side gate, footsteps. She froze, watchful, but it was only him, coming past the window and now through the door. A blue carrier bag hung from his fingers and this he lifted onto the counter and she watched him place the bread and eggs to one side and then take out the carton of milk and step towards the fridge. Anger propelled her forward and she snatched the carton from his hand and threw it to the floor.

'Why are you being like this? Why? Have I become so worthless?' Her eyes were white-wide, beseeching. She pressed a finger to her chest. 'What have I ever done to you? To anyone? I want to know. Why is this happening to me?'

He picked up the carton from the floor and put it on the shelf, next to hers. She'd moved to the cooker.

'There was a raid,' he said. 'Here.'

She turned round. 'That was months ago.'

'Three months ago.'

She didn't think she understood. 'And Randeep— What? He's been deported? But I'd have been told.'

'All I know is there was a raid. Sometimes they keep an eye on the house.'

'What does that mean?'

'He might have come back here too soon.'

'But he's got a visa.'

He took a few slices of bread and began to butter them.

'Are you going to leave now?' She realized she didn't want him to.

'If you stay quiet – if you quit the tantrums – they won't come again.' He took a dented, grim-looking tin from the cupboard – pilchards – and slopped it all into a pan.

'I'm making a fresh sabzi,' she said. 'I can make enough for two.'

'No.' Then: 'Thank you.'

*

A new girl had started at Crunchy Fried Chicken, replacing Kirsty, but for some reason to do with babysitters she could only work the late shifts. Tochi had been moved to earlies, finishing each day at 4 p.m. He'd argued with Malkeet over it, saying they didn't need anyone else and he'd been coping fine with the double shift.

'But I need someone who can banter at night,' Malkeet said. 'Someone who doesn't look like he wants to kill half my customers.'

A week on, he was still angry about it, about the cut in his income. He hauled the five-litre canister of oil into his arms and, to shake the dregs from the bottom, banged it against the steel fryers, hard.

'Very mature,' Harkiran said.

Then Tochi topped up the oil and chucked in the chips. But he'd forgotten to lower the temperature and the splashback was considerable. He managed to look away in time and felt only his forearm scald.

'You idiot!' Malkeet said, turning the gauge. He fetched a tube of soothing cream from the toilet room. 'See what happens when you do things in a temper? Turn round. Lift your T-shirt.'

'It's fine,' Tochi said.

'Your back got splashed to fuck. How can it be fine?'

'I said it's fine.'

His arm, however, was hot and sore and red, as if a whole world of heat was trapped inside it. For a moment, he thought he felt his back tense, his body remembering. He took the cream home and applied it again, then found a bandage and sat at the table and wound it crudely up from his hand. He tried tidying the ends in, but as soon as he stood up the whole thing unravelled. He was looking for a safety pin under the sink when she walked through the door.

'What happened?'

'Nothing.'

'Can I help?'

He carried on searching, knocking aside her stupid cleaning bottles.

'Do you want a pin?'

He stopped. 'Don't put yourself out.'

She fetched several from her room and told him to sit while she took the bandage and started at his elbow and worked tidily, carefully, down to his wrist. He checked, but she didn't seem to mind touching his skin. Maybe she didn't know. Or didn't care. In any case, each time he felt the soft scrape of her fingertips, he had to concentrate hard on the door straight ahead.

She used three pins to keep it all in place and said he should change it every day. 'But I can do that.'

He nodded.

'So you left work early?'

'Yes.'

'I see you sometimes. Walking home. Except you come a different way.'

He said nothing.

'Is it quicker? Your way?'

'Quicker?'

'I mean, why don't you just turn off the main road nearer the house?'

'I used to.'

'You don't any more?'

'No.'

'Why not?'

He sighed, impatient. 'Because of the police.'

She thought on this, in case she'd missed something. 'I don't think I've ever seen any police round there.'

'Perhaps because you don't need to worry about them.'

'Can I ask where you see them?'

'Are you calling me a liar?'

She didn't respond, and he seemed to regret the accusation.

'Near the school,' he said.

'The school?'

'That's what I said.'

She felt a smile coming to her lips. 'Do you mean outside the school?'

He looked across.

'At about four o'clock?'

'If you've got something to say, tell me.'

She explained what a lollipop lady was, that it had nothing to do with the police and was no reason for him to walk so far out of his way.

'Honestly. You don't have to do that.'

He nodded. He seemed embarrassed. 'Thank you for telling me.'

The following afternoon, at work, he pulled her crumpled notes from his pocket and asked Harkiran to read them for him, and when Narinder got back from work that evening she opened the fridge and saw that he hadn't bought his own separate carton of milk, and had instead drunk from hers.

Avtar felt a little fresher that evening as he sat down to eat. He'd washed in the toilets of the club, feeling a bit silly as he watched himself digging into his armpits with pink soap from the dispensers. He removed the steel plate covering the food bucket. There was still maybe half an inch of watery dhal left, enough for tonight. He'd top up at the gurdwara tomorrow. He spun the bread wrapper open and extracted two slices. Afterwards, he put the empty bucket in the corner and moved to the back of the Portakabin and lay on the bunk he'd made. Through the window, Leeds wore its evening lights: yellow office windows, a nightclub called Flares flashing crazily. He'd hitched a ride here straight from Jagdish's, three weeks ago now. He'd hoped the building work might have started up again. It hadn't. The foundations were still exposed. The cranes and scaffolding, the mesh sheeting and aluminium tunnel, none of it had changed. He should count himself lucky, though, because the very next day he'd found work cleaning a club called Parachute, for a young mussulman on the make. God was still looking over him. And he'd get his visa renewed soon, with his second year about to begin. Yes, it wasn't all bad, he told himself, as he drew his knees up and brought his face down to meet them.

It was still dark when he woke up, scrambling, scared he was about to piss himself. He hurried behind the cabin, clomping over the bushy grass, unzipped and held down the front of his jeans with his thumb. Nothing came, though the need was still there, pressing. He forced it out and the pain was a furious current firing up and down his cock. He had to keep stopping, pissing in short bursts, and when he finished and zipped up he was sweating. That was the third time this week, and the worst. It was the change in his diet, he kept telling himself, simply his body's way of asking for food stronger than watery dhal. He was too awake now; there was no point going back to his bed. He seated himself on the middle step, head tipped against the broken cabin door. It was a clear sky; the moon distant, the air thin. He needed to get a blanket soon. That probably wasn't helping either. The cold. He pulled his knees up to his chest, one leg at a time, and rested his cheek down. He was so tired. Far away, a plane silently climbed.

Arriving in London, he went straight to the college. They took his photo, added some notes to his computer file, and asked him to complete an application confirming his student visa status, which included an agreement not to undertake any paid work in the UK. He signed it hurriedly and slid it back across the counter. She'd changed her hair colour but it was the same woman as last year, when he'd walked into the college on bare feet. She seemed not to have remembered him.

'Now I just need your passport.'

There was an infinitesimal shift in Avtar's face. 'My passport?'

'I need to take a copy. You can have it straight back.'

'But you took copies last year.'

'Procedures, I'm afraid.' She smiled and looked to the line of students behind him.

'I left it at home.'

'Well, we will need original copies before we can enrol you. Until then you won't be able to sit the course. Sorry.'

Avtar nodded, as if in total agreement with their procedures. 'I'll bring them next time.'

'Marvellous,' and she passed him back his folder.

He returned to Cheemaji in the car park.

'Everything OK?' the doctor asked. 'Nothing about late registration?'

Avtar nodded, handing him the visa agreement.

'I'll take this to the embassy myself and renew your visa. Congratulations!'

He nodded again and tried to smile.

They reversed out and joined a queue at the exit barrier, which seemed to have broken. The security guard was turning a wheel to raise the bar.

'Are you not teaching today?' Avtar asked.

'Hmm? Oh, no. I'm on leave for a few months. A sabbatical.'

He'd grown his beard and his discreet steel kara had been replaced with a hefty gold band, as wide as his wrist. Avtar didn't ask after any of these changes. He had enough problems of his own. He turned his face to the window and tried to look forward to a night in a clean bed.

He'd told Cheemaji his return train was at one o'clock, an hour earlier than it was due.

'Thank you, uncle,' Avtar said, levering himself out of the car.

Dr Cheema undid his seat belt and leaned across. 'Are you sure you won't stay? We've hardly talked.'

'I have work tomorrow.'

'Well, make sure you come back soon, acha? Plenty of room now,' he added, laughing a little embarrassedly. Avtar hadn't said anything the previous evening, when they'd parked up outside the big house and Cheemaji told him he could sleep in his son's – Neil's – room. It was only this morning, over breakfast, that the grandmother confirmed she'd gone, taking the boy with her.

'The whore.'

'Biji, please,' Cheemaji said.

'It's what the world thinks.'

'She might come back,' he said, faintly.

Avtar had heard of people getting divorced, though this was his first experience of seeing someone going through it. If he was honest, he couldn't help but think that Cheemaji had brought it all on himself.

He entered Kings Cross and found a table at the same coffee shop as last time. He was nervous. He pulled his chair back and made for the toilets. Again, it hurt to piss and he had to chew his bottom lip to keep from crying out. He washed his hands and splashed his face and told himself to be strong. He would not show them his fear. There was a man in a suit at the hand dryer and when he walked out, shaking the water off his fingers, he left his mobile on top of the machine. Avtar nearly called after him. Then he pocketed the phone and returned to the table.

Bal arrived alone and Avtar shook his hand and invited him to please take a seat, as if he was chairing this meeting.

'No bhaji?' Avtar asked.

'He's busy.'

'Shall I order some tea?'

Bal looked surprised. 'You're getting confident.' Then: 'We thought you'd run out on us. Too scared to answer your phone?'

'I've been busy.' He took his hand out of his pocket and put a few sorry-looking notes on the table. 'For your uncle.'

Briefly, Bal inspected the notes. 'That's not even gunna touch the sides, bruv.'

'The rest will come. I'm working now. There's nothing to worry about.'

'You're weeks and weeks behind.'

'A little more time,' he said, feeling the confidence slip. 'You can have this as well,' and he put the stolen phone on the table.

'I don't want— You're just not getting the message, are you?' He lifted his finger to Avtar's forehead and accompanied each syllable with a prod: '*Are-you-too-thick-to-un-der-stand?*' He fell back against his chair. 'I think it's time we paid your family a visit. Navjoht, right? And the shawl shop in Gandhi Bazaar?'

'Please. I'm doing my best.'

'He's put whole families on the street if the son hasn't paid up.'

'Just a little more time. Please! Can't you explain it to him?'

Bal clucked his tongue several times, in thought, then shrugged. 'I guess you could buy yourself one last chance.' He looked across, with intent. 'You know?'

Avtar reached down inside his sock and pulled out another note. It was the last of his money and he'd intended on buying some meat with it, some strong food that might feed this body. He handed it over. 'Thank you.'

———

He avoided the guards at Leeds station, instead stealing through a delivery gate left unchained. He crossed the car park and made his way to the hotel. The makeshift stairs only took him halfway. He had to climb a ladder to reach the top tier of the scaffolding. The wind was loud up here, so loud you could almost put a face to it. He could see how the city worked, the roads, the one-way system. From here, the motorway bridge was a mouth, and the traffic poured into it. It was all clear. Easy. It was all easy and yet still he was losing. He breathed. The wind slapped his face. How easy it would be to fall. How nice. He dug out from his rucksack the mobile he'd stolen and switched it on. There'd been several calls, probably from the gora in the suit. He put the phone at his side and probed further into the bag and found his college folder. A phrase from somewhere came to him: *reaching beyond his dreams*. He lifted the flap and tore into pieces every handout and worksheet and note he'd made. He threw the white pieces into the air and watched them shower and drift, until they were caught by the wind and vanished into the night.

13. THE OTHER SIDE OF THE SKY

In a single stiff shudder the minute hand docked on twelve and Tochi untied his apron from behind his back and hung it across the handle of the toilet door.

'Off already?' Malkeet said. He'd come into the kitchen for some batter and stood there holding a sloppy white pail of the stuff.

'It's four.'

'I can see that. Set my bloody watch by you these days.'

He went through the gardens and up the main road, taking a left past the school and the lollipop lady.

For dinner he fried four aubergines into something that looked like a bartha. He ate half of it with bread and put the rest in the fridge for the next day. He was at the sink washing up when she came through the back door.

'Hello,' she said.

He nodded.

'You're early again.'

Was she making a joke? He said nothing.

She took off her coat and carried on through the beads and up the stairs. He heard a door shut and, perhaps a minute later, the toilet flush and then her feet on the stairs again.

'Right,' she said, re-entering the kitchen, and he hoped she might say something else. Instead, she set about making a start on her meal.

He ripped off the last square of kitchen towel and sat at the table, lifting his boot to his knee and spitting on the sheet. He worked at the dirt, scrubbing and polishing, sometimes spitting directly onto the leather. She brought her bowl of food to the table and sat opposite him. It looked like chickpeas. He glanced across to the counter and the opened tin confirmed that it was. She didn't seem that hungry, though, sitting there weaving the spoon through her soup. She looked over.

'I'll be a bit late tomorrow. I'm going to look at some flats.'

He nodded, scrubbed.

Nothing more was said for a long while. She seemed distracted, looking up, looking down, fiddling with the kandha at her neck. Perhaps it was something to do with her family.

Finally, she said, 'I can't eat this. Would you like the rest?'

He didn't think anything of it, but she seemed suddenly appalled at herself, her eyes wide, a hand to her mouth, and she apologized and dropped the lot into the sink.

There was a diversion further up, so the bus driver advised anyone wanting the top end of Ecclesall Road to get off outside the 'Tanical Gardens and walk. Narinder didn't mind. It gave her time to think. *Nothing can come out of nothingness*, the granthi had said. *So to know joy, compassion, sympathy – to feel love – means also to have in the world their opposites*. She'd been reassured with that at the time, returned to Waheguru's ship. It was only now, an hour later, that she felt the doubt and loss and fear whirling again, into a vicious storm. Stay strong, he'd advised. He knows what you are going through better than anyone. He'll send you a sign. A sign, she thought. A sign. Walking up to the house, she turned her gaze to the stars, half hoping for the moon to explode.

The kitchen light was off as she turned the key and took a single step inside. All was quiet. Darkest was the hallway beyond the beads, as if someone were lurking there. But then she heard him moving about upstairs and there was a sudden feeling inside her of being safe. It was a feeling she recognized. It was the same feeling she used to get inside the gurdwara.

The oven wouldn't work. She tried all four settings and then all four again after switching it off. It must be the mains. She pulled the oven away from the wall and saw that it was plugged into a wall socket, rather than straight into the circuit board. She sighed. The fuse, then.

He opened the door before she'd even stepped across the landing, as if he'd been listening out for her.

'The oven,' she said, one hand around the banister. 'It's not working. The fuse has gone and I can't find another.'

'I'll get one tomorrow.'

She nodded. 'Thank you.' She wasn't sure why she felt disappointed by his response.

'I suppose you don't have anything to eat,' he said.

'I'll find something. The gas is still working.'

He started closing the door.

'Unless you have something already made?'

He looked at her, and with the most surprising of sparks in his eyes said, 'As long as you don't mind eating leftovers.'

She smiled, and her smile widened in response to his own. He had such a quick, easy smile, as if it was something he did all the time.

There was still some of the bartha left, which she ate with toasted bread.

'It's better with roti,' he said.

'Not my rotis.'

'You can't cook?'

'A gurdwara aunty tried to show me. She said it was like teaching a horse to hop.'

Another quick smile. A lovely smile, she thought.

'I can teach you. If you like.'

She looked down at her food.

'It doesn't matter,' he said, brisk, retracting.

'No, no. I'd like that. Thank you.'

He went to the Londis to see if they sold fuses. She was putting away the dishes when he returned. His hands were empty.

'No?'

'Closed. I'll get one from the main road tomorrow.'

'Try Wisebuys. They look like they sell that kind of stuff.'

He poured himself a glass of water and sat at the table, still in his jacket and scarf.

'It is starting to get cold,' she said.

'There's blankets.'

'I can't walk around wrapped in a blanket the whole time.'

He drank half of the water. 'How good were the flats you went to see?'

She didn't know why she'd lied about that, about going to the gurdwara after work. But she knew what he meant: if she didn't like staying here, if it was too cold for her, she could move.

'I'm sorry,' he said. He was frowning, as if wrestling with some thought or idea.

'Can you leave the kitchen light on when you come back? It can't cost that much extra.'

He drained the rest of the water and said nothing for a long time. 'It's not the cost.'

She turned round from the worktop. She was more surprised by the fact of a response than by what he'd said. 'Do you prefer the dark?' Then: 'Like Panjab, isn't it? All those power cuts.'

'I'm not from Panjab.'

'Oh,' and she felt foolish for being so presumptuous.

'I'm from Bihar.'

He looked across so piercingly she felt herself pinned to the counter.

'My family's Kumar.' He kept his eyes on her but it was almost as if she didn't care. Perhaps these English-born types didn't understand. 'It's a chamaari name,' he clarified. Still he saw no change in her face, no recalibration in her eyes.

'Is your family still in Bihar?' she asked, warmly.

He stood up, both hands running through his hair. It was disturbing, dizzying even, not to get the response he'd always had, since time began. 'My family are dead.'

Half an hour passed. Nothing more had been said. She wiped down the table and prepared her lunches for the following week. He, meanwhile, went round with his screwdriver – the TV, an old kettle – to see if a suitable fuse could be found. It was as if the silence between them had swelled into a third being, sitting at the table, someone whose eye they were working hard to avoid.

Behind her, she could hear panels being loosened, the sound of metal on metal. She opened the fridge door, put her sandwiches on the shelf, and reached for a bottle of orange squash.

'Would you like a drink?'

He dropped the plugs, screws spilling. His hands were shaking. She came over and they gathered up all the screws and the wires and the plugs themselves and set them on the table.

He told her he was thirteen when he left home to find work in Panjab. A lot of Biharis did this, he said. *The Panjabis don't work their own farms any more. Their sons have left for America, Canada, UK. The parents need servants.* For six months he looked for work, travelling west from Ambala to Bathinda, then north as far as Amritsar. He slept in an aluminium tunnel he'd carried from home. For money, he scoured dump sites for plastic bottles and sold them to local recycling collectors. It was only when he reached Jalandhar that he found a good job, taking care of the farm for a family who lived about twenty kilometres outside the city. Their two sons had gone to Sydney, working in fast-food restaurants. *My family were doing well*, he said. *I was making good money. For the first time we could afford to rent our own land and house. But after three years it all started to go wrong.* He told her everything. About his father's accident, his sister's wedding, his attempts to make it as an auto driver. The riots that engulfed them and killed his family. His two years working in a brick factory in Calcutta and the travel across to Europe by plane, ship and truck. His weeks on the streets of Paris and the year in Southall and, finally, the trip up to here, Sheffield.

'Life,' he said.

On Monday, heading out to work, she left the weekly payment on the table as usual. It was still there when she came back.

'But don't you need it?' she asked.

'I've enough.'

She divided the sabzi and put a plate of white bread in the centre of the table. She sat down. He was looking at the food.

'Is something the matter?' she asked.

All at once he moved to the cupboards and pulled out the half-packet of flour. He shook it into a plastic bowl and added water from the tap.

'Are you making roti?' she asked, curious. She joined him at the sink.

He was using his hands, the wet dough hanging off his finger-tips in stiff peaks.

'You made the sabzi, I'll make the roti.'

She watched him work, adding water a little at a time – which she supposed was where she always went wrong – and she saw the concentration on his face, as if nothing in the world was more important than this task. She watched the muscles in his upper arms rise and fall and a slight sheen of sweat form across his brow. When he finished, he threw the ball of dough high up in the air, caught it, and turned to her.

'Done,' he said. And there was that quick smile again, and here was she, feeling herself blush.

That became the shape of their evenings: one of them cooking up the dhal or sabzi, the other making the rotis, and then a meal together, quietly, peaceably. At night he stood at his bedroom window, a finger absent-mindedly, repeatedly, tracing a crack in the wall. It really did feel like the two of them were alone in the world, as if the city was all lit up while they hid away in this pool of darkness. He moved to his mattress, listening. Her room was below his. There were small noises, creaks, light-footed and careful, unidentifiable in themselves, so painfully womanly when heard together.

Narinder pulled out from her suitcase the photo of Guru Nanak and stood it on the windowsill. She brought her hands together underneath her chin and thanked Him. He'd seen that she was in trouble and had given her His sign. Tochi. That's what this had all been about. That was why she'd been brought onto this path. So that she might help Tochi, a good man who'd been through too much. She understood now. She stood up, light-headed with relief.

She wanted to rush upstairs and knock on his door. But no. She'd wait until tomorrow. She hurried into bed. It took some effort to get to sleep, though. She was restless, like a castaway who imagines they've seen the prow of their ship coming over the horizon.

She didn't catch him in the morning – he was still in his room and she needed to get to work. The evening, then, she decided. But when they sat down to eat that night she was suddenly nervous of his reaction. She mouthed a silent waheguru.

'You not hungry?'

'Hm?' She gave the tiniest shrug, more a twitch of her shoulders, and put the roti down. 'Not really.'

'You should eat.'

'Later.'

He thought on this. 'You don't have to eat with me every night. You don't have to feel sorry for me.'

'I don't feel sorry for you.'

'I shouldn't have told you about me. It's put you in a difficult position.'

'It's not. I like spending time with you.'

He said nothing for a while, as if absorbing this confession. 'I'll do the meal tomorrow.'

She took a sip of her water. 'I went to the gurdwara at lunchtime and signed up for the kirtan tomorrow. And the rest of the week. I'll have langar there.'

'And if someone sees you?'

'God will protect me.'

His jaw paused in its chewing, then resumed its work.

'Why don't you come?' She'd tried to sound offhand.

He said nothing.

'It might help.'

She watched him lift his face to her. The look in his eyes.

'It might not help straight away. But in time . . .'

'In time what?'

She hesitated, then forced herself on. 'It might help if you let in His love.'

'If I let in his love,' he repeated, as if trying the words out. 'His love for us all.'

He laughed a little, and turned back to his roti.

He didn't see her for five days. He cooked his own meals – potatoes with a thin gravy, adding peas if he could steal some from work – and ate alone at the table. He'd be lying on his mattress by the time he heard her key rattling in the lock, her footsteps on the stairs. He held his breath – if she knocked, he'd answer – but always she turned down the landing and away from the second flight of stairs. He moved onto his stomach. He wished these feelings would go away. He wished things could be as straightforward as they once were.

His phone rang – Ardashir. They'd not spoken since the hotel work dried up.

'You still looking for work?'

'In London?'

'Would you go to Europe?'

Tochi was crossing the empty car park in front of the chip shop, on his way home. He switched the phone to his other ear. 'Get to the point.'

'Building offices. In the capital of Spain. For the city's rich.' There was lots of work, he said, enough for two years at least. He knew one of the contractors, and they'd get Tochi across no problem. The job was his.

'Are you going?'

'Me? No, I don't think so. I'll see out my days here.'

Tochi said nothing.

'What is it? When do you want to leave?'

He'd reached the gates to the Botanical Gardens. He curled a gloved hand around an iron bar. 'I'm staying here.'

'Why?'

'I want to.'

'You want to take this chance, Tarlochan. That's what you want to do. They're talking thousands. It'll make your future.'

'I've decided.'

'You'll never earn as much.'

'I know.'

'You're being stupid.'

'Maybe.'

He heard Ardashir sigh – 'I hope she's worth it' – and then he rang off.

He jumped the gates and was soon at the house, but one look at the unlit windows and he turned on his heel and set off back down the road.

The nishaan sahib fluttered above the gurdwara and for a long while he stood in the sudden icy rain. Inside, he removed his shoes and washed his hands and took a ramaal from the basket and tied it around his head. He could hear the kirtan playing upstairs, the plaintive chords of the harmonium, and, sort of under them, encouraging them, her voice. Slowly, he climbed up. It was his first time inside a darbar sahib since his family's murder. He didn't bow down before the book. He sat at the back and watched.

She had her eyes closed, her long lashes resting on her cheeks. Her necklace swung out, the kandha suspended in the air, and he allowed himself to imagine kissing her neck. She sang well, with feeling. He could see the strain on her face, as if she was working hard to dig right into the hymn, either to pull meaning from it or to force some back in. For a whole hour she sang like that, hymn begetting hymn, and when the last chords were played she bowed her head towards the book and picked up her songsheets and stood to leave. That was when she saw Tochi, watching from the back.

They walked home together in silence. The wind still contained grits of rain. As they turned up their road he said, 'The puddles in my village when it rains, some of them are as wide as this street.'

She could hear the effort he was making. She should respect that. 'In the monsoons?'

'Not only then,' he said, after a pause, and she wondered if she'd said something wrong. Did they not have monsoons in Bihar?

'You sing really well.'

'Thank you. And thank you for coming. I hope you got something from it?'

He said nothing. At the edge of his sight she looked beautiful, tired but beautiful. Her eyes were soft, her lips slightly parted. The wind turned her chunni into a sail behind her, exposing the small carriage of her breasts, the river of a back that flowed into the gentle roundness of her hips. More than anything he wanted to be with her tonight. They were nearing the house.

'I've enjoyed this walk,' he said. 'Thank you.'

'I'm singing for someone's akhand paat on Sunday. Perhaps you'd like to come? It'll be busy.'

He stiffened. 'I don't think so.'

She didn't try to persuade him as he'd expected her to – perhaps wanted her to. She just turned and made for the side gate.

He'd done it once for her. That was enough. She was expecting too much, he thought, as she came through the beads, putting on her coat.

'The paat starts at nine. Do you think it might snow?'

'Maybe.'

She picked up her gloves, quickly tugging them on. 'I'm guessing from your tone that you're not joining me.'

'That's right.'

She came to him. 'Please. I want to help.'

'I don't need your help.'

She put her hand on his shoulder. 'It would mean a lot to me.'

She'd been gone some half an hour and he could still feel her hand on his shoulder. Shaking his head, he put on his jacket and locked the door behind him.

It was busy, as she'd said it would be. Guests were filing out of the langar hall and heading up the stairs and into the darbar sahib. He joined the queue and sat at the back of the chamber, as far from the granth as was possible. She was kneeling at an angle to the palki, her harmonium in front of her, a tabla player on either side. Her head was bowed. Hands together in her lap. For now, all was silent save for the granthi's quiet reading.

The akhand paat was to celebrate some girl's upcoming marriage – three years ago, the granthi said, this girl's parents had come into this very gurdwara and vowed to hold a service if their handicapped daughter was blessed with a husband. And how God had listened! A boy from India, no less! Tochi had heard of these marriages. A marriage of desperates. As the ardaas ended, he watched Narinder lift her fingers to the keyboard, lean towards the microphone and begin the opening raag.

Afterwards, a vague sense of relief ran through the room. It was all over. Some started to leave; others milled at the back of the hall, chatting. He could see Narinder packing the harmonium into its large leather case. He started towards her. She hadn't noticed him yet; there'd been too many present for that. He was coming up past the canopy when he saw someone who seemed familiar. A very tall, very thin man with an oversized turban that tapered to a tight point. Instinctively, Tochi took a pace backwards. Better to assume trouble than wait to figure it out. Then he knew. It was the man from the shop. The one with the divorced daughter. Tochi made to walk behind him. The man spoke: 'It's you, is it? And who are you trying to deceive today?'

Tochi said nothing.

'Any more families you're trying to ruin?'

He turned round, started to walk away.

'Liars always run,' the man bellowed, so loud Tochi could feel the whole room turn and stare, conversations dwindling. 'Remember his face, everyone. He's a chamaar who pretends he isn't so he can marry our daughters and get his passport. Isn't that right? Come on, which poor girl have you got your eye on today?'

He felt Narinder at his side, whispering that they should go. He shrugged her off, violently, and barged through the embarrassed crowd.

He wasn't there when she got home. The lights were off and his room empty. She tried calling him but he didn't pick up. She waited all day in the kitchen. In the evening, she moved upstairs.

It was gone midnight when she heard him enter. She sat up in her bed, listened. A tap was running, and now he seemed to be climbing to his room.

She knocked once, then opened the door. He was lying in the squashed centre of his mattress, an arm across his forehead. Even in the dark she could see that his eyes were open. She remained in the doorway.

'Leave me alone.'

She didn't move.

'Don't you ever ask me to go there again.'

She nodded. 'I'm sorry.'

'Can I just ask you a question?'

'Please,' she said, but in a voice full of anguish, as if she knew what lay ahead. And yet still she had come. She knew what was going to happen to her and still she'd come.

He spoke evenly, as if detached from every word. 'Where was God when they set me on fire?'

'Please, Tochi.'

'When they knifed my sister's stomach open?'

'Tochi.'

'When they cut off my fifteen-year-old brother's balls?'

Her tears were falling. 'I don't know. I really don't know.'

'Where was your God when I couldn't even tell my parents' bodies apart?'

She carried herself down the stairs and into the kitchen. She tried the switch – she needed light, this darkness was plugging up her throat – but nothing happened. Water, then, and she gulped down a glass, breathing hard as she chucked the last inch down the sink. She turned round, tentatively, as though afraid of what awaited her. The room was still. The clock said it was a quarter past midnight. The blinds made a cage on the wall. She checked the silver tin in the cutlery drawer: empty. She fumbled about under the sink and found a box of candles, lit one straight from the hob and stood it on a red saucer in the middle of the table. She sat down. The candle cast the room in antique grace. She closed her eyes and bowed her head and brought her hands together on the plain wood of the table. She could feel her breath shaking inside her. *I am the dust at your feet. I am the dust at your feet.* She couldn't hear Him. *I am the dust at your feet. I am the dust at your feet.* No. No Him, him, no one, nothing. Only black silence and dead space. Her hands were trembling. She tried again. She couldn't. Birds flew past her shoulder and crashed through the wall. A river rushed out of her chest. The words dried away.

She raised her fingers to her head, to her turban. She lifted it off and put it on the table. She eased out the hairpin down by her neck and placed that on the table too. And then the pin above that, and then pin after pin and clip after clip and all the while her hair was coming down in ribbons, loosening, uncoiling, falling. She heard him on the stairs, and now he was holding aside the beads and standing in the doorway. She stared at him, her arms arranged over her chest as if she were naked. Candlelight on her long hair. He came forward and knelt beside her and put his head in her lap. He felt her hands lightly touch him and they both wept for all they had lost.

14. TOGETHER AGAIN

Avtar hauled his face out of his palms and tried to remember what he should have been doing. The mirrors, he thought, standing up, taking the cloth from his belt. He used a separate cloth for the basins and a third for the urinals. Lastly, he wiped down the cubicle doors and checked every toilet roll dispenser was full. Then he had to sit on the floor again. He slipped a hand under his T-shirt and pressed it against his stomach. That helped. But as soon as he let go the pain blazed.

Outside, he knocked on the window of the truck.

'What?' his boss said, as the glass slid down. 'I know I paid you right.'

'I need a doctor. I'm not feeling very well.'

The man lurched back. 'What you got?'

'Nothing. Just a pain in my stomach.'

'Hm. Well. You've got visas. Go to the doctor's like anyone else.'

'But I'm supposed to be studying. In London. Will they ask questions?'

'I don't know about that,' he responded, shoving into gear, eager to leave. There were about six mobiles on his dash. 'Not my problem.'

Avtar checked with some guys at the gurdwara and they seemed to agree that there was nothing to worry about. 'Janaab, you've got a visa on their computers. If I were you, I'd get everything done. Medicine, teeth, eyes. Everything.'

The woman behind the desk was young, with large teeth and a heavy fringe dyed purple. Avtar shook a hand through his own hair, flattening it at the back, and waited to be acknowledged. She seemed busy on the computer.

'Hi!' she said, beaming, as the printer started up beside her. 'Sorry. Do you have an appointment?'

'I would like to see the doctor, please.'

'You've come to the right place. Are you a patient with us?'

Avtar had rehearsed his response: 'I am visiting for a few days only. Normally I live in London, where I study. Could I see him, please?'

'Her,' she corrected, a little pointedly. 'So you're a visiting patient.'

She fished out a form from a two-tier rack bolted to the wall and placed it on the counter before him.

'Just fill this in, signing it here, here and – ' she flipped the form over – 'here. And then we can look to make you an appointment.'

'But I need to see the doctor today. Please.'

'What seems to be the problem?'

He hesitated. 'I am having pains. In my stomach.'

'OK. Well, we are booked out but if you fill the form in I can get you registered on a temporary basis, and then I'll slot you in between appointments. Does that sound fair?' She held out a pen.

Without really thinking, he did the little Indian wobble of his head – perhaps kindness had disarmed him momentarily – and he took the form and the pen and found a vacant orange seat in the busy waiting room behind him.

He sat there with the pen poised, writing nothing. Address. Current doctor. Non-UK national status (if applicable). Medical card number. He didn't know what to put for any of these. He returned to the kind woman behind the counter.

'I am sorry. But could I see the doctor only? I need bas five minutes.'

She glanced at the form in his hand. 'You do need to fill the form in first. Perhaps I can help?' Gently, she took the paper from him. 'They can be a bit confusing. We'll go through it together. Name?'

'Nijjar. Avtar Singh Nijjar,' and he wondered if already he'd gone too far. Said too much. They knew his name. They'd discover he wasn't anywhere near where he ought to be. That he was here working illegally. Fear began to rage.

'Address?'

Avtar gazed at her.

She smiled. 'Was it London you said?'

He shook his head, then ran down the escalators, tripping over at the bottom, and he didn't stop running until he was back behind the station and walking to the cabin.

He rang Lakhpreet. He thought it would help, hearing her voice, but when she answered he didn't recognize it. It sounded different. He kept the phone to his ear. She was talking. About what, he didn't understand.

'Jaan?' she said.

'Hm?'

'I said we've not heard from Randeep for ages. Is he all right?'

'He's fine.'

'Can I speak to him?'

'He's asleep.'

'Oh. OK. Tell him to call, will you? Mamma's frantic.'

He thought of his own mother. He imagined her being thrown onto the street. 'I need to go.'

'Wait! Can't we talk for a bit? How are you? Missing me?'

'I'm fine.'

'You sure? You don't sound yourself.'

'Don't I?'

He could see her frowning. 'Anyway, what have you been up to? Anything fun?'

He opened his mouth but no words came out. He had nothing, absolutely nothing, to say to her.

He couldn't sleep, and, the next day, he couldn't walk either. He sat up on the floor of the cabin, lifted his T-shirt and tightened the strap he now kept belted around his stomach. He had to get to work. Twice last week he'd arrived late and not once did he finish the job on time. 'Last chance, capiche? I got places to be, man. I'm losing money with every second,' his boss had said, clicking fingers. Avtar leaned in to the side of the cabin and with enormous effort heaved up onto his feet.

He'd be fine, he told himself, as he arrived at the club. Once he got his head on the job he'd forget about the pain. There was nothing to worry about. And after his boss drove off Avtar opened the broom cupboard and laid out very neatly the bottles and sprays and disinfectants he'd need. He went round and picked up all the litter, then raised the chairs onto their tables and vacuumed the entire hall, going right into the corners. He mopped away the standing piss in the toilets, polished up the urinals something pretty, and made a start on scraping the shit off the toilet bowls. He'd be finished soon. Then he could rest. The stains just needed a little more work. They weren't quite coming loose. He scratched harder, digging the scraper in. It made no difference. The pain was coming back. Nothing was going right. Why wasn't anything going right? He closed both hands around the wooden handle and started stabbing the ceramic bowl, chipping enamel. And then he was charging around the club, slashing the seats and smashing the mirrors.

At work, she was misfiling things – the wrong books on the wrong shelves – and several times she forgot that new library cards needed to be countersigned before they were laminated. She had to discard them and start again.

'You seem a bit preoccupied,' Jessica said.

'No, no. Just tired.'

On the wooden counter her phone rang, its incessant vibrations absurdly loud. The immigration inspector: she recognized the number. He'd been calling every day. She stared at the screen, at the shrieking telephone icon, and killed the call. Later, she rang her father, if only to hear his voice – as a comfort against the howling wilderness inside her.

'Is everything all right, beiti? I can hardly hear you.'

'I was – I hope people are treating you well? I hope they're not being hard on you because of me.'

'Let them say what they want. I know my daughter, I tell them. She'll be back soon. She'd never do anything to shame me.'

As she heard those words, words she'd heard all her life, she wished she'd not rung him after all. She said goodbye, quietly, and closed her eyes and tried to imagine herself weightless, without such expensive burdens. It was impossible.

Over dinner that evening, Tochi said, 'I fixed the oven.'

'Yes. I noticed. Thank you.'

'It should last us through the winter.'

She nodded. 'The winter. Of course.'

He looked across. Her hair was twisted up into the nape of her neck and he thought how, without her turban, she looked like a different woman altogether. Her eyes and mouth seemed smaller, as if the turban had amplified everything. 'It must feel strange, not wearing it.'

'Hmm? Oh, yes. Sorry. I'm not very good company tonight. I

was just thinking. You know, if you could go anywhere in the world, where would you go?'

He took another roti.

'Well?'

'I'm eating.' He lifted the side of his plate, the better to scoop up the sabzi. He could feel her waiting for an answer.

'You could go anywhere,' she said. 'I think that must feel wonderful. To have the freedom to go where you want. To do what you want.'

'If you're lucky. If you have the money.'

'But it's not about money,' she said, betraying a slight vehemence.

'Everything's about money.'

She frowned, as if he'd thwarted her attempt to get at something deeper.

'Courage, then,' he said. 'If you have the courage you can go anywhere. Do anything. Be with anyone.' He fixed her with a look. 'Just have the courage.'

She flushed and picked up her roti, signalling the end of the topic.

As they cleared the table, her phone rang, and again she cut it off.

'The inspector?' Tochi asked.

'He won't stop. I don't know what to do.'

'Keep ignoring it. They can't do anything if they can't find you. And then it's for him to sort out,' meaning Randeep.

'It's been a year already. This should be over by now. He should have his stamp and I shouldn't be here.'

He moved to the sink and started to fill it with water. He didn't look across as he asked, 'What will you do when it's over?'

She took her time answering. 'I'll go back home.'

He nodded. 'To your family?'

'I have to.'

She sat at her window, looking across the identical roofs of the houses opposite. Each slate was edged neatly under the one above it, and they all looked damp, lined with dew. She didn't let her eye wander too far above them. It was easier that way. If she looked up at the sky the loneliness was too large for her to carry. She heard Tochi standing in the doorway behind her. She turned away from the window. She seemed to know what he was going to say.

'Stay. Don't go.'

The streetlights threw one half of her face into shadow. The other half glimmered. Her chunni lay gently balled up between her hands, in her lap, as if she were caring for a small purple bird. He'd not lain with her or held her or touched her the way a man can touch a woman. He didn't know what explained this loose, unstructured love that pumped around his body. He only knew that he wanted to be with her. He wanted to protect her and never let anybody hurt her.

She looked down to her lap, to her hands. 'I was thinking about what you said. About courage. And I think it's more complicated than that. I think making a sacrifice so other people aren't hurt can be even more courageous.'

'You sound like you're trying to convince yourself.' Then: 'It's not complicated, Narinder,' and there was something about hearing her name in his mouth that made her gasp inwardly.

'We have duties. I have duties.'

'Forget them.'

She laughed unhappily. 'That's easy for you to say.' He had no family, no one he felt he owed anything to. 'I'm sorry.'

'I used to think I had duties. That I had to know my place. It doesn't work. People will be hurt. Don't hurt yourself instead.'

'It's easy to get over hurting yourself. Easier.'

'You're wrong. You won't. Stay.'

For a man like him, to talk like this was to beg. He was begging her to be with him and she knew that he loved her. All she had to do was take this chance that had been so delicately brought before her, on cupped palms. All she had to do was reach out and accept it. But below the cupped palms lay her baba's turban, on the floor and at her feet. She saw what her being with Tochi would do to him, the lifetime of disgrace. She closed her eyes. So this was what it felt like to be torn in two. It was amazing to think that she'd always had it wrong, imagining that they were the weak ones, the ones who took their chance. No. The weakest are those who stay put and call it sacrifice, call it not having a choice. Because, really, there was always a choice and she – one of the cowards, she realized – was making hers now. She turned back to the window, to the identical roofs. She closed her hands over the chunni and twisted it tight. 'Please. Go away.'

*

Randeep lifted the suitcase above the turnstile, slotted in his ticket, and pushed through the bars and out of the station. Avtar was sitting on the low wall by the water feature. He needed to shave. His hair was a mess. He stood up and beckoned him over. Randeep didn't move.

The bus dropped them at the bottom of the hill and Avtar walked on ahead. After ransacking the club, he'd not gone back to the Portakabin, fearing his boss. Instead, he spent a week sleeping in the car park of a Blockbuster's in south Leeds. He couldn't find work. And then Bal started texting, threatening. When the weather turned even colder the only option left was to contact everyone he knew until he found Randeep, head back to Sheffield and maybe ask Narinder to take them in again, just until he was better.

His gait, he knew, was uneasy. He couldn't apply any serious pressure on his left hip. But it would all be fine if he could rest up for a few days, eat well, bathe, and then get back to finding work. And once he was earning again, he'd clear his debts and after maybe three or four years return home and get a new flat, perhaps even buy one, and Navjoht would be earning too and the shop would be paid off. He held onto these thoughts as if they were all he had left.

'It's a new door,' Randeep said, stopping outside a brown one with a gold slip of a letter box.

He looked up to the window – unlit – then back at the door. He wondered if Tochi was still around. He wondered what she was going to say.

No one answered.

'She'll be at the gurdwara,' Randeep said, and they sat themselves down on the pavement, against the door.

'Are you sure she lives here?' Avtar asked. 'She might've moved. It's been a few months.'

'Three months,' Randeep said. 'Three and a half.'

He seemed different, Randeep, quieter, sombre. 'I'm sorry, yaar. I'm sorry for leaving you.'

Randeep nodded. 'I understand.'

'I owe money. I didn't know what to do.'

'You had no choice.'

'But once I've got rid of this stomach bug, we'll find work and it'll be fine.'

'I'm sure you're right.'

Avtar looked across. 'Were you on your own the whole time?'

He nodded, though he didn't seem to want to talk about it. 'I'm better now. I think I'm going to be OK.'

The darkness thickened and they didn't see the woman until they were gathering up their legs to let her pass. She halted at the house next door. The neighbour, then. An older white woman with small earrings like gold semicolons. Her bleached hair was duck-white at the roots, and her nose pitted with red spots.

'Can I help?' she said. She didn't sound friendly.

'We're waiting,' Avtar said.

'I can see that.'

'Excuse me?'

'Why don't you leave the poor lass be?'

'Do you know where she is?'

'Go on, get away. Hounding her like this. There were more like you last week. I'm calling the police.'

'You don't understand,' Avtar said. 'She's his wife.'

'Oh, I understand very well, don't you worry. I understand all about your arrangements.'

'He's her husband.'

At the threat of police, Randeep stood up and started pulling Avtar away and back down the hill.

They went to the gurdwara, where they charged their phones and slept on one of the mats inside the langar hall. In the morning they could only afford one phonecard between them. They topped up Avtar's – he had more work contacts – and then Randeep took the phone and said he was going to call her.

'What will you say?'

'That I want to meet.'

She was waiting for them at the back door, inside the kitchen. She wore no turban. Her hair was bunned up tight. It was the first time Randeep had seen her like that and this was a fact she seemed embarrassed by, as her smile showed.

She poured the tea into mugs and handed it to them sitting at the table. The kitchen looked different from when they'd lived there. The beads over the doorway were tied neatly to one side with a red curtain strap, and containers for tea, sugar and coffee stood on the counter, along with spice racks and chopping boards. The table was laid with square blue place mats, which Randeep rested his elbows on.

'You said you had to leave the flat?' he asked.

'My brother found me. But where were you, Randeep? That inspector calls every day. I rang you so much!'

'Nowhere,' he said, too ashamed to admit he'd been living like a tramp.

'You should've called.'

'You were worried?' Randeep asked.

Tochi walked in from the hallway. Clean, healthy, warm in his scarf and jacket and gloves. He looked like he was doing well. Next to him, Avtar felt like a dog come in off the street.

'They're here,' Narinder said, pointlessly.

Randeep nodded at him and looked over at Avtar, who said nothing. 'Is no one else here?' Randeep asked. 'Is it only you two?'

Narinder nodded. 'For over two months now.'

He felt himself flush crimson, maybe a little humiliated. His wife. 'We should go,' he said.

'We're staying here,' Avtar said.

'Is it safe?'

'Must be.'

'You're not staying here,' Tochi said.

'Who asked you?' Avtar said, rising.

Narinder stepped in. 'Stop it, all of you. Of course you're staying here.' She looked at Tochi, her lips parted in surprise. 'You can't expect them to spend winter on the streets.'

He said nothing and shut the door hard on his way out.

Narinder exhaled, as if at least one obstacle had been successfully negotiated. 'I should go to work, too.'

'Work?' Randeep said, smiling a touch to himself.

'Yes.' She put on her coat and took her bag from the doorknob. 'We'll talk more tonight. But eat what you want. And if you want to wash there are towels in the first floor cupboard. It's next—'

'We know where it is,' Avtar said. 'We were here first.'

Avtar suggested they share his old room, but Randeep said he'd take the one next door.

'You sure?' Avtar said, a little shocked.

'I'm sure.'

They washed and shaved and brushed their teeth with toothpaste for the first time in months. They even held their heads under the tap and ran several jugs of hot water through their hair, for the feel of it. Afterwards, Avtar tried calling home. No one picked up. It was late there, he supposed. He'd try again in the morning, to make sure they hadn't had any trouble.

Next door, Randeep lay on his mattress, on his side, on his own.

'We need to find work tomorrow,' Avtar said, coming in.

'How's your stomach?'

'Fine.'

'Was it something you ate?'

'You know,' Avtar said, changing the subject, 'if you want any chance of getting with her, you need to stop calling her Narinderji for starters. Like she's better than you.'

'I don't want to get with her.'

'Because girls don't go for boys who give compliments all the time.'

Randeep sat up. 'Can I ask you something? Are you in a relationship with my sister?'

Avtar looked across. He didn't feel surprise, though. 'Yes. We're going to marry. I'm sorry we didn't tell you, but I hope we can have your blessing.' He was her older brother, after all.

'Of course.' He held out his hand, which Avtar took. 'Congratulations. I think you'll be a fine brother-in-law.'

'I hope your mother agrees.'

Randeep chuckled lightly. 'Can I be there when you tell her?'

'You can take my place.'

They waited for Tochi – Narinder insisted – but eventually she had to give in and let them make a start before it got cold.

'I'm sorry it's not more,' she said.

'It's a feast,' Randeep said, though he spooned very little of the sabzi onto his plate, as if he'd got used to eating morsels. It made her wince to imagine how he might have been living.

'You've lost weight,' she said. His shoulders seemed even bonier, pointy under his thin turquoise shirt.

'It happens. Narinder,' he added, smiling at his food.

'We didn't have a kitchen,' Avtar said, pushing on. 'Of course we were going to lose weight.'

'Yes,' Narinder said, measuring out each letter of the word. Avtar seemed all too willing to be offended. 'It can't have been easy.'

'It's never easy when you don't have a job. Or when someone steals it from you.'

'Tochi . . .' Randeep explained.

She nodded. 'You said.'

'He's a thief,' Avtar said.

'I'm sure there's more to it than that,' Narinder said quietly.

Avtar looked up from his roti. 'Not really. He planned it. He told him – ' nodding at Randeep – 'that he was going to do it. And then he did, while I was away. He forced us onto the streets.'

'I'm only saying it's not easy for anyone. He's suffered as well. He's been through a lot.'

'And that gives him the right?'

'At least you have visas. If he gets caught, he doesn't have anything.'

'I'm surprised you're defending him.'

'I'm not, but—'

'My family is up to here in debt because I wanted to come here. If I don't have work God knows what will happen to them. Do you understand that? Do you know what they do to people in India that don't pay up? Do you?'

He shoved his plate with such force that it rattled to her side of the table. 'Stuff your food,' he finished, getting up, but the slowness of his exit took all the sting out of it.

'I'm sorry,' Randeep said. 'He doesn't mean it. He's worried about his family. And he's not well.'

'He should see a doctor.'

'That's what I said. He thinks they'll inform on him.'

They carried on with their meal. He hadn't asked her about the kesri, about why she'd discarded it and now kept her hair uncovered. Her slender wrists were bare, without their kara, and he'd not seen any images of Guru Nanak. The shrine, that too seemed to have disappeared.

'Have you spoken to your family?' she asked. 'How's your father?'

'It's been a while. I imagine they're fine.'

'Oh. Good,' she said, a little confused.

The side gate sounded – scraping the ground – and Tochi came in. If he was surprised that they were still at the table he didn't show it.

'There's plenty of food,' Narinder said.

'I've eaten,' he said, and carried on under the beads and up the stairs.

Randeep looked at Narinder, who was staring in the direction of the hallway.

—

It was getting better. He was sure of it. The yellowing along his left groin had lessened, definitely, and peeing didn't seem such a hardship any more. Only the flesh beneath his stomach felt worse: the soft patch of skin like old fruit, as if it might slip straight off if he pinched too hard. He soaked his bandage under the cold tap, wrung out the water and rewound it around himself, fastening the end with a safety pin he'd found in the kitchen.

He could even walk quite far without stopping for breath.

'Maybe you are getting better,' Randeep said.

They were heading for a timber yard in Manor Top, where they'd found a couple of days' work loading lorries with sawn-off wooden poles.

'The body is strong, janaab,' Avtar said, and did a muscleman pose.

But the wooden poles were thick and square and heavy, and soon Avtar was wheezing and Randeep asked if he wanted to take a break.

'Don't be stupid,' Avtar said, lowering his shoulder and then the pole onto the lorry floor. 'Can you afford to lose this job?'

'You seem to be struggling, that's all.'

'Well, I'm not.'

There were nine lorries and two vans in the yard, and when the last of them was loaded, Avtar collapsed against one of the huge tyres. His arms were quivering, as though his muscles wanted out.

Randeep jogged back from the low barn-like building, their pay in his hand. 'He said good job and he'll think of us for next time.'

'Nothing for tomorrow?'

'Nothing. He said there might be more work in some other factory. In Rotherham. We've been there, haven't we?'

Avtar managed to shrug, shake his head. 'Maybe. I lose track.'

The next day, Avtar couldn't get up from his mattress. He moved onto all fours and tried sliding his hands up the wall, climbing it, expecting his legs to follow. His knee shook and his leg buckled and he collapsed back down. Randeep was there to catch him.

'Rest, bhaji. We'll look for work tomorrow.'

He lay under his blanket all day. In the evening, Narinder boiled vegetables and he ate a little. Then he slept for a bit. When he woke it was dark and his armpits felt thick and oozy, tingling strangely, and a harsh drubbing went on behind his eyes. His insides were in agony. He thought he was going to shit them all out. He rose onto his knees, arms cradling his stomach, and felt a hot stream down his thigh, thudding onto the mattress. Shuffling sideways, crouched over, he made it off the bed and to the door, where he sat for a minute against the wood, sweating, wondering if this was it for him, then telling himself that it couldn't be, that he had work to look for in the morning. He reached up and opened the door. He tried standing but couldn't and crawled out of the room on his hands and knees. In the dark, disoriented, he started for the stairs across the landing, hands padding on ahead of him, knees scraping the carpet. He got as far as the banister when, dimly, he had a thought that the bathroom – because that was where he was headed, wasn't he? – was actually behind him, next door to the room he slept in. He turned himself round, hand by hand, knee by knee, each movement seeming to wring his stomach. But he couldn't go on. He was exhausted. He could hear himself panting. His elbows gave way, then his legs.

*

She worked late and had to catch the slow bus home. She didn't mind. She was in no hurry to get back to the house. She preferred sitting on her own by the window, letting the bus carry her through the city in the lovely pretence that she could stay sitting here forever, going round and round, observing. She noticed things more now, she realized. What people were holding, the way they spoke. She wasn't sure why. They passed the dark-green shores of Millhouses Park, the denuded trees and the brown *Y* of their mortification. She looked up at the sky and it really did seem full of snow. Everyone at work said it was coming, that it would be here before Christmas and last until the new year. *At least that's something you won't have to worry about*, Jessica had said. *You'll be back in London soon enough*, as if London had its own bespoke weather system. She knew that, by then, she wouldn't be able to marry Karamjeet. She'd lived her life by enough falsehoods.

Once back, she went upstairs and knocked on Tochi's door, not expecting him to answer, not surprised when he did. Every night, sitting on her bed, she'd listened to him in his room, trying to think what he might be doing, trying to think what he might be thinking, but this was the first time she'd seen him in five days, since the night of Avtar's collapse.

'I thought you'd be at work.'

'I'm on lates. I'm going in an hour.'

She nodded. 'Will you – will you let me in?'

He turned sideways on and she stepped past. He'd moved his mattress into the alcove, beside the chimney breast. A dirty plate lay beside it, a spoon atop that.

'How's the patient?' she asked.

'I've not seen them.'

'They're only in their room.'

He nodded, said nothing.

'This is for your boss,' and she held out an envelope. 'Avtar gave it me yesterday. So thank you. For the doctor.'

'Wasn't me.'

'Still.'

Too scared to dial an ambulance, Tochi had called Malkeet, who rang back a few minutes later to say a doctor was on his way and what payment they were both expecting.

'I'll leave it here,' Narinder said, placing the envelope on the windowsill.

'Thank you.'

She smiled flatly and nodded to leave. He wanted to punish her for denying them a chance. He wanted to hold her thighs apart and suck her cunt into his mouth. He wanted to make her happy. His hands jerked out of their pockets.

'Kanyakumari,' he said.

She turned round.

'Where I'd go if I could go anywhere.'

'I don't know it.'

'It's at the end of India. Nothing but sea from there.'

'It sounds very beautiful.'

'I wouldn't know.'

She tilted her head to the side. 'Why there?'

'Because it's the end and there can be no more false dreams.'

'Only real ones? Then are they still dreams?'

'I'm leaving,' he said.

'To go there?' she asked, lightly mocking.

'I'm leaving here.'

She didn't seem surprised. 'When?'

'Maybe two weeks. After Christmas.'

She nodded, wished him luck. He heard her on the stairs, then he picked up the phone to Ardashir and asked if that building job in Spain was still going, and when could he start?

The doctor – a baby-faced elder Muslim with a short, coarse beard, his upper lip hair-free – had advised going to hospital, saying that all the symptoms pointed to a severe lack of nephron reabsorption, which meant things weren't quite balancing out in his body. 'It'll be a small operation followed by a few weeks' rest. You don't want to risk septicaemia. And you've got a visa on file. There's nothing to worry about.'

In the meantime, to help manage the pain, he left them with some insulin which Randeep drew into the syringe and passed to Avtar. They'd got good at doing this over the last week, three times a day. Avtar passed the syringe back to Randeep and started to retighten his bandage.

'You should have told me about the operation,' Randeep said. 'Does Lakhpreet know?'

'No. And it's staying like that.'

'You should go to hospital soon, though. Before it gets worse.'

'Hmm.' He was worried about the recovery time. A few weeks. Which probably meant months. It might as well be forever.

He rang home again that afternoon and this time, at last, someone answered. His father.

'Thank God. Are you OK? I've been ringing every day for the last week.'

He said he was fine, his mother was fine, his brother was fine, the shop was fine. Everything was fine and Avtar wasn't to worry and should concentrate on his studies.

'Papa, what's happened? You're not telling me something. Put Navjoht on.'

'Nothing's happened. There was just some difficulty with some men last week.'

'What difficulty? Did they do anything to you?'

'We had to give them a few things.'

'What things? Did they hurt you?'

'The TV, the radio. Nothing important. Don't worry.'

'Did they hurt you?'

'Uff, it was nothing. I'm fine now.'

He called Bal straight away, shouting at him to leave his family alone, that he'd kill him if they went near his papa again.

'All your fault, man. We've given you chance after chance. You've got one week to settle up or we'll do more to your pop than just take his TV.'

He didn't sleep that night. He kept thinking of their old neighbours, Mr and Mrs Lal. How they'd been thrown out of their home, how broken and humiliated they'd looked.

He went to the chip shop in the morning, knocking on the rear door and asking the new gori if she could fetch Malkeet, please.

'Mal-kit!' she shouted. 'One of your lot!'

Malkeet emerged from the service area, telling the girl – Megan – to go out front. Avtar hadn't seen him since the drama with the chickens. He seemed to have got even fatter.

'How are you, my friend?' Malkeet said. 'Feeling better?'

Avtar held out the crumpled notes. 'Could you wire this across to my parents' account? They need it now.'

'Sure,' he said, taking the money. 'I'm going to the bank. I won't even charge you a fee.'

'Thank you. Is Harkiran here?'

'He's on afters.'

'OK.' Then: 'Is there any work, bhaji?'

Malkeet shook his head. 'It's quiet. Always is before Christmas.'

'I'll clean the floors.'

'Avtar.'

'The toilets.'

'Avtar.'

'You must have something.'

'Maybe in the new year.'

Behind Malkeet, Tochi came into view, working, earning, wiping the sweat from his forehead with the hem of his orange uniform.

In the afternoon, he and Randeep tried the takeaways on Ecclesall Road, the corner shops in Darnall. Someone mentioned a Muslim clothes outlet up in Ridgeway, but when they got there the car park was empty and the factory seemed to have been closed for some months. They came straight back to the house, Avtar slamming the bedroom door shut.

'What a wasted bhanchod journey.'

'Maybe we can sell something,' Randeep said, and they looked around the room and down at themselves and said nothing more about that idea.

Avtar didn't go down for breakfast – he had no appetite, he'd hardly slept – and lay on his mattress trying to think where there might be work. Nothing came to mind. He heard the kitchen door opening and moved to the window. It was Tochi, in the yard. He looked like he'd only come out to catch some air, head tipped up. He remained in that pose for several minutes, unmoving, as if in some staring contest with the sky, and then he zipped up his jacket, decisively, and went to work.

Avtar climbed to the landing and tried Tochi's door. It was locked, so, limping slightly, he fetched the metal pole from his rucksack. The first lock broke away and he listened out, for Randeep, for the girl. Nothing. He broke off the remaining two and then the gentlest of touches sent the door swinging open and he walked right into Tochi's room.

He called Bal, the five thick rolls of money stuffed into his jeans pockets.

'Come and get your money.'

'Great. We'll be there tomorrow.'

'Now. I won't have it tomorrow.'

Bal arranged for one his local cousins to meet Avtar outside the gardens. Avtar passed the cash over. Then he waited. He sat in the kitchen with the lights off and he waited.

Tochi stopped off at the station – he needed his tickets to London – but the counters were all closed, the green blinds laddered down. He spent some time trying to work the self-service machines, then gave up and went back to the house. He unlocked the kitchen door, not flicking the switch. He could see Avtar sitting there, at the table. Tochi said nothing and went through the beads and up the two flights. He saw that his door was broken. Inside, the bottom drawer of the wardrobe had been pulled out, the dummy panel smashed through. He went downstairs.

'Give me my money.'

'It's gone.'

'Give me my money.'

'I said it's gone.'

'Where's it gone?'

Avtar stared. 'You stole my job. I stole your money.'

'Where's it gone?'

'Fuck you.'

Tochi punched him, his knuckles slamming into Avtar's cheekbone. 'Get me my money.'

His nose was bleeding. His face ached. 'Fucking thieving chamaar.' He spat in Tochi's face and charged forward. But he was weak now, his blows thin, and Tochi easily pushed him off.

'Get me my money,' he said again, drawing his fist back behind his head and driving, catapulting it into Avtar's stomach. Avtar heaved, his head snapping back as if it was his face that had been hit. Another punch, once more into the stomach, where it was most tender. 'Get me my money.' Avtar staggered into the cooker, arms protecting his middle. He felt blood rise up his throat. He fell sideways onto the floor and could see his feet moving, scrabbling, though he had no sense of this.

All through the night he couldn't stop shaking. Randeep kept fetching him water. He gave him another shot of insulin, too, though it made no difference. He was still grimacing, in terrible pain. Randeep knelt beside him and cradled the back of his friend's head and brought his lips to the water. Avtar sipped, then flopped back.

'Maybe we should go to the hospital,' Randeep said.

Avtar didn't seem able to speak.

'You're not dying, are you?' Then, louder, 'Bhaji?' and this time Avtar opened his eyes and groaned weakly. 'Would you like some more water?' Randeep asked. A single nod. He laid Avtar's head back down on the pillow, gently, picked up the glass and hurried to the bathroom. When he returned, Avtar was shaking again, shaking violently all over, in a way that reminded Randeep of the jackhammer at the old hotel site.

The snow came at dawn, quietly, gracefully. She brought her hands together in prayer, then didn't know what to say, or to whom. She turned away from the window. Tochi entered the kitchen.

'Still no word,' she said.

He nodded. He withdrew two slices of bread from the fridge and spooned some cold sabzi onto each. He sat down and ate.

'Is that it? Aren't you even sorry for what you did?'

The side gate rattled and Randeep came past the window and into the house. His eyes were red, as if he'd been up all night.

Narinder stepped towards him. 'How is he?'

He had his back against the door, looking at Tochi at the table. 'They don't know. They operated. They say they have to wait. To see how far the poison has spread.'

'But he'll be all right? Randeep?'

He said nothing. She told him to sit down, that he must be

hungry, and got the tava out to make roti. Tochi washed his hands and reached for his boots.

'Are you going to work?' She looked at the oven clock. 'Already?'

'I'm going to the station first.'

Her face turned into a question.

'To get a ticket. I told you. I'm going to London. And then to Spain.'

'Spain? You mean you're not coming back?'

Randeep snorted. 'Running away.'

Tochi came right up to him, squaring up. 'I never run away.'

'I'm not scared of you,' Randeep said. He shoved Tochi aside and went up to his room.

'Did you have to do that?' Narinder said. 'Can't you see how he's suffering?'

Without a word, Tochi put on his jacket and shut the door behind him. She listened to him leave, then moved slowly to the table and stood with one hand on his chair. She thought of Tochi's face, of Randeep's, of Avtar lying in hospital. Who would be a man, she thought, in a world like this.

Upstairs, at the window, Randeep took the phone from his pocket. He could still see Avtar's terrified face when the doctor said he might very well have to lose his foot. He'd promised Avtar he'd contact his family and let them know what had happened. First, though, he had a call to make for Narinder. The receptionist transferred him through to Vakeel Sahib.

'Randeep!' the lawyer said. 'How's my boy?'

'Please start the divorce. It's been over a year.'

They went over a few details, the lawyer confirming he'd already applied for Randeep's stamp. 'I'll just need the girl to send me a copy of her passport. Fax or email will do. Can you ask her?'

'I'll do it now.'

He heard the lawyer laugh. 'You sound like you're in a hurry.'

'No hurry,' Randeep said, as he watched Tochi heading down the road, hands in his pockets, on his way to Spain. 'But there's no point in waiting.'

EPILOGUE

Tickets. She double-checked the reservation, what time she had to be at St Pancras, then slotted the orange cards back into her purse and put the purse under her pillow. Her suitcase was packed and ready at the side of her old dressing table. She went downstairs. The dishwasher needed emptying and after that she wiped down the kitchen surfaces. There was enough milk to last them another day and the fruit bowl held plenty of bananas, the only food that had never got stuck in her father's dentures. She wasn't sure why she still bought so many. She wrung out the dishcloth, left it by the sink, and went down the hall and into the front room.

'I'm still not happy about you going on your own,' Tejpal said.

'I'm sure I'll be fine.' She sat on the sofa, her reflection warped in the fifty-inch TV screen that dominated the room.

'We could have scattered the ashes here,' Tejpal said.

'It's not what he would have wanted.'

'Then maybe take Sabrina with you, if I can still get a ticket.'

Sabrina, Tejpal's wife of four years, looked up from her iPhone. She seemed horrified, as if she'd been asked to donate a limb. 'I really don't think so.'

'And what was wrong with Heathrow?' Tejpal said. 'Why are you going all the way to Manchester?'

'Maybe she's meeting someone,' Sabrina suggested, laughing. 'A secret affair. How funny would that be?'

'Sabrina!' Tejpal said. 'Don't be so rude.'

Sabrina sighed luxuriously and as she stood her emerald sari shimmered against her long brown arms. 'I want to go. The table's booked for eight.'

He started to lace up his shoes, presenting everyone with a view of his head. Forty this year, he was receding determinedly. So much so, it looked as if he'd taken to some sort of spray-on thickening agent. Narinder smiled discreetly and bent to her newspaper. She read a paragraph, until she felt forced to look up again, and saw Sabrina mouthing something to Tejpal. And then Tejpal spoke:

'Narinder, actually, I wanted to say that while you're away we thought we might get the place valued. You know, to get an idea.'

She nodded. She wasn't surprised. She'd overheard Sabrina on the phone to one of her friends about the matter, about getting out of this dreary old house, about the problem of the sister. 'That sounds good,' Narinder said.

'We've not decided anything, so I don't want you to worry. And of course you're part of this family as much as anyone.'

'But we wanted to be upfront with you,' Sabrina said, taking over, as if she thought her husband was pussyfooting. 'We want to move closer to my family. They can help with children and whatnot. If we ever get round to having any,' she added in a pointed aside. 'And there's nothing really keeping us here. Tej's office say he can get a transfer easily enough.'

'But nothing's been decided,' Tejpal said, a little desperately. 'And you can stay with us, you know, as long as—'

'Or you could start your own life,' Sabrina said. 'There are loads of great one-bedroomed flats around. I printed some off the net for you. And you could get a job or something. It's not too late. Because don't you think you should work? Like, live in the twenty-first century?'

'When did she have the time?' Tejpal said.

'I just think women died so we could work and be equal. It's disrespectful to their memory if we just sit around.'

'For God's sake, Sabrina! She was looking after Dad for ten years. What the hell did you do?'

'And what the hell did you do? And why should I? He wasn't my dad.' And then, muttering, 'Everyone loves a martyr.'

Tejpal had let Sabrina believe one version of the story. That she had forsaken her future to take care of her ill father. In reality, when she returned home from Sheffield, without her turban, her kara, her kandha, and told her family she wasn't going to marry – not Karamjeet, not anyone – Baba Tarsem Singh had slapped her. It was the one and only time in his life he'd done that. Tejpal bellowed, a frantic Karamjeet tried to talk her round, to the wedding, to God. She said she'd made up her mind and nothing could change that, however much she might wish it. Baba Tarsem Singh was forced to apologize to Karamjeet's parents, lowering himself in front of everyone. Less than a year after Narinder's return he had his second stroke, leaving him unable to care for himself. He lived for another ten years and then one morning Narinder came into his room, his toothbrush and glass of sugared water on her tray, and found him sitting up against the headboard, his heavy head sunk forward and turban falling off.

*

You'd think the rani was coming. His mother had said so at least a dozen times in the last week. He didn't care. He was excited. It wasn't often he had visitors, and he'd not seen her since that damp, formal day in the solicitor's office in Southall, when he'd waited for her to come and sign the divorce papers. Afterwards, they'd shaken hands and she'd hurried off down the road, unfurling her umbrella, hoping to catch the 2.15 back to Croydon. And now here he was, all these years later, waiting again.

A knock on the window startled him. Avtar. 'The door's locked,' he mouthed.

Randeep's hand went to his forehead, in apology, as if to convey he was losing his mind. He got up to let him in.

'Is she staying a few weeks?' Avtar said, eyeing all the food laid out on the kitchen counter.

Randeep carried on to the front room and sat down, clasping and unclasping his hands.

'What time's she coming?' Avtar asked, sitting down too.

'Her train gets in at 11.35. She said she'd get a taxi. Do you really think it's too much for lunch?'

'I think it's too much for Switzerland.'

Randeep frowned. 'Oh well.'

'Why so nervous, man?'

'Be serious, yaar.'

Avtar pointed. 'New haircut?'

The taxi turned into the cul-de-sac and parked outside a modern semi with a neat stamp of a front garden. She didn't remember ever coming to this part of Sheffield before. Beauchief, the address in her hand read. It was one of those new estates, where every house was of the same orange brick.

The front door opened before she'd even stepped out of the car. The bright sunshine pushed his face into shadow, but as she came down the driveway the light softened until he was standing before her and she could see him perfectly: the thin pockets of flesh that now cushioned his eyes, the inevitable downward turn of his full-lipped mouth. The hair at the side of his head, down to his sideburns, had greyed shockingly. He was still as thin and tall as ever, but looked perhaps a decade older than the thirty-one or so years she guessed he must now be.

'Narinder?'

'It's good to see you, Randeep. It's been a long time.'

He took her suitcase and showed her through to the front room, where she hugged Avtar. He'd run to fat. His face was bloated, pudgy, as if melted slightly in the summer heat.

'You haven't changed,' she said.

'Oh, I think we both know that's not true,' he replied.

Randeep brought in nibbles and glasses of mango juice, setting the tray on the coffee table. 'Lunch won't be long. I hope you'll stay.'

'I don't think so. The flights. And I've still to get to Manchester.'

He said he understood. 'It's great to see you. Really. It's made me very happy.'

'It doesn't take much,' Avtar said, popping peanuts into his mouth.

Randeep ignored him. 'I was sorry to hear about your father.'

She accepted this with a small nod. 'And I'm sorry I couldn't come to the twins' weddings. Thank you for inviting me, though. For contacting me.'

'It's because of you we're living here, Narinder. We would have invited you to Lakhpreet's wedding too – ' a nod at Avtar – 'but it was a very small affair.'

Narinder looked to Avtar. 'Congratulations. I didn't know.'

He shrugged, which she wasn't sure how to take.

'Do you live close by?'

'A twenty-minute walk for most people.' He tapped his foot against the table leg – a dull, hollow sound. 'Forty for me.'

A door opened, closed, and now someone was coming down the stairs. 'My mother,' Randeep whispered. 'For which I apologize in advance.' This elicited a smile, which was gratifying.

Mrs Sanghera welcomed Narinder with an embrace that had all the intensity of a puff of smoke. The white streak in her hair looked broader, fiercer, than Narinder remembered. Her face had lost none of its edge. If anything, the years seemed only to have planed it further. She sat beside her son.

They had tea, biscuits. Again Randeep mooted lunch, and again Narinder demurred.

'My son mentioned you are on your way to India?' Mrs Sanghera said. 'Is it a holiday?'

'Mum, I told you – Uncle passed away.'

'Oh ya. I'm sorry. You'll be going to Kiratpur, then?'

'Yes.'

'Good. And it's good you looked after your father so well. My Randeep is the same.' She patted his knee, as if she were praising a dog. 'My eldest daughter too,' she went on, gesturing towards Avtar but in no way looking at him. 'She lives with her in-laws. We must all perform our duty.'

'How is Dad?' Avtar asked, sharp.

Mrs Sanghera's smile threatened to collapse. 'He's well, Avtar beita. It's good of you to ask. Some might think you'd forgotten all about him.'

'Papa is in a home,' Randeep explained.

'He wanted to go,' Mrs Sanghera said. 'It was his choice.'

Avtar gave a faint snort of amusement.

'Perhaps with all your free time you could visit him once in a while?' Mrs Sanghera said to Avtar. She turned back to Narinder. 'My daughter is a nurse and is always working to earn money for her new family. So what excuse does he have?'

'None!' Avtar said brightly.

Narinder smiled. 'Still looking for work?' she asked.

'Oh, you know. Old habits.'

Mrs Sanghera huffed. 'It depends how you bring the children up. All my children have done well. My Randeep is Assistant Manager already. On his way to Director.'

'It's only an administration job,' he protested.

'And he has his own place,' Avtar said.

Slowly, as if measuring out her surprise, Narinder turned to Randeep. 'You don't live here?'

'No. It's not far. It's a very small studio flat. I prefer being on my own.'

'We all need our independence,' Mrs Sanghera said, sounding bitter about the whole arrangement. 'I only hope you'll at least let your mother find you a good girl. Unless that's another embarrassment you want me to bear.'

'Mum. Not now, OK? Not today.'

'Then when? Because you know—'

'When you start listening to me,' he cut in, silencing her.

She apologized, but said she really had to go. They called her a taxi and Randeep waited with her at the end of the drive.

'Your mother has some very grand plans for you,' she said.

'Worrying, isn't it?'

'I'm sure you'll take it all in your stride.'

He smiled in an automatic way. All through the visit he'd noticed her eyes. They seemed dulled, as if certain lamps had gone out. 'I hope you don't mind my asking, but are you happy?'

She took a while to answer. 'Happiness is a pretty precarious state, Randeep. I'm content. That's more than enough. That's more than most.'

'I'm sorry I never asked you what you were risking by helping me. I was too caught up in myself.'

'I think you tried. But I wasn't going to tell you then – ' she smiled – 'so let's not start now.'

As the taxi pulled up she pressed his arm and said goodbye, and he waited a long time after she'd gone before returning inside.

'I'm going, yaar,' Avtar said, coming into the hallway. 'Cards at the community centre. Come.'

Randeep shook his head.

'Dominoes, then. You'll only mope if you stay here.'

'I've got things to do.'

He locked the door after Avtar and turned round. He could hear his mother on the phone in the kitchen, at the end of the hallway. He went up to his old room, a tight boxy space, only large enough for a truncated single bed and thin MDF wardrobe. He sat down, hands on his knees. Beside him, on the floor, was a short stack of books he'd never removed to the flat, the bottommost one a dust-covered atlas. He fetched a glass of water from the bathroom and placed it on the floor, then sat down on the bed again. He should go home. He had some invoices to check before work tomorrow, tasks he'd been too anxious to complete the previous week. For some minutes he didn't move. Then he went downstairs and hurried into his jacket. He told his mother he was going, that he might catch a film, and would drop in on his father sometime tomorrow.

*

When Avtar got home from the community centre, his parents were cramped up on the settee watching their Indian soap operas. It was pretty much all they did, morning till night.

'Navjoht?' he asked.

'Working late,' his mother said, eyes not leaving the screen.

He carried on to the narrow kitchen where Lakhpreet was preparing dinner. She was still in her uniform of light-blue tunic and black trousers. He circled his arms around her waist and kissed her neck, bit it.

'How did it go?' she asked.

He paused, scoured his brain. She turned round.

'Did you call about the interview?'

'Oh. That.' He moved away, his good mood already dissolved. 'No.'

'Why?'

'I didn't want to. We don't need to.'

'You don't need to work?'

'We get money anyway.'

She turned back to the stove, banging pots. 'So we'll carry on living in this shithole, then.'

He grinned. 'At least it's our shithole.'

'Our rented shithole. And can you tell your brother to tidy away the sofa bed before he leaves? I don't have the time.'

'He wakes up early.'

'And I don't?'

He let this go. 'Your mother was on form today. Apparently I do nothing to help my family.'

'I could have told you that. How was Narinder?'

'Composed,' he said, after a while. 'She doesn't give anything away.'

'She might be dying inside.'

'We don't all live in a movie, jaan.'

She sighed heavily. 'Would that we did.'

'But I think it was good for your brother to see her.'

'Yeah. Maybe now he can put it all to bed.'

'Talking of bed,' he said, softly so his parents might not hear. He pushed off the counter, but sitting down playing dominoes all afternoon had stiffened his hip, and he had to exaggerate his limp horribly to get going. He saw the distaste in her face before she could hide it. It had always been an unspoken thing between them, that she'd married him partly out of pity. He admired her for it, and sometimes, at night, despised her too.

'I'm sorry,' she said, reddening.

He put his hand on her shoulder. 'It's OK,' he said. 'It's OK.'

He sold paper windmills and plastic chimes. Miniature models of the mandapam and pens topped with the statue of Thiruvalluvar. He sat beside his stall, feet lifted onto a second chair, ankles crossed.

'How much?' the American tourist asked, holding up a child's rattle, the central ball painted with a crude map of India.

He blew the beedi smoke out of his nose. 'Twenty.'

She nodded, put the rattle down. She wasn't going to buy anything. He could tell.

The sea was calm, the sunset dingy. The ferry made its final crossing back from Vivekananda. On the seafront some men were erecting a theatre, though the roof was nothing more than a large sheet of corrugated iron held down with seven unevenly spaced rocks. It was being built for a couple of days' time, when a local theatre group would be acting out the Ramayana. *With a modern twist!* as the posters all had it.

The American lady wandered off towards the tiny port, perhaps to meet someone off the ferry. Half an hour, maybe, and he'd call it a day too. He lit another beedi.

'How's things, anna?' It was Lavan, from the Red Palms Hotel up the hill. The light made the gold buttons of his uniform flash.

Tochi nodded.

'Ages ago, when you first came here, do you remember what you said?'

'Remind me.'

Lavan clicked his tongue. 'You said to tell you if any Panjabi Sikh woman from England ever stayed with us.'

He said she'd been at the hotel for three days now, and that he'd taken a photo of her with his phone. He showed it to Tochi. She was typing at a computer, behind a glass wall. Her hair was a single braid down her back. He looked closer. She'd not changed, not really. A little fuller in the face, maybe. A little thicker in the waist.

Still those clever eyes and gentle eyebrows. The same way of sitting: leaning forward a touch, engaged by whatever was in front of her with every cell of her body.

'So do you know her?'

'Do you always take secret photos of women?'

Lavan kissed the air.

'Has she asked if I'm here?'

'Why? What's the big secret? Did you use to be James Bond?'

Tochi removed his feet from the chair and sat up, throwing his beedi into the sand. 'How long's she here for?'

He didn't sleep well that night. The walls were thin and the neighbours arguing again. Beyond the window, work went on to get the theatre built in time – drills, hammering, men calling to each other in that round, tumbling language it had taken Tochi only a year to understand. He got up and off the bed, stepped over his wife and children and went down the metal staircase and on to the sea. The waves were loud, dark as his face, and the water rushed up over his feet, closing around his ankles and then slowly withdrawing.

In the morning, the receptionist shook her head and put the receiver down, hard. 'Not in. You'll have to wait outside.'

'How long is she staying?'

'Wait outside.'

'I said how long?'

'I cannot give that information,' she said, in English now, smiling.

It was nearly six when the auto dropped her at the hotel, and she was tired. She felt as if she'd spent more hours inside the tour bus than out, the rapidly speaking driver-cum-guide shuttling them from one museum to another. It had seemed a good idea back in Kiratpur, after finishing her father's rites, when she realized she didn't have to go straight back to England this time. She changed her flights and flew to Thiruvananthapuram and from there took a coach to Kanyakumari. She remembered Tochi mentioning the place and came because she wanted to, and because she could.

'Did you enjoy your trip, madam?' the receptionist asked.

'Yes. Thank you.'

'If you would like to go down to the beach to see the theatre show we have a party leaving in one hour.'

'I think I'll just go to sleep. My flight's tomorrow.'

'As you please, madam. Goodnight.'

She packed her suitcase and washed her hair. She checked what time the early train would get into Cochin and how long she'd have to wait before boarding the onward flight to Mumbai. Then she slipped the Mumbai to Heathrow tickets inside her passport and placed them on top of her luggage. She found that she was no longer tired. She unfolded Sabrina's printouts – a selection of grim high-rise apartments – and tried to focus on them. She couldn't. It was her last night in India – perhaps forever – and that thought seemed to be batting around her brain. She'd never been back to Anandpur Sahib. Until she arrived at Kiratpur with her father's ashes, she'd never been to a gurdwara again either. Not since her year in Sheffield. She went to the window. The beach was teeming, the theatre lit up.

She strapped on her sandals and smiled at the receptionist and said she was going out for a short walk. 'I don't think I'll be long.'

'Alone? Do be careful of pickpocketeers, madam. They like to bamboozle the tourists.'

She headed away from the lights and the crowds waiting for the play to start, and wandered down to a darker, quieter mile of sand. She bought a cone of pistachio ice cream and ate it while the sea purred at her side. The moon was low and enormous and the stars so many and so close that she felt as if she was walking among them. She was glad she'd done this. Glad she'd come to India to rest her father's ashes. He'd have liked the service, she thought. He might have wished that she'd assented when the priest asked her to give a prayer, but she couldn't. She was sorry, she told the priest, but if there was a God he'd know how false her prayer would be.

She stopped and turned round. The theatre lights were the tiniest bursts of silver and she realized she'd come further than she intended. She climbed up to the road and headed back. Down on the beach, people were taking their seats in front of the stage. There seemed to be a feeling of excitement, of expectation, a feeling that rose off the crowd and stroked its warm wing across Narinder's face. She descended the few steps leading off the road and felt her feet sink nicely into the sand again. A yellow banner ran along the roof of the theatre: *Kanyakumari Theatre Group. All Donation Wellcome*. She'd stay for a bit, she decided, and found a seat at the end of the back row. From here she could see into the wings, where a young boy in gold armour, mace in hand, nervously recited his lines.

People were still filling the aisle, then fanning into the rows of metal chairs. She didn't call out when she saw him. He was heading for the front row. He held a toddler high up in his arms and there was a woman with him too, vermilion in her hair, and one – no, three – children following on behind. His white kurta looked like it was glowing against the deep brown of his skin. His hair was longer, falling over his eyes, his stomach a little rounder. She was happy for him. Of course she was. What else had she expected? What else had she wanted? She looked down at her hands and smiled. She remembered that there was a night train which left Kanyakumari for Cochin at 2.30. She'd get that, she decided, instead of waiting for the morning. Trains were late all the time. Better to be safe. She stood up to leave. The lights dimmed and a hush spread over the audience. She could still see him, in the front row. He was saying something to his wife. Beside him, his children, who were whispering.